COUNT TO TEN

"Kept me up all night with the doors locked."
—**KAREN ROBARDS**, *New York Times* **bestselling author**

"Takes off like a house afire . . . There's action and chills galore in this nonstop thriller."
—**TESS GERRITSEN**, *New York Times* **bestselling author**

"Rose cranks up the heat in more ways than one . . . another winning mystery thriller . . . Emotional subplots, engaging characters, and a string of red herrings will keep readers hooked."
—*Publishers Weekly*

YOU CAN'T HIDE

"Suspense-filled . . . [an] action-packed serial killer thriller."
—*Baryon Magazine*

"A fast paced suspense novel with many twists and turns. Rose is a great suspense writer."
—*Midwest Book Review*

"Spine-tingling . . . Some writers can draw you in with the first sentence and keep you enthralled even if the house is burning down around you—and romantic suspense author Karen Rose is one of them."
—*NightsandWeekends.com*

"If there's one name synonymous with great romantic suspense writers it's Karen Rose—she just keeps getting better and better."

—BookLoons.com

"This novel is, in a word, riveting."

—Romantic Times BOOKclub Magazine

"Ms. Rose has done it again. She is one talented writer who can draw out a suspense read to the final spine-chilling end."

—TheBestReviews.com

"A chilling, fast-paced thriller."

—CurledUp.com

"As always, Rose delivers a masterful story of suspense."

—OnceWritten.com

HAVE YOU SEEN HER?

"Heart-racing thrills . . . Readers will . . . rush to the novel's thrilling conclusion."

—Publishers Weekly

"Terrifying and gripping."

—Romantic Times BOOKclub Magazine

more . . .

DON'T TELL

"As gripping as a cold hand on the back of one's neck."
—*Publishers Weekly*

"A definite page-turner that never lets up until the last page."
—*Romance Reviews Today*

"Action-packed [with a] story line [that] is character driven."
—*Midwest Book Review*

"Couldn't put it down."
—**Bookhaunts.net**

"Karen Rose's nail-biting delivery is unique."
—**Heartstrings.com**

"Will keep you on the edge of your seat . . . excellent writing and storytelling by Karen Rose."
—**TheRoadtoRomance.ca**

I'M
WATCHING
YOU

Books by Karen Rose

Don't Tell
Have You Seen Her?
I'm Watching You
Nothing to Fear
You Can't Hide
Count to Ten
Die for Me

KAREN ROSE

I'M WATCHING YOU

GRAND CENTRAL
PUBLISHING

NEW YORK   BOSTON

Copyright © 2004 by Karen Rose Hafer
Excerpt from *Die for Me* copyright © 2007 Karen Rose Hafer
All rights reserved. Except as permitted under the U.S. Copyright Act of 1976, no part of this publication may be reproduced, distributed, or transmitted in any form or by any means, or stored in a database or retrieval system, without the prior written permission of the publisher.

Grand Central Publishing is a division of Hachette Book Group USA, Inc.

The Grand Central Publishing name and logo is a trademark of Hachette Book Group USA, Inc.

Art direction by Diane Luger
Cover photography by Herman Estevez
Book design by Giorgetta Bell McRee

Grand Central Publishing
Hachette Book Group USA
237 Park Avenue
New York, NY 10017
Visit our Web site at www.HachetteBookGroupUSA.com.

Printed in the United States of America

First Printing: October 2004
Reissued: December 2006, September 2007

14 13 12 11 10 9 8 7 6 5

To my friends Kay and Marc Conterato—for the "Minnesota Buzz," for your often fiendish creativity, and for being there at all the important times in our lives. I love you both.

And as always to Martin. I'm the luckiest woman in the world to have such a man be both my husband and my best friend.

Acknowledgments

Kay and Marc Conterato, for help on all things medical.

Sherry and Barry Kirkland, for so kindly inviting me to the Tonitown Grape Festival and answering my questions about bullets with nary a raised brow.

Susan Heneghan, for information on the structure and cross-functional workings between the Chicago Police Department and their forensic and prosecutorial counterparts.

Jimmy Hatton, Mike Koenig, and Paula Linser, for modeling the epitome of teamwork. Those were good years.

Prologue

The sun had gone down. But then again, it tended to do that from time to time. He should get up and turn on a light.

But he liked the darkness. Liked the way it was quiet and still. The way it could hide a man. Inside and out. He was such a man. Hidden. Inside and out. All by himself.

He sat at his kitchen table, staring at the shiny new bullets he'd made. All by himself.

Moonlight cut through the curtains at the window, illuminating one side of the shiny stack. He picked up one of the bullets, held it up to the light, turned it side to side, round and round. Imagined the damage it would do.

His lips curved. Oh, yes. The damage *he* would do.

He squinted in the darkness, held the bullet up to the shaft of moonlight. Studied the mark his handcrafted mold had pressed into the bullet's base, the two letters intertwined. It was his father's mark, and his father's before him. The symbol meant family.

Family. Carefully setting the bullet on the table, his fingers ran down the chain around his neck, feeling for the small medallion that was all that was left of his family. Of Leah.

The medallion had been hers, once a charm on her bracelet that had jingled with her every movement. Engraved with the letters in which she'd once based her faith.

He traced them, one by one. WWJD.

Indeed. What would Jesus do?

His breath caught, then released. Probably not what he was about to do.

Blindly he reached to his left, his fingers closing around the edge of the picture frame. He closed his eyes, unable to look at the face behind the glass, then opened them quickly, the more recent picture in his mind too agonizing to bear. He never believed his heart could break yet again, but every time he gazed into her eyes, frozen forever on film, he realized he'd been wrong. A heart could break again and again and again.

And a mind could replay pictures hideous enough to drive a man insane. Again and again and again.

With his left hand he measured the weight of her picture in its cheap silver frame against the flimsy weight of the medallion he held in his right.

Was he insane? Did it matter if he was?

He vividly remembered the sight of the coroner pulling back the sheet that covered her. The coroner had decided the sight was too gruesome to be done in person, so the identification had been done by closed-circuit video. He vividly remembered the look on the face of the sheriff's deputy as her body was revealed. It was pity. It was revulsion.

He couldn't say he blamed him. It wasn't every day that a small-town sheriff's office discovered the remains of a woman intent on ending her life. And ended it she had. No pills or slit wrists. No veiled cries for help from his Leah. No. She'd ended it with determination.

She'd ended it with the business end of a .38 against her temple.

His lips curved humorlessly. She'd ended it like a man. So like a man he'd stood, nodded. But the voice from his throat was that of a stranger. "Yes, that's her. That's Leah."

The coroner had nodded once, acknowledging he'd heard. Then the sheet went back up, and she was gone.

Yes, a heart could break again and again and again.

Gently he set the frame back on the table and picked up the bullet, one thumb stroking the pressed mark that had belonged to his father, the other the mark that had been Leah's. WWJD. So what *would* Jesus do?

He still didn't know. But he *did* know what He *wouldn't* do.

He wouldn't have allowed a twice-convicted rapist to roam the streets preying on innocent women. He wouldn't have allowed the monster to rape again. He wouldn't have allowed his victim to become so wretchedly depressed that she saw taking her own life as her only escape. He certainly wouldn't have allowed that rapist to escape justice a third time.

He'd prayed for wisdom, searched the Scripture. *Vengeance is mine, sayeth the Lord,* he'd read. God would have the final justice.

He swallowed hard, feeling Leah stare at him from the picture frame.

He'd just help God grant His final justice just a little bit sooner.

Chapter One

"You've got company, Kristen." Owen Madden pointed toward the window to the street where a man stood in a heavy winter coat, his head tilted in question.

Kristen Mayhew gave him a brief nod and he entered the diner where she'd escaped the enraged protests inside the courtroom and the barrage of questions from the press outside its doors. She stared into her soup as her boss, Executive Assistant State's Attorney John Alden sat on the stool beside her. "Coffee, please," he said and Owen got him a cup.

"How did you know I was here?" she asked, very quietly.

"Lois told me that this is where you come for lunch."

And breakfast and dinner, too, Kristen thought. If it didn't come in a microwavable carton, it came from Owen's. John's secretary knew her habits well.

"The local station interrupted programming for the

verdict and reaction," John said. "But you held your own with the press. Even that Richardson woman."

Kristen bit the inside of her cheek, anger roiling at the memory of the platinum blond's microphone in her face. She'd so wanted to shove that microphone up Zoe Richardson's ... "She wanted to know if there would be 'repercussions' in your office because of this loss."

"You know this is not a performance issue. You've got the best conviction record in the office." John shivered. "Damn, I'm cold. You want to tell me what happened in there?"

Kristen pulled the pins from the twist that held her hair in severe check, a raging headache the price of curl control. There was enough compressed energy in her bobby pins to fuel downtown Chicago for a year. Her hair sprang free and she knew she was now Little Orphan Annie. With eyes. And no dog named Sandy. And certainly no Daddy Warbucks watching over her. Kristen was on her own.

She massaged her head wearily. "They hung. Eleven guilties, one innocent. Juror three. Bought lock, stock, barrel, and soul by the money of *wealthy industrialist, Jacob Conti.*" She singsonged the last, the press's description of Angelo Conti's father. The man she knew had corrupted the system and denied a grieving family justice.

John's eyes darkened abruptly and his jaw tightened. "You're sure?"

She remembered the way the man who sat in chair number three wouldn't meet her eyes when the jury filed back in after four days of deliberations. How the other jury members looked at him with such contempt. "Sure I'm sure. He's got a young family, lots of bills. He's a prime target for a man like Jacob Conti. We all knew Conti was prepared to do anything to get his son off. Can I prove Juror Three took money from Conti in exchange for a hung jury?" She shook her head. "No, I can't."

John's fist clenched on the countertop. "So we've basically got nothing."

Kristen shrugged. Exhaustion was beginning to set in. One too many sleepless nights before the culmination of a critical trial. And she knew she wouldn't sleep tonight either. She knew that as soon as she laid her head on her pillow she'd hear the tortured cries of Paula Garcia's young husband as the jury disbanded and Jacob Conti's son walked away a free man. At least until they could try him again. "I'll get started tracking Juror Three's spending habits. Sooner or later he'll spend the money to pay off his bills. It's just a matter of time."

"And in the meantime?"

"I'll start a new trial. Angelo Conti will go back to Northwestern and resume his drinking and Thomas Garcia will go back to his empty apartment and stare at an empty crib."

John sighed. "You did your best, Kristen. Sometimes that's all we can do. If only . . ."

"If only he'd wrapped his Mercedes around a tree and not Paula Garcia," Kristen said bitterly. "If only he hadn't been so drunk that pulling Paula Garcia from her wrecked car and beating her to death with a tire iron to keep her quiet seemed like a good idea." She was shaking now, a combination of exhaustion and grief for the woman and the unborn child that had died with her. "If only Jacob Conti was more concerned about teaching his son responsibility than keeping him out of prison."

"If only Jacob Conti had taught his son responsibility *before* giving him the keys to a hundred-thousand-dollar sports car. Kristen, go home. You look like shit."

Her laugh was wobbly. "You sure know how to charm a girl."

He didn't smile back. "I'm serious. You look like you're about to drop right off your feet. I need you back here tomorrow ready to go again."

She glanced up, her mouth bent in a wry grimace. "You sweet-talker, you."

He did smile at that, briefly. Then he was sober once again. "I want Conti, Kristen. He's corrupted the system, tainted the jury pool. I want him to pay."

Kristen forced her body to slide off the stool, forced her legs to hold her up, fighting gravity and exhaustion. She met John's eyes with grim determination. "No more than I do."

Wednesday, February 18, 6:45 P.M.

Abe Reagan walked through the maze of detectives' desks, well aware of the curious stares that followed him as he searched for Lieutenant Marc Spinnelli. His new CO.

He heard the conversation inside when he was three feet from Spinnelli's cracked-open door. "Why him?" a female voice demanded. "Why not Wellinski or Murphy? Dammit, Marc, I want a partner I can *trust*, not some new guy nobody knows about."

Abe waited for Spinnelli's response. He had no doubt the woman was his new partner and based on her recent loss, he couldn't say he blamed Mia Mitchell for her attitude.

"You don't want a new partner at all, Mia," came the level answer, and Abe figured that was true enough. "But you're going to have a partner," Spinnelli continued, "and since last I looked I was your superior officer, I get to pick who that partner is."

"But he's never done Homicide. I gotta have someone with some experience here."

"He's got experience, Mia." Spinnelli's voice was soothing without being condescending. Abe liked that. "He's been undercover in Narcotics for the last five years."

Five years. He'd gone under a year after Debra was shot, hoping the added risk would dull the pain of watching his wife exist in the life-support-induced limbo doctors called a persistent vegetative state. It hadn't. A year ago she'd died and he stayed with his cover, hoping the risk would dull the pain of losing her completely. That it had done.

Mitchell was silent and Abe had started to knock when Spinnelli's voice cut through once again, this time reproachful. "Did you read any of the information I gave you?"

Another half beat of silence, followed by Mitchell's defensive answer. "I didn't have time. I was making sure Cindy and the kids had food on the table."

Cindy would be Mrs. Ray Rawlston, the widow of Mitchell's former partner who'd been killed in an ambush that left Mitchell with a scar just above her ribs where a bullet narrowly missed every major organ. It would appear Mitchell was a lucky cop. It would also appear that Abe knew a lot more about her than she knew about him. No longer compelled to eavesdrop, he lifted his knuckles to the door in a hard knock.

"Come." Spinnelli sat behind his desk and Mitchell leaned against a wall, arms crossed over her chest, eyeing him sharply. At five-four, her 125 pounds was a well-distributed muscled mass. Her file said she was single, never been married, thirty-one years old. Her face looked a good deal younger. Her eyes, on the other hand . . . She might as well have been coming up for her retirement Timex. Abe knew the feeling.

Spinnelli stood, his hand extended in greeting. "Abe, so good to see you again."

Abe met Spinnelli's eyes briefly as he shook his hand but quickly resumed his study of his new partner. Her eyes met his even though she had to bend her neck to look up. She didn't blink as she continued to lean against the wall, every muscle visibly tensed.

"Good to see you, too, Lieutenant." He returned her stare. "You're Mitchell."

She nodded coolly. "Last I checked, that was the name on my locker."

Well, at least this won't be boring, he thought. He stuck his hand out. "Abe Reagan."

She shook his hand fast, as if sustaining physical contact was a painful thing. Maybe it was. "I figured that out myself." She shot him a hostile look. "Why'd you leave Narcotics?"

"Mia!"

Abe shook his head. "It's okay. I can give Detective Mitchell the *Reader's Digest* version since she's been too busy to read my file." Mitchell's eyes narrowed but she said nothing. "We closed a five-year sting operation, nabbing the bad guys and 50 million in pure heroin, but my cover was blown in the process." He shrugged. "Time to move on."

Her stare never wavered. "Okay, Reagan, you made your point. When do you start?"

"Today," Spinnelli said. "Everything finished up in Narcotics, Abe?"

"Almost. I have to tie up a few loose ends at the prosecutor's office, so I'll head over there when we're done." His grin was rueful. "I've been under so long, it'll be an adjustment, walking in the front door of the SA's office, introducing myself as a detective again." Abe sobered. "Do I get a desk?" he asked and saw the pain that flashed in Mitchell's eyes.

She swallowed hard. "Yeah. I still have to clean it out, but—"

"It's okay," Abe interrupted. "I can do that."

Mitchell shook her head hard. "No," she bit out. "I'll do it. Go tie up your loose ends. The desk will be yours when you get back." Turning on her heel, she headed for the door.

Spinnelli faltered. "Mia . . ."

She spun around, rage supplanting the pain. "I said *I'd do it*, Marc." She was breathing hard as she fought for control.

"Did they, Mitchell?" Abe asked softly.

Her eyes flew up to meet his. "Did they what?"

"Did Ray's wife and kids have food on the table?"

Her breath shuddered out. "Yeah. They did."

"Good." Abe saw he'd scored a point with his new partner. Her nod of response was jerky, but she was back in enough control that she didn't slam the door behind her. Still, the blinds on the window clattered and shook.

Spinnelli drew a breath. "She's not over him yet. He was her mentor." Spinnelli shrugged, and Abe could see he still had unresolved grief of his own. "He was her friend."

"Yours, too."

Spinnelli managed a smile before sinking back down into the chair behind his desk. "Mine, too. Mia's a good cop." His eyes sharpened and Abe had the sudden, uncomfortable feeling Spinnelli was looking straight into his own soul. "I think you'll be good for each other."

Abe was the first to look away. He jangled his car keys. "I need to be getting over to the prosecutor's office." He'd made it to the door before Spinnelli stopped him again.

"Abe, I *have* read your file. You were lucky to be alive at the end of that last sting."

Abe shrugged. It was the story of his sorry life. Lucky, lucky, lucky. If they only knew the truth. "Looks like Mitchell and I have something in common after all."

Spinnelli's jaw tightened. "Mia went down guarding Ray's back. You have the reputation of taking chances, riding in to save the day." Spinnelli's expression was severe. "Leave your death wish in Narcotics. I don't want to go to any more funerals. Yours or Mia's."

Easier said than done. But knowing what was expected, Abe nodded stiffly. "Yes, sir."

Chapter Two

Wednesday, February 18, 8:00 P.M.

Kristen jabbed the elevator button. She was late leaving the office *again*. "Go home and rest, my ass," she muttered. John wanted her fresh for tomorrow, but he'd also wanted a "quick check" on a case. One thing led to another, just like every night. And just like every night she walked out of the office after everyone else had gone home, including John. She rolled her eyes even as she noted the burned-out bulbs in the hallway that connected their offices to the parking garage elevators. She fished her dictating recorder from her pocket.

"Note to Maintenance," she murmured into the recorder. "Two bulbs burned out at elevator entrance." Hopefully Lois would type up that note and the twenty others she'd recorded in the last three hours. Lois never refused, it was just a matter of getting her attention. All the prosecutors had staggering caseloads and every request coming out of the Special Investigations Unit was life and death. Unfortunately, Kristen's caseload was mostly death. Which ended up taking most of her life. Not that she had much of one. Here she was, standing at the elevator to the parking garage, alone and almost too tired to care.

She let her head drop forward, stretching muscles strained from poring over case files when the hairs on the back of her neck lifted and her nose detected a slight shift in the musty smell of the hallway. *Tired, yes, but not alone. Someone else is here.* Instinct, training, and old tapes had her reaching for the pepper spray she kept in her purse while her pulse scrambled and her brain strained to remember the location of the nearest exit. Every movement deliberate, she spun, her weight evenly distributed on the balls of her feet, the can of pepper spray clenched in her fist. Prepared to flee, but ready to defend.

She had but a split second to process the sight of the mountain of a man that stood behind her, his arms crossed over his broad chest, his eyes glued to the digital display above the elevator doors before one of his huge hands was clamped around her wrist in a vise grip and his eyes were boring into hers.

Blue eyes, bright as a flame, yet cold as ice. They held her gaze inexplicably. Kristen shivered yet still she stared, unable to look away. There was something familiar about his eyes. But the rest of him was a total stranger, and the rest of him filled the hallway, his broad shoulders blocking what little light there was, throwing his face into shadow. She searched her memory, trying to place where she'd seen him. Surely she'd remember a man of his size and presence. Even wrapped in shadow, the hard planes of his face spoke of unmistakable desolation, the line of his jaw uncompromising strength. Each day she dealt with people in pain and suffering, and intuitively she knew this man had experienced a great deal of both.

It was another second before she realized he was breathing as rapidly as she was. With a muttered curse he ripped the pepper spray out of her hand and the spell was broken. He dropped her wrist and automatically she rubbed it, her heart slowing to a somewhat normal rate. He hadn't been rough, just firm. Still, she'd have bruises from the pressure of his fingers on her skin even through the layers of her winter coat.

"Are you insane, lady?" he snarled softly, his voice a deep rumble in his chest.

Her temper rallied. "Are you? Don't you know better than to sneak up on women in dark hallways? I could have hurt you."

One dark eyebrow quirked up, amused. "Then you *are* insane. If I'd been bent on assaulting you, there wouldn't have been a damn thing you could've done to stop me."

Kristen felt the blood drain from her face as his words hit home, and just that fast all the old tapes began to roll. He was right. She would have been defenseless, at his mercy.

His eyes narrowed. "Don't faint on me, lady."

Again her temper surged, saving her. She pulled herself upright. "I never faint." That much was true. She extended her hand, palm up. "My pepper spray, if you don't mind."

He grunted. "I do mind." But he dropped it in her palm anyway. "I'm serious, lady, that pepper spray would just have made me madder. Especially since you didn't get me right away. I might even have used it on you."

Kristen frowned. Knowing he was right just made her madder. "What do you expect a woman to do?" she snapped, exhaustion making her rude. "Just stand here and be a victim?"

"I never said that." He shrugged. "Take a self-defense class."

"I have." The elevator dinged and both of them jerked their eyes to the wall, waiting to see which set of doors would open first. The doors on the left slid open and the man waved his hand dramatically, gesturing her in first.

She assessed him with a shrewdness born of thousands of hours of associating with known felons who'd committed every unspeakable crime. This man was no danger, she could see that now. Still, Kristen Mayhew was a prudent woman. "I'll wait for the next one."

His blue eyes flashed. His square jaw clenched and a muscle twitched in his cheek. She'd offended him. Too damn bad. "I don't hurt innocent women," he said tightly, holding the elevator doors back when they began to close. His powerful body settled slightly and she got the sudden impression he was as weary as she. "Come on, lady, I don't want to hold this elevator all damn night, and I won't leave you here all alone."

Uneasily she glanced up and down the deserted hallway. She didn't like loitering there any longer than she had to. So she walked into the elevator, annoyed as always when faced with the reality that despite ten years and five times as many self-therapy books, she was still afraid to be alone in a dark corridor. "Don't call me 'lady,' " she snapped.

He followed her in and the doors slid closed. He faced her, his eyes now stern. "What was the first thing they taught you in that self-defense class, *ma'am*?"

She seethed under his patronizing tone. "Always to be aware of your surroundings."

He simply lifted an arrogant brow and Kristen's blood began to boil. "I was. I knew you were there, didn't I? Even though you sneaked up on me." And he had. She swore he had not been there a moment before she sensed him and he hadn't made a sound in his approach.

He snorted. "I'd been standing there for two whole minutes."

Kristen narrowed her eyes. "I don't believe you."

He leaned back against the elevator wall, folding his arms across his chest. " 'Note to Maintenance,' " he mimicked. "And my personal favorite, 'Go home and rest, my ass.' "

Kristen felt her face flood with color. "Why haven't we moved?" she demanded, then rolled her eyes. Neither of them had punched a button. Quickly she jabbed the button for the second floor and the elevator began to move.

"And now I know where you've parked your car," he announced with a satisfied nod.

He was right. She'd ignored everything she'd learned about keeping herself safe. She rubbed her throbbing temples. "You were right, I was wrong. Are you satisfied now, sir?"

His lips curved at that and the sight took her breath away. A simple smile transformed his face from devastating to . . . devastating. Her poor, abused heart skipped a beat, and she had the good sense to be surprised at herself. She didn't react to men, not *that* way, anyway. It wasn't that she didn't like them or notice them or even appreciate a good specimen here or there. And he was most definitely a good specimen. Tall, broad. Movie-star good looks. Of course she'd noticed him. She was human after all. Just slightly broken. The memory of a single word cut into her consciousness. No, there was no "slightly" about it.

"No, ma'am," he said. "And I honestly didn't mean to sneak up on you. You just seemed so pleasantly engaged in conversation with yourself and I didn't want to barge in."

Again her cheeks burned. "Don't you ever talk to yourself?"

His smile dimmed and the look of almost desperate desolation returned to his eyes, making Kristen feel guilty for even asking the question. "On occasion," he murmured.

The elevator dinged again, and the doors opened to a darkened cavern of automobiles and the smell of stale oil and exhaust. This time his after-you gesture was much more subdued and Kristen wasn't sure how to end the conversation.

"Look, I'm sorry I almost pepper-sprayed you. You were right. I should have been more aware of my surroundings."

He studied her carefully. "You're tired. People lower their guard when they're tired."

She smiled wryly. "So it shows, huh?"

He nodded. "Yeah. Just for my peace of mind, let me walk you to your car."

Kristen narrowed her eyes. "Who are you?"

"I was wondering when you'd ask. Are you always this trusting, carrying on conversations with strange men in deserted elevators?"

No, she definitely wasn't, definitely had the right not to be. "No, I normally pepper-spray first and ask questions later," she shot back and he smiled, this time in rueful acceptance.

"Then I guess I'm lucky once again," he said. "I'm Abe Reagan."

Kristen frowned. "I know you. I know I do."

He shook his dark head. "No, I would have remembered you."

"Why?"

"Because I never forget a face."

He said it matter-of-factly, as if there were no possibility of flirtation. And Kristen was annoyed to find herself disappointed.

"I have to be getting home." She turned on her heel, her key poking out from between two fingers as she'd been taught. She held her head high and looked and listened as she walked, but only heard his footsteps behind her. She stopped at her aged Toyota and he stopped, too. She looked up at his face, again in the shadows. "Thank you. You can go now."

"I don't think so, *ma'am*."

Enough was enough. "Excuse me?"

He pointed to her tire. "See for yourself."

Kristen looked and felt physically sick. Of all times, a flat tire. "Dammit."

"Don't worry, I'll change it for you."

Another day she might have refused, because she was certainly capable of changing a tire. Today, she'd let him knock himself out. "Thanks. I really appreciate it, Mr. Reagan."

He took off his overcoat and laid it across her hood. "My friends call me Abe."

She hesitated, then shrugged. If he'd planned anything evil, he would have done it by now. "I'm Kristen."

"Then pop the trunk, Kristen, and we'll have you on your way."

Kristen did, wondering when she'd last opened her trunk, sincerely hoping she had a spare, already anticipating Mr. Know-it-all's scathing response if she didn't.

And stopped short, staring at the interior of the trunk she'd left clean and empty.

To say it wasn't as she'd left it would be quite the understatement. She reached out a tentative hand, then snatched it back. *Don't touch anything*. She squinted, trying to make sense of the three large shapes that had not been there before. As her eyes grew accustomed to the dim illumination provided by the little trunk light, her brain began to process what her eyes were seeing. And the resulting message from her brain sent her stomach churning. She'd thought her day couldn't get any worse after the Conti mistrial.

She'd been very, very wrong.

Reagan's voice cut through the fog in her brain. "This should only take a few minutes."

"Um, I don't think so."

In an instant he was behind her, looking over her shoulder and she could hear him exhale on a hiss. "Holy shit."

Either his eyes were better than hers or fatigue had put her in slow-motion mode because it had taken Abe Reagan only a split second to comprehend what had taken her multiple seconds to process to the point of being well and truly horrified.

"I need to call the police." Her voice trembled and she didn't care. It wasn't every day her personal space was violated. It sure as hell wasn't every day she presided over her very own crime scene. And this one qualified as a real doozy.

Three plastic milk crates sat side by side. Each contained clothing topped by a manila envelope. Each envelope had a single Polaroid taped precisely in its center. And even from where she stood she could see the subject of each Polaroid was well and truly dead.

"I need to call the police," she repeated, grateful her voice was steady once again.

"You just did," Abe replied, his voice grim.

Kristen twisted, looking up at his face. "You're a cop?"

He pulled a pair of latex gloves from his pocket. "Detective Abe Reagan, Homicide." The gloves went on each hand with a surgical snapping sound that seemed to echo in the quiet of the garage. "This might be a good time to completely introduce yourself, Kristen."

She watched as he carefully pulled the envelope from the crate on the far right. "Kristen Mayhew."

His head jerked around, surprise on his face. "The prosecutor? Well, I'll be damned," he added when she nodded. He studied her face intently. "It's your hair," he announced and turned his attention back to the envelope in his hand.

"What about my hair?"

"It was pulled back." He held the envelope close to the trunk light. "I wish I had a flashlight."

"I have one in the glove box."

He shook his head, his eyes fixed on the Polaroid. "Don't bother. I'll have your car towed and dusted for prints, so don't touch anything. Son of a gun. This boy is dead."

"What, the bullet hole in his head tipped you off?" Kristen asked wryly and Abe Reagan shot her a brief but equally wry grin.

"Hey, what can I say?" Then he sobered, resuming his study. "Caucasian male, late twenties, early thirties. Hands tied in front of him . . ." He squinted. "Wonderful," he said flatly.

Kristen leaned over his arm to stare. "What?"

"If I'm not mistaken, somebody's stitched your boy up, stem to stern."

Kristen grabbed his arm and tilted the picture toward the trunk light. Sure enough, a line started at the man's sternum and stretched down his torso. "My God," she murmured. Horrified by a sudden thought her eyes flicked to the milk crates, then up to meet Reagan's eyes. "You don't think . . ." She let the question trail off when his face twisted into a grimace.

"What, that whatever body parts that were removed are

in these crates? Well, Counselor, I suppose we'll find out soon enough. Do you recognize this guy?"

She squinted, shook her head. "It's too dark. Maybe I will when we get it in better light." She looked up at him, feeling stupid and helpless and hating both. "I'm sorry."

"It's okay, Kristen. We'll figure this out." He flipped his cell phone open and punched some numbers. "It's Reagan," he announced. "I've got a . . ."

"Situation," Kristen supplied, feeling hysterical laughter building down deep. She shoved it deeper. Someone had committed murder and stowed the evidence in the *trunk* of her *car*. There could be hearts and spleens and God-knew-what-else in the *trunk* of her *car*. She'd been driving around, blissfully unaware that an entire crime scene resided in the damn *trunk* of her *car*. She took a deep breath, relieved to smell stale oil and exhaust instead of putrid rotting internal organs.

"A situation," Abe was repeating. "I'm here with Kristen Mayhew. Someone left what looks like evidence of a multiple homicide in the trunk of her car . . . We're on the second floor of the parking garage next door to the courthouse. Seal the exits, just in case he's still around." He listened, then looked down at her, and his eyes which she'd thought to be cold flared to life with heated interest. His eyes slid to her hands which she realized were still clutching his arm as if he were a lifeline. Quickly she stepped back and looked away, dropping her hands to her sides just as he said, "I'll tell her . . . Yeah, I'll be waiting." He snapped his phone shut and dropped it in his pocket. "You okay?" he asked.

She nodded, hoping her face was only peony pink and hadn't progressed to ruby red which clashed with her hair. Striving for dignity, she asked, "Tell me what?" Then she looked up and whatever forced nonchalance she'd managed to work into her face just drained away.

He was still looking at her, his eyes intense, his jaw tight. A tingle started in her chest and sped to her extremities making her shiver and to her mortification she had to clench her hands to keep them from grabbing his arm again. "Spinnelli says to tell you that you didn't have to go to so much trouble for department attention," he said, his voice low and rumbly. "Flowers and candy would have sufficed." The timbre of his voice alone intensified the sensation of fingertips trailing the back of her neck, and she suddenly wondered what it would be like if he did just that. But he'd turned back to her trunk and the other two crates, breaking the almost tangible connection between them and Kristen shivered again. "He's sending a CSU team. This could take a while."

Wednesday, February 18, 9:00 P.M.

Finally. He sat in his car safely out of the flurry of uniformed activity taking place inside the parking garage. Lights flashed and yellow tape was strung everywhere. Either some political dignitary had been murdered in the garage or Kristen Mayhew had finally looked in her trunk. He was pretty certain he could disregard the former.

He'd been busy in the last weeks. He was up to six. Six down, about a million to go.

He'd taken his first in secret, painlessly and quietly.

And had discovered it wasn't nearly enough. Not enough that he'd done such a thing for the world. For the victims. For his Leah. It wasn't enough that he be the only one to know. It wasn't enough that he be the only one to celebrate.

So he'd abruptly changed his plan and once done, it was easy to determine who else would know what he'd done. The person who most deserved to know.

Kristen Mayhew.

He'd been watching her for some time. Knew how vigilantly she worked to get justice for every victim who crossed her path. And how destroyed she was whenever she failed. Today had been a bad one. Angelo Conti. Vicious, vicious, cold-hearted bastard.

His hands clenched around the steering wheel. Conti had murdered a pregnant woman with no remorse, but was home tonight, sleeping in his own soft bed. Conti would wake up tomorrow and go on with his life.

He smiled. He himself would wake up tomorrow and add Conti's name to the fishbowl. It was full, his fishbowl. Full of slips of paper, cut precisely, folded precisely. Each holding a typed name, representing so much evil. But they would get their due, one at a time. He'd get to Conti sooner or later. And like all the others, Conti would pay.

He was up to six. Six down, about a million to go.

Chapter Three

Wednesday, February 18, 9:30 P.M.

Spinnelli was waiting for them in the lab, slapping a pair of latex gloves against his palm as they entered in single file, looking like three kings bearing gifts for the Christ child.

"What took you so long?" he snapped as Abe set the crate he carried on the stainless-steel table that dominated the center of the room.

"We were waiting for Jack to finish," Mia snapped back, setting her crate next to his.

Crime Scene Supervisor Jack Unger was the leader of the CSU team sent to comb the parking garage. His team had been thorough and professional and Abe had to respect their skill even as he grew more restless by the moment. There was likely evidence of multiple homicides in these crates, but the light was too poor in the garage to see a damn thing. Jack had insisted they wait to examine the contents of Kristen Mayhew's trunk until he'd finished his initial sweep. Jack placed his crate at the end of the table and turned to face Spinnelli.

"You want it done fast or right?" Jack asked, unperturbed.

"Both," Spinnelli said. "Where's Kristen?"

"I'm here." Kristen brought up the rear and closed the door behind her. "I was trying to get John Alden on the phone to let him know what happened, but I just got his voice mail."

"Well, I'm here in person so how's about telling *me* what happened?" Spinnelli demanded, pulling on his gloves.

Kristen pulled off her coat and Abe's memory was confirmed. Her bulky winter coat had concealed a petite, slender body in a tailored suit of black that contrasted sharply with her ivory skin and those green eyes that gripped him from the moment he'd seen her at the elevator, wild-haired and wide-eyed. He remembered the first time he'd seen her, the only other time, two years ago. She'd worn black that day as well. She'd apparently seen him too, but hadn't connected the memory yet. He wondered if she would. That she remembered anything about that meeting, he found remarkable. He hadn't recognized her in the elevator, not with her auburn hair curling in every which direction. That day two years ago she'd worn it up in a severe twist that looked so tight it had to hurt, just as she wore it now.

He watched as she ran a hand over her hair as if to assure

herself it was in no danger of escaping the twist she'd managed just before Mia and Jack had arrived on the scene. It didn't take a detective to figure out she was buttoning herself back into her prosecutor persona. She had a reputation that didn't include wild hair, fear, or clutching the arms of total strangers.

"I met Detective Reagan while waiting for the elevator." She lifted one shoulder in a half shrug. "It was late and he offered to see me to my car, but when we got there, the tire was flat. When I opened the trunk for the jack, I saw this." She gestured to the three milk crates, then extended her hand, palm up. "Got another pair of gloves?"

Jack gave her a pair and she pulled them on, taking a position at the table as physically far from Abe as possible. She'd maintained her distance in the hour since they'd discovered the crates filled with clothing and envelopes. Not once had she gripped his arm or anyone else's, and Abe knew she was embarrassed that he'd seen her vulnerable and frightened. She was no longer either of those things, now sober and wary. He found the utter turnaround fascinating.

"Let's take a look at what your secret admirer left for you," Jack said. "Any preference on where to begin?"

Abe watched as Kristen's eyes flicked to the crate on the end, the one with the Polaroid of the stitched-up torso. The one she'd worried might hold body parts as she clutched his arm. The one he'd carried in himself.

"It wasn't any heavier than the others," Abe said and her eyes lifted to his, and for a moment he saw relieved gratitude before the professional shield rose once again.

"Then let's start with the way he had them placed in my trunk. Left to right."

Jack picked up an envelope from the first crate, examining it. "I'm willing to bet we get nothing from the envelopes. Probably stock you could buy at any office supply store. But I'll slit the top just in case he was stupid enough to lick the envelope and leave me some DNA."

Spinnelli grunted. "Don't hold your breath."

"Jack's the eternal optimist," Mia said. "He still buys season tickets to the Cubs."

Jack just grinned at Mia in the way of very old friends. "They'll win the pennant this year." Sobering, he handed the envelope to Kristen. "You recognize this guy, Counselor?"

Kristen hesitated. "It was too dark in the garage." Drawing a breath, she held out her hand. "Let's take a look." Abe saw her hand tremble, saw her quickly control it as her eyes dropped to the grainy Polaroid stuck to the envelope. "Anthony Ramey," she said quietly.

"Shit," Mia muttered.

"Who is Anthony Ramey?" Abe asked.

"Serial rapist," Kristen answered and she swallowed. "He seized his victims in parking garages up and down Michigan Avenue. Targeted women walking alone to their cars after hours." Her green eyes flicked to his. He thought about the wild fear in her eyes in front of the elevator, that pathetic can of pepper spray in her hand, and found himself angry on her behalf. It was no wonder she'd been afraid of him. It was little wonder she ventured out onto the streets at all, given the crimes she'd seen. It was little wonder any of them could. "I prosecuted him two and a half years ago," she said, "but the jury acquitted."

"Why?"

Regret shadowed her face. "Unlawful search of Ramey's apartment. The judge threw out the only piece of physical evidence we had, and his victims were unable to make a positive ID."

"Warren and Trask executed that search," Mia said, tilting the envelope so she could see the picture, leaving it in Kristen's hands. "They still haven't gotten over it."

Kristen sighed. "Neither have I. Those three women didn't want to testify, but they did because I told them we could put Ramey away for good."

"Well, now someone has," Abe said and Kristen looked troubled.

"I'd say so." She gave the envelope back to Jack. "I don't think I'm going to like this, but let's have the next one." Jack handed her the next envelope, the equally grainy Polaroid showing three bodies lined up shoulder to shoulder. Kristen blinked and brought the picture closer to the overhead light. "You got a magnifying glass, Jack?" Wordlessly Jack handed her a small glass. She peered and squinted. "Oh, God."

Mia looked over her shoulder and hissed a curse. "Blades."

Abe's brows went up. "Blades? Those three guys are Blades?" He'd had dealings with the gang in his undercover role. The Blades were well-known for dealing in weapons and drugs. They'd been small-time when he started in Narcotics, but they were growing rapidly. If someone had murdered three Blades, there would be hell to pay.

Again Kristen met his eyes from across the table. "They have Blade tattoos. See for yourself." She handed him the envelope and the glass. "I prosecuted three Blades last year for the murder of two elementary school children waiting for their school bus," she continued as he noted the tattoo of three braided snakes on the upper arm of one of the bodies. She had a good eye. Or perhaps she had never been able to put the sight from her mind. "The children got caught in gang cross fire. They were only seven years old."

God. Seven years old and mowed down like they were

nothing because a crowd of punks had a turf war going.
"And these guys were acquitted?" he asked tightly.

She nodded and once again he saw regret in her green
eyes. Regret and anger and growing apprehension. "We had
four eyewitnesses."

"Who promptly got amnesia the day of the trial," Mia
added bitterly. "That one was mine." She looked away.
"And Ray's."

"You did your best, Mia," Spinnelli said. "All of you
did."

Abe handed the envelope back to Jack. "Let's see the last
one."

"I'm not sure I want to," Mia muttered.

Kristen squared her shoulders. "We're two for two. The
last one will probably be one of mine, too." She took this
envelope herself. "This one's been sewn up, breastbone to
abdomen." Her mouth tightened. "And it couldn't have happened to a nicer guy." She glanced at Spinnelli over her
shoulder. "Ross King."

Spinnelli's lips curled in distaste. "Hell's got new company tonight."

Abe reached across the table and took the envelope from
her hands. She was right, but he had to strain to see it. The
battered face in the Polaroid bore little resemblance to
the face that had been plastered across the front page of the
Tribune for weeks leading up to King's trial. "You've got
good eyes. I wouldn't have recognized him with all those
bruises on his face."

"Maybe it's because that's how I imagined him," Kristen
returned, her voice hard. Brittle. "After all the parents of his
victims got done with him."

Abe looked up in surprise and her lips curved bitterly.
"We're not immune, Detective. We see the victims, too. It's

hard not to hate a man who preyed on boys who trusted him."

"I read about it in the paper when I was under." Abe handed the envelope to Spinnelli who'd been waiting his turn. "Softball coach and pedophile."

"With a damned clever lawyer." Kristen's jaw clenched. "Put King's brother on the stand and coached him to let it slip that King had priors for sexual misconduct. His lawyer got a mistrial, but we had to plead him down from rape to misdemeanor assault because the boys' parents refused to put their sons through a second trial."

"Which was what his sonofabitch lawyer had planned all along," Spinnelli gritted.

"Like I said, his lawyer was damned clever." Kristen leaned forward, bracing her gloved fingertips against the table, staring into the crates. "So now we know the cast of characters. Five dead bad men. Let's get on with the play, Jack."

They all watched as Jack carefully sliced open the first envelope and slid its contents on the stainless-steel table. He switched on a tape recorder. "This is the envelope with the Polaroid of Anthony Ramey," he said for the tape. "Inside we find four more Polaroids. Views of the victim from various angles. Looks like a concrete floor in the background."

Abe sifted through the pictures. "Here's a close-up of his head. Bullet was probably a twenty-two." He looked up at Kristen. "Anything bigger wouldn't have left much face."

Jack was back to the envelope contents. "Four Polaroids and . . . one map with a nice little 'x.' Looks like it's down by the Arboretum."

Spinnelli's mustache bent down. "That's where we picked Ramey up."

Jack set the map on the table, leaving one piece of paper

in his hand. He went still, only his eyes moving, back and forth as they scanned the page. He looked up uncertainly. "And one letter that starts 'My dearest Kristen.' "

Kristen's eyes widened. "Me?"

She was alarmed, Abe thought, as well she should be. Their killer had just gotten a little more personal. "Read the letter, Jack," Abe commanded softly. "Out loud."

Wednesday, February 18, 10:00 P.M.

Jacob Conti didn't glance sideways when the door to the club was opened for him. He was rich beyond most people's ability to count. Everybody held the door open for Jacob Conti. He had almost forgotten a time when he would have been surprised at the gesture of respect. He scanned the throng of bodies gyrating on the dance floor, his eyes narrowing as he located Angelo. His son was easy to spot. He'd be the one with a whore on each knee and a bottle in his hand. You'd think after narrowly escaping prison his son would toe the line for at least an evening. But no, there he was. Celebrating his innocence, no doubt.

Angelo's celebrations were legendary. And they would soon stop.

Jacob stood in front of Angelo for a full minute before his son realized he was there.

"Hello, Father," Angelo slurred, lifting the mostly empty bottle in salute.

"Get up," Jacob gritted. "Get up before I pull you out of here."

Angelo stared a moment, then slowly ambled to his feet. "What's wrong?"

"What's wrong is you being seen here getting drunk."

Angelo grinned. "So? I was acquitted." He ran his

tongue over his teeth as if surprised he could even say the word. "I can't be tried again. Double jeopardy, you know."

Jacob grabbed Angelo's lapels and hauled him on his toes. "You idiot. You weren't acquitted. You got a hung jury. That means they get another shot at you. That means Mayhew is watching you like a hawk. That means one wrong step and you're back in jail."

Angelo pulled away, flattening his lapels with damp palms, his courage mostly bravado and booze. "I wouldn't mind seeing Miss Mayhew again. She hid a really nice ass under that black suit." He raised a surly brow. "But I won't be going back to jail."

Jacob clenched his fists at his sides. He'd hit Angelo here and now, but Elaine didn't like him to raise his hand to their boy. Their "boy" was twenty-one years old and headed for trouble, but Jacob held his temper. "And what makes you so sure, Angelo?"

Angelo sneered. "Because you'll always be there to bail me out."

Jacob watched his only son weave through the gyrating bodies and knew Angelo was right. He loved his son and he'd do anything to keep him safe.

Wednesday, February 18, 10:00 P.M.

"That's it," Jack said after he'd read the last word of the letter.

Kristen stared at it, glad it was in Jack's steady hands, because hers were anything but. Knowing the others were waiting for her to say something, she tugged at the latex gloves that encased her sweaty palms and reached for the letter, willing her hands not to shake.

"May I?"

Jack handed it over with a shrug. "You're the celebrity, Counselor."

She shot him a sharp look. "That's not funny, Jack."

"I didn't mean it to be," Jack replied. "What does he mean, blue stripes?"

Her heart pounding against her rib cage, she scanned the page, hoping Jack had left something out. He hadn't. She turned the page over and stared at the back, hoping there would be something to alert her to the writer's identity. There was nothing. Just a plain piece of paper from a generic printer, just like thousands of printers in the city. No name, no mark, no nothing. Just three paragraphs of the most elegant, chilling words she'd ever read.

"I take it you've never received a similar letter?" Mia asked, gently pushing at Kristen's wrist until the letter lay flat on the table where she could see it, too.

Kristen shook her head. "No, not like this." She drummed her fingertips on the table. "Never like this." She lifted her eyes and found Abe Reagan's blue eyes fixed on her with an intensity she found more disconcerting now than when he'd gripped her wrist in front of the elevator. "What?" she asked, and he frowned.

"Read it again," he said.

"Fine." Kristen made herself utter the first line. " 'My dearest Kristen.' "

"He knows you," Spinnelli murmured, sending a new set of chills down her spine.

"Or thinks he does," Abe mused, then gestured with his hand. "Go on."

She splayed her gloved hands flat on the tabletop on either side of the simply printed page to keep her fingers from drumming. " 'My dearest Kristen, There comes a time in a man's life when he must take a stand for his beliefs and acknowledge a law higher than the law of man. This is that time. For too long have I watched the innocent suffer and the guilty go free. I can watch no longer. I know you of all people can appreciate this. For years you have worked to avenge the innocent, to make the guilty pay for their crimes. But even you cannot win them all. Anthony Ramey preyed on innocent women, battered their bodies, stole their confidence and their trust, and though they bravely confronted their attacker in your courtroom, they found no justice. Today they have their justice, as do you. Tonight you can sleep well, knowing Anthony Ramey has met his final judge.'" She drew a deep breath. "It's signed 'Your Humble Servant.'" Her fingers drummed, just once and she splayed her hands flat again. "Then there's the P.S." She opened her mouth, but no more words came out.

Perplexed, Mia read the last line for her. "'And if for some reason you can't sleep well, I recommend the blue stripes.'"

There was silence in the room until Reagan tapped the table. She looked up to find the same frown on his face. "What does that mean, Kristen, 'the blue stripes'?"

Kristen fought back a bubble of what would most certainly be hysterical laughter. "What do you do when you can't sleep, Detective Reagan?"

Reagan studied her thoughtfully. "I usually get up and watch TV or read."

"Mia?"

Mia looked at her strangely. "Sometimes TV. Sometimes the treadmill. Why?"

Kristen pushed back from the table and peeled off the gloves that were sticky with her sweat. She grabbed a paper towel and dried her hands. "I do home improvements."

Mia's blond brows jumped to the top of her forehead. "Excuse me?"

Kristen's lips curved in a self-deprecating smile. "I work

on my house. I've painted walls, refinished hardwood floors and put in a new bathroom. Last month I wallpapered my living room. I hung samples on the walls for a week, trying to decide which pattern to go with. Pink roses, green ivy, or . . ." Exhaling, she threw the paper towel away. "Or blue stripes." She turned to look at the group who looked collectively troubled. "I see you understand."

"He's a vigilante murdering peeping Tom," Mia said, disbelief in her voice and this time Kristen couldn't control her laugh, which thankfully didn't sound too hysterical.

"Jack, I need another pair of gloves. Let's see what else he left in the crate."

Jack obliged and she pulled on the dry gloves while he gingerly removed folded clothing from the crate and placed each item in a specially prepared plastic tub. A rank odor filled the air and Kristen was suddenly glad she'd had no dinner. "We'll unfold them in the lab, look for fibers, that kind of thing," he said. "We've got a shirt, very bloody." He flipped the collar to check the tag. "No famous brand. One pair of jeans, slightly bloody. Levi's. One belt." He grimaced. "One pair of jockey shorts. Fruit of the Loom."

"Would his mother be proud?" Spinnelli asked dryly and Jack chuckled.

"You mean are they clean? May have been when he put 'em on. Sure aren't now. One pair of socks, one pair of Nikes. And finally . . ." He frowned at the bottom of the crate. "I don't know. Some sort of tile. Considerate of your humble servant to put a bottom in the crate, Counselor. That way nothing of importance slipped out." He lifted out a thin slice of stone, turning it over and sideways. "Well, this is one for the books. I think it's marble."

"This whole case will be one for the books," Kristen said. "How about the next crate, Jack. The one with the Blades? I want to see if there's another letter."

Jack sliced open the next envelope and more Polaroids and papers slid free. "He's methodical," he said as they gathered closer. "Close-ups of the tattoos, bullet entry wounds."

Kristen clenched her fists to keep her fingers still. "Is there a letter, Jack?"

"Patience, patience," he admonished.

"You wouldn't say that if he was peeping in your living room window," Mia said and Jack had the good grace to look chastised.

"One map, 'x' marks the spot . . . And one letter." He handed it to Kristen, soberly.

"Wonderful." Kristen scanned the page, swallowed back the lump that rose in her throat at the P.S., this one more personal. " 'My dearest Kristen. It would appear you haven't yet found the first token of my esteem.' " She looked up, found Reagan studying her with the same concern as before. "He sounds pissed."

Reagan's black brows furrowed. "Go on."

" 'No matter, it's only a matter of time, after all. I suppose we're fortunate it is winter. They should keep.' " Her own brows crinkled at that, then glancing at the map she understood and her stomach quickened at the thought. "He means their bodies should keep."

"Aren't we the lucky ones?" Mia asked, tongue-in-cheek.

" 'These three hoodlums and their kind savage the peace every day. They've stolen the lives of two precious innocents and for that alone they should die. The fear and misery they caused the good people who would have done the right thing and testified makes their sin all the worse. You fought a good battle in the courtroom, Kristen, but this one was lost before you began. Again, sleep well knowing these heartless murderers have been rendered final justice . . . Your Humble Servant.' "

"And the P.S.?" Abe asked.

Kristen drew a careful breath, trying to keep the words from sticking in her throat. " 'The blue stripes were a good choice and your workmanship admirable. You may, however, choose different attire when you begin work on your next project. I would hate for anyone to believe you anything but a lady.' "

Mia hesitated. "What did you wear to the wallpapering extravaganza, Kristen?"

Kristen's cheeks heated as her hands grew clammy once again. "A sports bra and biker shorts. It was three A.M. I didn't think anyone in my neighborhood was awake to care."

Reagan pushed back from the table and paced the length of the room, his big body tense. "That isn't the point," he said tightly. "Jack, I want to see that last letter."

Again Jack obliged, slitting open the envelope, sliding the contents to the table. He bypassed the Polaroids and the map and handed Reagan the letter without a word. Reagan scanned it, creases of color appearing on his cheekbones, a scowl bending his features. " 'My dearest Kristen, I grow impatient for you to share the satisfaction of my labor. Ross King was the lowest of criminals, preying on young children, stealing their youth, their innocence, then conspiring with his debased lawyer to further pervert the system. What he has received at my hand is a thousandfold less than he deserves. Sleep well tonight, knowing the children he ruined are vindicated and countless others are now safe from harm . . . Your Humble Servant.' "

"And the P.S.?" Kristen asked, hearing her voice tremble.

He looked up, his eyes narrowed and questioning. " 'Cherry, dear.' "

Kristen closed her eyes, her empty stomach churning. "I've been stripping the paint off my antique fireplace mantel and I'm about to start the staining. Choices are oak, maple, or cherry." She opened her eyes. "The fireplace is in my basement. You can't see in from the street. You have to be standing at the window, looking down."

"Then he's venturing up to your house." Spinnelli was grim. "When was the last time you worked on the mantel?"

"This past Saturday." She flattened her hands on her thighs. "I've been too busy with the Conti case to do any work on the house the last few days."

"Then we have a time frame. He must have been frustrated that you didn't check your trunk." Spinnelli looked from Abe to Jack to Mia. "You check the tire for vandalism?"

"Puncture in the sidewall," Abe responded, his fists jammed in his pants pockets.

"Was the tire punctured while the car was parked in the garage?" Spinnelli asked.

"Almost certainly," Jack said, then turned to Kristen. "Do you mean you really haven't opened your trunk for a month, Kristen? Not even once?"

Kristen shrugged. "I never carry anything large. Any home improvement materials get delivered by the store. I just put little stuff in the backseat."

Mia frowned. "Don't you buy groceries or anything?"

"Not a lot. I don't cook very often, so no."

"If you don't cook, what do you eat?" Spinnelli asked.

Kristen shrugged again. "I eat most of my meals at a diner near the courthouse." She found herself addressing the next question to Abe Reagan. "What next?"

Reagan was looking at the maps. "Let's put some uniforms at each of these locations until we can get your guys out there, Jack. I want to start at dawn. First light."

Spinnelli was looking at the Polaroids. "We have five dead men. Suspects?"

Mia sucked in one cheek. "First stop would have to be the victims of the . . . victims."

"How many victims are we talking about, Kristen?" Spinnelli asked.

Kristen sat back. "Ramey had three that we know of. The Blades had their two. Ross King had six boys come forward, ranging in age from seven to fifteen. So all totaled we have eleven victims, plus families and friends." She lifted her eyes once again to Reagan's intense gaze. "I can get you a list of names and last-known addresses."

"But that one victim would kill all five," Jack wondered. "Does that make sense?"

"Perfect way to muddy the waters." Abe noted the coordinates of each map on his notepad. "Get your revenge, pop off a few for the road, give the defense attorneys room to introduce reasonable doubt if you're caught. There's a certain poetic justice in it."

"I'm surprised our humble servant didn't pick off a defense lawyer or two while he was at it," Mia muttered.

Kristen took in the photos, the clothing, the maps. The letters. "Don't discount it," she said quietly. "I don't think he's anywhere close to being done yet."

Chapter Four

Wednesday, February 18, 11:00 P.M.

Abe stopped short at the base of the stairs. There she was, once again. Standing at the glass doors that led to the street, nearly swallowed up in her bulky coat, her rich red hair still in the tight twist that made his head ache just looking at it. Her profile could have been hewn from stone, she was so still. He was surprised to see her. He thought she would have left half an hour before, when the meeting had disbanded and they'd all gone their separate ways. Spinnelli had gone back to his office to order uniformed watch over the three sites indicated by the maps. Mia disappeared with a large box filled with Ray Rawlston's personal effects.

His new partner was efficient, eradicating all traces of the man who'd owned that desk for twenty years. He didn't envy her the task of taking personal effects to the widow of a fallen officer. He'd done it himself, once, before making detective. It was his partner's baseball cap, and he'd held the woman left behind, awkwardly patting her back as she sobbed, clutching the baseball cap to her breast. His partner's wife hadn't cried at the hospital or the funeral, but it was somehow holding that damn cap that lowered her floodgates. He'd gone home and pounded the punching bag in the garage until Debra had come to find him, worried. She'd kissed his sore knuckles, then held him, murmured in his ear the comforting things that only a wife can. *Could.* Past tense. Debra was gone, truly gone.

God, he missed her. He let himself yearn for just a moment, to wish for what might have been, to wonder what if. Then realized he still stood in the same spot. Still stared at Kristen Mayhew's profile as she stared out onto the darkened street. And he wondered what went through her mind. He assumed she was scared. She had every right to be. Even though Spinnelli had ordered a unit drive by her house every hour and even though she had every one of their personal cell phone numbers, she had every right to be afraid.

He approached slowly and cleared his throat. "Am I out of pepper spray range?" In the window's reflection he saw her lips quirk in rueful amusement.

"You're safe, Detective," she said quietly. "I thought you'd be gone by now."

He stopped a few inches from her right shoulder, closer than he'd intended. But he caught the scent of her fragrance and his feet refused to move. When she'd clutched his arm in the garage she'd been this close, but his head had been filled with the odor of stale oil and exhaust. She smelled good, he thought. Pretty. And he wished he hadn't noticed. "I'm on my way home. I thought you'd have been out of here a half hour ago."

"I'm waiting for a cab."

"A cab? Why?"

"Because you have my car at Impound and the rental car place is closed."

Abe shook his head. Of course. He couldn't believe one of them hadn't thought about that before going their separate ways. "Don't you have a friend you can call?"

"No." It wasn't a bitter retort, just no. *No, you don't have a friend you can call, or no you don't have a friend?* The thought hit him out of nowhere, accompanied by a profound need to protect. From a vigilante murdering peeping Tom? From having no friends? *From me?*

"I'll take you home. It's on my way." It was a lie, of course, but she didn't have to know.

She smiled. "How do you know? You don't even know where I live."

He recited her address, then shrugged a little sheepishly. "I was listening when you told Spinnelli your address for the patrol drive-bys. Let me drive you home, Kristen. I'll check out your house and make sure no vigilante peeping Toms are hiding in the closets."

"I was worried about that," she admitted. "Are you sure it's no trouble?"

"I'm sure. But I do have two favors to ask."

Instantly her green eyes went wary and he wondered why. *Or who.* A woman that looked like Kristen Mayhew would find it impossible to escape opportunists who wanted special favors. "What?" she asked sharply.

"First, stop calling me Detective Reagan," Abe said simply. "Please call me Abe."

He could see her shoulders relax through the heavy winter coat. "And the second?"

"I'm starving. I'd planned to stop someplace for a quick bite. Join me?"

She hesitated, then nodded. "I never ate dinner, either."

"Good. My SUV is parked across the street."

Wednesday, February 18, 11:00 P.M.

He was ready. He ran a soft cloth down the matte barrel of his rifle. It was like new. It should be. A wise man cared well for his tools. It had served him well these past few weeks.

He pulled the photo in its cheap silver frame just a little closer. "Six down, Leah. Who will be next?" Carefully he laid the rifle on the table and stuck his hand in the fishbowl. Once the bowl held Leah's goldfish. Ever since he'd known

her, Leah had a goldfish. Cleo had always been its name.
When one died, a new one would miraculously show up in
the bowl the next day and it would be named Cleo. Leah
never acknowledged one fish was dead, never made a fuss.
She just went out and bought a new fish. He'd found a dead
Cleo in Leah's fishbowl the day he'd identified her body.
He hadn't the heart to buy a new one.

Now the fishbowl held the names of every person who
had escaped justice under Kristen Mayhew's watch.
Murderers, rapists, child molesters, all out walking the
streets because some morally bankrupt defense attorney
found a loophole. The defense attorneys were no better than
the criminals themselves. They just wore better suits.

He riffled his hand through the little slips of paper,
searching, pausing when his finger caught a dog-eared
edge. He'd worried over whom to target first. Over which
crime was more serious than the rest, which victims
deserved justice before the others. He'd only have so much
time, especially now that the police were involved. He'd
known that Kristen would involve the police before he'd
tipped his hand, but it seemed a justifiable risk for the satisfaction he'd receive just by knowing she knew. So he'd
put all the names in the fishbowl and let God guide his
hand. He pulled out the folded piece. Looked at the corner
he himself had turned down. He'd given God a little help,
that's all.

What was the punishment for that dog-ear? he wondered. There *were* crimes that were worse than others. Rape
and child molestation had a premeditation, a wickedness
that must be punished, eliminated. So he'd gone back and
dog-eared all the sexual crimes.

He stared at the folded paper for another long minute.
The last pick had yielded a prime target. Ross King
deserved to die. There wasn't a decent person that would

disagree with that. He hadn't died easily, or quickly. And in the end he'd begged so piteously. He'd often wondered, in the past, if he could beat a man who begged for mercy. He now knew he could.

He'd done well that night, ridding the world of a parasite too dangerous to live with decent people. God would be pleased. The innocents were just a little safer today. So his decision was made. He'd choose all the dog-eared names first. There was still a random nature, the choice in the end was still God's. When there were no more dog-eared names, he'd go on to the lesser crimes. And if he never made it that far, at least he'd go on to his reward knowing he'd gotten the biggest bang for his buck.

He unfolded the little piece of paper and his smile turned grim. *Oh, yes. I'm ready.*

Wednesday, February 18, 11:35 P.M.

"It's good."

Abe chuckled. "You sound surprised."

"I am." Kristen studied the gyro in the strobing light of the passing streetlamps. They were just a few miles from her house, but she'd torn into the sandwich less than a minute after leaving the drive-thru saying she was hungrier than she'd thought. "What's in it?"

"Lamb, veal, onions, feta cheese, and yogurt. You've never had one? Really?"

"Ethnic foods weren't exactly a staple where I grew up."

"Where did you grow up?"

She studied the sandwich for a long moment, so long he thought she wouldn't answer. "Kansas," she said finally and he wondered what she'd left there that bothered her so much.

He forced his voice to be light. "No kidding. I took you for East Coast."

"No." She looked out the window. "Turn left at this light."

He was quiet as she gave terse directions to her house. Bringing his SUV to a stop in her carport, he shifted in his seat so he could see her face. Her profile, really, as she sat resolutely looking forward, not looking at him. Not looking at her house. "I could take you to a hotel if you want," he said and she stiffened. "I'm serious, Kristen. No one would blame you if you didn't want to sleep here tonight. I could do a walk-through while you pack a bag."

"No, I live here. I won't be thrown out of my own house." She wrapped up the remains of her gyro and gathered her laptop from the floorboard. "I appreciate the gesture, but he doesn't appear to want to do me harm. I have an alarm system and Spinnelli's patrol will be driving by every hour. I'll be fine. Besides, I have to feed my cats. But I would appreciate you giving the place the once-over." One side of her mouth quirked up and he admired her pluck. "The cats aren't much in the way of protection."

He followed her to the side door and waited as she stepped inside and disabled the alarm. She turned on the light and he let his eyes wander around, taking in the goldenrod appliances, the garish foil wallpaper, the cabinets of chipped fiberboard. It appeared she hadn't had insomnia enough times to have started renovations on this room. His gaze came back to where she stood, ramrod straight with her coat still on. Even in the dim light he could see her swallow hard. The need to protect again welled, but even after only a few hours he knew her well enough to know she wouldn't welcome his touch, no matter how reassuring it was intended to be. So he made himself stay where he was, his hands in his pockets.

"You want the lights on or off?" she murmured.

"I'll turn them on as I go," he answered, wishing she'd agreed to go to a hotel. He didn't know if she was in danger, but she was still clearly frightened and it unsettled him.

He made his way through her house, flipping on the living room light, noting the blue-striped wallpaper. She had done a good job. His sister Annie was a professional decorator and she couldn't have done any better. He found both spare bedrooms devoid of vigilante murdering peeping Toms, as was the bathroom with its neat stacks of makeup and hairspray. She'd left it so neat, almost as if she expected company. He instantly wondered who, irritation pricking at the thought of shaving cream and a razor littering the neat vanity top. But there was none. No sign of a man. He laughed at himself. Harshly. If there existed such a person, she would have called him to pick her up instead of trying to take a cab.

And even if there existed such a person, it was none of his damn business.

Abe pushed open the door to her bedroom, his eyes scanning for any sign of movement. There was none. He hadn't expected there to be. He flipped the light switch and saw Kristen's skill lent itself to picking furniture as well. Art deco pieces filled the room, giving it a solid feel. There was no lace, no trace of ribbon, but still there was a feminine air. Perhaps it was the old-fashioned quilt on her bed. Or maybe the scent of her perfume, still hanging in the air. A sleek black cat sat on her pillow, watching him with eyes as green and cautious as Kristen's.

Abe swept his flashlight under her bed and around the closet filled with black suits, dark navy suits, charcoal gray suits. Her knack for color didn't extend to her wardrobe, or maybe there was an unwritten dress code for officers of the court. Still he wondered at the absence of party dresses, evening gowns, shiny shoes. He paused long enough to scratch the cat behind the ears before making his way back to the kitchen where Kristen stood spooning loose tea into a china teapot with big pink roses. She still wore her winter coat and he wondered if she planned to stay after all.

"This floor is clear," he said and she nodded mutely. "Basement door?"

She pointed to the wall behind him. "Be careful. It's a bit of a mess down there."

Kristen Mayhew's mess was cleaner than any of his siblings' houses, he thought. The fireplace mantel was scraped and sanded down to its natural wood. A set of stained wood samples rested on the top, propped against the wall. Abe sighed. Their humble servant was indeed correct. The cherry was the best choice.

Kristen jumped when his footsteps sent the stairs from the basement creaking. She wasn't sure what made her more nervous, the knowledge that a killer routinely stalked her movements in her own home, or that there was a man in the house for the very first time ever. She drew a breath, the aroma of the brewing tea settling her nerves enough that she didn't appear insane. Abe Reagan reappeared, sliding his pistol into his shoulder holster.

His pistol. He'd drawn his weapon. A shiver raced down her spine. "All clear?"

He nodded. "No one's here except for you, me, and the black cat on your pillow."

Kristen smiled, just a little. "Nostradamus. He lets me sleep in his bed."

Reagan choked on a laugh and her heart did a little trip that had nothing to do with vigilante psychos. He was an incredible-looking man. And he seemed kind. But he was still a man. "You named your cat Nostradamus?" he asked with a grin.

She nodded. "Mephistopheles hasn't come home yet. He's out chasing mice."

His grin widened. "Nostradamus and Mephistopheles. The Prophet of Doom and the Devil Himself. Whatever happened to Fluffy or Snowflake?"

"I never could bring myself to name them something cute," she said dryly. "It just wasn't in their nature. The first week after I adopted them they destroyed the carpet in three rooms."

"So if you ever got a dog, you could name him Cerberus and have a full set."

Her lips twitched as he'd meant them to and she felt a sudden rush of appreciation for his effort to lighten her mood. "The three-headed guardian of Hades. I'll certainly keep it in mind. Would you like some tea? I drink it at night when I'm all wound up. I'm hoping it will settle my nerves so I can sleep tonight."

"No thanks. I have to get home and catch a few hours' shut-eye. I have to meet Mia and Jack at dawn at the first site."

Kristen's hands stilled on the teapot. "Which one will you do first?"

He shrugged his wide shoulders. "Ramey. We'll do them in the order he did."

Kristen made herself pour the tea, grimacing when her hands shook, sending tea over the cup's edge and onto the old countertop. "That makes sense." She looked up at him to find him watching her with the same intense expression he'd worn in Spinnelli's office. It was concern, she realized and her back went straight. She wasn't weak. She might be many things, but weak was not one of them. "I'd like to be there as well."

He considered it. "That makes sense," he echoed her words. "Wear sensible shoes."

She looked down into her tea, then back up at him. "I don't have a car."

"I'll be by to pick you up at six A.M."

The volley was over and it was her serve. "Thanks. I'll get a rental car tomorrow, but—"

"It's all right, Kristen. I don't mind."

He really didn't, it was clear to see. And that bothered her. "Then . . ."

He pushed himself away from the wall against which he'd leaned. "I'll be going." He stopped at the kitchen door. "You've done a wonderful job on your house."

Her hands cradled the steaming cup, absorbing the warmth. She was so cold. "Thank you. And thank you for driving me home. And for the gyro."

He studied her face, his expression uncertain. "You're sure you want to stay here?"

She smiled with a hell of a lot more confidence than she felt. "Positive. You should get some sleep. Six A.M. is only a few hours away."

Abe took a last uncertain look before backing out the door and into the carport. Through the gauzy curtains on her kitchen door he watched her lock the door and set the alarm. For a moment he debated going back inside and dragging her to the relative safety of a hotel, but knew it was none of his business. Kristen Mayhew was a grown woman and entirely capable of making her own decisions.

He started his car and had pulled into the street before he realized she hadn't called him Detective. Nor had she called him Abe. They'd talked for almost an hour and she hadn't called him anything at all. He shouldn't let it bother him. He shouldn't let *her* bother him. She was pretty, that was true, but he'd meet many pretty women now that he was no longer working undercover. For five years he'd held no attachments, stealing time to see his own family, his brothers, sisters, his parents, Debra, all the while worrying that he'd been followed, that just by visiting he'd place them in jeopardy.

Now he was out from under the burden of constant secrecy and isolation, working in an environment where people developed social and professional relationships. It was natural to be tempted on his first day out. And it would be unnatural not to find Kristen Mayhew tempting. She was as beautiful now as she'd been the first time he'd seen her.

And unlike the first time he'd seen her, he was now free to feel the lust that clutched at his gut like a slippery fist without the shadow of guilt. Debra was gone now. Truly gone. After five years of existing in hellish limbo, Debra was finally at peace. It was time to get on with his life. Step one would be getting Kristen Mayhew to call him by his first name. Then he'd take it from there.

From her living room window, Kristen watched as Reagan's taillights disappeared around the corner, troubled. *I should be,* she thought and uneasily glanced up the street, wondering if the man who'd killed five people was watching her at that moment. But the street was empty, all her neighbors' windows dark. The troubled feeling persisted and Kristen wasn't sure how much she could attribute to a man who called himself her humble servant versus a man who was unwilling to leave her in a darkened corridor unprotected.

Slowly she walked to her bedroom, sat down at her vanity. As men went, Abe Reagan was quite a specimen. Tall, dark. Very handsome. She was not so naive that she failed to recognize the interest that flared in his blue eyes. She was honest enough to admit it had affected her. Methodically, she pulled out her hairpins, dropping them into the little plastic tray where they went, searching her reflection in the mirror. She was not a beautiful woman. She knew that. Nor was she inordinately unattractive. She knew that, too. Men looked at her sometimes. Never had she looked back, never given the smallest hint of encouragement.

She'd heard the whispers. They called her "Ice Queen."

It was true enough. On the surface anyway, which was all she let anyone see.

She was not so cold that she didn't recognize the good men, because they were out there. She was not so blind that she didn't recognize Abe Reagan was probably one of them. But even good men wanted more than she was able to give. On so many different levels.

From the vanity drawer, she pulled out the small album that was perhaps her greatest treasure and deepest regret. Flipping from page to page, her eyes lingered on one photo, then another. Then, as always, she resolutely closed the album and put it away. She needed to sleep. Abe Reagan would be by tomorrow at six A.M. to take her to where they would ostensibly find the body of Anthony Ramey.

She wished she could be sorry he was dead, but she was not.

Anthony Ramey was a rapist. His victims would never be the same.

She ought to know.

Thursday, February 19, 12:30 A.M.

Zoe Richardson closed and locked her front door, having sent her lover home to his wife. She turned on the TV, having taped the ten o'clock news as she'd been otherwise occupied during the time slot. She stretched languorously, still as pleasantly surprised as the first time. She'd set out to seduce him for who he was and the connections he possessed, but damned if the man wasn't a wonder in bed. She hadn't had to fake it, even once.

But fun was done. It was time to work. She rewound the tape until the perky ten o'clock anchors appeared. Her good mood suddenly dimmed as it did every time she saw another sitting in the seat she'd earned. She'd paid her dues, dammit. She'd taken every insipid little human interest story they'd thrown her way. But no matter. With her new connections it was only a matter of time before she snagged the big one, the story that would put her face on every TV screen in America. And once there, she didn't intend to leave.

Ahh, she thought. *Here we go.* Her own face appeared on the screen. She was reminding the viewers of her interview with ASA Mayhew that afternoon, of Mayhew's failure to get a conviction against the son of the wealthy industrialist Jacob Conti. She managed to sound earnest and concerned when in reality she was inordinately pleased with Mayhew's very public failure. Then she turned, *nice profile, Zoe,* she thought, and the camera panned back to show the famous Jacob Conti himself.

"Can you tell our viewers your reaction to your son's verdict, Mr. Conti?"

Conti's handsome face took on an expression of abject relief. "I can't tell you how relieved and happy my wife and I are that the responsible members of the jury could not find my son guilty. This empty accusation has nearly ruined his young life."

"Some would say the lives that are ruined are those of Paula Garcia and her unborn child, Mr. Conti." His face changed, seamlessly transforming to one of abject sorrow.

"The Garcias have my deepest and most profound sympathy," he said. "I cannot imagine their loss. But my son was not responsible."

She watched her head nod, her own lips droop for just a moment before she went in for the kill. "Mr. Conti, can you address the rumors of jury tampering?"

She'd caught him by surprise with that one. Hah. But he covered his temper quickly and with admirable aplomb lifted a brow. "I choose not to give credence to rumor, Miss Richardson. Especially rumor as preposterous as that one." He tilted his head in a half nod, a smooth and graceful exit move. "Now I must be getting back to my family."

Her image turned back to the camera. "That was industrialist Jacob Conti with sympathy for the family of Paula Garcia, but relief that his son is home tonight. Back to you."

Zoe stopped the tape and ejected it. She'd dupe the segment onto her master later, the tape she used to capture all her more interesting moments. A portfolio of sorts. She stood, absorbing the feel of silk sliding down her legs as her robe fell into place. She loved silk. This robe had been a gift from one of the mayor's aides. They'd scratched one another's political backs for a while. She smiled. Then they'd scratched other itches for a while longer. In her honest moments she could admit she missed him, but she mostly just missed the silk.

Soon she'd be able to afford her own silk. Soon she'd be able to afford anything she wanted. Because soon it would be *her* face, *her* voice America trusted for its news. She paced her small living room restlessly. She needed a story. So far she'd done pretty well shadowing relentless pursuer of evil and overachieving Girl Scout, ASA Kristen Mayhew. Her gut told her that if it wasn't broke, don't fix it. She tapped a French-manicured nail on her silk sleeve, wondering what was first up on Kristen's agenda tomorrow.

Thursday, February 19, 12:30 A.M.

The computer monitor glowed in the darkness of the room. The Internet had made the world a very small place indeed. The name he'd drawn from the fishbowl resided on Chicago's North Shore, in one of the city's most affluent communities.

He wouldn't be able to get to Number Seven where he lived or worked, he thought. He'd need to draw him out, to lead him to the place he'd chosen for just such a purpose.

He glanced at the stack of envelopes, gleaming an unnatural white in the streetlight that filtered through the curtains. But first he had some work to do.

Chapter Five

Thursday, February 19, 6:30 A.M.

CSU had the site prepped and ready when Reagan pulled his SUV up to the Arboretum. Inside the building, tropical plants flowered. Outside, what little grass could be seen was brown and shriveled. A light rain fell. Jack had erected a tarp beyond the parking lot, over a narrow span of grass in the shadow of the El tracks above. CSU must have found something.

Bracing herself against the cold, Kristen slid down from the high seat of the SUV and picked her way across the icy sludge in her sensible shoes, Reagan's big body beside her. He slowed his pace to match hers and she was grateful, for he acted as a windbreak. He'd pulled up to her house at one minute 'till six this morning, a bag of bagels and lox on the front passenger's seat of his SUV. So she was treated to yet another ethnic delicacy and found she liked the lox nearly as well as the gyro the night before.

Jack was pacing outside the yellow tape when they approached, his face grim. "Come and see," was all he said. One of Jack's men knelt, shining a flashlight at the ground.

No, not the ground. What the light illuminated was not snow-covered dirt. Horrified, Kristen could only stare as her blood ran cold. *He wouldn't. He couldn't. It just didn't fit.*

"I'll be damned," Abe muttered under his breath. "Who are Sylvia Whitman, Janet Briggs, and Eileen Dorsey?"

"Ramey's three rape victims," Kristen heard herself reply, still staring at the beam of the flashlight. At the marble marker bearing the three names. And dates.

It was a grave marker.

Her eyes jumped up to meet Reagan's. "The dates are their birth dates to the day of their assault. He . . ." She swallowed back bile.

Reagan shook his head. "It doesn't make sense."

Mia jogged up behind them, her breath turning to fog in the air. "What doesn't make sense?" Then a quiet, "Oh, God."

Kristen shook herself. "You're right, it doesn't make sense. Besides, if something had happened to even one of these three women, I'd have been informed." By one of their irate boyfriends or husbands who had so bitterly blamed her for dragging their women through the hell of testifying only to suffer again when Ramey was acquitted. She still felt the sting of their anger, of the accusations she hadn't tried to defend. She pushed back the guilt and stared at the marker at her feet. "It's for remembrance," she said. "For the victims."

Abe nodded to Jack. "Let's start digging. Be careful with the marker. The dirt under it might have retained some trace evidence. Are there markers at the other sites?"

"I'll find out." Jack gestured them back, out of the way of the team. "This is going to take a little while. The ground is pretty frozen."

They backed up, still standing under the tarp which provided shelter from the light rain. And they watched as the team carefully dug.

"I made a list of the victims, their families, anyone associated with the three cases," Kristen said as a shovelful of frozen earth landed in the growing mound close to her feet.

"Another bad night?" Mia murmured, her eyes trained on the diggers.

"You could say that." She'd tried to go to sleep, but visions of *him* staring in her window kept her far too tense to sleep. Every creak and whine of her old house just made it worse. Finally, she'd given up. "I also ran a list of all the defendants I unsuccessfully prosecuted and separated them out by the ones who got off on technicalities versus legitimate defenses."

"How many were there?" Reagan asked.

"I had to replace my printer cartridge midway through," Kristen answered dryly. "Did wonders for my professional self-esteem."

"So how many could you have won?" Reagan asked, his tone practical. She'd wondered the same thing herself and had been compulsive enough to do the math. "Twenty-five percent, maybe," she said honestly.

"Twenty-five percent with the benefit of twenty-twenty hindsight." Reagan made a humming sound in his throat.

"That means on seventy-five percent you wouldn't have changed a thing. That sounds pretty significant to me."

Her first instinct was to take his words as lightly as he'd likely meant them. But she glanced up, found his blue eyes trained on her face, and knew he'd been quite serious. Awkward pleasure warred with a nagging feeling of déjà vu. And because dealing with the déjà vu was far less uncomfortable than accepting his praise, she focused on his face with a frown. "I know we've met. Last night you said my hair was up. What did you mean?"

His mouth opened, but his first words were drowned out by Jack's shout.

"We've got something. Come and see."

Reagan and Mia lurched forward. Kristen's approach was a little more tentative, hindered by her skirt even in her sensible shoes. She rounded the pile of dirt and gingerly stepped to the edge of the three-foot-deep hole. And swallowed hard.

He was right, was her first thought. *We're lucky it's winter.* Had it been summer, the flesh would have been so decomposed it would have been unrecognizable. But being winter in Chicago, the body was fairly well preserved. Enough that she could provide a positive ID.

"It's him. Anthony Ramey." Her voice was shaky, but she doubted anyone would fault her for it. Jack's men wore identical grimaces that said they'd rather be fingerprinting anything anywhere than be here, in the hole with a decomposing body. Mia pressed a handkerchief to her face and walked around the hole to get a view from a different angle.

"Most of him, anyway," Mia said through the handkerchief. "Hell, Kristen, your humble servant sure did a job on Ramey. Nothing like a little vigilante justice with a biblical twist."

It was true. Nude and rotting, the body of Anthony

Ramey had been laid to rest minus his pelvic region. In its place was about a baseball-sized expanse of nothing.

"Eye for an eye," Kristen murmured, wishing to high heaven she'd brought along a handkerchief of her own. Even with the benefit of Nature's freezer, the body's odor was enough to turn her stomach and suddenly she felt like cursing Reagan's kind breakfast gesture. Bagels and lox threatened to gag her.

"Shotgun?" Reagan said to Mia, and she nodded.

"Probably." Mia crouched to get a closer look. "Definitely not the same gun that brought him down. Probably done after he was dead. The Polaroids don't show any pelvic damage."

"The ME can tell us for sure," Reagan said, crouching beside Mia. "What's that?"

Mia squinted over the edge of the handkerchief. "What's what?"

Reagan pointed to Ramey's throat. "That pattern around his neck." He got down on his knees and bent down for a closer look, then looked back up at Mia. "Could be ligature marks from strangulation," he said. "Jack?"

Ligature marks. *Oh, no,* was all Kristen could think. *No, no, no.*

Jack brushed some dirt from Ramey's neck with a soft-bristled brush. "Looks like it."

Mia swung around to look at Kristen, her eyes narrowed. "Kristen, didn't Ramey—"

Kristen's mind was already there. Her gut tightened, the implications far too disturbing to contemplate. But contemplate they must. "He would come up to his victims from behind and strangle them with a thick necklace-like chain, but only to cut off their air supply so they couldn't scream. When they stopped struggling, he stopped strangling, then dragged them off to a dark part of the parking garage to rape them. It was the chain that the defense said police obtained through an unlawful search of Ramey's apartment. If we'd had that evidence, I could have gotten the conviction. But the jury never saw it."

"So we have a copycat," Reagan said, still staring at the ligature marks.

Kristen shook her head, seeing from Mia's expression that she understood, that any way it turned out, this would be very bad. "That was a detail we never gave to the press."

Reagan's head turned slowly, his expression as dark as Mia's. "Then—"

Kristen nodded. "He's got access to restricted data."

Mia stood up and brushed at her slacks. "Or he's one of us."

Reagan's breath hissed out. "Shit."

Thursday, February 19, 7:45 A.M.

The bagels and lox were still in her stomach, but they weren't happy to be there any more than Kristen was happy to be standing at the makeshift grave of three young men who'd taken the lives of two children so heedlessly. Once again their humble servant's map had been accurate and once again he'd left behind the headstone.

Carved with the names of two little kids who'd never see the age of eight.

Jack had radioed ahead to the uniforms guarding the final scene, where they'd presumably find the body of Ross King, and sure enough, waiting for them was a headstone with the names of six innocent victims of a hideous theft of their childhoods. Their trust. Those six boys had testified so bravely, it still made her heart ache. They'd relived their terror and trauma to a closed courtroom, empty but for the boys' parents, the judge, the defense attorney, Ross King, and herself. *And the jury.* She'd forgotten about the jury.

"Their names weren't released," Kristen said out loud, and both Mia and Reagan turned to stare at her. She blinked, bringing their faces into focus. "The names of King's victims were never released. They were minors. The arresting officers knew and the lawyers knew and the jury knew. I forgot about the jury." From her briefcase she pulled out the printouts she made during the night. "Here's the list of anyone associated with the three trials. Victims, family members, anybody who testified. I ran copies for both of you." She handed each detective a stack. "But I forgot the jury. It may not mean anything, of course. The Ramey jury wouldn't have known about the chain, but the King jury knew the names of his victims."

Mia flipped through her stack. "Wow. How long did this take you?"

"To get the list, about ten minutes. I keep a personal database of all my cases so the hard work was already done. It took three hours to print it all up because my home printer is ancient." She frowned, watching Reagan's face darken. "What?"

He looked up, his blue eyes cold. "There are cops on this list," he said too softly.

Kristen felt her stomach gurgle, a sure sign of stress. As always, she pulled into herself, growing still. It was one of the most valuable skills she possessed. She met Reagan's gaze unflinchingly. "Of course there are. They participated in the investigation."

Twin flags of dark color appeared just above Reagan's clean-shaven cheekbones. "And for too long they've watched the guilty go free?" he said, quoting the killer's letter.

Kristen clenched her jaw, but kept her voice level. "You

said that, not me. But it's true. And now we know he has an inside track." A glance from the corner of her eye showed Mia watching the exchange with a puckered brow.

Reagan riffled through the pages impatiently. "Where are the lawyers, Kristen?"

"They're on there. All defense attorneys and their staff."

He dipped his head, an intimidating move she wasn't entirely sure he did on purpose. "What about your office? What about the prosecutors?" he asked, his voice falsely calm.

She let out a quiet breath. "You're looking at her, Detective Reagan."

"But you have assistants, right, Kristen?" Mia asked neutrally. "Secretaries?"

Truthfully, she hadn't considered that fact, but it was only fair and complete to add everyone to the list, especially now they knew he had an inside track of information. "I'll revise the lists and send them over to your office after lunch." She shouldered her laptop case, readjusting the weight. "I'll see you later."

"Where are you going?" Reagan demanded and irritation had her straightening.

"Motion hour is at nine." She leveled him a stare. "We all have jobs to do, Detective."

He nodded stiffly and lifted the printout in the air. "Thank you. This would have taken us hours to complete." It was an olive branch and she accepted it with a civil nod.

"Days," Mia corrected. "We'll get started interviewing the original victims later today."

Kristen's gut clenched. "So they get steamrolled by the system yet again." She looked at Mia. "I'd like to come along, especially for Ramey's and King's victims."

Her expression sympathetic, Mia opened her mouth, but Reagan cut her off before she could utter a word.

"Why, Counselor?" he asked, his tone one step from caustic. "Think we'll bully one of them into confessing?"

Mia blew out a frustrated breath. "You're outta line, Reagan. She—"

Kristen held up her hand. "No, Mia, it's all right. I can understand Detective Reagan's misperception under the circumstances." She looked up at him, challenging him to meet her eyes, waiting to speak until he did. "Let's get a few things straight, Detective. I have a good working relationship with Spinnelli's office. Anyone will tell you I'm fair and thorough. I don't know if we're dealing with a cop or a lawyer or just some nutcase with really good sources, but at this point none of us can afford to overlook any potential suspect. Even if it's a cop. Especially if it's a cop. *Because* I respect your badge and don't want to see it tarnished by one bad apple who doesn't represent any of you."

He opened his mouth and this time she cut him off. "I'm not finished," she said, her voice still calm. If people only knew how hard she practiced to keep that calm voice even when her insides were shaking like Jell-O in an earthquake. "Based on my limited personal experience, I don't believe you'd bully a rape victim who's already been through hell, but based on the last few minutes, the jury's still out on your sensitive side." He looked away, abashed, and she sighed. "I do know those people depended on me to get justice and nine out of ten of them blame me because I didn't. I don't want to feel like I owe them, but I do. So I want to go. Call me a masochist or a bleeding heart if you want, but don't call me unfair, because that's what you've done."

"I'm sorry," he said quietly. He looked at her, his blue eyes piercing. "I was out of line."

For just a moment, Kristen stared, his gaze almost as palpable as a physical touch. She swallowed and shook her head, whether to break the tug of his stare or to deny his words, she wasn't sure. "It's all right, Detective. I understand."

Mia cleared her throat and Kristen started. She'd almost forgotten Mitchell was there. "We'll call you when we're ready to start talking to the victims, Kristen," she said dryly.

Kristen felt her cheeks heat. For heaven's sake. Caught staring like a brainless teenager. It was just that the man had the most intriguing eyes. And she was sure she'd seen them before. "Thank you," she said briskly. "I've got to go now or I'll be late." She turned on her heel and had made it halfway to the Arboretum's parking lot when she felt a hand on her shoulder. He didn't need to say a word for her to know it was Reagan. Her shoulder tingled with awareness, even through the layers that separated his hand from her skin.

"Do you need a ride, Kristen?" he asked and she shook her head.

"No," she said, mortified when her voice came out husky. Resolutely she kept her gaze forward. "I'll take a cab. I'll have a rental car delivered this morning, so I'll be fine. I really need to go, Detective."

His hand lifted and she made her way to the street without looking back. But even still, she could feel his eyes watching her all the way.

Thursday, February 19, 8:15 A.M.

"Well, isn't that interesting," Zoe mused, sipping at a cup of black coffee.

Her cameraman yawned. "What?"

"Mayhew, walking up the courthouse steps. Get some film of her, okay?"

"Why?" He frowned. "You're not getting one of those stalking complexes are you?"

"Just do it. And get a close-up of her feet."

"You're creepy, lady," Scott groused, but did as he was told, his video camera following Kristen all the way up the stairs until she disappeared into the building.

Zoe took the camera from his hands. "Let's take a good look." She rewound the tape and stared into the viewer. "See that? Look at those shoes."

Scott reached for his own coffee. "I did. Nike high-tops. Didn't match her suit."

Zoe rolled her eyes. "No. *Look* at her shoes. They're all covered in mud."

Scott shrugged. "So? She went for a morning run."

Zoe shook her head. "No, she doesn't run. She does aerobics twice a week at her neighborhood Y." She looked up to find Scott's unshaven face twisted in a disgusted grimace.

"You *have* been stalking her."

Zoe blew out a breath. "Don't be an idiot. Of course I'm not stalking her. I'm just acquainting myself with her usual routine. So I know when something's up, like now. She went someplace this morning before motion hour." Her eyes narrowed, her mouth all but salivating. The fine hairs on the back of her neck stood straight up. Good investigative reporting was instinct and persistence. And preparation. This morning all that preparation was about to pay off. "Something's cooking with our devoted public servant." She turned to Scott with a satisfied smile. "We're about to hit pay dirt."

Thursday, February 19, 10:15 A.M.

John stood staring out the window, his back visibly tense. His hands gripped his upper arms and Kristen saw his knuckles grow whiter with each new detail she told him.

"I had a message on my voice mail from Detective Mitchell when I got out of motion hour," she finished. "They'd uncovered the bodies of three gang members. Everything was the same except the pelvic shot." Watching his reflection in the glass, she saw his mouth tighten. "They were on their way to the final scene, Ross King."

"Do you know what time it is, Kristen?" John said flatly.

He sounded like an annoyed father asking her if she was aware she'd missed curfew and that, in turn, annoyed her. "Yes, John. My watch is accurate to the second."

"Then why did you wait until now to tell me? Twelve hours later?"

Kristen frowned. "I did try to call you. I left three voice mails telling you it was urgent."

He turned from the window with a frown of his own. "Three voice mails? I didn't get any of them." He pulled his cell phone from his pocket and punched buttons. "I'll have Lois call the wireless company. This is unacceptable service." His frown smoothed from angry to worried. "You're all right?"

Kristen shrugged. "I kind of hope somebody else in the office gets a special surprise—then it won't be just me he's chosen." She vividly remembered every creak her house made during the night, wondering if he was out there, watching her. Relieved that Reagan had checked every closet and under every bed, then pushing Reagan and his intriguing eyes right out of her head. "I don't necessarily feel like I'm in danger, but it's unsettling all the same."

John buzzed Lois on his intercom. "Lois, please set up an emergency department meeting this afternoon. One o'clock. Mandatory. Those in court need to see me before they leave tonight." He looked at Kristen. "If he tries this with one of the rest of us, we'll be ready."

Thursday, February 19, 12:00 P.M.

"Thanks for squeezing us in, Miles," Mia said, leading the way into the office of Dr. Miles Westphalen, their staff psychologist. "We've got a unique situation."

"What's happened?" Westphalen's eyes focused on Mia as she filled him in. "Let me see the letters," he said and Mia handed him copies of all three. He read them twice before looking up and removing his glasses. "Interesting."

"I thought you'd think so," Mia said. "Well?"

"He's sincere," Westphalen said. "And smart. He either has an academic background in literature or he's an avid reader. There's a . . . poetic cadence to his writing. Refinement and . . . culture. He writes like a cultured grandfather passing wisdom to his grandchildren. He's religious, even though he never mentions God or any specific organized religion."

Abe's mouth tightened. "He's a hypocrite, claiming to avenge victims yet preying on ASA Mayhew."

One gray brow lifted and Westphalen turned to Mia. "What do you think, Mia?"

Mia pushed out a breath. "He has a special hatred for sex offenders. We found five bodies today. The rapist and pedophile both had their pelvis blown away while the murderers just had the head shot. And the last guy, King?"

"The pedophile," Westphalen supplied.

Mia grimaced. "Yeah. Anyway, either he walked into

one hell of a wall or our humble servant beat him to a bloody pulp. His own mother wouldn't have recognized him."

"Kristen did," Abe commented.

Mia frowned, swinging around to look at him. "What's that supposed to mean?"

Abe shrugged uneasily. "Just a comment. She has a good eye."

Mia's eyes narrowed. "You're still pissed with her."

Abe shook his head. "No, I'm not. I was, but I'm not now." Westphalen was waiting and damned if Abe didn't feel compelled to explain himself. "She made a list of everyone connected with the original crimes and added the cops. I was just . . . surprised."

Pivoting in her chair, Mia faced Westphalen. "He knows details that he shouldn't."

"Details? Such as?"

"Ramey had evidence of strangulation with a chain," Mia said. "That was his M.O. It also wasn't public knowledge."

Westphalen leaned back in his chair and looked at Abe. "And this troubles you."

Abe's brows bunched. "Of course it does. It's a security breach."

"Or he could be one of us." Mia used the same words she'd used this morning standing over Ramey's makeshift grave. *One of us.* It irritated Abe now as much as it had then. The thought that a cop could take the law into his own hands, could stalk a woman in her own home. It was repugnant. What was more unsettling, though, was that he wasn't sure which crime bothered him more, stalking Kristen or the murder of five people.

"Why did he give us their clothing?" Abe asked, changing the subject.

Westphalen steepled his fingertips. "What else should he have done with it?"

"Thrown it away," Mia said. "Why didn't he destroy it?"

Abe paced. "If he'd thrown it away, somebody might have seen it. A dog might have pulled it from the trash. If he burned it, we might look for ashes if we ever caught up to him." He looked at Mia with a wry smile. "Where safer to leave it than with the cops?"

Mia returned the smile, grimly. "He is smart. Why the grave marker?"

"Now that I consider truly fascinating," Westphalen commented. "Such symbolism, and he went to so much trouble. He used real marble?"

Abe stopped pacing and took the chair next to Mia's. "The lab will know for sure. We made some calls, looking for anybody that makes headstones. There weren't that many."

"We're trying to find someone to see if they recognize the work," Mia explained. "So what about the symbolism?"

"The day of their assault is the second date," Westphalen said, "as if it's the day they died. To him, the lives of the victims ended the day they were raped, even though they lived. He says he's watched the guilty go free for too long. He could mean from afar, like on television, or he might even live where people die every day." His shrugged. "Or he could mean from up close, like a cop. Regardless, he's had a trauma of his own, and recently. This is all so very personal. I'd look for someone who's recently suffered a terrible loss."

"A recent victim," Mia mused.

"Maybe, maybe not." Westphalen frowned. "The passion is sporadic, like beating King's face and blasting the pelvis of the two sex offenders. It's almost like he gets them in his grasp and just can't help it. But hunting them and disposing of them after they're dead and the letters . . . very calculated. I doubt you'll find anything of use at the crime scene. Not at first anyway. Maybe later, after he's gotten careless, but that could take a long time."

"Wonderful," Abe muttered.

"Sorry, Detective. I save my ESP for the track. No, I think that even though the loss or trauma that triggered this killing spree is recent, I don't think the *crime* he's suffered is recent at all. It takes a long time to build up such anger."

"Any guess on our guy's age?" Mia asked and Westphalen shrugged.

"Don't know. He writes like an aged scholar, but he had to have physical strength to move the bodies. I'd have to say he's younger versus older."

"Why did he target Kristen?" Mia asked and Westphalen's face became grim.

"I don't know that either. It could be no more than the fact she's a pretty face that the reporters like to put on television. But this man is obsessive. Does Kristen have protection?"

Mia slid Abe a slow look. "Do you think she needs it?" she asked.

"Perhaps. If the other state's attorneys start getting little gifts, I'd say no."

"But you don't think that's going to happen," Abe said.

Westphalen's expression of disturbance expanded to worry. "No, I don't."

"Wonderful," Abe muttered.

Chapter Six

Thursday, February 19, 1:30 P.M.

"Next time I pick lunch," Mia grumbled, taking the stairs to their office two at a time.

Abe followed her up. "It was good. Best Indian curry I've had in a long time."

Mia turned to him with a frown. "It was vegetarian." *Ray would never have*—She stopped herself midthought. Ray wasn't here. She had a new partner now. A new partner whose file she'd finally taken the time to read before going to bed the night before.

"It was one meal, Mitchell, not a disease. What's this?"

Mia picked up the thick stack of papers on her desk, identical to the one he held in his hand. "Kristen's new lists. She keeps her promises."

She thumbed to a page marked with a little neon green Post-it and had to chuckle. At the head of the list was Kristen's own name, bolded and italicized, followed in normal type by the names of her secretary, three other prosecutors, and her boss, John Alden himself.

"It'll take us hours to go through this," Abe said, flipping through the pages. Mia could tell when he reached the green neon Post-it because his face turned red. "I didn't mean to insult her. I was just surprised."

"I think she understood." Mia looked up to see an unfamiliar face crossing the bullpen. Unfamiliar in and of itself, but there was too much resemblance to Abe's to belong to a stranger. "Looks like you've got company."

Abe looked up and a smile lit up his features. Mia sucked in an involuntary breath. Abe Reagan with a smile was enough to make her forget all her own rules about not dating cops. Except that she'd seen the look in his eye every time he looked at Kristen. The boy had some serious work to do there. Kristen Mayhew would be a hard nut to crack.

"Sean," Abe said. The two men embraced in an awkward hug, Abe shooting her a don't-get-this-wrong grin. "My brother, Sean."

"I figured that out for myself," Mia said dryly. Abe's brother had the same dark good looks, but, unfortunately, a wedding ring on his finger.

"I was in the neighborhood," Sean said and Abe snorted.

"Since when do you slum in this neighborhood? He's a stockbroker," Abe explained.

"Since Mom told me to come down and check on you. She wanted to be sure you were getting treated right. Dad wouldn't let her come herself."

Abe's lips twitched. "I'll just bet. It's good to see you. How's Ruth?"

"Better now since the baby's sleeping through the night."

A shadow passed over Abe's face, and then it was gone, replaced with a smile that was strained, but sincere. "Good."

Sean's smile faded. "Abe . . . About the christening next Saturday."

Again, the fleeting shadow and another strained smile. "I'll be there. I promise."

"I know. It's just . . . Ruth feels just terrible, but her parents invited Jim and Sharon."

The strained smile disappeared and Abe's jaw clenched. Mia knew she shouldn't be listening, but figured if they really wanted privacy, they'd go somewhere else. Jim and Sharon weren't names she'd read in Abe's file, but they seemed pretty damn important.

"Tell Ruth it's all right," Abe said. "I'll still come and there won't be any trouble from me. Surely the church is big enough for the three of us."

Sean sighed. "I'm sorry, Abe."

"It's okay." Abe forced a cardboard smile. "Really."

"But on the upside, Mom's making a ham for Sunday. She wanted me to tell you."

"I'll call her tonight and tell her I'll be there." There was another short silence in which Sean's face became pained.

"Ruth and I were out at Willowdale last weekend. The roses were nice."

Abe's throat worked, and this Mia understood. Willowdale was a cemetery and according to Abe's file, he was a recent widower. "It's the first time I've dared go."

What must it have been like, she wondered, being so deep undercover that you couldn't risk visiting your wife's grave? She felt a stirring of compassion, of respect. Abe Reagan had given up a great deal to bring some very dangerous drug traffickers to justice.

Sean clasped Abe's arm, his knuckles going white. "I know. I'll see you on Sunday."

"Thanks for coming by," Abe said, subdued. When his brother had left the bullpen, he sank into his chair and picked up Kristen's new list.

Mia studied him unabashed. "So he's the moneymaking black sheep of the family?" she asked, and made Abe huff a good-natured chuckle.

"Go figure. Whole damn family of cops and he has to go play with money all day."

"Blue genes, huh?"

"Yeah. My dad's a cop. Retired. Beat cop his whole career. My grandfather, too. And one of my brothers." He raised a brow. "Aidan's single."

"I don't do cops," Mia said with a smile.

"Smart lady."

She lifted her brows. "Smart enough to figure out that Ruth is Sean's wife, and that Debra who was your wife is buried at Willowdale. But who are Jim and Sharon?"

Abe's eyes widened in mild amazement, more than likely at her cheek than at her powers of deductive reasoning. "Debra's parents," he answered anyway. "We don't exactly get along. Are you always so nosy?"

"You're my partner now," she said. "How long ago did Debra die?"

"Depends on your philosophy of life," he said, then sighed when she frowned. "Debra was injured six years ago. Technically, she was brain-dead from the moment they wheeled her into the ER. She never woke up."

That hadn't been in the file. "How was she injured?"

Abe's face went carefully blank. "A bullet meant for someone else hit her by mistake."

"Meant for who?" As if it wasn't written all over his face. Poor guy.

"Me. It was some punk bent on cheap revenge because I arrested his brother." He swallowed impatiently. "Damn punk was a lousy shot."

Her eyes softened in sympathy. "So when did she die? Technically."

"Technically? A year ago."

"I'm sorry," she said.

Abe nodded stiffly. "Thank you."

"How much time did the kid do?"

Gritting his teeth, he looked away. "Six fucking months."

Mia sighed. "The piece of shit that got Ray? Plead down. Good behavior'll have him walking the street again in two years."

Abe lifted his eyes. "Then I guess we'll be waiting for him in two years, Mitchell."

Ray would have liked you, Abe Reagan, she thought. *Despite your tendency to play the cowboy and take stupid risks.* But now she understood why Abe had taken so many chances. Grief sometimes made a man do things he might never otherwise do. "You planning on doing any more stupid stunts like you did in Narcotics?"

His lips quirked up. "No."

"Good."

Thursday, February 19, 2:30 P.M.

From his van he watched as an old woman in a maid's uniform opened the door and took the box he'd left on the doorstep after ringing the bell.

He started the van's engine with a satisfied smile. He rounded the corner and pulled into an alley, hopped out, and pulled the magnetic sign from the side of the van, revealing the painted sign beneath. Crossed to the other side and did the same, then rolled both signs and stored them in the van before climbing back in.

He had to get back to work. To his day job, anyway. The real work would commence when the sun went down.

Thursday, February 19, 3:30 P.M.

Kristen sat in her car, dreading what she was about to do. Mitchell and Reagan would be here soon. Then she'd have to face the accusing eyes of Sylvia Whitman once again.

She remembered the day of the Ramey trial. It had been a cold day, like this one. The three women, dressed in the conservative clothes they wore every day to work, looking petrified and nauseous. Their husbands, boyfriends barely containing their fury at the sight of Ramey sitting next to his defense attorney. The way each woman took the stand retold her story, her hands clenched together so tightly. The look of shame none could hide. The way they couldn't look anyone in the eye. *Except for me,* Kristen thought. Each woman had fastened her gaze on Kristen's face, as if she was the only anchor in the courtroom.

How brave they'd been. Even as the defense attorney battered and chipped at their esteem, at their composure. Not one of the three cracked. Until the jury read the verdict and Ramey walked away a free man. They'd cracked then.

Kristen drew an unsteady breath. So had she. The crack had widened this morning when she looked down at the body of Anthony Ramey, his pelvis blown away.

What she'd felt had not been outrage for Ramey the victim nor a sense of loss for his family. She'd denied the feeling standing there with Mitchell and Reagan, but later alone she could admit it to herself. It was quite simply . . satisfaction. And gratitude.

Their humble servant killed a man who didn't deserve to live, whose death she refused to mourn. It was wrong, but human. And she was still human, after all. After everything.

Mitchell's dark sedan pulled up in front of her, parking along the curb and Kristen watched the passenger door open and Reagan step out, straighten his body, then his tie. Her throat thickened as her eyes noted his wide shoulders, trim body, the faintest shadow of a beard on his cheeks and she swallowed hard. Yes, she was still human.

Reagan glanced up the hill at the house, then without warning turned his eyes on her. Her heart stuttered and skipped a beat as the tips of his dark hair lifted and the hem of his unbuttoned overcoat tossed in the wind. He made quite a picture, she was forced to admit.

Which forced her to admit something else. Her blood really could still rush, her pulse could still pound from something other than fear. Which was ridiculous. Especially ridiculous was the way she could never seem to look away from his eyes, she thought, so she did just that, opening her door just as he arrived to open it for her. She climbed out on her own, shaking her head politely at his outstretched hand. "I'm fine," she said aloud. "What's new?"

Mia waited by the sidewalk. "We've informed the next of kin. They'll be coming to identify the bodies over the next few hours. King's mother wailed loud enough to break my eardrums and Ramey's girlfriend nearly ripped Abe's pretty face with her finger-claws."

Abe rolled his eyes at the reference to his pretty face. Which it was.

"And our Blade friends?" Kristen asked.

"We found next of kin of two of the three. Nobody seems to know anything about the third." Mia frowned. "The girl-friend of one swears she was with him on January 12, but that he was missing the next day. The second one's brother swears he was home January 20, but that he was missing the next day. A full week apart."

Abe shrugged. "Hopefully the ME can give us a reasonable estimate of time of death." He looked up the hill. "Are we ready?"

"What are you going to ask Mrs. Whitman?" Kristen asked. "You don't have a time of death on any of them yet, so we're not asking her to provide an alibi."

"Yet," Reagan answered. "I'm more interested in her reaction to the news."

"I wouldn't expect tears," Kristen said flatly.

"Of sorrow?"

"Of any kind. Sylvia Whitman's not the tears type."
Kristen squared her shoulders. "Let's get this over with."
Mia and Reagan stood back, allowing Kristen to ring the
bell. Sylvia Whitman opened the door, her expression one
of contempt, but not of surprise.

"You don't seem surprised to see me, Mrs. Whitman,"
Kristen said quietly.

"Because I am not." The older woman stepped back.
"Come in, if you must."

As welcomes went, that one left a lot to be desired, Abe
thought, but at least Whitman hadn't ordered them to go. In
the car on the way over, Mia had filled him in on the after
effects of the trial, of the scathing letters Mr. Whitman had
written to Kristen's boss demanding she be fired for incompetence.

That Kristen still felt guilty for not convicting Ramey
had been clear as she'd stood on the street, her dread almost
palpable as she'd stared up at the house. But once inside
she was composed, her face as still as Whitman's, and Abe
had to give her credit for that.

"Forgive me if I don't offer you tea," Mrs. Whitman
said, leading them into the living room, and Abe chose a
chair that gave him a good view of Whitman's face. He'd
been serious last night when he'd said one of the original
victims could have killed all the men. *Original* was how he
now thought of the eleven names inscribed in marble. That
the five dead men deserved their fate didn't change the fact
they'd been murdered. One of the originals could have mas-
terminded the whole plot, taking out a few other deserving
accused felons on the way. What an ironic dilemma for the
prosecution.

Sitting, Kristen folded her hands together in her lap.
"These are Detectives Reagan and Mitchell. Mrs. Whitman

why aren't you surprised to see me?" she asked levelly and Abe felt a spurt of pride on her behalf.

Pursing her lips, Mrs. Whitman rose to her feet and retrieved an envelope from a desk. *More envelopes,* Abe thought. Without a word she handed the envelope to Kristen, who slid the letter out and, holding it by one corner, scanned it, and sighed.

" 'My dear Mrs. Whitman,' " she read, " 'what you have suffered defies articulation, so I will make no attempts to do so. I want you to know your tormentor has received justice at long last. He is dead. This doesn't begin to restore what you've lost, but I hope you can now go on with your life.' " She looked up. " 'Your Humble Servant'."

"So it's true?" Whitman asked. "Ramey is dead?"

Kristen nodded. "Yes. When did you receive this letter, Mrs. Whitman? And how?"

"It was on the welcome mat under my newspaper this morning."

After Kristen had found the offerings in her trunk, Abe thought. The timing was interesting, the method of delivery conveniently untraceable. He'd bet they'd find no prints on the letter or its envelope, but they could get delivery time from the paperboy. "Was there anything else with the letter?" Abe asked and Whitman met his eyes unflinchingly.

"No. Just the letter and the envelope. Why?"

Kristen slid the letter in the envelope and handed it to Mia. "The detectives will need you to verify your whereabouts at the time of Ramey's death, Mrs. Whitman."

Mia bagged the letter. "We'd be grateful if you and your husband would come down to the station and provide us with fingerprints. Then we can separate yours from the letter writer's."

"I'll save you the trouble, Detectives," Whitman said entirely too softly. "If Ramey was killed at night, I was here alone. I've no one to corroborate my alibi. I didn't kill him, but I salute the man who did."

"And Mr. Whitman?" Kristen asked.

"He's gone." For a moment Abe thought Whitman's composure might crack, but with a deep breath she held it together. "He filed for divorce a year after the trial."

"We'll need his address, ma'am," he said. Whitman's eyes flashed with pain and anger and humiliation, and Abe felt a stirring of pity. "I'm sorry."

Thursday, February 19, 6:00 P.M.

If the interviews with Sylvia Whitman and Janet Briggs had been stiff and formal, the conversation with Eileen Dorsey and her husband had been anything but. Kristen's ears still rang from the shouting. Her heart still raced like a wild thing in her chest.

"Well, that was pleasant," Mia said, rubbing her forehead wearily.

Kristen leaned back against her rental car, barely controlling her trembling.

Reagan's voice came rumbling from just behind her. "Are you going to be all right, Kristen?" She let the sound of his voice, his very nearness, seep in. Felt the trembling begin to subside. Didn't let herself think about how or why he made her feel so safe. For now she'd just take what he offered and leave it at that.

She threw Reagan a weak smile. "I'll be fine. But I'm grateful you were there. Having two armed detectives certainly helped diffuse them. At least we know they own a gun."

Mia whistled. "Or fifty. Man, I've never seen a personal arsenal so well equipped."

Reagan moved to lean one hip against the hood of Mia's car. "'Yes, I have a gun, Detective,'" he mimicked and Kristen snickered as the adrenaline high started to subside. He sounded just like the outraged Stan Dorsey as the man had slapped an enormous revolver on his dining room table, followed by two semi-automatics, a hunting rifle covered in camouflage paint, and an AK-47. Then he'd opened his custom-made oversized gun cabinet, revealing another forty weapons, his eyes angry and wild.

"And yes, they'd all been fired lately," Kristen added lightly. She could still taste the fear she'd felt when Dorsey advanced, standing toe-to-toe, icily declaring that he dreamed every night of filling Ramey's body full of holes. That he hadn't killed the bastard, but if he had, he could only hope he landed her as his prosecutor. That her ineptitude would ensure he made it home for supper. Then Dorsey had leaned in close and lobbed the final verbal grenade. That he wished Ramey had picked her parking garage that night. Then she'd know what it was like to be a victim.

Then there had been heat at her back as Reagan moved behind her. He hadn't touched her, hadn't said a word, but something in his face caught Dorsey's attention and in a slow, measured movement, the man took a step back, fists at his sides. Reagan handed Dorsey his card over her shoulder, instructing them to call if they had more information.

Mia shook her head. "I wonder if their neighbors know they're living next door to a fucking armory. He's a 'collector.' How clever."

Reagan shrugged. "They're all registered. They aren't breaking the law."

"They got a letter, too." Kristen tried to put Dorsey's wild eyes from her mind. He was angry enough to have killed, but probably too passionate to have done it so methodically.

"As did Janet Briggs," Mia said.

"Our humble servant either used one hell of a discreet delivery service or he was out last night himself," Abe said. "Assuming the other victims received letters, he made eleven deliveries. Somebody must have seen something somewhere. We'll do a canvass of the neighborhoods to see if anybody remembers a car or a person lurking."

"Good idea." Mia's cell phone rang, a simple non-musical beep. "Yeah." Her eyes narrowed. "When? . . . Fine, we'll be there." She pocketed her phone and looked up. "Spinnelli says the ME has news. We're meeting back at the office ASAP. You coming, Kristen?"

Kristen nodded, just as her stomach growled. "I am, but first I'll stop and grab some dinner to go. You bought the gyros last night, Detective Reagan. I'll pick up something from Owen's and bring it to Spinnelli's. Don't let the ME start until I get there."

"What's Owen's?" Mia asked. "Please tell me it has meat."

Reagan rolled his eyes. "The Indian curry was *good*."

"I gotta have meat, Reagan, or I'll get anemic."

He snorted. "Yeah, you look real anemic to me, Mitchell."

Mia turned toward Kristen, ignoring him. "If Owen's has meat, I'm in."

Kristen smiled. "Owen's is the diner where I eat. You want to try his fried chicken?"

Mia sighed. "Best offer I've had all day."

Thursday, February 19, 6:15 P.M.

Zoe snapped her cell phone closed. "Bingo."

Scott yawned. "I have a date tonight, Richardson."

"So did I." Zoe made a mental note to cancel it. If she hurried, she might have a story ready for the ten o'clock slot. She watched two cars pass, the first with Detective Mitchell at the wheel, accompanied by a man she didn't recognize but fully intended to get to know much better. The other car was manned by Kristen Mayhew, driving solo. "That's not her car."

Scott yawned again. "So maybe she got a new one."

"Are you kidding? That woman plans to drive her old Toyota into the ground and it still has a few good years on it." She shrugged when Scott's head turned, his brows scrunched in a frown. "I know her mechanic. He tells me stuff."

"Pillow talk," Scott said with a sneer and Zoe bit her tongue. Like it or not, she needed him to make the damn film.

Ignoring him, she pulled her mirror from her purse. Her makeup was still flawless. "Besides, the car had an Avis sticker in the window. Come on, we're doing an interview."

"With who? Your hero just drove away."

Again Zoe bit back the retort. The day Mayhew was her hero . . . Meal ticket, maybe. Hero, never. "Haven't you been paying attention? She visits three houses with Detective Mitchell. Aren't you the least bit curious as to why?"

"I'm sure you'll tell me," Scott drawled, and the tips of her nails bit into her palms.

"Records says that this house belongs to Eileen Dorsey. The last house was Janet Briggs, the one before that Sylvia Whitman. Three victims of Anthony Ramey," she said and watched his eyes widen. Scott wasn't stupid, just a man who foolishly believed a single night of sex months ago should become an ongoing relationship and was mad because it hadn't. "So you do watch the news," she said, swallowing a smirk.

Scott straightened. "Ramey never went to jail. He's either reoffended or he's dead."

Zoe slid out of the van and tugged at her skirt. "Well, let's go find out which."

Thursday, February 19, 6:30 P.M.

"Kristen, so good to see you." Vincent pulled a brown bag from behind the counter. "You're order's ready." Vincent had worked for Owen for as long as she'd been coming to the diner. A sweet, unassuming man. Everybody loved Vincent.

A loud crash had them both wincing. "Another new cook?" Kristen asked.

Vincent sighed. "I give this one two days. Tops."

Owen had hired so many cooks in the last month, Kristen stopped trying to remember their names. "Any news from Timothy?"

"Nope. Wish his grandma would get better, though. Owen's been fit to be tied lately, dealing with all those new fry cooks."

"Maybe we could get Timothy some help for his grandma and he could come back."

Vincent shrugged. "We asked, but Owen says Timothy doesn't want the help. You know how Tim is about accepting help anyway."

Kristen nodded. "I know." A highly functional adult with Down's syndrome, Timothy had a great deal of pride and independence. She could see him refusing Owen's help.

"You know what?" Owen came out of the back, drying his hands on the towel he kept tied around his thickening middle. He was solid and dependable and he made a hell of a chicken potpie. A smile creased his face when he saw her. "I missed you at lunch today."

She made a face. "Peanut butter crackers."

He scowled. "You'll get sick if you don't eat right."

She crossed her heart. "I promise. I called in a take-out order."

Owen scanned the order slip. "Three fried chickens and three chicken potpies?"

Kristen licked her lips. "Plus potatoes and gravy."

"It's all here. What's going on tonight?" Owen gathered the bag in his arms and started for the front door.

"Meeting. I offered to bring dinner." She held open the door and shivered while Owen stood in his shirtsleeves with hardly a tremble for the cold, looking around with a frown.

"My car." She pointed to the rental and his face changed to a beaming smile.

"You finally listened to me and got rid of that old thing."

"It was not old. It was just well used." She opened the rear passenger door and he put the bag on the seat.

"It was a bucket of bolts that Vincent prayed for daily. We worried about you driving around at night in that rust heap."

"This is just a rental. Mine's in the shop." Kristen bit her lip over the little white lie.

The scowl returned. "Bucket of bolts, Kristen. It's going to leave you stranded on the side of the road some night and . . ." He shook his head, disgusted. "Stubborn girl."

"With no monthly car payment. Go in out of the cold, Owen. You'll get sick."

Chapter Seven

Thursday, February 19, 7:00 P.M.

"Where's Spinnelli?" Mia tossed her jacket onto a chair at the same table they'd used the night before. Abe saw that someone had set up a whiteboard for their use as they cataloged evidence. A young woman in a white lab coat already sat at the table, and Jack's coat hung on the back of the chair next to her although Jack was nowhere to be seen. The woman rose and extended her hand.

"I'm Julia VanderBeck," she said as she shook his hand. "I'm the ME."

She was thirty-five or so with wide brown eyes and hair the color of coffee with heavy cream. She was pretty, he thought. He should be interested, he thought. But all he could think about was ivory skin and green eyes and wild, curling hair.

"I'm Abe Reagan," he said. "Do you have all five bodies in your office?"

"Yes, I do, but if you don't mind, let's wait until everyone gets here so I don't have to say it twice." The request was made politely, but wearily.

Mia dropped into her chair. "Where's Spinnelli?" she repeated. "And Jack?"

"We're here," Spinnelli said, coming through the door, holding a casserole dish. "We have a visitor." His eyes were amused.

"Who's welcome anytime," Jack added, his arms laden with Tupperware bowls.

Abe recognized the dishes and bowls even before he heard his mother's voice, before she bustled into the room.

"Abe!" She pulled his head down for a loud smacking kiss on his cheek and ignoring the grins of his co-workers, he let her do it.

"Mom." She smiled up at him, so happily that he didn't have the heart to tell her she shouldn't have. He smiled back. He'd wondered when she was going to show up. Sean said their father had told her not to come, but Becca Reagan generally followed her own mind. "What have you done?"

"Now don't you be telling me I shouldn't have," she clucked. "I called your Lieutenant Spinnelli to get your telephone extension and he kindly informed me that you all would be working late tonight so that I wouldn't worry."

Spinnelli lifted the cover from the casserole dish and Abe could smell his mother's cabbage casserole from across the room. It was one of his favorites.

Spinnelli took a deep breath of appreciation. "Your mother offered to bring supper." He grinned. "How could I refuse?"

Abe leaned down and kissed his mother's cheek. "Thanks, Mom." Her cheeks blushed, and he thought she looked as beautiful today as she had when he was a first-grader and she'd arrived at school with chocolate cupcakes on his birthday. "This is so sweet of you."

"Sweet, my eye." She swept away to retrieve paper plates and plastic cutlery from the enormous handbag she was never without. "Couldn't let you go hungry, now could I?"

Mia was leaning over the dish, sniffing. "Does it have meat?"

His mother looked affronted, then concerned. "Of course it does. You're not a vegetarian are you, dear?"

Mia laughed. "No, ma'am. I'm Detective Mia Mitchell, Abe's new partner."

His mother looked even more worried. "You're his partner?"

Mia chuckled, apparently taking no offense. "Don't worry. He's safe with me."

Spinnelli nodded his reassurance. "Mia takes care of her own."

Still doubtful, she moved to the door. "Well, then, I'll leave you to your meeting, now."

Abe watched Mia heaping casserole on a dangerously full paper plate and growling at Jack, who backed away, hands held up in surrender. "I'll walk you downstairs, Mom."

His mother waited until she got to the bottom of the stairs. "So who was the other one, the one with the white coat?"

"She's the medical examiner." Abe had to chuckle at the look on his mother's face. "I'm sure she washed her hands before she left the morgue."

"Oh, my." She shrugged. "Well, I suppose someone has to do it. So what about your new partner?" She looked up at him through her lashes. "She's cute."

Abe laughed. "Cut it out, Mom. You don't want her thinking about me that way. She'll get all befuddled and won't be watching for the bad guys."

His mom grinned. "You've got a point there. You'll bring back all the dishes?"

"On Sunday when I come for ham, if not sooner."

"Ah, you've talked to Sean." Her smile dimmed. "Then you know."

He knew. He'd managed to push it to the back of his mind, but the thought had nagged him all day. Now the thought of seeing Jim and Sharon slid to the front of his mind and his stomach twisted. He and Debra's parents had never been on friendly terms, but their relationship had deteriorated to litigiously hostile by the end of his wife's life. He squeezed his mom's arm. "Don't worry. I promise I won't ruin the christening for Sean and Ruth."

"I didn't think you would, Abe. I just didn't want you blindsided."

No, she wouldn't. Faithful to her children to the bitter end was his mother. And he loved her for it. "Consider me warned." He dropped a kiss on her cheek. "Thanks for dinner, Mom. I'll drop by as soon as I can."

She pressed her palms against his face, keeping him in the slight bow that put him in her reach. "I'm so glad you're in a new job," she whispered fiercely.

"I know."

"I worried about you every day."

She was the wife of a career cop, the mother of two cops. She knew the danger and lived with it, but the undercover work had taken a toll on his family, and he knew it. Early in his undercover career, he'd chanced visits home once a month, but the deeper under he went, the further apart his visits became. The last time he'd risked a trip home had been the night Debra died. A full year ago. In secret, under cover of darkness. But all that was over now. As of this week, he could go home whenever he chose. "I know, Mom. But I'm fine. Really."

Her hands didn't budge, and his neck started to develop a cramp from bending so awkwardly, but he made no move to straighten. "I hope I didn't embarrass you too much by coming down tonight. I just couldn't seem to help myself."

"I love you, Mom. You did a wonderful thing." Her eyes glinted and he grinned to break the solemnity. "But you probably don't want to make it a habit. It'll be like feeding a stray—you'll never get rid of them."

She laughed shakily and released him, then pointed at the window to the street. "Abe, help that woman. She's too small to be carrying such a load."

Kristen was trying to open the door with one hand, the other grasping at a large paper bag, and he remembered her errand. Dinner from the diner. He hoped she wouldn't mind refrigerating it. He doubted anyone would be hungry after finishing his mother's food. That anyone would choose diner food over his mom's home cooking never even entered his mind. Quickly opening the door, he plucked the bag from her hands. "I'll take that."

Kristen rolled her shoulders. "Thanks. It didn't seem that heavy when Owen was carrying it out to my car." She glanced over to where his mother waited expectantly for an introduction, then glanced back, her brows lifted in question.

"Kristen, this is my mother, Becca Reagan. Mom, this is Kristen Mayhew. She works in the prosecutor's office."

His mother eyed Kristen up and down. "You look taller on television," she said.

Kristen smiled politely. "You're the first person to ever say that. Thank you."

"Some days I'd like to smack that woman reporter, teach her some manners."

Kristen's smile warmed from polite to sincere. "What a kind thing to say, Mrs. Reagan. Most days I want to do the same."

"My daughter wants to be a lawyer," she said thoughtfully.

"Annie?" Abe asked in surprise.

"No, not Annie," his mother returned with a frown. "Annie's got a career. Rachel. Keep up, Abe."

"Rachel can't want to be a lawyer. She's just a little girl." His parents' late-life surprise. Actually, more of a shock. There were twenty-two years between himself and his youngest sister, so she was more like a daughter to them all.

"Rachel's thirteen," his mother pointed out sharply.

"And you'd do well to remember it on her birthday come May. No silly stuffed animals this year, she's grown out of it."

Abe huffed in frustration. Rachel couldn't be thirteen. It just wasn't possible. Thirteen meant makeup and boys and . . . boys. He shuddered at the very thought. He and his little sister needed to have a talk. "Then what does she want for her birthday?"

"Cash." She turned back to Kristen. "She's talking about being a lawyer like you."

Kristen's eyes widened. "Like me?"

"Sure. She sees you on the TV. Would you be willing to have a chat with her?"

Kristen's mouth curved in amusement and Abe's breath caught in his throat at the sight. It was impish and fun and not like any expression that had crossed her face so far. "You want me to talk her out of it, Mrs. Reagan?"

"I don't know. Should I?"

Kristen shrugged. "Some days yes, some days no. But I'd be glad to talk with her. Your son has my office number."

Your son. It rang of the same formality she'd used in addressing him all day, since last night. It was starting to annoy him. He had a first name, dammit. She called Mia and Jack and Marc by their first names. It was a damn courtesy. "We need to be going, Mom. They're waiting for us to start the meeting. Be careful driving home."

His mother blinked at his brusque tone. "I will. Don't forget to return my dishes." With a wave she was gone.

Kristen looked up at him warily. "What dishes?"

"Dinner plans have changed. Mom brought a little snack."

Kristen started up the stairs, unbuttoning her coat. "How little of a snack?"

"How does fried chicken strike you as a breakfast meal?"

She shrugged. "Like normal."

Thursday, February 19, 7:15 P.M.

Spinnelli was just scraping the last morsel from his plate when they came in. "I was about to send a search party."

"Not me." Mia licked her fork. "If you never came back, there'd be more for me."

"Did you leave any for us?" Abe asked, peering into a casserole dish.

Mia grinned. "Only the vegetables."

Abe set Kristen's paper bag on the table and retrieved two of the Styrofoam containers. "Well then, let's get started. Julia, what can you tell us about the bodies?"

Julia drew out a notepad. "I received all five bodies by two o'clock this afternoon."

Handing Kristen one of the containers, Abe took the seat next to her and once again she felt the heat of his body, reminding her of how he'd stood behind her at the Dorsey house. Of how safe she'd felt. What she felt now was crowded. He took up all his space at the table and some of hers, but to scoot her chair a few inches out of his way seemed rude so she stayed where she was and focused on the subject at hand. There were five new dead bodies in Julia's morgue. And the man who put them there was still walking around, likely planning number six. "Cause of death, GSW to the head?" she asked.

Julia shook her head. "If only life were that simple. This is going to get complicated so everybody get your score-cards ready. Five bodies. All had gunshot wounds to the head, but the head shots only killed your three gang boys.

Head shots on Ramey and King were inflicted postmortem and by a different gun."

She had the attention of everyone in the room.

"Ramey was strangled. X-ray shows his larynx was crushed. I was able to get a good picture of the ligature marks. Your killer pulled hard. The grooves are deep." She handed a photo to Jack, who studied it before passing it down the line. "I may even be able to make a plaster cast of the chain links. I'll let you know. Ramey also had a fracture at the base of his skull. It looks like your killer hit him with a blunt object before he strangled him."

"Any idea of what kind of blunt object?" Mia asked.

"Not right now. I'll let you know if I do. Ramey has no defensive wounds, nothing under his fingernails. I found traces of gunpowder residue around the hole in his head. He has abrasions on his wrists and ankles."

"So he knocked Ramey out, tied him up, strangled him, popped a bullet in his head, then moved him and buried him." Spinnelli noted the details on the whiteboard with a frown. "The head shot is overkill." He rolled his eyes at the snickers that rippled through the room. "You know what I mean."

"He gets his revenge, but it isn't enough," Reagan said thoughtfully. "Then he gets him to the burial site and has one more go at him. Being dead isn't enough, so he puts a shotgun shell through his pelvis."

"We sifted the dirt at the site," Jack said. "Found shotgun pellets. Same with King."

"He couldn't have silenced that," Mia mused. "Somebody heard something."

Spinnelli nodded. "We'll canvass the area tomorrow." He crossed to the board, drew three columns, labeling them *Ramey*, *Blade*, and *King*. "When was Ramey last seen?"

Mia flipped open her notepad. "His mother says she last

saw him on January 3. His girlfriend confirms it. She was sure because Ramey stood her up for a date that night."

Kristen drew a breath as Spinnelli noted the date in Ramey's column, his squeaking marker grating on her nerves. *Blue stripes.* She'd decided on the blue stripes that night, but hadn't taken the samples down until two nights later, when insomnia prompted her to start papering that wall. "He would have put the Ramey crate in my trunk the next night or the night after at the latest." She glanced at Spinnelli whose mustache bent down in concern. "That's when the samples came down. You can try asking around my neighborhood to see if anyone saw anything, but everybody is usually in bed by eleven."

"What samples?" Julia asked sharply.

Spinnelli tilted his head in Kristen's direction, indicating she had the floor. She blew out a breath. "The killer left letters in my trunk."

"I heard that part. What samples?" Julia repeated.

"In the letter he refers to some wallpaper samples I had on my living room wall."

Julia leaned back in her chair with a frown. "He's been watching you?"

"Looks that way." Kristen felt a shiver of new worry slide down her spine. "Don't stare at me like that, Julia."

Shooting her an intense look, Julia brought out new photos and Ross King's bruised face stared up from the glossy film. "Ross King had blunt force trauma to the head and shoulder area." She held up a photo and pointed with her pen. "Fractures behind the right ear and the left temple. Based on the shape of the bruising, I'm thinking it was a bat."

"He was their softball coach," Kristen said softly. "More poetic justice."

Reagan pulled one of the pictures toward him. "Wood slivers?"

"No, not a trace. I'm thinking it was an aluminum bat."

"He beat him to death?" Mia asked.

Julia shook her head. "I don't know. I won't know until I've had a chance to open him up, but King may have died from a bullet to his chest." She held up another photo, an enlarged close-up of the stitches running up King's torso and pointed to a half-moon-shaped area of missing skin.

"Could be a bullet hole," Reagan agreed.

"I'm guessing he went after the bullet." Julia handed him the photo. "His X-rays show no bullet, but half his left lung is gone. Also, there's no exit wound. As to why your killer wanted the bullet back, that's your bailiwick, not mine."

"And the material he used to stitch him up?" Spinnelli asked, coming to look over Reagan's shoulder.

"Linen twine." Julia shrugged. "Available at any hardware store."

"A bullet for his head and a bullet for his heart." Kristen stared at Julia. She knew the woman well enough to know there was more. "What else?"

Julia stared back, her eyes worried now. "King's knees were popped, Kristen." She pulled another photo from her stack and handed it to Jack, who sat to her left.

"We saw the knee damage when we dug him up," Jack mused, "but we didn't know what caused it."

"A bullet caused it," Julia said. "My information is from X-rays, because I haven't had a chance to probe inside. The films show both kneecaps are shattered. Pulverized, actually. The shot was a direct hit. Whatever weapon your guy used had one hell of a kick."

"He immobilized King so he couldn't get away," Kristen murmured. Somehow, the thought of it bothered her more than the actual killing itself.

Julia brought out one more set of photos. "That's what I thought. One more piece of data for your board, Marc. Your gang boys were brought down with a single bullet to the forehead. No powder residue. No blows to the head like the others. No defensive wounds of any kind." She looked up and caught Kristen's eye. "Again, you'll want to get an opinion from ballistics, but from the angle of entry and exit wounds on each boy, I'd say your killer shot from above. Coupled with the absence of powder residue, well above."

Mia leaned across the table to look at the photos, her face intense. "How far above?"

Julia shrugged. "Twenty, thirty feet maybe."

"He could have cleaned the residue away," Mia said, but her tone said she didn't believe her own words.

Kristen let out a breath. Now Julia's worried frown made sense. "He didn't knock them out first, so they were conscious when he shot them. I can't imagine even a junior Blade going down without a fight." She looked up to find Reagan's blue eyes fixed on her face and this time found it oddly comforting. "They never saw him," she said quietly. "He waited for them on a rooftop."

Reagan nodded soberly, then said the words they were all thinking. "We have a sniper on our hands."

Mia leaned back in her chair. "Who disables his victim with premeditation, then beats him senseless."

Kristen shivered, suddenly ice-cold despite the heat radiating from Reagan's body beside her. "And he's watching me," she murmured.

Spinnelli capped his marker. "Shit."

Thursday, February 19, 7:45 P.M.

The whiteboard was covered with Spinnelli's notes and
Kristen had the feeling they'd only touched the tip of the
iceberg on their humble servant.

"So we know he killed his victims in one place, moved
them somewhere indoors where he took the Polaroids and
cleaned them up, then moved them to yet another place
where he buried them." Kristen stared at the facts on the
whiteboard. She'd been shaken, knowing the man watching
her had a sniper's rifle and scope, but she'd pulled herself
together with the help of a slice of lemon meringue pie
Reagan's mother had left behind. Mrs. Reagan was a good
cook, better than Owen, she was forced to admit.

"You forgot the postmortem pelvic-ectomies," Mia said,
tongue-in-cheek.

Kristen sighed. "No, we can't forget about that."

Reagan sat back, crossed his arms over his chest. "The
murderers he dealt with cleanly and efficiently. The sex
offenders got something extra."

"Maybe he's a victim, too," Jack said.

"Or someone in his family was," Spinnelli countered.

"Or both," Kristen said quietly. She looked up and her
eyes skirted away from Reagan's. "The family members
exhibit a different kind of victimology, it's true."

Abe frowned. There was something in her tone, in the
way she wouldn't meet his eyes. "Stan Dorsey is proof positive of that," he said, wondering if she was still shaken by
Dorsey's display. He knew he was, and he'd faced Dorsey's
kind before. The sight of those crazed eyes and all those
guns . . . He didn't imagine it was a sight Kristen Mayhew
saw every day.

Her smile was distant, brittle. "He certainly is." She

turned to Mia, effectively shutting him out. He wanted to take her by the shoulders and turn her back, but of course he didn't. "What did Miles Westphalen say this morning?" she asked.

Mia shot him a look over Kristen's head before answering. "He thought our guy had a life-altering event recently which caused him to snap. That if he'd been a victim or had a family member that was a victim, the actual crime happened some time ago. But that something happened recently to trigger all this." Mia looked over her shoulder at Spinnelli, then back at Kristen. "Miles wanted to know if you had protection."

Kristen kept her composure. "He thinks I need it?"

"Yes," Mia said unflinchingly.

Her fingers drummed against the table once before she flattened her hand. Abe would have missed the slight tremble in her fingers had he not been looking. No wonder she was so good in the courtroom. Kristen Mayhew had control down to a science. "He hasn't threatened me specifically."

"If it were me, I'd request it, Kris," Julia said earnestly. "The idea of a peeping Tom with a scope scares me."

Her jaw hardened. "I'll cross that bridge when I come to it. For right now I don't intend to be a prisoner in my own home or be forced out of it. What else did Westphalen say?"

Mia apparently knew when to concede. "He was interested in the grave markers."

"So let's talk about them," Spinnelli said. "Jack, anything on the stones?"

Julia stood up. "I don't have anything more to give you until I start the autopsies tomorrow, and I have a babysitter on the clock at home. Do you need me anymore?"

Spinnelli shook his head. "Go on home, Julia. You want some of this pie?"

Julia shook her head. "No, thanks. I'll be starting the

autopsies at nine A.M. if anyone wants to join me." She gathered her purse and notepad. "Night, everyone."

"Jack?" Spinnelli tapped the table and Jack's head whipped around.

"Hmm?" Jack's face heated. "Sorry. What did you say?"

With humor and pity, Abe noted how Jack's gaze had followed Julia's every movement as she left the room. Jack was smitten, and Julia either didn't know or didn't care. Poor guy.

Spinnelli blinked at him. "The grave markers? What did you find?"

Jack cleared his throat. "The markers are made from marble. The inscriptions are sandblasted versus hand-carved, which makes sense. He would have needed a week to hand-carve just one."

"Sandblasting?" Kristen asked. "How does it work?"

Jack settled back in his chair. "Generally the craftsman makes a template from rubber or a vellum film, like a photographic negative—the parts he wants inscribed are cut out. He puts the template on top of whatever he's blasting, then puts it through a sandblaster. Fine sand is blasted at the rock, eating away everything but the rubber. When he's done, he peels off the template and the inscription is complete. But it's harder to get all the template material off the flat surfaces when the letters are blasted deep into the rock, like these markers."

Mia looked impressed. "You've done this?"

Jack's smile was wry. "I gave up handcrafts after I almost cut off my thumb in high school shop class. No, I did an Internet search on sandblasting. There are a few major memorial manufacturers in the area, but I don't think this guy went outside. I'd bet he did these himself. From what I read, with the right equipment it wouldn't be that hard to do."

"Where would he get the equipment?" Spinnelli asked.

"Again, there are only a few major manufacturers of equipment powerful enough to do such a big job. There were traces of the template material on King's marker, and the lab says it's not rubber. It's vellum. That narrows it down a bit."

"I'll follow up on this one," Mia said. "Jack, I'll get the names of those companies from you tomorrow, then I'll get a list of Chicago customers."

"He could have bought the equipment some time ago," Abe said.

Mia nodded contemplatively. "Perhaps. But these guys have to buy materials somewhere. I'll ask about that, too. I mean, I don't think you're going to get tombstone-quality marble at the local Wal-Mart."

Spinnelli noted it on the whiteboard. "What else?"

"We're still checking the clothing we found in the crates. I expect some results in the morning. We'll also run the notes the Ramey victims got through the lab tomorrow," Jack said. "Though if we find anything, I'll be shocked."

Kristen sighed. "We still have to visit King's victims and the parents of the two kids killed by the Blades."

Abe could see it was something she was dreading. "I can go by myself, Kristen."

She shook her head, just as he'd known she would. "No, I need to do this. Can you wait until after ten in the morning? I have motion hour at nine." Her cell phone jangled, a digitized Pachelbel's Canon. "Mayhew . . . Hi, John, yeah we're almost finished." She paled and jumped to her feet, moving to the television in the corner. "Oh, hell. What channel?"

The set came to life, revealing Zoe Richardson reporting from a familiar street.

"Fuck," Mia snarled.

"Bottom-feeding bitch," Jack muttered.

Abe studied Kristen, standing in front of the flickering screen, the remote visibly shaking in her hand. But this time it wasn't fear on her face. It was rage. He understood how she felt. Richardson must have been following her all afternoon, lurking in the shadows until they were gone and she could get her pound of flesh.

"And so a chilling chapter in the lives of three women comes to a close," Richardson said, her hair barely moving in the brisk evening breeze. The camera zoomed to frame Sylvia Whitman's home. "First they were victims of rape, then denied justice by what many termed incompetence within the State's Attorney's Office, but today these women are finally vindicated. Today each of these three innocent women received visits from Assistant State's Attorney Kristen Mayhew accompanied by two CPD detectives to inform them that Anthony Ramey, the man who allegedly terrorized and victimized them has paid the ultimate price."

The anchor's voice cut in, sober and concerned. "What do the police and the State's Attorney's Office have to say about this, Zoe?"

"We were unable to reach the police for comment this evening. We can only assume they are working to uncover clues to the identity of Ramey's killer."

"Were the three women able to provide any additional information, Zoe? Anything that might be helpful to the police?" the anchor asked.

"Son of a bitch," Jack muttered. "Like we need her kind of help."

"Not the letters," Mia urged under her breath. "Don't mention the damn letters."

Richardson widened her eyes, as if she'd only just remembered something important and Mia smacked her palm against the tabletop. "Dammit."

Kristen flung her hand up, signaling for quiet and Mia gritted her teeth.

"Yes, Andrea. Each of the three women received an anonymous letter today, saying Ramey was dead and that justice had finally been done." Zoe's eyes gleamed. "He signed each letter 'Your Humble Servant.' This is Zoe Richardson, reporting."

The camera flashed back to the serious face of Andrea the Anchor. "Thank you, Zoe. We'll be anxiously waiting for more details on this exclusive breaking story." Her face brightened, almost comically. "Now back to our regularly scheduled program."

Viciously, Kristen turned off the television and for a long moment no one spoke.

"How did she know?" Spinnelli finally asked, his own temper under an obviously tight leash. "How the hell did she know?"

Kristen stood staring at the dark screen, her rigid back to the rest of them. "She was following us." Her swallow was audible. "Me." She placed the remote on top of the television with precise care. "I don't believe this."

"My mom can smack her for you," Abe said lightly. "I have it on good authority that she packs a wallop when she's mad." He let out a silent breath when Kristen's back slumped and she turned to him with a tight little smile.

"And just how many times did you make your mom mad, Reagan?" she asked.

Abe forced a grin. "More times than I can count."

The tight smile relaxed to a wry grimace. "Now, *that* I can believe."

Spinnelli dragged his palms down his face. "Well, the cat's out of the bag, people. I'll schedule a press conference tomorrow. Abe, you make sure we get whereabouts for all the vics for the times of the murders, as close as you can and find out if any of them are sharpshooters."

"Besides Stan Dorsey?" Abe asked dryly, and Spinnelli lifted his eyes heavenward.

"God help us. I want to know every step Dorsey took on the days in question. I'll start checking all the cops and lawyers on the list for anyone with enough skill to make those shots. Mia, see what you can find on the sandblasting angle. Hopefully Julia will come up with something more when she's done with the autopsies."

"What about his next victim?" Kristen asked. "Are we going to wait for another crate to appear on my doorstep?"

Spinnelli shook his head. "I'm going to get surveillance cameras installed around your place tomorrow. If he visits you again, we'll know."

She shook her head, hard and fast. "No, that's not what I meant. We know he has a special rage for sex offenders. I can get you a list of all the sex perps I've prosecuted. Maybe we can head him off at the pass."

Spinnelli nodded. "It's a good start. And Kristen?"

Warily, she eyed him. "What?"

"Do you have a dog?"

She shook her head. "No."

"Then I'd advise you to get one."

"And make it big," Mia added. "No cute puppies."

"And make it a barker." Jack bared his teeth. "With sharp teeth."

Kristen turned to Abe, one russet brow lifted. "Any more recommendations?"

He tucked his tongue in his cheek. "Cerberus would give you a matched set and would get on well with Mephistopheles and Nostradamus."

To his surprise she laughed. Not a chuckle, but a full,

throaty laugh that went all the way up to her eyes. And listening, it was like he'd been slugged in the chest.

Thursday, February 19, 9:00 P.M.

Zoe topped off her wine, her bones finally warm after a soak in the tub. When she hit the big time, she was going someplace warm. To hell with Chicago in the dead of winter.

Dead. Her lips curved. Anthony Ramey was dead and CPD had a vigilante on their hands. And she, Zoe Richardson, had made the scoop.

Mayhew will be furious, she thought gleefully. *How very marvelous.* Zoe carefully removed the tape from the VCR. This piece was definitely a keeper. She'd neatly printed half the date on the label when she was startled by loud banging on her front door. Eyeing the peephole, she felt the smallest bit alarmed, but quickly dismissed it.

He couldn't, wouldn't say a word. She could and would expose him. He was putty in her hands. She opened the door, feigning her surprised doe look. "I wasn't expecting you. Didn't you get my message canceling tonight?"

He pushed open the door and closed it hard before grabbing her shoulders even harder. His face was dark and angry, a vein throbbing at his temple. Excitement shivered down to her toes.

"What the hell do you think you're doing?" he demanded, shaking her.

She blinked, even as her mouth watered. Who would have guessed he'd had it in him? "What do you mean?"

"This is Zoe Richardson, reporting," he mimicked nastily. He shook her again. "What the fucking hell are you doing?"

"You're hurting me." Instantly he released her, but his chest still heaved like a bellows. She met his eyes, all pretense gone. "I am doing my job. I am a reporter. I report the news."

"Don't treat me like one of your imbecilic groupies," he snarled. "I know you are a reporter. But why follow Mayhew? Do you have any concept of the trouble you'll cause?"

With a careless shrug she retrieved her wineglass. "That's not my problem. Would you like some wine? It's a wonderful Chardonnay."

He was looking at her as if she'd gone insane. "You don't care, do you? You don't care that you've stirred up a hornet's nest that could ruin my career."

She hoped her smile was sincere. "I simply don't see the connection between your job and mine." Of course there was a connection. She was counting on it. She approached him, well aware of the way the silk draped over her skin, scented from her bath. Of the way the silk parted to reveal just enough cleavage to make his eyes drop, flash, and burn. "Don't pout, darling." She lifted herself up on her toes and pressed a kiss to his hard mouth. Felt his shoulders soften, just a little. Felt him harden elsewhere, quite a lot.

Like taking candy from a baby. Men were so wonderfully predictable.

"You knew I was a reporter before you managed to be introduced to me." She'd been the one to manage an introduction to him, but letting him believe he was the aggressor was part of the charade. She touched her tongue to the corner of his mouth, felt him shudder. "I reported on Mayhew for months before you met me and will continue to do so after you grow tired of me and go back to your wife." She kissed him, the briefest nibble. "So how is she?"

His hand slipped under her robe, against the bare skin of

her back. "Who?" he murmured, lowering his head for more.

"Your wife, darling," she purred.

"Most likely she's asleep." His other hand toyed with the ties between her breasts. "And once she's asleep, she doesn't wake until morning."

Zoe blindly set the wineglass on the lamp table and reached over his shoulder to flip the deadbolt on her front door. "Excellent."

Chapter Eight

Thursday, February 19, 9:00 P.M.

Adjusting her rearview mirror, Kristen cautiously looked both ways before exiting the parking garage, feeling alone and very vulnerable. Looking over her shoulder, wondering if he was following. And if he wasn't, where was he, what he was doing? Who was next for his vigilante justice? Her hands gripped the steering wheel and she squinted at the onslaught of headlights coming in her direction. So many people, most engaged in perfectly legal pursuits. But for every twenty who were honest citizens, there was one who was not.

The sum total of that one in twenty was enough to keep her gainfully employed for the rest of her life. She blew out a breath, watched it turn to vapor, then disappear. He was out there, somewhere, hunting for the one in twenty.

And for some reason, he brought the fruit of his labors to her.

Fruit of his labors. "I'm starting to sound like him," she murmured. "All pomp and circumstance." She bit her lip, glanced up to her rearview mirror once again. With teeth. Their humble servant was pomp and circumstance with very sharp teeth.

Which made her think of Jack's funny face as he'd urged her to get a dog with sharp teeth, and it made her smile. They'd tried so hard to lighten her mood, to lessen her fear. They'd walked her to her rental car, all of them. Mia and Jack and Marc. And Reagan. She couldn't forget about Reagan. With his intense blue eyes and dry wit. *Cerberus.* She chuckled out loud. The three-headed guardian of the gates of Hell. How apropos. Maybe she would get a dog at that. This weekend, perhaps. A dog that barked, wasn't cute, and had big sharp teeth. That didn't eat cats.

She entertained herself with the notion all the way home, but when she pulled into her driveway, the lighthearted thoughts fled, leaving her staring at her own house with dread.

He could be anywhere. Anger mixed with the dread, fury that her fear had her still sitting in her driveway. She was afraid in her own home. Dammit.

A knock on her car window nearly sent her though the roof. With her hand on her racing heart she turned to find Reagan's frowning face. He twirled his fingers and she rolled down the window, shuddering from the cold blast of frigid air.

"It's ten below out here," he hissed, mindful of the darkened windows up and down the street. "If *he* doesn't get you, you'll die of exposure."

She narrowed her eyes at him. "It *was* warm in the car."

"Well, I'm freezing my keister off out here. Give me your keys."

"Excuse me?"

He shoved his gloved hand through the open window, palm up. "Give me your keys and I'll check your closets. Dammit, Kristen, hurry up."

She yanked her keys from the ignition and slapped them in his palm. "I didn't ask you to come." But she was suddenly, fiercely glad he had. Cursing her unsteady legs, she followed him up the sidewalk.

"You're welcome," he muttered. "You should have a spotlight by your door."

"I did," she muttered back, wincing as he missed the keyhole and the key skittered across the door she'd so painstakingly painted last fall. "The neighbors complained it was keeping them awake and signed a petition to make me get rid of it."

He pulled a flashlight from the pocket of his overcoat, shone it on the lock, and unlocked the door to the kitchen. "Your neighbors need to get a life." He waited for her to follow him inside before closing the door. "Disarm the alarm, then stay here."

"Yes, sir."

He threw a lopsided grin over his shoulder at her caustic reply and her heart took off at a canter once again. Not with fear this time. Not the same kind of fear anyway. But just as fast and just as hard. She watched as he drew his weapon and his grin faded. "Stay here," he repeated, softly this time. "I mean it."

"I'm not stupid," she muttered to the empty kitchen. To keep herself occupied she fed the cats, then busied herself with the teapot, willing her hands not to rattle the china.

Her tea was steeped and poured and he still hadn't returned. She tiptoed to the archway to the dining room and peered out. Just as he had the night before, he'd left every light blazing in his wake. She'd grumbled about her electric bill the night before, but made no move to turn off a single light. She suspected tonight would be much the same.

Behind her the door opened and slammed shut and Kristen swallowed a shriek just as his deep voice rumbled through her kitchen. "Damn, it's cold."

She turned to find Reagan stamping his snow-covered feet. "Don't scare me like that."

Abe looked up, his expression grim. She stood still as stone, holding a fragile china teacup so tightly it seemed fused to her hands. She still wore her winter coat, buttoned up to her neck even though her kitchen was warm. "Sorry. I didn't mean to sneak up on you." He tossed her keys to the countertop and more carefully put her laptop bag beside them. "I closed your car window and locked it up."

She drew a deep breath. "Thank you. What took you so long?"

He slipped his flashlight in his overcoat pocket. "I used the basement door to get to the backyard and did a lap around the house."

"And?"

His lips thinned. "Somebody was here. There's a set of fresh footprints in the snow up by your basement windows. What's in the little shed out back?"

"It's the detached garage, but I use it for storage. Why?"

He shrugged. "Just curious. That's one hell of a padlock for a storage shed. Somebody might think you've got valuables in there."

Her smile was shaky, and totally false. Now that he'd seen the real thing, heard her truly laugh, he recognized all the other smiles for the frauds they'd been. "One man's trash is another man's treasure," she said lightly. Which of course meant she had no intention of telling him what she'd stored in the shed. The realization stung a little. She lifted her cup. "Can I pour you some tea?"

Abe looked down at her for a moment. She was trying. She was uncomfortable having him here in her kitchen, of that he was certain, but she was making an honest attempt at hospitality. He should leave her in peace, allow her to get what would obviously be much needed rest, but somehow he couldn't make himself leave.

He wanted to hear her laugh again, so much it was almost a palpable ache.

"Sure. Maybe it'll warm me up." He sat down at her table and pulled at his gloves and scarf. "Aren't you going to take off your coat?"

She looked down, as if surprised she was still wearing it. Awkwardly she shrugged out of it, laying it across one of the chairs, but made no move to take off the jacket of her dark charcoal suit. "Thank you for following me home." She concentrated on pouring tea into a big mug, totally at odds with her fragile little cup. "I was scared to come inside by myself and that made me mad, so I took it out on you." She looked up, met his eyes. "I'm sorry."

He tilted his head, studying her as she placed his mug on the table in front of him. She didn't look away while apologizing and he respected that. "It's okay. I'm used to women getting mad and taking it out on me. I have two sisters. Sit, please."

She sat self-consciously and he wondered if she was always so ill at ease in her own home, or if being stalked by a homicidal vigilante was a special cause.

"Annie and Rachel, right?"

He nodded, pleased that she'd remembered. "And two brothers. Aidan and Sean." He blew on his tea, enjoying the feel of the warm mug between his cold hands. "Aidan's also a cop. So was my dad before he retired. And all of his friends."

Her eyes sharpened. "I understand now. I'm sorry if you

thought I was singling out police as potential suspects. I would have added John's staff from the beginning, if I'd thought of it, but I'm so accustomed to doing things by myself." She pressed her fingertips against her nape, massaging her neck. "I meant no disrespect."

"I was too sensitive." His lips quirked up. "In some households IA is the postal code for Iowa. In my house 'Internal Affairs' was worse than the worst four-letter word."

She smiled, small, but real. "Well, I'm glad that misunderstanding's out of the way." Her eyes sobered. "But you do realize the chances of him being a cop are higher now that we know he's a marksman."

Abe nodded. "I know. I think I knew it this morning, but that a cop could go bad isn't an easy thing for me to admit." She massaged her nape again and he tightened his fingers around the warm mug to keep from taking over the task. "Just let it down."

Her eyes widened. "Excuse me?"

He sipped at his tea. "Let your hair down. Those pins are giving you a headache. Besides, it isn't like I haven't seen it down before, and you are in your own house now."

After a moment's hesitation she did, pulling out a handful of pins, letting her hair fall to her shoulders. Well, *fall* was the wrong word, he thought. It *boinged,* like so many springs, sending fiery curls in every which direction. He chuckled into his tea, imagining she'd be none too pleased with his thoughts.

"What?"

Her face relaxed as her fingers threaded through her curls and Abe tightened his fingers around his mug, wondering if her curls were soft or coarse, knowing that the scent of her hair would linger on his hands if he was ever brave enough to find out. Instead he shook his head. "You'll be mad."

She tucked her tongue in her cheek. "What, little Orphan Annie? Looks like I stuck my finger in a light socket? I've heard them all before."

"I like it."

Her eyes narrowed as if she suspected him of lying but was too polite to voice it aloud. "Thank you."

They were quiet for a few minutes, then, sipping their tea in the absolute quiet of her kitchen and Abe wondered if there was ever noise in Kristen Mayhew's house. His own parents' house had been so noisy that he'd often yearned for quiet, but the silence in Kristen's house was oppressive. Despite her efforts to renovate room by room, the house had an empty feeling. "How long have you lived here?" he asked.

"About two years." She looked around fondly. "It's been fun making this place over."

"You do good work," he said and she smiled in genuine pleasure. "My sister Annie has her own interior design business. She'd love the challenge of an old place like this."

"It was built in 1903. I uncover hand-carved wood in every room I redo, but I haven't even contemplated the kitchen yet. I've kind of been waiting for one of the appliances to die so I have a good excuse to buy new ones. But I don't cook often, so the oven's safe, and the refrigerator seems to be immortal."

"Annie would show these old appliances the door with no remorse. My mother fought her for years over redoing our kitchen at home, but Annie finally won. Mom complained every day the kitchen was out of her hands, but in the end she loved it."

Kristen's mouth curved, a little wistfully, he thought.

"Your mom seems like a nice woman. Takes good care of her baby."

"I'm not the baby," he corrected. "That would be Rachel."

She lifted a brow. "Ah, yes. Rachel that wants to be me. She's thirteen?"

Abe shuddered dramatically. "Apparently so."

"A bit of a late-life surprise, huh?"

"More like the shock of the century." He grinned at her. "I remember us all being appalled to find our parents still did it at all." She chuckled in answer, but said nothing and within a minute the quiet became suffocating once again. "How about you?" he found himself asking. "Family in the area?"

She shook her head. "No."

He leaned forward slightly, waiting. "And?"

She leaned back, so slightly he was sure she didn't realize she'd pulled away. She'd maintained her distance, consciously or not. "No, I don't have any family here in Chicago."

Abe frowned. Her tone had become flat, her eyes blank. "Where then? Kansas?"

Her eyes flashed at the mention of her home state and her teacup slowly lowered to the table. "No. Thank you for escorting me home, Detective Reagan. It's been a long day for both of us." She stood up, and irked, he would have done the same if he hadn't seen her hands tremble just before she locked them behind her back. Still dressed in her dark suit and heels, he imagined this was how she stood in court, seemingly impervious.

With her hands trembling behind her back. So he kept his seat.

Yesterday she said she had no friends. Today, it was no family. It struck him that in both times he'd made a sweep through her house he'd seen no pictures, not a single personal memento, with the exception of the law school diplomas that hung over her desk. "Sit down, Kristen." He pulled her chair closer to where she rigidly stood. "Please."

Her jaw clenched and she looked away. "Why?"

"Because you've got to be exhausted."

She shook her head and her curls bounced. "No, why is it so important to know about my family?"

"Because . . . it's family."

She turned to look at him and her eyes were no longer angry, but weary. "You're close to your family, Detective?"

Detective. She seemed determined to keep him at arm's length. He was equally determined to see the wall she'd erected torn down. "I haven't seen much of them over the past few years because of the job. But yes, we're close. They're my family."

"Then I'm happy for you. Truly. But you should know that the majority of families aren't close, tight-knit little units. The majority of families have problems."

"You're awfully young to be so jaded."

Her shoulders sagged. "I'm a hell of a lot older than you think."

He stood up then. "What I think is that you're tired. Try to get some sleep."

Her mouth twisted. "Sleep well, Kristen?" she mocked bitterly. "Somehow I don't think so." She lifted a hand when he opened his mouth to speak. "Don't say it."

"Say what?"

"Don't tell me to go to a hotel. This is my home. I will not let him make me leave."

He picked up their cups and put them in the sink. "I wasn't planning to. I was planning to offer to run to the drugstore and get you something to help you sleep." She closed her eyes, one hand clutching the back of the chair.

"Why are you being so nice to me, Detective?"

It was a damn good question. Because she seemed so alone? Because he'd seen her scared and vulnerable when the face she showed everyone else was confident and brave? Because he wondered why there were no party dresses in her closet and no family pictures on her nightstand? Because he found her fascinating and couldn't get her out of his mind? Because her laugh was like a sucker punch to his gut?

"I don't know," he answered grimly. "Why won't you call me by my first name?"

Her eyes flew open, suddenly wary. "I . . . I don't know."

"Fair enough." He pulled on his coat, conscious of her eyes following the movements of his hands as he buttoned up. When he reached the button at his throat, her eyes rose to meet his and he could see she was still troubled by his question. Good, because he was troubled by hers as well. "I'll swing by the courthouse tomorrow morning to pick you up. I'd like to visit the rest of the original victims before the families of our five dead guys make a connection with tonight's report and contact your friend Richardson."

At the mention of Richardson, her lips thinned. "I'll be ready."

Thursday, February 19, 10:30 P.M.

He was cold. Very cold. His hands ached and he glanced longingly at the fur-lined gloves sticking up out of his bag. Soon. For now he'd have to make do with the thin leather gloves. The warm gloves were so thick he couldn't feel the trigger.

He wriggled a little on his stomach, trying to get comfortable on the hard concrete. Fought the urge to check his watch. No more than an hour could have passed since he arrived. He'd spent three times that long crouched in duck blinds on cold mornings waiting for feathered prey. He could wait a little longer for a prize infinitely more valuable.

He expected his guest to show at any moment. That Trevor Skinner wouldn't show up hadn't even entered his mind. The bait was entirely too enticing.

So enticing that even a man like Skinner would risk coming at night, to a place like this. He'd staked out this place weeks and weeks ago. Location, location, location, he thought. This one had it all. Deserted, dark alley. Commercial property. A two-story abandoned building with easy roof access. And a neighborhood bad enough to discourage anyone who actually did hear anything from coming out to investigate.

He heard the car before he saw it pull around the corner, headlights dimmed. He watched, silently waiting as Skinner stepped out of his Cadillac. He dipped his head, checked the sight. Ensured it was the man he sought.

It was.

Quickly he dropped the sight to Skinner's knees and pumped the trigger—once, twice—and Skinner went down with a scream. Just as King had. He felt the surge of triumph, dismissed it, his eye still on the sight, still on Skinner so when Skinner's hand moved, he pumped again. Skinner's hand went flying in an arc to the pavement, empty. He'd been going for something in his coat pocket, but he wasn't any longer.

He waited another half minute until he was satisfied Skinner wasn't moving. Quickly he gathered his things, including his shell casings, wincing as they burned his hand. The police were going to catch up to him sooner or later, but he didn't intend to make it any easier for them than he had to. In another minute he was at street level, stowing his gear in the small hidden compartment in the back of his van. Again, the cops would find it if they looked hard enough, but a passing glance revealed nothing but the hollow inside of a delivery van. Now he did check his watch—so that he could time the rest of the act. Lifting from the back of the van the platform on rolling casters that he'd made just for this purpose. Lowering the ramp. Rolling platform to the mark, sliding the writhing body onto the platform, click, click, buckling him down. Seat belts saved lives, he thought, patently ignoring Skinner's moaned insistence to know who he was. Skinner's weak curses of retribution made him smile.

No, if anyone would have retribution this night, it was to be himself. And the young woman whose brutal rape went unpunished a year ago. Renee Dexter.

And, of course, Leah.

He rolled the platform up the ramp into the van on top of the thick plastic he'd laid down. Bloodstains were so difficult to remove from carpet fibers, and the police had ways of detecting trace amounts even after a carpet had been thoroughly cleaned.

As a final step, he patted down Skinner's pockets, retrieving a set of keys, an electronic organizer, and a gun that looked more like a water pistol than a real firearm.

"Why . . . why are you . . . doing this?" Skinner demanded, his face a contorted mask of agony. "Take . . . my wallet . . . please . . . just . . . let me . . . go."

He chuckled, closed the van doors, pocketed the organizer, and tossed Skinner's keys onto the front seat of the Cadillac. Left with the keys in view, the car would be gone by dawn.

He checked his watch a final time. Less than seven

minutes for the whole second act. King had been eight minutes twenty. He was improving.

Thursday, February 19, 10:30 P.M.

From his car Abe stared up at his apartment building, at the dark concrete that seemed to loom into the sky. In reality it was only a twenty-story building. His apartment was on the seventeenth floor. He had a bed, a recliner chair, and a television set. With cable—250 channels. He hadn't turned the television on in more than six months. It was an empty shell, a place he came to sleep.

He sighed, the sound rife with frustration. He didn't have pictures of family in his place, either. They were all in boxes, in storage. He'd put them there himself the day before he'd transferred the keys to the house to its new owners. The house he'd bought with Debra, with the swingset in the yard and the nursery Debra had just started to decorate in baby blue.

Kristen Mayhew had her little shed in the backyard.

He had the Chicagoland U-Store-It in Melrose Park. *I am a first-class hypocrite.*

He glanced at the clock on his dash, then at the empty bowls on his passenger seat. His mom stayed up late sometimes, usually when Aidan or his dad were pulling night patrols. *Or me,* he thought, remembering all the times he'd dropped by for breakfast after his shift to find her dozing in her favorite chair, the movie she'd started watching long since over.

Without another glance up, he backed out of his space. Twenty minutes later he pulled into his parents' driveway. Sure enough, the light was still on and his key still worked in the front door. It had been a long time since he'd let himself in after midnight, before he and Debra were married. Sure enough, his mom was dozing in her favorite chair. Some things truly didn't change. He put the empty bowls in the kitchen sink, then covered his mother up with an afghan. She stirred, then jerked awake, her eyes widening at the sight of him.

"What's wrong?"

He crouched down. "Nothing. I needed to bring back the bowls."

Her eyes narrowed. "It could have waited till Sunday. What's wrong?"

He took her hand, linked his fingers through hers. "Nothing. I just missed you."

She smiled, squeezed his hand. "I missed you, too. How was your meeting?"

"Busy. Your cabbage casserole was a big hit."

"Good. Nobody teased you about your mommy bringing dinner?"

He grinned. "Hell, no. They want you to join the team."

She grinned back, then her expression went sly. "So . . . what about Miss Mayhew?"

Abe went for obtuse even though he knew exactly what she meant. "She got there too late to try the casserole. Mia had eaten everything but the vegetables."

His mother shook her head. "Not what I meant. She's pretty. Smart, too."

He should have known her sharp eyes had missed none of his and Kristen's exchange. "Yes, she is, Mom."

"You didn't like it when she ignored you."

She knew him so well. "No, I didn't."

Her face settled to serene. "Do you want me to fix you a snack?"

He pulled her to her feet. "No, I want you to go to bed."

She grimaced. "Your father snores."

"I do not." Kyle Reagan appeared, scratching his broadening belly.

"He does, too!" The scornful shout came from behind Rachel's closed bedroom door.

"What're you doing awake this time of night, young lady?" his father demanded.

Rachel stuck her head out the door and Abe blinked at the sight of his baby sister in nothing but an oversized T-shirt. She *had* grown up. *My God. She's only thirteen and she looks seventeen.* He wondered if his father had cleaned his gun recently. She'd done something different with her dark hair and there were traces of smudged mascara around her blue eyes, which were rolling in a display of great patience. "Like I could sleep with all this noise," she said. "Not." She eyed Abe carefully. "Hiya, Abe. Good to have you back."

She wanted something. That much hadn't changed in the last year. "Hi, Rach."

"So can you get me an interview or not?"

Abe blinked again. "With who?"

"Whom," Rachel corrected archly, and it was Abe's turn to roll his eyes.

"Whatever. With whom?"

"With Kristen Mayhew. Mom says the two of you are tight."

Abe winced at the idea. "You want to interview Kristen Mayhew, like with a camera?"

"No, not *like* with a camera. *Like* with a pencil. We have to do a project on the career we want and interview somebody who's doing it. I want to be a lawyer. Miss Mayhew is a lawyer."

"Damn lawyers," Kyle grumbled. "Cops arrest 'em, lawyers in suits let 'em go."

Rachel shook her head. "Not this lawyer, Daddy. She has

the highest conviction rate in her office." She lifted eyebrows that Abe sworn hadn't been that severely tweezed last time he'd been home. "So? Can you get me an interview or not?"

I can't even get her to call me by my first name, Abe thought. "I don't know," he answered honestly. "I can ask."

"She spoke last year at the University of Chicago Law Commencement," Rachel said and Kyle disappeared into the kitchen, still grumbling about lawyers.

Abe had trouble picturing that. "She did?"

Rachel nodded vigorously, her dangling earrings dancing wildly. "I did an Internet search and found her speech in one of the university's newsletters. She said that mentoring young people was one of the greatest things the graduating class could do to keep the pipeline full of diverse talent."

"She did?"

Rachel rolled her eyes again and Abe caught his mother smothering a grin. "What, is there an echo in here?" Rachel asked, sounding just like their father. "Yes, she did. So I'll bet she'd just love to help a young person like me." Her face softened into a winsome smile that he'd never been able to deny. "Please, Abe, pretty please?"

Abe exhaled helplessly. "I'll ask her, Rach. But don't be disappointed if she says no. She's a busy lady."

Rachel tilted her head forward conspiratorially. "I bet you could invite her over for Sunday dinner. Mom's making a great big ham. Everybody's got to eat."

"No. No. No." Abe scowled, but not at the thought of looking at Kristen's face across his mother's table. That would be no hardship at all. His scowl was for the withering look of disdain she'd give him when she rejected his invitation. "Did I say no?"

Rachel's face fell. "Well, ask her about the interview. I'd get an A for sure."

"I'll ask."

"I think it's way past time you were in bed, sweetie," Becca said and Rachel frowned, but obeyed, first lifting on her tiptoes to kiss Abe's cheek.

"I'm glad you came," she whispered. "Even if you can't get me an interview."

He kissed her forehead. She was a good kid, all in all. "Me too, squirt. Now go to bed. You're going to fall asleep in school tomorrow."

His mother slipped her arm around his waist as Rachel's door closed. "She was so excited to hear you knew Miss Mayhew. I told her to wait to ask you, but you know how she is. The bed in your old room is made up, Abe. If you want to sleep here, I'll make you waffles for breakfast. From scratch, not those disgusting frozen things."

"You never make me waffles from scratch," Kyle complained from the kitchen.

"You don't need waffles from scratch," his mother shot back. "You're on a diet."

Abe had to grin at his father's muffled muttering. "No, Mom, I need to be in the office early tomorrow. I just wanted to see you tonight."

With a sigh she walked him to the door. "You're still coming over on Sunday?"

"Unless something really important comes up on this case, I'll be here."

Friday, February 20, 1:00 A.M.

"*Why?*"

It was an agonized cry, and no less than the bastard deserved. He spared a cool glance. "Renee Dexter."

Skinner twisted his head to follow him as he gathered his tools, eyes widening in terror. "Who?"

He stopped. Turned his full attention on Skinner's pathetic form, still strapped down. His bleeding had slowed, his Armani suit was soaked. It would be the most expensive clothing he'd packed into a crate up until now. Skinner hovered on the brink of consciousness, holding on with an effort. "You truly don't remember her, do you?"

"No. *Dammit*. Where . . . am I?" Skinner gasped. "Who are you?"

He turned away, ignoring Skinner's line of questioning. "Renee Dexter was a college student, driving home from her part-time job at the campus library." He opened a drawer, studied its contents. "She had car trouble, and no cell phone to call for help." He made his choice and held it up for Skinner to see before placing it on the table next to him, gratified when Skinner's eyes went glassy with fear. "Do you remember her yet?"

"Oh, God," Skinner moaned, twisting, trying to escape. "You're insane. Insane."

He considered it. "Perhaps. God will be the judge of that, I suppose." He rolled a cart holding a vise across the room, positioning it at Skinner's head. Adjusted the grips of the vise on either side of Skinner's skull and twisted the knobs. Skinner moaned.

"Renee Dexter was terrified." His voice hardened. "Nineteen years old and terrified. A car stopped and two clean-cut young men got out and she drew an easier breath. She'd been afraid of thugs, of criminals, but fate had been kind and sent two nice young men her way." He twisted the knobs once more and Skinner began to sob. "Unfortunately, they were not nice young men, Mr. Skinner. When the police found Renee Dexter the next morning, she was weaving through traffic on foot, her clothes torn. They thought she was drunk, but she wasn't. Is your memory improving now, Mr. Skinner?"

"Why?" Skinner sobbed. "Why are you doing this to me?"

His lips twisted grimly. "Ironic. Renee said the very same thing to the two young men as they held her down all night, raping her by turns. She said they laughed and said 'Because we can.' The police were able to catch the two men using descriptions Renee gave them from her hospital bed and the State's Attorney's Office filed charges." He lifted his tool of choice, twisting it in the overhead light, watching it shine. "That's where you came in, Mr. Skinner." He chuckled dryly as Skinner's eyes flickered in recognition. "I see you remember now."

"You . . . weren't there."

"Are you sure, Mr. Skinner? Are you very sure about that? You sat at the same table with those two animals." His voice shook with anger. "And when Renee came to the stand, you decimated her, assaulting her a second time. Not with your fists or your . . ." He waved a hand toward Skinner's lower regions. "But you assaulted her the same. She was a party girl. The boys had met her the weekend before. Not true. She'd agreed to meet them. Not true. A drug test showed she'd smoked some marijuana sometime in the previous two weeks, confirming what kind of girl she was. So you said she'd asked for it, allowed them to do it. Then accused them falsely." He leaned close, his body vibrating with fury. "*Do you remember now, Mr. Skinner?*"

"I—"

"Answer the question, Mr. Skinner. Yes or no?"

Skinner moaned. "Oh, God."

He straightened. "Not so comfortable now, Mr. Skinner? I've contemplated this, long and hard. Those animals went free because you painted Renee Dexter as a girl with loose morals. When she tried to defend herself you tripped her up again and again until she finally had no voice at all." He was calm again, and ready to do what needed to be done. "Now you'll learn what it is like to have no voice, Mr. Skinner."

Friday, February 20, 3:45 A.M.

Zoe ripped the sheet away from his sleeping form. "Up you go." She shook his shoulder impatiently. "Rise and shine, big boy. Time to go home."

He rolled over onto his back and blinked up at her. "What time is it?"

"Almost four. Your wife's alarm will be going off in less than two and a half hours."

His eyes flew open at that. "Shit." He rolled out of bed and grabbed his boxer shorts. "Why the hell did you let me go to sleep?"

Zoe looked away, under the pretense of gathering the items that had fallen from his pockets until she managed to control the gleam in her eye. She turned back, her hands filled with his belongings. "Because I fell asleep, too." She smiled, alluringly. "You tired me out."

He looked up from tucking in his shirttail into his pants, a smug grin on his face. He'd earned it, so she let him be self-satisfied for now. "You were fucking amazing."

She brushed her lips against his. "Hmm. I know. But it's time to go home."

"I'm going. You want to meet me tonight?"

Not if I can help it, she thought, but smiled nevertheless. "I'd love to." If she had her way, by sunset she'd be ass-deep into what was becoming a more interesting case with every new tidbit she learned.

Grabbing her chin between his fingers, he placed a hard kiss on her lips. "I'll call you."

She walked him to the door. "You do that." Then she closed the door behind him and, sliding the deadbolt into place, let the Cheshire cat grin take over her face.

She wondered if he knew he talked in his sleep. She suspected his wife did.

She grabbed the phone. "Scott . . . Of course I know what time it is. Meet me at the station in an hour. We're going to have a very busy day."

Chapter Nine

Friday, February 20, 8:30 A.M.

"You don't look so good, sugar."

Kristen looked up from the pile of papers on her desk, bleary-eyed. John's secretary stood in the doorway of her office, her lower lip pushed out in a worried pout, a stack of folders in her arms.

"Thank you so much, Lois." She eyed the folders balefully. "Don't say those are for me."

" 'Fraid so." The pile landed on her desk with a thump, leaving Lois's hands free to plunk down on her generous hips. "Did you sleep last night?"

No, not a wink. "A little." She unscrewed the cap from the thermos Owen had filled that morning and refilled her cup. "But I have enough coffee to keep me going."

"Any new letters?"

She shook her head, thinking of the footprints Reagan

had found in the snow next to her windows. "No, but it will happen. It's only a matter of time."

Fellow prosecutor Greg Wilson poked his head in the door. "Did you ask her, Lois?"

Lois turned around with a frown. "I was getting to it."

Greg ambled into the room. He'd just celebrated his fortieth birthday, but retained boyish good looks that made all the women in the office by turns sigh in admiration and grumble in envy. "We're all worried about you, Kristen."

Kristen felt a prick of annoyance. "I can take care of myself, Greg."

He waved his hand as if she hadn't spoken. "Come stay with us. We have an extra room since my mother-in-law ran off with that man from her bingo parlor."

Kristen's mouth dropped open. "What?"

"Yeah, my mother-in-law met this guy and—"

Kristen shook her head, as much to clear her brain as to shut him up. "No, you want me to come stay with you?"

"We all know you live by yourself," Lois rushed to explain. "We drew straws to see who would ask you."

Kristen raised a brow. "And you lost, Greg?"

"No, I won. We want you to come stay with us. Until all this blows over."

Touched, she found a smile. "I don't think your wife will approve."

"It was my wife's idea."

Kristen's eyes widened. "You told her about the letters?"

Greg frowned. "Of course not. I told her your house was being renovated and you needed a place to stay." He grew a little sheepish. "Then she saw Richardson's spot last night and confronted me about it over breakfast this morning. But I still didn't say anything. What do you say?"

Kristen looked up at the two of them, their faces so earnest and concerned and her heart clenched, just a little. It had been a long time since someone went out of their way to take care of her. *No, it hasn't. Reagan did last night.* "I say it's a wonderful gesture."

Greg scowled. "But?"

"But I won't be driven from my own home. Besides, Lieutenant Spinnelli is having a surveillance camera installed today."

Greg looked resigned. "I think you're making a mistake."

She smiled at the two of them. "Thanks. I mean it."

Lois leaned over the desk to give her a quick hug and Kristen stiffened. It had been a long time since she'd been cared for, still longer since she'd been embraced in any way. Lois immediately pulled back, her cheeks reddening slightly, but she made no apology for her unexpected gesture. "You'll tell us if we can help you, Kristen."

"I will. I promise." With an effort Kristen lightened her voice to soften the dismissal. "Now, I've got less than an hour to review all these new files before I have to be in court."

Lois exited, shaking her head. Greg stopped at the door for a last comment, his normally pleasant face grim. "Kris, we're seriously worried. Don't underestimate this guy."

She met his eyes. "I won't."

Then she sank back down into her chair, staring at the new files she'd add to her caseload. After a minute she shook herself and lifted the first folder from the stack. And sighed. Another rape case.

Some days were better than others. This wouldn't be one of those days.

Friday, February 20, 11:00 A.M.

"Thanks for waiting for me."

Abe looked over at Kristen in the passenger seat. Those

had been the first words she'd uttered since climbing up into his SUV, her coat unbuttoned, her cheeks flushed from a combination of cold and exertion. She'd run down the courthouse stairs so fast he'd been shocked she hadn't tripped on her high heels. For the first twenty minutes of the drive she glanced nervously behind them until he assured her that although Zoe Richardson had been following, they'd lost her a few miles back.

Now she sat unmoving, her eyes fixed on the passing scenery of the quiet little neighborhood in the suburbs that was home to the first of Ross King's young victims.

"It's all right," he said. "I used the time to make some calls."

Another thirty seconds passed, then she murmured, "Anything new?"

"Jack found traces of dried milk on the inside of one of the crates. Two percent."

She didn't move a muscle, her eyes still glued to the window. "Wouldn't you expect to find milk in milk crates?"

"Not unless they'd recently been used for a milk delivery."

"So he has access to a person or business that gets milk in crates?"

"Versus using them to hold up his stereo equipment. Yeah."

"He could have picked them up from anywhere."

Abe shrugged, a little unnerved by her lack of animation. Something had happened that morning, and he had no illusions she'd trust him enough to be forthright with the information. "Maybe. It's one more piece of the puzzle though. Jack also found ground marble on all the crates, but that was no surprise since the killer lined the crates with marble tiles."

He pulled the SUV to the curb in front of their first stop.

"Are you going to tell me what happened?" he asked sharply and she stiffened. "Another letter?"

Her head whipped around, her green eyes wild and turbulent. "No. I would have told you that. I'm not stupid, Detective."

He wanted to touch her, to soothe her, but of course he did not. "Then what?"

Her eyes quieted. "I got a new sexual assault case today. The victim and her father were waiting for me outside my office when I got back from motion hour."

So that explained her terse tone when she'd called his cell phone to ask for another half hour. He said nothing, just waited for her to continue. After a few seconds and a weary slump of her shoulders, she did.

"She broke down in my office, terrified to testify. Her father all but threatened her if she didn't. Said he wouldn't rest until the scum was behind bars."

"She won't make a very compelling witness if the jury thinks she's being coerced."

She looked back at the house beyond the curb. "No, no she won't, even though I think she's telling the truth. Plus, the physical evidence isn't very strong. I have to decide if we have enough to charge the man she's accused."

"And if you do, you'll have to put her on the stand." He followed her gaze to the little house. "Like the boys in the King case."

She sighed, deep and long. "And the Ramey case and all the other cases. Every time a victim of sexual assault goes on the stand, they live it all over again."

"Maybe that's how they heal. Learn to forget. Go on with their lives."

She turned again, met his stare, her eyes now filled with sorrow and a vulnerable regret that made his heart clench. "They never forget," she said quietly. "They might heal and they might go on with their lives, but they never, ever forget." She opened the door and hopped down. "Let's get this over with," she said without looking back at him.

Stunned, he simply sat watching her back as she faced the house, then made himself move to where she stood on the sidewalk. "Kristen—"

She shook her head, a hard, resolute movement that made him leave it alone. He wasn't sure what he'd been going to say anyway.

She gestured at the driveway. "The Restons have company," she said.

It was true. Cars lined the driveway and the other side of the street.

"Mr. Reston was their spokesman. They stood together then," she explained and started up the front walk. "All the parents. I guess that hasn't changed."

She didn't even have to knock on the door. It opened as they stepped onto the front porch. Standing inside was a man in his sock feet wearing a Bears sweatshirt and a battered pair of jeans. On his face he wore weary resignation.

"Miss Mayhew," he said softly. "We've been expecting you." He opened the door wider and they entered. Abe looked around the room where nine more adults sat. All studied him with curiosity, then lowered their gazes to look at Kristen with hostile accusation.

Which made Abe madder than hell. He drew a deep breath and reminded himself why they were there. Their children had been horribly victimized, not only by King, but also by the judicial system that failed to give them justice. Standing behind Kristen, he touched her shoulder lightly. She flinched at the contact, then cleared her throat.

"This is Detective Reagan. He's been assigned to this case."

Which case didn't need to be said. Not one of the parents said a word.

Her shoulders rigid, Kristen continued. "Ross King was murdered. We'd planned to spend the morning informing the families of his victims, but you've made our job easier by being here all together."

"So happy to make your job easier, Miss Mayhew." The sarcastic sneer came from one of the men on the sofa and Abe again had to remind himself of why they were there.

Kristen ignored the jab. "You all have obviously been informed."

Reston gestured to the coffee table where five envelopes sat in a neat row. "We all received these yesterday morning. And we saw that reporter on the news last night."

Kristen searched the room. "Where are the Fullers?"

"They got divorced last year," Reston answered. "She moved back to L.A. with their boy. His company moved him to Boston. Their marriage just couldn't take the strain."

A woman rose from the love seat and came to stand beside Reston, sliding her arm around his waist in the way of a supportive wife. "We knew you'd been to see those women yesterday. We figured it was only a matter of time before you came to us." She looked up, met Abe's eyes with challenge in hers. "We used to be a normal, happy family, Detective Reagan. Until Ross King. Not one of us is sorry to see him dead."

Abe searched the faces of each parent, choosing his words carefully. "I won't insult your intelligence by acting as if I assumed otherwise. I won't debase my own integrity by acting as if Ross King deserves my compassion. But it's my job to investigate murder, regardless of how I feel about the victim. I don't expect you to accept that, but that doesn't make it any less of a reality."

There was absolute silence in the room. Then one of the

women started to cry. Her husband stood, helpless rage on his face. "Tell us this, Miss Mayhew. Did he suffer?"

The woman looked up, tears streaming down her cheeks. "You owe us that much."

Kristen looked up at Abe over her shoulder and for a moment the sobbing mother's anguish was reflected in her eyes. Then it was gone. She looked back to the waiting parents. "I can't give you details on an ongoing investigation."

"Goddamn you to hell!" Still another father jumped to his feet. "We did what you said. We put our boys through *hell* because *you* said you could put him away." Dropping back into his seat, his chin dropped to his chest and his shoulders started to shake. "Goddamn you," he whispered.

Abe could feel her hesitate, then her breath left her in a silent sigh. "I can't give you details," she repeated. "But . . ."

The father looked up and Abe felt his own eyes sting at the man's sheer misery. "But?" the man whispered.

"He suffered," Kristen said simply.

"A lot," Abe added flatly, wondering what the parents would do next. They looked at each other, grim relief the predominant theme. "I realize that when we find King's murderer you all are likely to send him a thank-you card, but—"

"Try a twenty-year-old bottle of scotch."

"A week in my Florida time-share."

"Season tickets to the Bears."

Abe held up a hand to quiet them. "I get the picture. Still, I hope you'll give me your cooperation. Did anyone see anything that would help establish the time the notes were delivered?" No one said a word and Abe sighed. "You are obviously smart people. You know from the news that King is not the only one that's been killed. You also know that we can't condone vigilante justice. If you did condone it, you would have offed King yourselves."

"How do you know we didn't?" Reston asked carefully.

"I don't," Abe said. "But like I said, you're smart people. You know you're all on my suspect list. You also know your being there won't make this any easier for your kids. They've already been through hell. Now, I'm thinking the only reason you didn't off King yourselves three years ago was because you didn't want your kids to grow up visiting you in Joliet." He saw them flinch at that and knew he'd made his point. "I need to know when you got the notes, then I'll need to know where you were the night King disappeared."

"What night did he disappear?" Mrs. Reston asked.

"First things first." Abe took out his notepad. "Since I only know the Restons here, I need to know your name, where you found the note, and when did you receive it?"

Mr. Reston shrugged. "I fell asleep on the sofa the night before last. I woke up at three A.M. and opened the front door to lock the storm door and saw the note stuck in the frame."

"Good." He wrote it down. "Next?" All the other parents said they'd seen the notes when they woke up. One at six, then others at seven A.M.

He'd gotten responses from all but the man who'd shouted at Kristen. That man was still sitting with his head hung low. Abe waited, but the man didn't say anything.

Kristen had said nothing since during the questioning. Now she bent over and touched the man's shoulder. "What time did you get home, Mr. Littleton?"

He looked up, narrowed his red eyes. "What are you talking about?"

His wife sighed wearily. "You know what she's talking

about, Les. He got home about one-thirty." She glanced up at Abe. "Les and Nadine Littleton."

"Was the note there then, Mr. Littleton?" Kristen asked.

"Yes." Littleton turned away. There was more, Abe knew it.

"Did you see anyone deliver it?" Kristen pressed, but gently.

Littleton hesitated, then nodded. "He slid the envelope through the mail slot."

Abe waited, but the man said nothing more. "And? What did he look like?"

Littleton shrugged tightly. "Dressed in black. Average height. Nothing else."

"A car?" Kristen touched his shoulder again. "Please, Mr. Littleton."

"White van. That's all I know."

Kristen straightened. "Can I speak to you alone for a moment, Mrs. Littleton? You can start on whereabouts," she murmured to Abe. "We'll be right back."

As she led Mrs. Littleton into the kitchen, he turned back to the group. To a couple they all swore they were at home with each other on the night in question. Kristen returned with Mrs. Littleton and pulled on her gloves.

"I have the Littletons' whereabouts, Detective Reagan."

He shot her a puzzled glance, then closed his notepad and bagged the five envelopes on the table. "I'd like to ask you all not to speak to the press."

"And if we do?" Reston asked.

Abe sighed. "It's your right, of course. But Zoe Richardson isn't interested in anything more than a sound bite. You kept your kids' names out of this the first time. I hope your priorities are still in the right place." He left them with that and he and Kristen walked back to the SUV in silence. When they were both buckled in, he started the engine. "I'm waiting."

She sighed. "Mr. Littleton has developed a drinking problem since the trial. He was arrested a few months ago for a bar fight. Mrs. Littleton came to me and asked me to help."

"That must have been hard for her to do."

One russet brow lifted wryly. "You have no idea. Anyway, I worked with the ASA on the case to plead Littleton down to a lesser misdemeanor with probation and participation in a sobriety program. I just guessed he was out drinking last night. Mrs. Littleton gave me the name of the bar and the cab service that brought him home. Maybe the cab driver saw something. Mr. Littleton was also out the night of King's disappearance. He was at the bar until the cab brought him home." She looked away, back up at the Restons' house. "I didn't see the need to make him air his problems in front of the others."

Abe put the SUV in gear. "Well, I've learned a few things here."

Her face was still turned to the window. "Such as?"

"Our boy drives a white van, goes for the trite statement in black evening wear, delivered the notes sometime between one-thirty and three A.M., and . . ." He waited until she met his eyes. Warily.

"And?"

"And you are a very kind person, Kristen Mayhew."

Her eyes widened in undisguised surprise and her cheeks reddened, but she didn't look away and the moment stretched on, Abe suddenly aware of the quickening of her breath. It matched the beating of his own heart. She swallowed hard, her whisper coming out husky. Incredibly sexy. "Thank you, Abe."

His eyes dropped to her slightly parted lips, then lower to where her pulse fluttered at the hollow of her throat. And because the air was undeniably charged and because she pulled her full lower lip between her teeth and especially because getting back to work was absolutely the last thing on his mind, Abe resolutely turned in his seat and pulled the SUV away from the curb. "You're welcome."

Friday, February 20, 1:00 P.M.

Zoe was seething, even the information she'd managed to pull from a technician inside the ME's office a bitter victory. Here they sat, in front of the courthouse waiting for the queen to emerge from hiding. Dammit. "I can't believe you lost them."

Scott pinched the bridge of his nose. "I said I was sorry every one of the ten times you said that. You think you can keep up with a cop who doesn't want to be followed, fine. You drive next time and I'll shove a mike down some poor bastard's throat."

Zoe rolled her eyes. At least she had the name of the cop from the license plates on his SUV. Detective Abe Reagan. A call into Records revealed he was career CPD with a cop family and a dead wife. He'd look good on tape. Great profile, and those linebacker's shoulders. Mmm. Made her envious of Mayhew sitting in his passenger seat. "Well, she's got to come back sometime."

Scott squirmed, impatient from the waiting. "You got the names of the bodies they pulled up yesterday. Why don't you get film of that?"

It was true. One small indiscretion after an office holiday party had given her an eternal fountain of information inside the ME's office. It was amazing what men would do to keep their wives from learning about their flings. She figured she'd earned it. She still shuddered at the thought of being touched by hands that routinely cut up dead people.

So now she knew there were three crimes vindicated by Kristen's vigilante and five dead bodies in the morgue and their names. She could have gotten film of the families of the children killed by the Blade Trio, but she didn't want to miss getting film of Mayhew's face when she popped the question of the day.

"Well?" Scott demanded. "We going to the house with the dead little kids or not?"

"Not," Zoe snapped. Then she straightened in her seat as Detective Reagan's SUV pulled up in front of the courthouse. "Showtime, Scott. Let's go."

She waited until Kristen was out of the SUV and halfway up the courthouse steps before jumping from the car, Scott at her heels, tape rolling. She stepped into Kristen's path and took great pleasure in the way the woman's eyes flashed in anger.

"No comment, Richardson," she ground out. She moved up a step, but Zoe headed her off smoothly while making it look as graceful as a dance step. It was a gift.

"I haven't asked the question yet, Counselor."

"But you will."

"I will. How about now?" she pulled the mike close to her own mouth. "Can you confirm you now have five murders, ASA Mayhew?"

Mayhew's eyes widened in momentary shock, then narrowed. "No comment." She started walking, Zoe keeping up step for step, Scott catching the whole dance on film.

"Is it true that the killer has sent you personal letters, offering the murders as a gift?"

Mayhew stopped abruptly, her mouth drawn in a tight line. "No comment." But the abrupt halt had said it all. She darted up the steps and Zoe let her go with one last jab, shouting her final question at Mayhew's retreating back.

"He signed the notes to Ramey's victims 'Your Humble

Servant.' Is that how your letters were signed, ASA Mayhew?"

Kristen stopped and turned, now completely composed. "Perhaps you didn't comprehend me the first three times. No comment, Miss Richardson."

"Keep rolling," Zoe commanded, and Scott kept rolling until Kristen had disappeared inside the courthouse.

Scott lowered the camera. "How did you know she personally got letters?"

Zoe smiled serenely. "I'm good, Scottie. And don't you forget it."

Friday, February 20, 1:30 P.M.

The words on the pages in front of her blurred. She hadn't read a single word.

It just wasn't fair.

Kristen bit her lip. How many times had she heard that phrase in the five years since she'd joined the State's Attorney's Office? Too many times from too many victims, which most of the time didn't make it any less true. How many times had she said it herself? Not recently, she had to admit. At least not when it came to her own life.

Which right now well and truly sucked.

But her life had been worse. A couple of times. Seriously worse. Even so, she wasn't one to complain. She kept her personal life personal. *So why today? Damn.* She clenched her teeth, dabbing at her lip with the tissue. Whatever possessed her to say that to Reagan? *They never, ever forget. Am I freaking insane?* She closed her eyes, looked away from her desk as if that would erase the image of Reagan's shocked eyes from her mind. Of the sound of his voice when he called her name. *Like he knew.* Or the look later, after the Restons' house. He'd looked at her with those blue eyes, bright as the center of a gas flame.

He'd called her a nice person.

God. *If he only knew. Really, truly knew.*

He'd wanted more. The way his gaze had heated, the way the air had grown so charged it chased goosebumps up and down her arms, shivers up and down her back.

She'd been called a number of things, but naive generally wasn't one of them. Frigid, yes. Ice Queen, yes. Naive, not lately. Reagan had considered kissing her. Right there in front of the Restons' house.

She huffed an empty, mirthless chuckle. *If he only knew. He'd run so fast—*

He'd thought about kissing her. And for one insane moment, she'd wondered how it would feel having him touch her, wondered if his lips were hard or soft, wondered how it would feel to put her arms around his strong neck and hold on. Tight.

For that one insane moment, she'd considered kissing him back. Perhaps that was what had her so shaken.

"Kristen, you have a visitor."

She jerked around to find Lois standing in her doorway, looking concerned. Kristen drew a careful breath and glanced down at her Day Timer. Her calendar was free for another fifteen minutes.

"Can you have them come back later this afternoon?" After the press conference. After Richardson blew the roof off their case in front of every microphone in Chicago. *I should've told Reagan*, she thought. *I should've prepared him.* It was the least she could do for the man who thought she was a nice person. Hah. "I'm kind of busy now."

"No, it can't wait." Owen stepped around Lois holding a large paper bag. "You didn't come by for lunch."

Kristen sat back in her chair in weary relief. She gestured to the stack of folders on her desk. "Too much paperwork."

Owen frowned his displeasure. "Paperwork is no reason to skip lunch, Kristen. I brought you some beef stew." He put the bag on her desk and lifted his bushy brows. "With some cherry pie for dessert."

She looked up at him with a smile. "You didn't have to go to so much trouble."

He looked stern. "What trouble? I dished some stew in a plastic bowl and walked a few blocks. Besides, I had a few other orders here in the building." From the bag he pulled a plastic bowl, placing it in front of her. "I saw that Richardson woman on the news last night."

She sighed. "Yeah, I caught the end of it."

Owen frowned. "Is it true, what she said? That there's a vigilante killer out there?"

Kristen pulled the lid from the bowl. It smelled wonderful. "Now, Owen, you know I couldn't tell you anything whether I knew anything or not." She looked up, tried for a grin that fell miserably flat. "Can I still eat the stew?"

He didn't smile back. "I've been watching the news all morning, Kristen. There's been a lot of talk about vigilantes because of that Richardson woman's account last night."

Terrific. "So what's the word on the street?"

His lips thinned. "That finally somebody's taking a stand against crime in this town."

Kristen winced. "So much for all this." She gestured at the pile of reports. "I'll have to remember that when ten o'clock rolls around tonight and I'm still here."

"Things could get ugly, Kristen." Owen zipped up his coat. "Me and Vincent are worried. We just want you to be careful."

Just wait until Zoe airs her next report, Kristen thought.

Ugly will take on a whole new meaning. "I always am
Owen. Thanks for lunch."

Friday, February 20, 1:50 P.M.

Abe set a bag on his desk. "You hungry?"

Mia looked up, sniffing deeply. "Depends. What is it?"

"Gyros and burgers." He peered into the bag. "And
baklava."

Mia licked her lips. "I take back every bad thing I said
about you."

Abe chuckled. "I doubt that."

She chose a burger. "Did you get anything from the cab
bie?"

"He said he saw a white van with a big flower on the side
right after he dropped off Littleton early yesterday morn
ing."

Mia's brows jumped. "A florist delivery van? Any
name?"

"Said it had 'flowers' in the name," Abe said dryly
unwrapping his gyro. He took a deep appreciative breath
He hadn't realized how hungry he was.

"Well, *that* oughta narrow it down."

"To 460 places in Greater Chicago. I already checked."

"Did Jack find anything floral on the stuff from Kristen'
car?"

"Nope, and it bothered him. Jack thought that if the kille
used a flower delivery van to transport the bodies or the
crates, we would have found something on the clothes a
least. Pollen or something." He pointed to the faxed lists o
Chicago area customers who'd purchased sandblasting
equipment. "How's it coming?"

Irritably, she pushed the papers away. "It would help if I

knew what the hell I was looking for. There are hundreds of names here. I've got Todd Murphy helping run names for priors, but somehow I don't think our guy's been in trouble before."

Abe was inclined to agree with her. "Well, let's see if any of these people work in one of the florists in Chicago with 'flower' in the name. Give me a couple pages."

She handed him a handful of paper, wincing when a loud shout came from Spinnelli's office. "He's not happy."

Abe glanced over, saw Spinnelli pacing, holding a telephone to his ear and gesturing wildly. "What, stage fright over his press conference?" It was scheduled for three o'clock.

"Hell, no. He's trying to explain to the captain how Richardson got the scoop." She tilted her head, frowning when he just looked at her. "Oh, boy. I thought you knew."

He felt a spear of sharp heat in his neck, a sure sign of stress. "Knew what?"

"Richardson knows that Kristen got letters, too, and that we've got five bodies in the morgue and their names. Apparently Richardson ambushed her going into the courthouse. Kristen called Spinnelli right after that. I thought she'd told you, too."

His appetite disappeared. "No, she didn't." In fact, she hadn't been able to get out of the SUV fast enough. The hours after they'd driven away from the Restons' house had been awkward, to say the least. She'd pulled back into herself, saying nothing until they reached the house of the first child killed by the gang's gunfire. Then it was all business. And not once did she call him Abe. They talked to the families of the slain children, endured more anger and accusation, retrieved two more letters from their humble servant, then he'd driven her back to the courthouse in silence, thick and heavy.

She hadn't called him about Richardson, hadn't trusted him. It hurt. But it *had* been interest he'd seen in her eyes, sitting there in front of the Restons' house. Interest and heat. He'd been a heartbeat away from kissing her, right there in front of the Restons' house, which would have been completely unacceptable. Unprofessional. Probably wonderful.

But she'd pulled away. She was afraid, he knew. *So am I*, he thought. But Kristen's fear ran deeper and he was afraid to contemplate its source, because he thought he knew. And if he was right, they had one hell of a long row to hoe.

I have to be insane to even consider hoeing any rows with Kristen Mayhew, he thought. *So why am I?* Because she had pluck and courage. Green eyes and subtle curves. A quick mind and quiet grace. And a laugh that made him catch his breath.

Maybe it was just because she was a nice person. Maybe it didn't have to be any more complicated than that Kristen Mayhew was a beautiful woman and a nice person.

Bullshit. It was way more complicated than that.

Mia finished her burger in thoughtful silence. She wiped her mouth with a napkin, then folded it into a tiny square. "I've known Kristen for a long time, probably about as well as anyone knows her," she finally said. He looked up and saw understanding in Mia's blue eyes and felt his cheeks heat. "But nobody really knows her that well," she went on. "She's always been a bit of a loner." She frowned. "They call her the Ice Queen in the locker room, which is so totally unfair."

Abe remembered the anguish in her eyes when the mother broke down in the Restons' living room, how Kristen had never uttered a word in her own defense when the parents' words had been cruelly accusing. The way she'd said the victims "never, ever forget" just before they'd gone in. No one who had seen what he'd seen could ever conceivably call her icy and cold.

"Yes, that is very unfair." His voice was calm. Much calmer than he felt. Kristen Mayhew brought out something in him that he hadn't felt in years, the fierce desire to protect, to take care of anyone that hurt her.

The killer felt the same way. The realization was sudden and clear. *That's why he'd targeted her for his gifts, why he watched her in her own home.*

"The killer knows her," he said.

Mia looked puzzled. "We know that."

"No, he *knows* her. He's seen her interact with the people, the victims." The compassion, the anguish. "And he doesn't hate her."

"What do you mean?"

Abe leaned forward, intense. "I watched her with all these victims and their families for the last two days. They're aloof at a minimum, hostile at the most extreme."

"Like Stan Dorsey."

"Yeah. But no one was warm, certainly not admiring." Not even Les Littleton, who she'd gone out of her way to help and who still damned her in his pathetic misery.

Mia's eyes lit up. "So either she didn't represent them, or she didn't lose."

"He lost," Abe said, "regardless if Kristen represented him or not. Remember what Westphalen said. And my gut says he's connected to Kristen in a real way, more than just seeing her on television. He's met her in person, I'm certain of it. I wonder if we could find any victim who'd lost in court that didn't blame her."

Mia tilted her head, considering. "She gave us the list of all the cases she lost. I wonder if she noted customer satisfaction in that database of hers."

Abe picked up the phone. "One way to find out."

Friday, February 20, 2:00 P.M.

The man who'd originally built his house played the trumpet. The man's wife apparently held little appreciation for her husband's musical gifts and insisted he either give up the trumpet or soundproof the basement.

He carefully pushed the basement door closed behind him.

Luckily for him, the man had really loved his trumpet. Without the soundproofing he most certainly would have been reported by a neighbor by now.

But now, there was no sound. Skinner was dead. Rigor mortis had come and gone, leaving the body limp. He approached the body, wishing a man could be killed twice. In Skinner's case, perhaps a hundred times. The bastard had made a career of defending scum who preyed on the innocent. Skinner's eight-bedroom house on the North Shore, his luxury cars, the fancy private schools for his children—all were bought with blood money, all paid for by the suffering of the innocent and the vile pandering of the guilty.

He drew his pistol from the drawer, knowing it was impossible to kill a man twice, knowing he'd have to be satisfied with the symbolic gesture. With little fanfare he centered the barrel of the pistol on Skinner's forehead.

Pulled the trigger. And nodded once. It was done. And done well.

Just a few details to wrap it up, and he'd be ready to visit Leah's fishbowl once again. He pulled on his gloves and prepared to divest Mr. Skinner of his Armani suit. After all, Skinner would find it unbearably hot when he arrived at his final destination.

Chapter Ten

Friday, February 20, 2:15 P.M.

Kristen and Jack watched Julia pull the linen string from Ross King's torso. Her appointment completed, she'd come down to watch Julia autopsy King. Hell, if an autopsy couldn't clear her mind, nothing could. She'd met Jack on the way in, his face grim. He'd found nothing new on the clothes or crates or dirt from the gravesites. He was there to find anything to point him toward another lab test that might turn up something.

And because he has a thing for Julia, Kristen thought. *Too bad everybody knows it but Julia.*

"Whoever did this sure as hell knew what they were doing," Julia said. "Nice, neat stitches, even placement, no tearing." She looked up and met Kristen's gaze, her eyes distorted by the goggles she wore. "He's either a doctor or queen of the quilting bee."

"Or a hunter," Jack added from where he stood on Kristen's right. He shrugged when Kristen and Julia looked at him in surprise. "I used to hunt with my uncle. Lots of deer and ducks. He could dress a duck with nicer stitches than a surgeon."

"It explains the clean incision," Julia remarked, looking back down at the body.

Kristen moved closer, watching Julia's gloved hands. "What do you mean?"

Julia pulled back a flap of King's skin. "There aren't any indications of hesitation."

"No jagged edges," Jack said and Julia nodded.

"Exactly. The incision only goes as deep as it has to."

She pulled both flaps back, exposing the anatomy beneath. "There's no damage to the organs . . . from the knife anyway. Here's where the bullet went in. Whoever did this was damn good with a knife. I wouldn't have thought of a hunter, but you could be right."

"It's a possibility." The deep voice behind her set off warning bells in her head, and she had barely a moment to compose herself before turning to find Reagan standing in the doorway. Filling the doorway, Mia barely visible behind him. Awareness buzzed between them and the morning memory still burning, Kristen looked away.

"Detective Reagan," Julia said. "Did your mother bring lunch?" she asked hopefully.

Reagan moved into the room and it suddenly became that much smaller. "Maybe next time," he returned. "So our boy's a sharpshooter with a quick needle. Did the autopsy turn up anything else?"

"Not yet." Briskly, Julia bent back down to the body.

"What did you find out about the white van?" Kristen asked and Reagan turned, his eyes narrowed in reproach and for a moment he said nothing. She knew he knew about her call to Spinnelli and that she'd offended him by not calling him first. Possibly even hurt him.

But she hadn't been able to call him. The wounds she herself had raked open that morning were still raw, the humiliation still too fresh. He thought he knew, but he didn't. And even if he did, there was no way he'd ever understand.

"It was a flower delivery van," he finally said, just as quietly. "Spinnelli's got a few men canvassing the Arboretum area where King's body was found to see if anyone saw a similar van. Hopefully it hasn't been so long that the trail's gone cold."

One of Julia's techs came in with a clipboard. "Well, this

is something you don't see every day," Julia said. "Two of your Blade vics have evidence of cellular damage. From the look of these slides, I'd say your gang boys at one time were frozen solid."

Mia tsked. "Freezer burn. Shoulda' used Saran Wrap."

Reagan shot Mia an amused look before turning back to Julia. "That makes sense."

Julia raised a brow. "It does?"

Mia nodded. "The three Blades were in the photo together, but they were last seen at different times. We wondered what our humble servant did with the first bodies while he killed all three. He wanted them all in the photo together, since they did the crime together."

Reagan crossed his arms over his chest. "This could mean that he's storing them in a place where he can't risk detection. If he hadn't frozen them, the first two bodies would have started to stink before he bagged all three."

Mia scrunched her mouth. "Or he could just be the fastidious type."

"This could also support his being a hunter," Jack said. "A hunter would have a big freezer for his game, especially if he went for deer."

Reagan nodded slowly. "You've got something there," he said, then looked over at Mia. "After the press conference, let's pay a visit to the local target range. I'll bet they have a club for hunters or know where we can find one."

"Ask for members that go for deer and fowl," Jack advised. "You don't sew up deer after they're dressed, but you might stitch up a bird. I've got to get back now. Bye, Julia."

Julia looked up from King's body with an absent-minded smile. "Bye."

Mia rolled her eyes as Jack left with a backward wave. "Idiot," she muttered, but Kristen wasn't sure if she meant

Jack or Julia and frankly was in no mood to care. All she was looking for right now was escape from Reagan's eyes that seemed to follow her every move. She'd pulled on her own coat and was two steps from the door when Mia stopped her with a lifted hand. "Wait. We actually came to talk to you about that database you keep. The one of all your cases. Did you keep track of whether or not the victim was satisfied with the outcome of the case?" Mia asked.

"Or more importantly," Reagan's voice rumbled softly, "with you. We're looking for someone who didn't blame you for losing."

Kristen swallowed, the sound of his voice sending prickly tingles up and down her spine. He was too close, way too close, but there was no room to back away. So she drew a deep, steadying breath instead, unwillingly drawing in the smell of him. Soap . . . and gyros. He'd had gyros for lunch. "They all blame me, one way or another. But I'll go through my list and try to remember everything I can." She glanced at her watch and felt the tension already throbbing in her neck spike, this time at the thought of Zoe Richardson's planned conversion of Spinnelli's press conference into a three-ring circus. "It's showtime, people."

Friday, February 20, 3:00 P.M.

This is better than sex. The thought struck Zoe as funny, even as she acknowledged the truth of it, but she didn't smile. Cameras were poised, the stage set with microphones and two straight-backed chairs. A door on the left opened and two men walked to the podium. One was John Alden, Kristen Mayhew's boss, the other Lieutenant Marc Spinnelli.

And speaking of the devil . . . As Alden and Spinnelli

took their places on the stage, Mayhew entered, flanked by Mitchell and Reagan. Zoe frowned inside her head at the sight of Reagan who thought he was pretty hot stuff, giving them the slip this morning. Still surrounded by her honor guard, Mayhew moved to the sidelines, her face devoid of any signs of their earlier altercation until she spied Zoe sitting in the front row. Mayhew's response was quickly masked, but not before Zoe saw her green eyes flash.

Spinnelli stepped up to the microphone and the vague murmurs ceased.

"You've heard we are investigating a string of connected murders," Spinnelli announced without preamble and Zoe felt more than saw the heads turning her direction.

Thank you, thank you, Zoe thought.

"Yesterday we recovered five bodies. All were declared homicides. As you know, all the victims had within the past three years passed through the justice system, but were either acquitted or released by way of plea. The investigation is being led by Detectives Mia Mitchell and Abe Reagan of my office and supported by the State's Attorney's Office. We currently have no statement on the status of the investigation other than to say we are applying all urgency to its resolution." He paused and cameras flashed.

Next to her a man from a competing station popped to his feet. "What can you tell us about the letters that were received by the victims of the five dead men?"

"We are not commenting on that at this time."

Zoe rose to her feet and pretended not to listen to the rustling murmurs of her peers. "Lieutenant, can you comment on the personal letters received by ASA Mayhew dedicating the murders to her and declaring himself her humble servant?"

She'd guessed the part about the murders being dedicated to Mayhew, but quickly saw she'd guessed right.

Murmurs became mutters and exclamations and from her plum spot on the first row she could see Spinnelli's jaw clench hard in anger, if not in surprise. Showing her hand to Mayhew this morning had been necessary to confirm her lead, but unfortunately it had also given Spinnelli time to mentally prepare. It was still a direct hit and she let herself bask in the thrill of the scoop.

"We have no comments at this time," Spinnelli said evenly, but the deed was still done. Zoe looked at Mayhew from the corner of her eye. Mayhew stood straight and tall, her face perfectly composed as the flashes now aimed at her face. Damn, but Zoe had to respect her for keeping her cool when it was important. It was probably why Mayhew was Alden's top prosecutor. She knew when the public was watching and played it well.

"But all the victims had been defendants unsuccessfully prosecuted by ASA Mayhew," Zoe pressed. "Do you have any words for the other men and women who are out on the street because Mayhew was unable to get a conviction?"

One of the men behind her said, "Duck!" which sent skitters of laughter through the press, but it was obvious neither Alden nor Spinnelli was amused.

Spinnelli pointed at a reporter from WGN. "Next question."

Zoe sat, pleased. Sometimes a blatant dismissal said more than a direct response.

"Are you looking for a single killer or a group?" asked WGN.

"No comment," Spinnelli said. "Next?"

"You only have two detectives assigned to this case when you've put teams of four or more on other serial murder cases." The observation came from a *Trib* correspondent and brought more murmurs. "Should the public assume you've placed less significance on the murders of these men because they were accused criminals?"

Spinnelli's jaw clenched harder and Zoe could see a muscle twitching in his cheek. The *Trib* had struck a chord. *That would be an interesting angle*, she thought, *the conflict of interest in this case.* How many cops *really* wanted this vigilante caught?

And how scared were Mayhew's lost cases likely to be right now? She thought about Mayhew's most recent loss. Angelo Conti would be sure to have a response, especially if she caught him coming out of a bar. It wouldn't be real news, but it would be great copy. And sometimes great copy created great news. What a deal.

Amid the mutters and flashes, Spinnelli said evenly, "We have assigned Detectives Reagan and Mitchell to this case. Both are experienced and well-qualified. They are backed up by the full resources of CPD. This case is staffed appropriately."

John Alden rose to his feet. Spinnelli moved to one side to allow Alden to speak.

"Lieutenant Spinnelli and I are in full agreement on the staffing and plans for this investigation. We have no further comments at this time."

Together the two men left the podium and Zoe had to admit they were both fine, fine specimens of pure American male, Spinnelli in his dress uniform, Alden in his expensive suit. But now was not the time for idle wandering.

She had a report to prepare before six o'clock. She hoped Angelo Conti was drunk.

Friday, February 20, 4:15 P.M.

The guy behind the glass counter was built like a Sherman tank, which was a good thing because under the glass was a most formidable display of firearms.

"Guy's almost as well stocked as that Dorsey idiot," Mia muttered behind him and Abe chuckled. She was right. Unfortunately both the Dorsey idiot and his wife had rock-solid alibis for the nights King and Ramey disappeared and for the hours they believed their humble servant delivered his notes early Thursday morning.

The tank behind the counter narrowed his eyes. "Can I help you?"

Abe flashed his shield, Mia following suit. "I'm Detective Reagan and this is Detective Mitchell." The man's eyes flickered in recognition, his mouth bent in a sneer.

"Only a matter of time," he declared bitterly.

"Why do you say that, sir?" Mia asked.

"Some guy pops a few and suddenly the cops are crawling all over legitimate gun owners." He shook his head in disgust.

"Actually, we're here to ask your help," Abe said and the man scoffed.

"Right. So what?"

Abe leaned his hip against the counter, lifted his shoulder in a shrug. "So, you obviously know why we're here. We're looking for the guy who popped a few and who's getting ready to pop a few more. We picked your store because you host a marksmanship competition and we're hoping you'll cooperate and give us the list of entries without making us go to all the trouble of getting a warrant."

The Sherman tank got smug. "Get a warrant."

Abe sighed. "I was hoping you'd be reasonable."

"He will be. Give the man the list, Ernie." A tiny old woman appeared from the back of the store, her arm in a sling. "I'm Diana Givens, the owner of this store. This is Ernie, my nephew. He's been helping me run things while I was laid up." She extended her uninjured hand and Abe shook it. "I saw the press conference, Detective. I know who you are and why you're here." She turned to Ernie. "Get the folder from the upright cabinet in the office. Now, Ernie," she snapped and Ernie did her bidding, slouching and muttering all the way. "Damn boy thinks he's the next president of the NRA," Givens muttered. "I run a clean place here, Detectives. I obey gun sale laws and run all buyers through the system. I don't think it does a damn to stop crime, but I obey the law. I'll cooperate with you however I can."

"Then maybe you can help us a little more," Mia said, staring at a display case on the wall. "You've got a great collection here. My dad's a collector. He's got a LeMat, mint."

Diana Givens visibly softened, her eyes taking on a possessive light. "Mint?"

"Um-hmm."

"If he wants to sell it, I'm interested."

Mia turned with a half smile. "He's leaving it to me someday. I don't plan to part with it, but thanks. We're looking for a marksman who hunts."

The old woman stuck her tongue in her cheek. "That narrows it down, honey."

Mia smiled. "I know. He likely hunts duck and deer. Do you keep track of ammo sales by customer? We'll look for someone who buys both kinds."

"You hunt?" Diana Givens asked her.

Mia looked amused. "I have. Not a lot, but I know my

way around the forest. Bagged a three-point buck once with my dad. Mom made venison stew for a month."

"Why didn't you say anything back at the morgue when Jack suggested hunters to Julia?" Abe asked.

Mia grimaced. "Because I wanted Jack to have his moment in the sun in front of Julia. She barely notices his existence and he's been practically tripping over his damn tongue for the last year." Mia leaned on the counter, eye to eye with the diminutive Givens. "Can we check your records, Miss Givens?"

Givens hesitated, then nodded. "I kind of hate to say yes, you know? Your boy took down some very bad players. I hate to see him stopped."

"But we have to stop him, ma'am," Abe said quietly and Givens sighed heavily.

"I know. But I don't have to dance a jig over it. Records are in the back."

Friday, February 20, 4:30 P.M.

"The Myers girl is here with her father, Kristen."

Kristen looked up from her paperwork. The headache from hell was brewing behind her eyes. Lois was looking over her shoulder toward the waiting area with a frown.

The Myers girl was her newest sexual assault case, the one where the father was insisting they press charges. All she needed to make this day perfect was to have that young girl break down in her office again. "I don't suppose they'll come back later."

Lois snorted her displeasure. "No, I don't suppose. Kristen, that dad makes me nervous. He's twitchy. You want me to call Security?"

"Yeah. Just tell them to be ready. Tell Myers I'll see them

in five minutes. I want to finish this first." Hell, she just wanted to finish something today. Her phone had been ringing off the hook since the press conference, every reporter in town wanting a comment.

"Okay, Kristen. Oh, here." Lois dropped a thick stack of paper bound with a big black clip on her desk. "E-mails from all over. Some want information, most are rooting for *him*." She sighed. "Don't leave by yourself tonight. Call Security to walk you down to your car. I'm going home soon. I have a headache."

Join the club, Kristen thought, staring at the bound stack of paper. There wasn't a news service that hadn't picked up the story since the press conference this afternoon. They'd been on CNN every half hour, and even the Yahoo! home page had a photo of Spinnelli and Alden at the podium. She massaged her temples wearily.

She'd see Myers and then she'd go home. After all, who needed an overworked prosecutor when they had a humble servant? Maybe she should just let him mop up the cases she lost, she thought sarcastically. She could work fewer hours.

Hell, she might even take a vacation.

Her mouth twisted at the image of herself on a sandy beach in a bathing suit, sunglasses on her eyes and an unread book on her lap. Like she'd ever take a vacation. Alden was always urging her to take one, but the few times she'd asked he'd always found a reason she had to stay in the office. She'd covered for him enough times when he'd gone on vacation, she thought, resentment making her head throb harder. So she drew a deep breath and let her mind drift, trying to let the image of crashing waves and crying seagulls relax her. It's what the therapists recommended. She ought to know, she'd seen it on late-night cable when she was refinishing the hardwood floor a few months back.

Find your happy place and all your worries will just slip
away . . .

So she leaned back in her chair and closed her eyes.
Then in her imagination opened them and rolled her head to
one side to the lounge chair beside her.

Where Reagan lay, his body tanned, muscled . . . and
perfect. As if sensing her stare, he turned those intense blue
eyes her way and flashed a white smile. And covered her
hand with his.

Kristen sat back up with a hard jerk that sent new waves
of pain coursing from her head down her neck. Dammit.
The man wouldn't leave her alone, checking her closets,
buying her dinner, ruining a perfectly good autopsy viewing. Now he was invading her mind. She rubbed her hand
hard, trying to still the tingles caused even by an imagined
touch. She cursed the hard beating of her heart and pushed
away the feelings she'd be foolish to label anything but
futile longing.

It wouldn't do to long for things she'd never have. If she
ever let Reagan close enough, he'd run so fast . . . He
would.

But damn, he looked good lying there on the beach.

She frowned at her own idiocy. *Face it, Kristen, you'll*
never have anyone. You'll never even get to a vacation on
the beach.

Resolutely she picked up the phone. "Lois, send in the
Myers girl now."

Friday, February 20, 4:30 P.M.

The hat with the earflaps hid his face, and given the wind
chill, nobody would think twice about it. Now, if he was
able to evade the police and keep his work going until

spring, he'd have to get a little more creative if he wanted to walk around undetected.

The thought made him smile, as did the brown box left neatly on Kristen's front porch. The boy had done well. He imagined the surveillance cameras around Kristen's house would capture the boy's face clearly. Tracking him would give Reagan and Mitchell something to do for a day or two, but when they found him, the boy wouldn't be able to give anything more than the most basic of descriptions. Any police artist sketch they got would be able to pass for 10 percent of the men in Chicago, at least.

The news would pick it up and the boy would be linked to, in the hire of, a serial killer. He'd chosen the boy carefully. If there were any negative repercussions to being involved with the "Vigilante Killer" as the news was calling him, this kid deserved them. If nothing came of it, no harm, no foul. But if the kid got into some trouble, it would be a good thing.

Without slowing, he continued down Kristen's street and obediently stopped at a stop sign, left blinker flashing. No bad behavior to make him memorable to anyone that happened to notice his white van, which today sported a sign for an electrical contractor. He thought the happy face on the cartoon electrical plug was a cute touch.

Leah would have been amused.

Friday, February 20, 6:50 P.M.

Spinnelli leaned his head back, weariness etched in his face. None of them had had a great day, but Spinnelli's had been the most publicly bad. "So you've got lists of sharpshooters, hunters—duck and deer, florists and tombstone makers." He dragged his hands down his face. "Sounds like some kind of rabid children's rhyme."

Totally frustrated, Abe stared at the lists covering the conference room table. There were a hell of a lot of hunters in the Chicago area, and they'd only tapped a handful of the ammunition stores. "It will take days to get through all this, even if we had more people. Can the guys in IT help us out? Maybe scan the names in, look for connections?"

Mia stared at Spinnelli. "I heard somebody say today that we have the resources of CPD at our disposal."

Spinnelli shrugged. "I'll ask them. They should be able to do something with all those fancy computers up there."

Abe pushed away from the table and walked to the whiteboard where they continued to note evidence that continued to be unconnected. "We've accounted for the whereabouts of all the original victims on the nights our new victims disappeared. The only ones with shakable alibis are Sylvia Whitman and Paulo Siempres, the stepfather of one of the murdered children."

"Do you think either of them was involved?"

Abe shook her head. "Not Siempres. He wouldn't have had the strength to strangle Ramey. His right arm is withered. Polio as a kid."

"And Mrs. Whitman?"

"Nope." Mia crossed her ankles on the table's edge. "She talks a big talk, but I don't think she's capable either. She might have paid somebody to off Ramey, but if she did, it was from a source nobody knows about. I've checked all their finances. Nobody's made any large contract-killing-sized payments lately."

"Besides," Abe said, "somebody had to know the names of King's six victims to sandblast them into the marker, and there's no reason to suspect Whitman or Siempres had access to that information."

Spinnelli sighed. "I've got Kristen's list of lawyers and cops associated with all three cases. Here's the list of marksmen."

"Poor Marc," Mia said sympathetically. "The press and IA."

"I prefer the damn press," Spinnelli muttered. "Anyway, take a look at this list and see if you can find any ties to your florists, hunters, and tombstone makers."

Abe scanned the list and let out a low whistle. "Check this out, Mia."

Mia's eyes widened. "John Alden."

"Kristen's boss was in the military, qualifying as a marksman." Abe looked up at Spinnelli. "You want us to check this out, or do you want to?"

Spinnelli shrugged. "Get whereabouts for everyone just as a matter of course. I'll talk to Alden myself.

"We'll start first thing Monday," Mia said.

Spinnelli frowned. "What's wrong with now?"

Mia threw a pointed gaze at the clock. "It's Friday. I have a date."

"So?" Spinnelli retorted. "I haven't even seen my wife and kids for a week."

"Then you should go home, too," Mia snapped. "Just because—"

Abe's cell phone vibrated in his pocket and one look at the caller ID had him waving his hand for silence. "What's wrong?" He listened as Spinnelli and Mia abruptly quieted. "Just stay there with the windows rolled up and the doors locked. I'll be there in ten minutes." He snapped his cell phone closed. "Kristen just got attacked. Somebody ran her car off the road into a pole. Two guys with knives wanted to know the identity of her humble servant."

Mia paled. "Shit. Sounds like Blades. Damn that Richardson."

Spinnelli jumped to his feet. "Is she hurt?"

"Where are they now?" Mia demanded.

"I don't think she's hurt," Abe said grimly, "but she's scared." And for that some punk would pay. "She pepper-sprayed their faces and locked herself in her car, then leaned on the horn until other drivers started slowing down and the assholes ran away." He grabbed his coat. "I'll take care of it and call you."

Friday, February 20, 7:10 P.M.

Now that it was over Kristen wanted to scream.

Her shoulder burned from where they'd grabbed her out of the car. Her whole face throbbed from the impact of the deployed airbag and she knew she was lucky not to have a broken nose. The rest of her body ached from holding herself rigid since she'd gotten away and locked herself in the car, but she knew if she let go, she'd start to cry, and that wasn't an option. Not with Richardson perched outside with her toady cameraman. Rage simmered. If she ever found out Richardson had seen the whole thing and just let the camera roll as she screamed for help . . . There wouldn't be a pit deep enough for that bitch to climb out of.

Someone tapped at the window and she muffled a yelp. A uniformed officer stood by her locked door. "Are you all right, Miss Mayhew?" he said loud enough to be heard through the glass. He was the response to her 9-1-1. The call she'd made after the one to Reagan. She refused to consider the significance of the order of her phone calls for help, instead jerking a nod that made her want to whimper in pain. She kept it in, still in control. "Yes."

"Do you need me to call an ambulance?"

Wouldn't that look just great on the ten o'clock news? "No. Did you find them?"

He shook his head. "We'll keep looking, but I think they took off on foot through the business park across the street." He straightened abruptly and Kristen knew without looking that Reagan had arrived. Seven and a half minutes. He must have run a few stop signs along the way. She couldn't help but be grateful.

His face appeared in her window, anxious and worried. "Open the door, Kristen."

She did, willing her hand not to shake, biting back the wince at the burning pain in her shoulder. He pulled open the door, frowning at the loud creak it made.

"They hit me on this side," she murmured. "I think they bent the frame."

He crouched down, his face level with hers, his expression grim. "Your airbag deployed." He bit out the words, as if somehow that made it worse.

"That normally happens when you hit a telephone pole going forty." She lifted a brow, still in control. "I pepper-sprayed them, right in the eyes."

His mouth curved, and she was suddenly so glad he was there. "Good for you."

"They ran away." She pointed to a spread of bright lights and concrete. "Through the business park. I guess the car they used was stolen." They'd abandoned it, its front fender still hooked with hers. "They were Blades. They wanted to know who killed their brothers. When I said I didn't know, they said it didn't matter, that they'd keep me until he came for me."

Reagan's eyes searched her face. "They didn't hurt you."

She shook her head. "Just a little soreness in my shoulder and knee. A few ibuprofen and a hot bath and I'll be fine in the morning. Please . . ." Her voice started to wobble and she swallowed hard. "Please, just take me home."

He offered his hand and let her pull herself out of the car. For a split second she teetered, held by his eyes, then it was out of her hands. She gave in to a need she couldn't admit and leaned into him, into the hard strength of his body. She felt him stiffen, then a half beat later his arms were around her, pulling her in, holding her. She shuddered at the sensation of it, of feeling so utterly safe before allowing the sharp pain in her shoulder to intrude. She couldn't hold back the small moan and his body tightened.

"You *are* hurt. You're going to the ER."

"No. Please." She dragged in a breath and pulled away, the brief respite over. He reached for her face, but she shook her head. "Not here. *She's* here."

His eyes took on an unholy light, and she saw no further explanation was necessary. "Where?"

Kristen gestured to a small unmarked minivan. "Her minion has us in his sights."

"Her minion will turn over that goddamned tape," Reagan snarled. "Can you stand on your own for a minute?"

"Do I get to see you rough up Richardson?" Kristen asked with a quirk of her lips, and as Reagan bared his teeth in response Kristen couldn't help but think of him on the beach. Somehow, he looked a great deal more appealing right now than in her daydream.

"Only if she makes me mad."

"Then I can stand on my own." She watched Reagan take the distance between her car and Richardson's van in great, ground-eating strides. He threw open the sliding side door and blocked the camera's shot with his big body. Richardson scrambled out, her hands on her hips, but Reagan didn't move, and a minute later Kristen saw a black cassette in his hand.

Then he was back, helping Kristen up into his SUV.

"I need a statement, sir."

Reagan drew a deep breath, visibly restraining himself before he turned to the hapless young uniform who had responded to her 9-1-1.

"Do you know who this is?"

The officer met her eyes over Reagan's shoulder. "Yes, I do."

"Then can you meet us at her house in half an hour? She'll give you her statement then. And, Officer? Can you keep that viper from following us?"

The young man looked over at Richardson's van with contempt. "It'll be a pleasure, Detective. Miss Mayhew, are you sure you don't need medical attention?"

She smiled down at him, relief sinking in. "I'm sure. But thank you."

He walked away and Reagan looked up and Kristen's heart caught in her throat at the raw caring she saw in his face. It was so difficult to resist. "My brother Sean's wife is a pediatrician. You're bigger than her normal patient, but I bet she'd make a house call."

"No, but thank you, really. Please, just take me home."

He slammed her door and swung up into the seat next to her, and for a long moment neither said anything. Then, very gently, "Why didn't you call me before you left the office? I would have kept you safe."

To her horror tears burned at her eyes. He saw them, but said nothing, just sat there waiting for her answer.

"Remember the new case I mentioned this morning?" she finally answered unsteadily, but Reagan's gaze never flickered.

"The sexual assault who didn't want to testify but whose father was insisting?"

She nodded. "Yeah. That one. They came to see me this

afternoon and the father said . . ." Her voice broke and sucking in a panicked breath, she pushed the tears back. "For a minute I thought he wanted a different prosecutor, because of all the media attention his daughter would get right now. But he didn't."

Reagan pulled a pack of tissues from the console between their seats and offered it silently. She took the whole pack and clutched it in her hand. "He said that he hoped I lost because then the 'humble servant' would take care of the bastard that raped his daughter. Three days ago I was the prosecutor. Now I'm a surrogate gun for a vigilante." She released her hold on the poor pack of tissues and tried to restore it to its original shape. "I needed to be alone." She looked away from his eyes. "I'm sorry."

He started the car. "You're all right and that's all that's important now." He pulled away from the curb. "I'm going to sleep on your sofa."

She understood he wasn't making a request. She watched the mangled rental car disappear from her side mirror and for the first time let it sink in how truly close she'd come to serious harm.

They could have done anything. They could have . . . Would have . . .

It was like the lid lifting from Pandora's box, releasing memories she'd kept locked away for so long. She shuddered. Hard.

"It folds out," she murmured, closed her eyes, and tried to dream about beaches and sun and waves. But once released, only one image filled her mind, replaying over and over like a horrific video of someone else's life. But it wasn't someone else's. It was hers.

Friday, February 20, 7:30 P.M.

As Reagan's vehicle drove away he let out an angry breath. She was safe now, but she might not have been. He'd almost stepped in, but then she'd taken care of the matter herself, spraying their eyes, making them run, tails between their legs like the curs they were.

She wasn't hurt. But she could have been. Despicable worms. Forcing a woman off the road, planning God-knows-what.

He jumped at the sound of tapping at his window. A police officer stood outside.

"We're trying to clear this area, sir. Could you please move along?"

He smiled. Just nice and easy, and no suspicions would be aroused. He nodded, saying nothing. He pulled the van away and slipped into traffic. He couldn't be caught, not yet. He still had work to do. He wasn't even close to emptying the fishbowl.

Chapter Eleven

Friday, February 20, 8:00 P.M.

"Give me your keys."

Kristen said nothing, moved not a muscle, just sat staring out the window as she'd done the entire way to her house. She was in shock, Abe realized and cursed himself for not following his gut and driving her straight to the ER.

He crossed around to her side of the SUV and gently grasped her chin. "Kristen." He snapped his fingers and she blinked. "Let's go inside. Can you walk?"

She nodded dully and slid down, her face contorting in pain as her foot touched the ground. Ignoring her muted protests, he swung her up into his arms and carried her as if she were one of Sean's kids.

He eased her in through her kitchen door, careful not to jar the knee he'd seen her favoring as he'd stalked off to relieve that bitch Richardson of her ill-gotten gains. He couldn't stop Richardson at the press conference, but he'd be damned if he allowed her to portray Kristen scared and hurt for all Chicago to see.

Because even through her bravado, the woman he held in his arms had been both hurt and scared. Terrified. He thought about the look in her eyes that morning. Had it just been that morning that they'd sat outside the Restons' home?

Impossible to believe, but true. She'd said victims never, ever forget. And he'd suspected she'd been one. Was still one. Now, he knew for sure. How that made him feel was something he wasn't ready to analyze. He was still too pissed off by the here and now to even think about the past.

"I need to turn off the alarm," she murmured. So he set her down long enough to punch the buttons on the console, then guided her to the overstuffed sofa in her living room, stretched out her legs, and slipped a pillow under her knees.

He unbuttoned the top button of her coat and her hands sprang to his. "No." She looked up, her eyes carefully blank in the darkness of the room.

"Okay." He switched on the overhead light and they both blinked. "I'm going to make you some tea." He hoped she had tea bags, because he had no idea of how much loose tea to put in her china teapot with the big roses. "Stay here."

She did have tea bags and he completed the task with reasonable competence while he placed calls to Spinnelli, Mia, and his physician sister-in-law Ruth, his voice steady. But when he picked up the cup of tea his hands trembled.

Abe turned, leaning against her ancient refrigerator, her fragile teacup clenched in his hands, his stomach churning. And once again he was back *there*, with Debra the day she'd been shot, stuck in the scene he'd replayed in his mind too many times to count. It had been cold, a late-spring storm dumping five inches of snow the night before. The sidewalks were still icy, and he'd worried she'd slip and fall. Hurt herself or their unborn child. How ironic.

"I'll drop you off in front of the store," he'd said, worried that the walk from the parking lot to the baby store would be too much for Debra, round in her eighth month.

She'd laughed, that husky sound that he'd found so incredibly sexy. "Don't be such a daddy," she'd said, playfully reproachful. "I'm pregnant, not disabled. The exercise is good for me. Ruth said so." So he'd driven on to find an empty metered space on the street two blocks from the baby boutique on Michigan Avenue. The gift certificate she'd received at her baby shower the night before was burning a hole in her pocket, she'd said, and jumped from the car before he'd had a chance to come around and open her door.

And then everything happened so fast. The shot, the way Debra's body just crumpled to the ground, the look of surprised disgust on the face of the teenaged gunman before he ran to his waiting car. The sound of squealing tires as he escaped.

Then everything moved so slowly. The way her blood pooled in the gutter, a bystander calling for help, his own futile attempts to stop the blood spilling from the hole in the side of her head, his own voice, pleading. "Debra. Please, baby, open your eyes." Again and again.

But she didn't. Not then, not ever again. The doctor delivered the baby at the hospital an hour later, still and lifeless. Never in his life had he felt so helpless.

Until tonight. Driving up to two wrecked cars, knowing Kristen was locked inside one of them, knowing two bloodthirsty gang punks had threatened her for something she'd had no part in causing.

But she's all right. She took care of herself.

He huffed a mirthless chuckle. With a pathetic can of pepper spray. And thank God she had it, that she had the guts to use it. That she hadn't frozen, helplessly.

"Abe."

He looked up to find her standing in the arched doorway, her brow creased in concern. She'd called him Abe. "You shouldn't be up," he said.

She limped across the tired old linoleum and took the cup from his hands. "I'm not hurt. I'm all right."

She was better, he could see right away. Her eyes were sharper, her face less pale. But she wasn't all right, not by a long shot. "Right. That's why you haven't taken off your coat in your own house." His voice was harsher than he'd intended, but she just quietly removed her coat, revealing a charcoal suit with a bright fuchsia blouse that should have clashed with her hair, but somehow did not.

"Is this my tea?" she asked.

"Unless it tastes bad, then it's mine."

She sipped. "It's fine. Can I get you something? You look worse than I do."

He supposed he might at that. "Do you have anything stronger than tea?"

"I don't drink, but I might have something." She searched a cupboard and brought out an unopened bottle of scotch, a really good brand. "I won the door prize at John's office Christmas party last year. If it's no good, blame him."

He followed her to the kitchen table, taking the seat across from her. "It is good," he said after the first sip. Alden had good taste. "Why don't you drink?"

She blinked at him over her teacup. "You are a nosy man."

He sipped at the scotch, feeling it warm his belly, settling the residual nerves still buzzing from his stroll down memory lane. "It's a job requirement."

She acknowledged the point with a wry nod. "My sister was killed in a drunk-driving accident when I was sixteen. I've never touched the stuff."

"I'm sorry."

"Thanks."

They said nothing more after that, just sat drinking their beverage of choice. It was not an uncomfortable silence, Kristen thought, watching Reagan watch her from across the table. Actually she'd become accustomed to seeing him in her kitchen after the last few nights. It had an air of intimacy that she savored even though she knew it was a product of her own imagination. And fruitless wishing.

The front doorbell rang and Reagan stood up. "That'll be Officer McIntyre. He'll want your statement."

"Have him come in here if you don't mind."

Kristen heard him open the door, greet McIntyre. Then curse loudly and she knew what he'd be holding before he came back into the kitchen, a plain brown box in his hands.

"Sonofabitch," Reagan snarled. "At least we'll have him on tape this time."

Kristen stared at the box, utter exhaustion making her limbs heavy. "We knew it would happen sooner or later. You want to open it here or down at the station?"

Reagan flipped out his phone. "I'll let Spinnelli decide." He walked out of the kitchen, leaving her with the box and an agitated Officer McIntyre.

"This is a really bad time, Miss Mayhew," McIntyre said, and she couldn't say why, but the young man's earnest words struck her as incredibly funny and the laughter just rolled. She laughed and laughed, slumping down in the chair when her breath simply gave out. McIntyre was eyeing her teacup suspiciously.

"It's just old-fashioned Earl Grey, Officer," she said when her gasps had refilled her lungs. "The scotch is Reagan's."

"Yes, ma'am. Could I take your statement now?"

Kristen pulled out a chair and gestured him into it. "Go right ahead. I'm not under the influence, Officer McIntyre, just damn tired and worried sick." She straightened in her chair. "You just delivered the punch line to a very bad day."

He looked sympathetic as he took out his notepad. "I'll make this quick."

And he was true to his word, not asking stupid questions or making her repeat anything. He'd slipped his notepad back in his pocket when Reagan came back.

"Got everything you need, McIntyre?"

"Yeah. I don't know that we'll catch anybody, but we'll send some men into the neighborhood tomorrow. Maybe somebody heard somebody bragging. We'll see."

Reagan grimaced. "They'll try again."

Kristen's stomach rolled over. "Wonderful."

Reagan gently squeezed her uninjured shoulder. "Try not to worry." He removed his hand before she gave in to the temptation to lean into him. "Spinnelli and Jack are coming here. McIntyre, you'll need to confirm the location of the box on the front porch."

McIntyre snugged his hat on his head. "No problem, Detective. Miss Mayhew, I'll call you if there's anything more."

Reagan walked him out, but she could hear him welcoming someone else and opened her eyes wide when a thirty-something woman with light brown hair and a black bag appeared at his side. Her house had seen more visitors in the last hour than in the last two years. Reagan shot her a cautious look. "This is my sister-in-law, Ruth."

The pediatrician. Kristen pursed her lips. "I told you I wasn't hurt."

"And you're probably right, Miss Mayhew," the woman said. "Let's check it out, and we can both go to sleep."

"Please call me Kristen." She glared at Reagan, who looked not a whit apologetic. "I'm sorry Reagan dragged you away from your house, but there's nothing wrong with me."

"It's her shoulder and knee," Reagan said, ignoring her. Kristen exhaled in frustration, but Ruth just looked amused.

"Call me Ruth or Dr. Reagan, but don't call me Dr. Ruth, that's all I ask. Abe, scram." She waited until he'd obeyed, then smiled. "Slip off your jacket and your hose if you can."

The jacket was painful enough, but manageable. The hose, however, were a different matter. Annoyed, Kristen acknowledged defeat. "It's a good thing you came by, I guess. I can't imagine sleeping in these things."

Ruth grinned and knelt by her chair. "I can't imagine wearing them at all. Like being stuffed into sausage casings. Let me help." A few tugs and Kristen sat bare-legged, her skirt hiked above her knees. Ruth poked gently for a few minutes, then sat back on her haunches. "You've probably twisted your knee and strained your shoulder socket. Neither one is life-threatening though you'll feel really sore tomorrow."

Kristen frowned. "Worse than now?"

"Oh, a lot worse," Ruth said cheerfully. "But considering the alternative I'd say you're lucky." She rose and looked down, her expression shifting from cheerful to concerned.

"Abe's a fine man. He was afraid you'd gone into shock. Don't be too hard on him."

Kristen tugged her skirt to her knees. "I'm just sorry yo got dragged out here."

"It's okay. Have you eaten?"

Kristen frowned, trying to remember. "Yes, I did. stopped at Owen's for dinner. It was on my way home fror the diner that those guys stopped me."

"Well, then I'd say the best idea is to take some ibupro fen and a nice bath."

Kristen snorted. "That's what I told Reagan, but he's to thickheaded to listen."

Ruth laughed. "Runs in the family, honey. Wait till yo meet his dad."

Kristen shook her head, sincerely panicked that Rut thought . . . "Oh, no. I don't want . . . I mean . . ." She gav up when Ruth just looked more amused. "Never mind."

"It was nice to meet you, Kristen." Ruth's smile fade and she glanced at the door. "He'll need to take care of you Please let him. It's very important."

Kristen remembered the look on his face when she' entered the kitchen. Such desperate desolation. And he' clutched her teacup so tightly that she'd thought it woul shatter, right there in his hands. "Why?"

But she got no answer as Reagan picked that moment t return.

"She's fine, Abe," Ruth said, patting him on the shoul der. "You, on the other hand, look like you could use a ho meal and a good night's sleep."

He smiled down at his sister-in-law with such genuin affection, Kristen's heart ached a little at the sight. What i must be like to have a family so close that you could cal and know they'd come at a moment's notice. Wishes, onc again.

"Don't worry about me," he said.

Ruth sighed. "That's what you always say, but I always do. You're still coming on Saturday, right? A week from tomorrow, don't forget."

"Wild horses couldn't keep me away from my newest niece's christening."

Ruth bit her lip. "I'm sorry about Debra's parents, Abe. My mother invited them. I couldn't un-invite them without causing a huge family row."

Who was Debra? And why did the mention of her parents make his eyes harden?

"It's okay, Ruth. I'm sure we can manage to coexist peacefully for one evening." He pushed a lock of hair behind her ear, the movement practiced, as if he'd done it many times before. "If it looks like trouble is brewing, I'll leave. I promise."

"I don't want you to do that, Abe." Ruth's voice thickened and she closed her eyes. "I'm sorry. It's just that you've missed so much. I don't want you to miss this."

He glanced over at Kristen, his expression slightly embarrassed. Good manners dictated she look away, but again she remembered the look of desolation on his face and gave him what she hoped was a supportive smile instead. He'd been good to her, this relative stranger. Caring for her when he hadn't needed to. Ruth said that it was important he take care of her and whatever his reason, Kristen believed that was true.

"Now don't go getting squishy on me," he said. "You know how much I hate that."

Ruth grinned tearily. "It's just the damn hormones. Kristen, it was so nice to meet you. Keep your foot elevated." She leaned up and kissed Reagan's cheek. "Dinner on Sunday?"

Kristen watched in fascination as Reagan's stubbled

cheeks reddened at the little kiss. "Me miss ham? I don't think so. Let me walk you to your car."

Kristen gave Ruth a little wave. "Thank you." And she watched them leave, Reagan's arm around Ruth's shoulders, the sight making her eyes sting. Hating herself for wishing for things she could never have, she turned and stared at the box.

He was here because of the damn box. Because of all the damn boxes. And as soon as their humble servant was safely put away, he'd be gone. She drew in a deep breath and let it out. And focused on the damn box.

She wondered who the vigilante had targeted this time and tried to make herself care, but it was hard to care about the loss of such twisted, evil people. Harder still after tonight. It didn't take a genius to figure out what those men would have done to her had she not gotten away. It didn't take imagination to conjure the picture of herself at their mercy.

Memories sufficed.

"Spinnelli will be here soon," she murmured to herself, and it wouldn't do to be sitting here bare-legged when he arrived. She needed to change her clothes. Summoning all her energy, she pushed herself to her feet.

Friday, February 20, 9:15 P.M.

He didn't knock. He banged hard enough to wake the damn dead.

Zoe opened her door. "Do you have any concept of self-control?" she snapped.

He pushed inside and slammed her front door so hard the building shook. "Obviously not, since I was stupid enough to get tangled up with you." His body shook with barely suppressed rage and for the first time, Zoe was afraid.

"Calm down, for God's sake. Do you want a drink?"

"No, I don't want a drink." He grabbed her arms hard and she cried out. He hauled her up on her toes. "What I want is for you to back off. No more stories about Mayhew or vigilante killers." He pulled harder and she bit back a whimper. "Understand?"

She struggled, but he held firm. "It's my job. I'm doing my job."

"Then go find another story, because you doing your job will make me lose mine."

"You're overreacting. Nobody's going to lose their job."

He shook her, hard. "That's because you're going to stop."

She threw her head back, stared him in the eye. "Or what? What could you possibly do to back up your spineless little threat? Tell the world I'm sleeping with you? *I'm* not married. *I* don't care." She narrowed her eyes. "Or maybe I'll turn up as one of Kristen's gifts."

He paled as she'd known he would. "What are you talking about?"

She lifted a shoulder in a careless shrug. "The power of the press, the spoken word. A whispered allegation. Association with a vigilante. It could ruin a man's career."

He stared at her for a moment, then threw her away as if she burned him. She hoped she had. Nobody threatened Zoe Richardson. Nobody.

"You're insane," he whispered.

"Unfortunately for you I am quite sane." She settled her hands on her hips, well aware of the picture she made. "You want to stay or what?"

Horror flickered across his face. "You think I'd sleep with you now? My God."

"Pity. Press conferences and interviews with the Contis really get my blood stoked. Sleeping hadn't crossed my mind."

His eyes narrowed. "Conti? What does that sonofabitch have to do with anything?"

Zoe laughed. "So sanctimonious suddenly. Go on home, sugar. You can probably just catch the interview if you leave right now."

He shook his head. "You're poison."

"Probably. Oh, and I'd be careful about that sleep-talking thing if I were you, sugar."

He paled and went still. "What are you talking about?"

It was too rich for words. "You talk in your sleep, honey. I'm sure your wife knows all about us. Or will soon." She tilted her head, her smile patronizing. "Sleep well."

Friday, February 20, 10:00 P.M.

He'd chosen the next name from the fishbowl. It was a good choice. He stared at the name, thinking of the vileness of the man's crimes. It would be too much of a pleasure to see this man dead.

He sighed. He really should admit it, if to no one but himself. He'd started this mission to avenge Leah and the countless other victims denied justice. After the second one, Ramey, he'd felt satisfaction, and that was okay. With King it had been more than satisfaction, it had been almost . . . exhilarating, beating that man's face to a bloody pulp. But with Skinner . . . it had been pleasure.

Watching Skinner's eyes, so horrified. The way Skinner tried to struggle, gasping and gurgling at the very end. And he'd felt pleasure.

Was it wrong? Would God be displeased?

No, he told himself. God's people often were command-ed to kill and afterward, celebrated. There was precedent. Even Skinner would have appreciated precedent.

He stood up to go to the computer when the flickering television caught his eye. He'd been watching it all day, off and on. Watching for mention of himself, gauging public response. He was ahead in the polls if the public demon-stration at the courthouse had been any indication, he thought, then stilled when Zoe Richardson filled the screen.

He hated that woman. She was vile also, prancing around, portraying Kristen as an incompetent. He was glad Reagan had taken her videotape earlier this evening. If Reagan hadn't, he would have done it himself. He sat down, grabbing for the remote and turned up the sound. Richardson was interviewing that murderer, Angelo Conti. "So what was your reaction when you learned of the 'Humble Servant'?" Richardson asked and Conti swag-gered in place.

"I wasn't too surprised," Conti replied.

Richardson tilted her platinum blonde head. "Why were you not surprised, Angelo?"

"The way she went after me, like she was crazy or some-thing. I was innocent."

"Actually, the jury was undecided, Angelo. ASA Mayhew could try you again."

Angelo's face flushed dark red. "Yeah, and she'll lose again. She's incompetent, you know? That's why she hired this guy. She can't win, so she takes the fight outside."

Richardson looked taken aback. "Are you suggesting that ASA Mayhew somehow hired this vigilante to kill the people she was unable to convict? Like a hit man?"

His stomach roiled as Richardson's accusation rolled from the television. "*No*," he whispered, his hand clenching the medallion around his neck. "It wasn't like that."

Angelo Conti shrugged. "Call it what you like. I'd just like to see somebody checking her financial records the way she's checked mine."

"An interesting perspective." Richardson turned back to the camera. "This is Zoe Richardson in Chicago."

He switched off the television, trembling. He looked at the name on the paper he'd drawn from the fishbowl. It would have to wait. He had another target to eliminate first.

Friday, February 20, 10:30 P.M.

"Where's Spinnelli?" Jack grumbled. "I wanna open the box."

Abe's smile was wry. Jack sounded like a little kid on Christmas morning. "He'll be here soon. You'll have all day tomorrow to analyze what he's left this time."

Jack grunted. "Where's Mia? I would have thought she'd want front-row tickets to this."

"She had a date. I called her to tell her Kristen was all right, but when I called her a half hour later, her phone was turned off."

Jack huffed. "Well, at least one of us will be smiling tomorrow."

Kristen looked up from her seat at the end of the kitchen table. She'd changed into a sweat suit, but her hair was still fiercely pinned to her head and Abe fought the urge to release her curls, knowing it was likely the last semblance of control she possessed.

"Why should Mia be any happier than the rest of us?" she asked. Then her eyes widened as she caught Jack's meaning, and her face blushed a pretty pink. "Never mind."

Jack grinned. "Sorry, Kristen." Then sobered. "You

know there won't be a hell of a lot to analyze tomorrow. He wasn't even here, we know that."

They did. The bastard must have seen the cameras because the surveillance tape showed only a young boy delivering the box. They had a good picture of the kid's face and of the name of his high school on his letter jacket, so they could find him pretty easily.

Nevertheless, Jack's team was currently dusting Kristen's front porch for prints and combing every square inch of her front yard for anything that might have been left behind. A call to her neighbors revealed the box had been there when they got home from work at five o'clock, and beyond that, nobody had seen anybody.

Jack pointed at the box. "Let's just open it, okay?"

Abe sighed. "Okay. Go for it."

Jack had already covered Kristen's kitchen table with white paper. "I don't expect to find any prints on this box either, but you never know. Here goes." He sliced open the box and pulled out an envelope. And sat down hard in his chair. "Dear God."

Kristen jumped to her feet, wincing. "What?"

Jack looked up, every ounce of color drained from his face. "It's Trevor Skinner."

"Oh, no." Kristen sank back down, her face white as the paper on the table. "I was afraid of this," she whispered. "He's added defense attorneys to his target list."

Abe reached for the envelope in Jack's trembling hand. He'd heard of the man by reputation only. A real piece of work. "Did you know him well?"

She nodded, stunned. "We butted heads quite a few times. He was ruthless. I hated being in the same courtroom with him. He was merciless to the victims, pounding away until they were . . . nothing." She pressed her fingertips against her lips. "I can't believe this."

Abe shook the envelope's contents on the table, found the letter. "'My dearest Kristen, I am so glad the proverbial cat is now out of the bag. I hope you've taken comfort knowing these monsters are dead. I'll continue for as long as I'm able. By now you're probably wondering why I'm doing this, why I've set out on this mission to rid the city of the festering filth that roams its streets. Suffice it to say that I have my reasons. I've watched Mr. Trevor Skinner at work in the courtroom, the way he so skillfully turned opinion away from the victim, often rendering them incapable of speaking on their own behalf.'" Abe paused and looked up at Kristen.

"Yes, that's very true. I would object and object, but he never stopped. He's a favorite among the defendants with money. He could make a victim look worse than the accused. The rape cases were so painful." Her lips quivered and she pursed them. "He made those women feel so worthless and dirty," she finished on a whisper, met his eyes, hers shiny and wet. "I'm sorry he's murdered, Abe, but I'm glad he can never do that to a woman again." She blinked, sending two fat tears down her cheeks and Jack reached out to take her hand.

"We should have done this in my lab," Jack said softly. "This is too much for you, after what happened tonight."

She drew a steadying breath, gently pulling her hand away. "I'm okay, just shaken up. Let's hear the rest of it."

"'So in the spirit of an eye for an eye, I devised a punishment that was fitting. Sleep well, Kristen, knowing Mr. Trevor Skinner died unable to say a word in his own defense. Please ensure the criminals of Chicago know that I am watching, I am angry, and I am not bound by the laws of man. I am as always, Your Humble Servant.'" Abe sighed. "'P.S. You really should finish one job before you start another.'"

"What new job did you start?" Jack asked.

Kristen's mouth thinned to a grim line. "Last night I started making curtains for my damn windows."

Jack's lips twitched. Then he began to laugh and after a moment she joined him. She had a wonderful laugh, Abe thought, once again feeling as if he'd been kicked in the gut. His face must have shown it, because she quickly sobered, looking guilty.

"I'm sorry, really. It's just . . . been a really long day."

"It's about to get longer," Spinnelli said from the doorway. "You catch the news?"

"We've been a little busy, Marc," Kristen said wryly. "We were at the press conference. What more harm could she have done since then?"

Spinnelli pulled a tape from his coat pocket. "Where's your VCR?"

"It's in the living room," she said, worried now.

Spinnelli looked at the box. "Who was it this time?"

"Trevor Skinner," Abe said and Spinnelli's face went as pale as everyone else's.

"And I thought my day couldn't get any worse."

Saturday, February 21, 2:00 A.M.

"You should be sleeping."

Startled by the sound of Reagan's rumbly voice on the basement stairs, Kristen jerked her attention from the mantel she was sanding, putting a pause on the delightful fantasy of Zoe Richardson dipped in honey and tied to a thriving anthill. Vicious red ants that bit hard. She was still angry, hours later. Angry that Richardson had insinuated she'd hired a killer. Angry that the bleached blonde bitch had given the criminal community yet another reason to come after her with knives. Angry that Angelo Conti got another chance to posture in front of a camera. And at this very moment, angry that just the sound of Reagan's voice could make her pulse race.

But none of her anger was his fault. He'd been more than kind, refusing to leave after Spinnelli and Jack left, worried that the men who had accosted her would be back. "I'm sorry," she said quietly. "I didn't mean to wake you up. I was trying to be quiet."

"I wasn't asleep." She watched as he descended the stairs in a slow, deliberate way. He still wore his hard shoes, as if he expected to go chasing after an intruder any moment. His trousers were still creased, despite all the hours he'd worn them. The only sign he'd relaxed at all was the absence of his tie and the shirt he'd pulled out of his pants, unbuttoned just past the hollow of his throat. Her eyes lingered there, probably longer than they should have. She lifted her eyes to his face where dark stubble shadowed his cheeks, then to his eyes which were shadowed with concern. *For me,* she thought, and tried not to let it mean too much. "Doesn't that hurt your shoulder?" he asked and she looked down at her sandpaper.

"It's okay. It's my left shoulder, and I'm right-handed."

"Oh. I thought you were sewing curtains," he said.

"The sewing machine makes too much noise, and I—

"You were trying not to wake me. Got it." He walked over to the little windows that lined her basement wall. Unlike herself, Reagan was tall enough to look through the glass without standing on a chair. There was something settling in his size and strength. "Where's your sewing machine?"

"Up in my spare bedroom."

"Then he could have seen you from the street."

Kristen dropped her sandpaper, her palms suddenly

clammy. She wiped her hands on her sweatpants. "Yeah." She stood up, wincing at the soreness in her knee. "Look, I know this sounds weak and lame, but could we not talk about him right now? It's driving me insane, wondering if he's out there, looking at me." She rubbed her upper arms, suddenly cold. "Watching me. God, it's like some kind of Hitchcock movie. I've been afraid to get in the damn shower."

His mouth quirked up, and it wasn't the first time she noticed how nice a mouth he had. It suited his face which at the moment he was turning her way. "Well, if you want to take one tonight, I'll stand guard outside your door and I promise I won't look."

She went still, every muscle in her body going taut. He'd meant it as a silly tease, intended to make her smile, but she could see his words had affected him as well. His only movement was the rhythmic rise and fall of his chest as his blue eyes flared and held her. The very air between them was suddenly charged. She could almost feel the sparks.

Sparks. Her chin came up as her mind clicked into gear. "You were working the Sparks case, weren't you? That's where I saw you before. It was two years ago, in the summer. You were undercover and got arrested with everybody else they'd picked up for possession. I saw you in the holding area." She'd heard him before she'd seen him, as she recalled. It would have been impossible not to.

That mouth of his curved in a smile that was almost smug. "I was wondering if you'd remember. Took you long enough."

She advanced a limping step. "No fair." She chuckled, remembering. "You were something else. You had a ponytail, a beard, a shiner, and a really big mouth."

He grinned and her breath caught at the sight. "I was in

character that day. You should have heard what I said about you after you'd gone."

She was alone with a man she'd known only three days, who made her feel safe and who, if she was not mistaken, was flirting with her. She'd been flirted with before, but had always been left with cold nerves. She now felt the nerves, but she was definitely not cold. "I'm almost afraid to ask." *How true.*

He lifted a dark brow, making him look devilish and to her mortification, her mouth watered and the warmth in her face spread down. *Don't wish, Kristen. It won't happen.*

"Let's just say my cover was very heterosexual and leave it at that," he said dryly, but his eyes never left hers.

Kristen swallowed hard and looked away. She picked up the sandpaper and began working a small section of mantel carving where decades of paint stubbornly clung. "I was bringing some papers to the precinct that day," she said. "I heard you, then saw you. You were watching me." With those piercing blue eyes she'd never truly forgotten. "Why?"

She heard him approach, felt his heat at her back. And wondered how she ever could have been cold. "I don't know," he answered seriously. "I just looked up and there you were in your black suit with your hair pinned up. I was . . . stunned."

Stunned. Kristen made herself laugh. "Oh, please, Reagan. 'Stunned' is a bit dramatic, wouldn't you say?"

"You asked, I told you," he answered tersely. "I wasn't happy about it myself."

He sounded positively grim and her stomach gave a nasty twist. *That hurt.* She renewed her efforts on the stubborn paint until she was sure her voice would be steady. "That's good to know. I think I'm ready to talk about vigilante stalkers now."

"My wife was alive then." The words cracked out, seemed to hover between them.

His wife. Slowly she turned around. He was standing too close, and she pressed back against the mantel to put a few more inches of distance between them. He'd noticed her when he was still married. She hadn't believed him to be that kind of man. *And that hurt even more.* "Your wife?" Her voice came out a whisper.

He was staring at her, his eyes intense. Challenging. "Yeah. Debra, my wife."

Debra, whose parents' coming to the christening on Saturday made him angry. She moistened her suddenly dry lips. "She's no longer alive, I take it?"

"She died a year ago."

Kristen waited a moment, but he said no more. "Of?"

His expression became angry. "I guess the official cause of death was heart failure, but after five years in a vegetative state, any failure would have been sufficient."

Her breath caught in her throat as the enormity of his admission hit home. *Five years.* Five years of painful limbo. Her heart ached for him, for what he'd endured. Her first impression had been an accurate one, she thought, thinking of that night in the elevator. Desperate desolation. "You loved her, then."

His eyes flashed. "Yes." He bit it out, the one little word that said volumes. She knew that if she wanted to know more, she'd have to ask. She wondered if she did want to know more. She had enough troubles of her own without taking on those of another. *But he took on yours, Kristen, without a second breath.* And in a flash of insight she realized what he was offering. The opportunity to share burdens.

A relationship. Something she'd longed for over the

years. Something that terrified every bit as much as it beck-oned.

He was watching her think, which was unsettling, as if he knew her thoughts. Maybe he did. *Maybe he won't care.* The thought came, childish and hopeful, and she dashed it immediately. No, he'd care. It would make a difference. Later, it would. But now, he needed to talk and she wanted to listen. They would be friends.

But no more than friends. It would be his choice, not hers. He would be the one to walk away, not her. She knew it, even as she stared into his eyes. They'd be hurt, both of them. But not tonight. She tore her sandpaper into halves and offered him one.

"Tell me about her. Debra."

He took the bit of sandpaper that looked pathetically small in his large hand. He stepped away, moving down to the other end of the mantel and she took in a deep breath, filling her lungs. Then turned back to her stubborn paint.

"She was . . ." His voice roughened, broke. "She was everything."

Kristen's heart cracked as she wondered what it would be like to be "everything" to someone. Someone like him. She sanded harder. "What happened?"

"She and I were going to the store. She got out of the car, and she was shot."

She glanced at him from the corner of her eye. He just stood there, staring at the sandpaper in his hand. "Was it a mugging?"

His jaw clenched. "No. Just some punk retaliating against the just-promoted detective who arrested his brother."

She closed her eyes briefly. He'd only been doing his job and somebody ruined his life. There was a parallel here, his past experience with her current situation, but she wasn't going to touch it now. "Tell me about *her.*"

"She had brown hair and brown eyes." He was quiet for a moment, and she could almost feel him grappling for the memory of the woman who'd been his "everything." "She was tall," he continued, his voice steadier. "She was a pre-school teacher, loved little kids."

"She sounds like a very nice woman."

"She was." She heard the rueful smile in his voice and turned to find it reflected on his face. Still he stood, just holding the sandpaper. "She put up with me."

Kristen made her own lips curve. "A hardship, I'm sure."

His smile dimmed, draining her energy with it. "You have no idea."

Suddenly too weary to stand, Kristen abandoned the mantel. "I'm tired, Abe. I think I'm going to call it a night. You should sleep, too. Please."

He turned only his head, studying her from her head to her toes and back again, his eyes hot and her weariness evaporated, replaced by tingling awareness. He'd been stunned, he said. So was she, she admitted.

"Do you ever plan to take those pins out of your hair?" he asked and her breath left her in a hard exhale that left her head spinning.

Breathe, Kristen. Breathe. "Why?"

He shook his head and the spell was broken. "Never mind. Go to sleep. Morning will be here soon enough."

"And what will happen then?"

He lifted a brow. "We dig up Trevor Skinner."

Chapter Twelve

Saturday, February 21, 7:00 A.M.

The press was a barely suppressed horde, led by none other than Zoe Richardson who was currently tempting fate by brandishing a microphone way too close to Abe's face.

"The public has a right to know the identity of this victim," Richardson demanded. "You can't keep this quiet."

"We will until we've notified the victim's family," Abe said in a warning tone, cognizant that his every move was being recorded for the public's "right to know." He motioned to the officer assigned to crowd control at the scene. "Just keep them behind this line." He walked back to the scene, sheltered by some trees just off the main road.

Julia stood beside Jack next to the shallow grave that had been topped with a marker that read RENEE DEXTER. Mia stood next to Kristen who had quietly told them the details of the case. It was much as she'd described the night before in her kitchen. Dexter was a rape victim who Skinner had verbally eviscerated on the stand.

"I objected and objected," she'd murmured, staring at the woman's name forever inscribed in marble. "But the judge let Skinner tear that woman to shreds."

Jack's team was bringing the body up now, under Julia's watchful eye. Once Skinner was on the ground the five of them gathered close and Mia knelt next to the body.

"He's got something in his hand," she explained. "His fist is wrapped with duct tape." Jack carefully slit the tape, opening the hand. With a look of revulsion on her face Mia looked up and met Abe's eyes. "Looks like the proverbial cat our humble servant let out of the bag got Skinner's proverbial tongue."

" 'He died without saying a word in his own defense,' " Kristen quoted from the letter. "You've told his wife?"

Abe nodded. "Spinnelli arrived at the Skinners' house at the same time we arrived here. We didn't want the press to tell her first."

Still kneeling next to the body, Mia looked up at Julia. "Can a person die from having their tongue cut out?"

Julia knelt on the other side of Skinner's body. "No. But look at these depressions on both sides of his skull. Same size, same placement just behind his ears."

"Vise grip," Jack said and Julia looked up at him with approval.

"That would do it."

"Do what?" Abe asked.

Julia stood up. "I'll be able to confirm it after the autopsy, but if your boy is consistent and this bullet hole in Skinner's forehead is postmortem and not the cause of death, I'm thinking we'll find blood in his lungs."

Abe sighed. "Meaning he cut out Skinner's tongue and immobilized his head with the vise so that he drowned in his own blood."

Mia rose to her feet, brushing her knees. "I think we need to put a watch on the guy that was acquitted for Renee Dexter's rape. It's logical that that's where he'll strike next."

They all stepped back as the ME's office zipped Skinner into a body bag.

"He's crossed the line," Kristen murmured. "Skinner was a bastard in the courtroom, but he never broke the law."

"What's next?" Jack asked bitterly. "Judges?"

"Or prosecutors who don't win," Abe said and Kristen's

eyes widened, meeting his. "This guy has no boundaries, Kristen. He doesn't blame you yet, but that could change."

"We asked Spinnelli to give you twenty-four/seven protection," Mia said and Kristen opened her mouth as if to protest, then closed it.

"Thank you," she said instead.

"And until then," Abe said, "you stay with one of us."

Mia's phone beeped and she flipped it open. "Mitchell." Her lips curved in a feral smile as she listened. "You don't say. Ain't technology grand? Hold on." She looked at Abe, blonde brows lifted. "They found Skinner's car across town. It has one of those global positioning systems."

Abe's pulse jumped. *Finally a break.* "Ask them if they can track the car's movements Thursday night."

Mia looked satisfied. "They can and they did. Looks like we have our own little x-marks-the-spot."

Saturday, February 21, 7:00 A.M.

He staggered back against his basement wall, nauseous. He slid to the floor. Gasping. His heart thundering as if it would claw its way out of his chest. His hands, his arms, his chest, his face . . . all covered in blood. *I did this. Dear God . . . I did . . . this. This.*

He closed his eyes. *Relax. Take a deep breath. Get control of yourself.*

He drew in the air with deep gulps, shuddered it out, felt control return in slow spurts. He was finished. Angelo Conti was dead. Very, very dead.

Bracing his feet on the cement floor, he pushed against the wall, forcing himself to his feet. And surveyed the carnage he'd left in the process. He'd lost control. He mustn't allow that to happen again.

But Conti deserved it, the cocky punk. It had been no great mystery finding him last night. He'd just waited until Angelo came out of his favorite bar just off Northwestern's campus, weaving drunkenly. He'd headed for his brand-new Corvette, obviously intending to get behind the wheel. Conti hadn't cared that he was too drunk to walk. One would think the boy would be minding his manners after narrowly avoiding prison for the murder of Paula Garcia and her unborn son, but obviously Angelo thought himself charmed.

Angelo had been wrong . . .

He never saw me coming. He could have just hit Conti on the head and dragged him into the van, but something about that drunken swagger and the brand-new Corvette made his blood boil. So he'd popped his knees. Both of them.

Then he'd coshed him on the head and dragged him to the van.

He'd savored the anticipation of Conti's return to consciousness, the fear that would make the boy's eyes go glassy and his tongue finally stop flapping. But no. Angelo had roused from his stupor surprisingly alert and in seconds had figured out where he was.

And who I was.

He hadn't stopped talking, *and before I knew it, the tire iron was in my hand.* The first few blows were to get his attention. But still Conti wouldn't *shut up.* Then he started talking about Kristen.

And I lost control.

The things Conti had said . . . vicious, vile things. *"How did she pay you for doin' her dirty work, huh? How was she? I bet there's a real tiger under that prissy suit."* He kept talking, saying perverted, vile things about him, about Kristen. He just wouldn't stop.

And then neither could I.

He drew a breath. No one would recognize Conti now. Most of his face was gone. There would be no sense in taking any Polaroids. He walked to where he'd left Conti's things and found the boy's wallet. His driver's license had been taken away for too many DUI's. But Conti did have a university-issued photo ID. That would have to do.

He busied himself, taking care of Conti. The sharp crack of his pistol and the acrid odor of a fired weapon soothed. It was routine by now.

He checked his watch and grimaced at the time. "I'm late," he murmured. He had to clean himself up and get back to work. Later, he'd return and make the marker. Paula Garcia and her unborn son deserved that much.

Saturday, February 21, 9:30 A.M.

Trevor Skinner's wife was a thin, pale woman who looked as if she'd collapse at any moment. She was no help when it came to any questions about her husband's whereabouts, any strange visitors, nothing that would explain how Skinner was lured to the place where he'd been shot Thursday night.

They'd found the ambush site easily, thanks to modern technology. Skinner subscribed to one of those global on-call services that track motorists by satellite so that they can send help should there be an emergency. The service also provided driving directions. Luck was with them. Skinner called for directions to an abandoned factory site, where the killer shot his kneecaps and moved him elsewhere. Apparently the car was then stolen by passing teens who drove it to where it was found that morning.

Abe was ready to call it quits with the hysterical Mrs.

Skinner when an elderly housekeeper tentatively tugged at his jacket sleeve. "Sir?" she whispered. "There was a package delivered."

At instant alert, Abe and Mia escorted the housekeeper to the next room where they could hear her soft voice over Mrs. Skinner's understandable hysteria.

"When was this package delivered, ma'am?" Abe asked.

"Thursday." She shrugged uncomfortably. "Maybe two o'clock."

"Did you see anyone deliver it?"

"No, sir. Someone just rang the doorbell and left it there."

"Can you describe this package, ma'am?" Mia asked.

"It was wrapped with plain brown paper. There was a label, typed, just with Mr. Skinner's name. It was very light, like air. About so big." She gestured with her hands.

Light like air. A single piece of paper, another letter, most likely and Abe wondered what could have been compelling enough to lure Skinner out. "Did you see a car, ma'am?"

"Yes, yes I did. It was a white van. I remember thinking it was odd because it was a florist van, but there were no flowers."

"Yes," Mia muttered. "A flower by any other name smells just as sweet. Did you open the box?"

The housekeeper's eyes widened in something akin to horror. "No. Mr. Skinner didn't like us touching his things. He was very particular." The housekeeper looked over her shoulder at the sobbing Mrs. Skinner. "He's really dead?"

Oh yeah, thought Abe. *Mr. Skinner is very dead.* "Yes, ma'am. We're very sorry."

Saturday, February 21, 4:00 P.M.

"Diana Givens won't be able to help us." Mia's pronounce-
ment from the backseat of Reagan's SUV was glum.
"Nobody can help us. The bullet's too damaged."

CSU had found the bullet in the wood frame of a doorway in the old factory where Skinner had been abducted
Thursday night. Analysis of the blood they'd found on the
street would provide certainty that that's where he'd been
shot, but they were already pretty sure. The bullet was a
huge find, especially since the killer had taken such pains to
remove the bullet from King's body, cutting him open and
sewing him back up.

The bullet had some kind of a mark, a maker's mark, ballistics had called it. But unfortunately the mark was severely marred, to the point of being unrecognizable.

"You don't know that, Mia." Reagan smoothly parked
his monster SUV in the lot of an older-looking gun shop and
Mia hopped out.

"You coming, Kristen?" Mia asked.

Kristen sighed. She'd been everywhere else in the city
today. This would be their seventh gun shop. "Why not?"

Reagan shot her a sympathetic look. "I can take you
home. Spinnelli should have your shadow assigned by
now."

The thought irked as much as it comforted. Her neighbors were already in a tizzy over having CSU's bright lights
illuminating the neighborhood half the evening. Now there
would be a black-and-white stationed outside her house
until . . . Well, until something changed, Kristen supposed.
Until her humble servant was no longer watching her. Until
she was no longer the target of rage-filled gangs or raven-
ous reporters. Until she was no longer a victim waiting to

happen. She eyed the big sign in the gun shop window and made a decision.

"No, I'm coming."

Reagan helped her down from the high seat and she held her breath until she was solidly on her own two feet. Her knee throbbed like hell, but she'd be damned before she let it show in case any cameras were lurking. "Any cameras?" she murmured and Reagan looked up and down the street.

"No, I think everybody with a camera is at Spinnelli's press conference." Reagan grimaced. "Better him than us. Especially now that our boy has widened his repertoire."

"I've gotten fifteen calls on my cell from defense attorneys since Richardson broke the story on Skinner." Kristen took a test step and winced. "Everybody is scared to leave their houses." And if she felt a certain satisfaction in visualizing them all hiding in their homes, quaking in their boots, Kristen thought she was entitled. She'd never been able to understand the mentality of defense attorneys. They knew that most of their clients were guilty as hell, yet defended them as if the scum-suckers had been the victims themselves.

Reagan just grunted. "Serves the bastards right. Maybe it'll be good for them, being scared for a day or two. We should have taken Mia's car. Climbing up and down all day can't be good for your knee."

She chanced a glance up at him, but couldn't see his eyes behind his dark sunglasses. It was better that way, she thought, swallowing the pang of regret. She was becoming too accustomed to the caring look in his eyes. "You heard Ruth. I'm not hurt."

He said nothing, just offered his arm as they followed Mia into the store. "What's that?" Kristen asked, eyeing the case Mia carried by its handle. She'd insisted they stop at her apartment before starting their canvass of the gun stores and emerged with the case.

Reagan chuckled. "You'll see."

A big man stood behind the glass counter, glaring. "You're back."

"So it would seem," Mia said dryly. "Is Diana here?"

"No," the man snapped.

"Oh, Ernie, for God's sake." An elderly woman appeared from the back, her arm in a sling. "Yes, I'm here, Detectives. What can I do for you today?" She eyed Mia's black case cagily, then openly appraised Kristen. "You've brought famous company."

"Yeah, yeah, she's a regular celebrity." Mia leaned on the counter. "It's like this, Diana. We found a bullet in the course of our investigation." She brought out a bag and set it on the glass counter. "It's not beautiful, but right now it's all we have. What can you tell us about it?"

The old lady pursed her lips, sending wrinkles from the corners of her mouth like rays of the sun. She fidgeted with the bag holding the bullet. "So what's in it for me?"

Mia tapped the black case she'd brought. "Be a good girl, and we shall see."

"What is it?" Kristen whispered to Reagan, but he shook his head and shushed her.

Diana's eyes had warmed considerably. "Long time since I've been called a girl."

"Consider it part of the service," Mia said. "We think this bullet is hand-cast."

Diana bent her mouth in a speculative frown. "It is. But it's too mangled to get any specifics on the mold that made it." She picked up the bullet and narrowed her eyes. "It has a maker's mark."

"I know. My ballistics guy told me that much. He didn't recognize it. Do you?"

She brought out a magnifying glass and examined the bullet with precision. "No, it's too mangled, like I said. Not many people make their own bullets anymore."

"Any of your customers?" Mia asked. "Any on the list of marksmen you gave us?"

The old woman thought. "There are a handful, but none have a mark." She eyed the black case. "So what's inside, Detective Mitchell?"

Mia popped the latches. "My dad's gun." And she smiled when Diana's eyes grew wide and reverent. "It's a real treasure." Then she snapped the case closed when Diana reached out to touch it. "Maybe later."

Diana lifted a brow. "Quid pro quo, huh?"

"Depends. Me and my partner need information on the mark on this bullet. If I can get a decent sketch, can you post it on your bulletin board?"

Diana conceded with a dignified nod. "I'm the cooperative sort, Detective Mitchell. In fact, I'll do you one better. I'll ask all my most enthusiastic sharpshooting friends to come in for a little get-together, and we'll make you a list of all the marks we recall."

Kristen heard Reagan's laugh rumble softly above her ear. "She's good, isn't she?" he asked and Kristen leaned her head back to look up at his profile. His eyes were focused on Mia, his mouth bent in a smile that held pride as well as amusement. He wasn't a man to be threatened by the skill of another, even when the other was a woman, and that alone set him apart from most of the men she knew.

"Yes. Yes, she is. Where are we going next?"

"Mia and I are going to King High School. We got a picture off the surveillance video of the kid who delivered that box to your house and we want to pass it around. There'll be kids on the basketball court across from the school all day since it's Saturday."

"If you're thirty minutes late, is that a problem?"

He looked down at her with a puzzled frown. "I guess not. Why?"

Kristen turned to the glass counter. "Because I'm going to buy a gun."

Saturday, February 21, 5:00 P.M.

"Can I talk to you for a minute, Jacob?"

Jacob Conti looked up to find Elaine standing in the doorway of his office, wringing her hands. "What is it, Elaine?" But he knew.

She approached in that timid way of hers. She'd made him think of a delicate bird when he'd first met her, twenty-five years ago now. She still did. "I've been trying to reach Angelo all day. I'm starting to get very worried. He was supposed to meet his friends at the club for racquetball and he never showed up. Can you send Drake to search for him?"

Conti nodded. "Certainly, dear. Try not to worry."

She came closer and kissed his cheek. "I'll try. Thank you, Jacob."

He let her leave without telling her that he already had Drake Edwards and three others searching for Angelo. So far, they'd turned up nothing.

A sick feeling settled in his stomach. *Angelo, you had to go and open your big mouth. As if you weren't a target in the first place, you had to go on television, for God's sake.*

If anything happened to his son . . . Someone would pay.

And Jacob Conti was not a man accustomed to making idle threats.

Saturday, February 21, 7:00 P.M.

She'd surprised him once again, Abe thought as he watched Kristen order their meal in Italian, then go on to converse fluently with their waiter. He'd brought her to Rossellini's, an Italian place his family had loved since he was a boy. There was a cozy warmth here, and tremendous food. And unlike Mia, Kristen seemed to have an open mind for new culinary experiences.

Watching her smile as Italian flowed from her lips, he couldn't help but wonder if she had an open mind for other experiences as well. All day as she'd sat next to him in the SUV he'd breathed in her fragrance, watched the play of emotions across her face, some subtle and others not so. He'd watched her tense every time her cell phone rang, knowing she endured harassment from the frightened defense attorneys who'd had the misfortune to share her courtroom. He'd watched her look over her shoulder all day, wondering if she was the subject of scrutiny of cameras or gang members or her humble servant.

And all through the day, Abe replayed the events of the night before in his mind. The heated interest in her normally wary green eyes. The simple compassion when she'd urged him to talk about Debra. And he'd wondered what it would be like.

With her.

He wondered what it would be like to see her solemn face smile every day, to hear her laugh, unfettered by worry. Then he wondered if he was being foolish, latching on to the first wholesome woman he'd come across since coming out from undercover. Kristen was a woman of integrity, intelligence. Beauty and grace. He'd met very few women with those qualities in the last five years. They didn't tend to hang around drug and weapons dealers.

He kept remembering the day he first saw her. He hadn't lied the night before. He had been stunned. Then captivated. Then aroused. Incredibly, unmistakably aroused. He'd stayed in the character of his cover that day, spouting innuendo and earning a few slaps on the back from his underworld accomplices. But the mental images hadn't faded, had stayed fixed in his mind as he'd completed the arrest that had been staged to give his cover credibility. He was one of them then, arrested, with a record. He'd been released on bail shortly thereafter and had returned to the dark, dirty part of the city his cover called home.

But as soon as he'd been able, he slipped away to see Debra in the hospice center, sitting by her bed, massaging her hands and feet, quietly speaking her name while mentally tormenting himself with guilty self-recriminations. He'd lusted after another woman while his wife lay in a silent hell.

Now, his wife was at peace, finally. And he still lusted after Kristen Mayhew.

It was with obvious regret that the waiter broke off their conversation to get back to his other customers. Kristen turned to him, then her green eyes widened and he realized what he was thinking must be written all over his face. For a moment he considered casually laughing it off. But her eyes slowly heated and a rosy blush darkened her cheeks. The tip of her tongue appeared, wetting her lips and Abe almost groaned aloud.

"I'm sorry," she said. "That was rude of me to ignore you. It's just been a long time since I've had a chance to use my Italian."

"Don't apologize. I enjoyed listening to you. I didn't know you spoke Italian."

She lifted one shoulder in a half shrug. "I spent a year in Italy when I was in college. I picked up a lot of conversational Italian, but I'm sure my grammar is atrocious. I know I'm rusty as hell." She picked up her menu, fidgeting with the corner. "You didn't have to take me to dinner, you know. Spinnelli has a cruiser stationed outside my house. I think I'll be all right on my own."

Something inside him stirred, hot and restless. "Did it occur to you that I might want to be with you? That my bringing you here has nothing to do with this case?"

She looked up and met his eyes. "Yes." Her voice had dropped, gone husky, sending tingles of sensation racing across his skin. "Yes, it did."

He swallowed hard. A thousand responses ran through his mind, all of them completely inappropriate and guaranteed to make her pull away.

"Ah, signorina."

Abe bit back a curse at the interruption as Kristen's face lifted to a beaming Tony Rossellini, the heart and soul of the restaurant and one of his parents' oldest friends. He made himself smile. "Tony, it's so good to see you."

Tony's eyes widened in surprise, and with amusement Abe realized the old man hadn't come by to see him. "Abe. Abe Reagan. My nephew did not tell me it was you with this beautiful signorina tonight. It is good to see you. Your parents were in just last week and never mentioned you were back in town."

It was the family's story, one they'd told to all their friends and even their own small children. Abe had moved to Los Angeles and came back only periodically for visits. As far as he knew, even Rachel believed it. It would have been too dangerous for one of the kids to inadvertently mention his true movements. He shot Kristen a look and saw she understood the subterfuge and would not expose it.

"Yes, sir. I'm back now, assigned to the Homicide Division. This is Kristen Mayhew."

Tony's wizened old face scrunched in concentration as he struggled to place the name, then his brows shot up his forehead when he did. "Ah. Well, we'll not speak of such things tonight. Tonight is not for work, but for play." He produced a bottle of red wine from behind his back. An excellent label, Abe could see at a glance. "My nephew told me only of a pretty lady who had spent a year in the beautiful city of my father and grandfather." With the skill of the well practiced, he whipped the cork from the bottle. "It has been some time since I have been to Firenze, but it is always in my heart." He set about filling their glasses with pride, and it was then Abe remembered Kristen didn't drink.

He opened his mouth to say something, but stopped, his entire body stiffening when he felt her hand slide across his. He looked at her and she shook her head, a minute movement meant only for him. Then her hand was gone and she lifted her glass to Tony in a toast. She spoke in Italian, and whatever she said made Tony beam even brighter. He responded in kind before turning to Abe with a great smile.

"Now that you are home you will come often, yes, Abe? And when you come, you will bring the signorina."

"I will." Whether Abe meant the first or both, he couldn't say. "Tony, we've been followed all day by reporters. If anyone comes in that looks suspicious, could you . . . ?"

Tony frowned. "Say no more, Abe. They will not bother you here." He went back to the kitchen, not waiting for a response.

Kristen carefully set the wineglass on the table and looked away. "A nice man."

"Mmm, yes. Tony is an old friend of my parents."

He tilted his head, willing her to look at him, but she didn't. His fingers itched to touch her, to slide across the table and cover her hand as she had his. But he didn't, instead lifting his own wineglass to his lips. "I thought you said you didn't drink."

"I don't, but I didn't want to insult him by denying his hospitality. I'll have a sip or two over the evening, and you'll be the only one to know."

And there it was again, her simple regard for the feelings of others. He thought of the look in her eyes the night before as she'd torn the sandpaper in two and handed him half. He'd seen compassion and understanding, but also something more. That something more had kept him awake most of the rest of the night.

"Kristen." He waited, but she kept her eyes steadily focused on a point across the restaurant. "You could have gone home at any point after Spinnelli assigned your shadow. Mia offered to drop you off on her way to meet her date. Why are you here with me?"

It was another long moment before she met his eyes, but when she did he saw both interest and a vulnerability that made his heart stutter even as his blood kindled. "Did it ever occur to you that I'm here because I wanted to be with you, too?" she asked quietly.

"I'd hoped," he answered honestly and her lips curved, so slightly he would have missed it had he not been staring. He covered her hand with his, feeling her quick flinch. But she didn't pull away and he took that as a positive sign. "Why Italy?"

She blinked, clearly not anticipating the question. "Excuse me?"

He slipped his thumb beneath her hand, sweeping back and forth against her palm in a gentle caress. She grew rigid, but still didn't pull away. "Why a year in Italy?"

Her eyes dropped to their joined hands. "I was studying in Florence."

"Art?"

She looked up, a little smile on her face, and his heart stuttered again. "Does anyone go to Florence to study anything else?"

"I thought you had an eye for color," he said. "So if you studied art in Florence, how did you end up a lawyer? Why aren't you painting or sculpting or whatever you studied?"

Her smile dimmed. "Life doesn't always end up the way you plan. But I suppose you know that, too."

That he did. "Yeah."

She visibly shook herself. "I'm being selfish here. You invite me to share a nice dinner and I go all maudlin on you. Let's talk about something else."

"Okay, something else." He tilted his head, scrutinizing her. "You surprised us this afternoon at the target range. You never told us you could shoot." But she could. He'd watched her standing in front of Diana Givens's glass counter methodically choosing her weapon, his mind thinking about how pleasurable it would be to show her the fundamentals of handling a firearm. How it would feel to put his arms around her, to feel her slender body against his. His body had responded instantly to the fantasy, leaving him almost relieved when she'd declined his and Mia's offers of help. Instead, she'd emptied the magazine into the paper target with speed and accuracy, leaving them all momentarily speechless. "You hit the chest cavity every time."

"I'm no sharpshooter, but I can hold my own with a tin can on a fence rail."

"So you lived on a farm in Kansas?" he asked, pulling together the scant details about her life she'd let drop over the last few days.

She shifted uncomfortably, but nodded. "My father had an old .38 we used to use for target practice."

She'd effectively sidestepped that question about the old

Mayhew family homestead. "So who got your father's gun when he died?"

Her expression chilled. "My father isn't dead."

Abe frowned. "But you said you don't have any family."

"Because I don't." Once again she drew a breath and visibly shook herself. "I'm sorry. There I go again. I'm just mad I have to wait three days to get my gun. The reality of gun laws hit me pretty squarely when I was filling out the paperwork."

"What do you mean?"

She grimaced. "Just that the guys I'm protecting myself against will have purchased theirs from a dealer that doesn't exactly comply with gun laws. They're armed while I wait."

"You probably could have the waiting period waived."

"And wouldn't that look just peachy in Zoe Richardson's report?" She shook her head. "I don't think so. No, I'll just keep a tire iron under my pillow until I get my permit."

He opened his mouth to say more, then closed it on a groan when the restaurant door opened. Kristen instantly sat up and pulled her hand back to her side of the table. "What?" she asked, twisting to look behind her, alarm on her face. "More reporters?"

"No, worse. My sister." It was true. Rachel came in with what appeared to be a busload of teenagers, and the volume in the restaurant became suddenly overwhelming.

That Rachel wouldn't see him was too much to hope. That she wouldn't recognize Kristen was just pipe dreaming. From across the restaurant he could see Rachel's eyes grow wide, and in less than a minute she was standing beside their table.

"Abe!" She leaned down and pecked his cheek. "I didn't know you were going to be here tonight. Did you ask her? Did you?"

Abe sighed. Rachel's request for an interview with Kristen for her school project. In all the activity it had simply slipped his mind. "No, Rach, we've been busy."

Rachel frowned her displeasure. "Then at least introduce me so I can. Please?"

Abe sighed, more heavily this time. "Kristen Mayhew, this is my youngest sister Rachel. Rachel, this is Assistant State's Attorney Mayhew."

Saturday, February 21, 7:30 P.M.

"He doesn't want to be disturbed."

Jacob Conti could hear the voice of his butler outside the door of his darkened office where a tenor's voice soared from the speakers to greet the final notes of his favorite aria. Normally he found this the most relaxing way to end the day, but today it was a farce. Angelo was missing, Elaine was in tears and Jacob knew what came next would be bad.

"He'll want to see me," Drake Edwards said.

No, I don't want to see you, Jacob thought. But he silenced the aria with the remote. "Let him in." He rose, furious that his legs trembled. He took one look at Drake's face and sank back down into his chair. His head of security looked grim.

"I'm sorry, Jacob," Drake said quietly. He brought a set of keys from his shirt pocket and Jacob instantly recognized the Northwestern emblem hanging from the chain. "We found the Corvette. Some kids say they found the keys on the front seat and were taking a joy ride."

"And Angelo?" Jacob's voice was hoarse.

Drake shook his head. "He was last seen at a bar off campus. His friends say he'd had a lot to drink, but he wouldn't let anybody call him a cab."

Stupid, stupid boy. "No, I guess he wouldn't. Not Angelo."

"Jacob, we . . ." Drake closed his eyes, his expression pained. "We found blood spattered on the driver's seat."

Jacob drew a breath. He'd have to tell Elaine. This would kill her. "I'll wait to tell Mrs. Conti until we're certain. Keep looking, Drake. And put men on Mayhew and those two detectives . . . Mitchell and Reagan. According to Richardson, the killer sends Mayhew letters. If Angelo's—" He forced the word from his mouth, "*hurt*, they'll know soon enough."

Drake nodded stiffly. This was hard on him, too, Jacob thought. Drake had been with him for a long time, long before he was Jacob Conti, wealthy Chicago industrialist. Drake had been his right-hand man since he was running two-bit cons on lonely old ladies and doing the dirty work of others on the side. Drake was family. He'd changed Angelo's diapers, taken him to the circus when he was just a kid. Drake's heart had to be breaking.

"I already put men on the three of them and their bosses and the Richardson woman," Drake said. "Jacob, try to get some rest. I won't stop until we find Angelo."

No, Drake wouldn't stop looking. Jacob knew it as well as he knew his own name. *But when he does find Angelo, will I still have a son?*

Chapter Thirteen

Saturday, February 21, 9:30 P.M.

With a wave to the cruiser, Reagan pulled into her driveway, his headlights illuminating another vehicle sitting under her carport. "Looks like you have company," he said.

"I don't think so." She never had company. Except for him. "I think the rental car company brought me another car." Kristen squinted to see the make and model in the darkness. "It's a Chevy." She glanced over to find him studying her, his expression as intense and expectant as it had been the whole way to her house. There had been an air of anticipation hovering between them that made her jumpy and wistfully anxious all at once. "Maybe it'll come with a global positioning system just like Skinner's."

The corner of Reagan's mouth lifted. "Couldn't hurt."

The silence between them grew heavy and still his eyes held hers. He was waiting. For what she wasn't sure. Yes, she was. Trouble was, she had no idea how to begin.

"Thank you," she said. "I had a good time." She really had. She'd met his sister and what seemed like four dozen of his sister's friends. The kids had been noisy and brash, but their youthful enthusiasm served to dissolve her depressed mood. They'd been curious about the case, which thanks to Rachel everyone knew about, and asked questions, most of them surprisingly pertinent. Rachel lapsed into an imitation of Zoe Richardson so irreverently funny that Kristen laughed until her ribs ached. Then the middle school crowd took over the other half of the restaurant, leaving Kristen and Reagan to talk in relative peace.

Reagan liked art, he told her, and they found they had

Impressionists in common. Music was a slightly different matter. He preferred seventies rock while she admitted owning every Bee Gees' album ever made, much to his disdain. She'd found Reagan's company utterly charming. And comfortable. And enticing.

Once again he'd held her hand. No one had simply held her hand in a very long time. It made her crave more. And that frightened her even as it beckoned.

"I'm sorry about my sister. She can be . . ."

"A teenager?" Kristen supplied and his smile flashed.

"Yeah, I suppose that's as good a word as any. You don't have to do her little interview tomorrow afternoon, Kristen. I know she bugged you into it."

Kristen shook her head. Rachel Reagan was quite the salesperson, she thought. One minute she was politely declining the girl's request for an interview and the next minute she was accepting an invitation to a Reagan Sunday dinner tomorrow afternoon. "It's okay." And she found it really was. "I don't mind." *In fact if I'm honest, I'm looking forward to it.* "Besides, I can use all the good press I can get."

Reagan grimaced. "Tony felt just terrible about that."

"It was bound to happen. It wasn't his fault the reporters were lying in wait outside. I just wish I knew when Richardson sleeps. She seems to be everywhere all the time."

"At least, the uniform in front of your house can keep her from bothering you here."

There was another heavy pause, and Kristen wished she was comfortable with the social words. She wished she could invite him in for tea without making it seem like a big deal. Even though it would be. Her skin still tingled from the sweep of his thumb across her palm. And she wanted him to do it again. She blew out a hard breath.

"I'm no good at this."

One dark brow lifted, giving him a rakish look. "At what?"

Kristen rolled her eyes. "Do you want to come in for a cup of tea or not?"

His eyes gleamed in the darkness and her heart thumped as she waited for his answer. "Yes, I do," he said huskily, and she had the definite impression he was talking about more than tea. "I need to talk to your uniform down on the street. I'll be right back."

He slammed the door, leaving her in the dark with her thoughts.

He's going to kiss you, Kristen. You stupid idiot. Now he'll know.

She wasn't that naive. Yes, he'd try to kiss her. Nor was she a woman to deny the inevitable. Yes, he'd know. With a man like Reagan, all it would take would be one single kiss to expose her. *So he'll know. So what? Maybe he won't care.*

Hah, she ridiculed herself. *You really* are *stupid. All men care.*

She sighed. Even a nice man like Abe Reagan would want what she couldn't deliver. After one kiss, he'd realize she was too cold . . . Too frigid to give him what he needed, wanted. He'd quickly conclude this wouldn't work, and though he'd try to be kind about it, they'd quickly find themselves back in a purely professional relationship. Which was better. The sooner they caught this killer, the sooner Reagan would be gone and she'd have her life back to normal. *Normal is lonely. Normal is all you'll ever have. Get over it.*

He opened her car door, letting the cold air rush in, a fitting end to the lecture she'd given herself. She looked up at him bleakly. "Any action while I was gone today?"

"No. Charlie Truman's assigned to night shift. He's a

good cop, friend of my brother. You'll be safe with him outside. And remember McIntyre, the guy who took your statement last night? He's got day shift. You should see him tomorrow morning." He frowned. "Kristen, what's wrong?"

"Nothing."

In silence he helped her down, opened her kitchen door and flicked on the lights while she disabled the alarm. "I'll take a rain check on the tea," he said quietly. "You must be tired."

"No." The word exploded from her lips, surprising them both. She drew a breath and unbuttoned her coat. *Let's just get this over with.* "No, stay. Please." She tossed off her coat and busied herself with the teapot, listening to the rustle of his coat hitting a chair, cursing the trembling of her hands when half a spoonful of tea ended up on the counter.

"Kristen." His voice came from behind her. Deep and rumbly and soothing. "It's all right."

No, it's not all right. She dropped her chin to her chest. "Maybe you were right. I am tired." *I am so not good at this.*

She flinched when his hands covered her shoulders, but his hands didn't force, they soothed, massaging her shoulders in wide circles that made her want to sigh and beg him never to stop. He slipped her jacket from her shoulders before returning to his task and she could feel the heat of his hands through her blouse as her body slowly began to relax.

You are so good at this, she thought.

"Thank you," he said and she realized she'd voiced her thoughts aloud. His voice had gone deeper, huskier, and a hard shiver racked her body, head to toe. For just a moment his hands tightened on her shoulders, then let go, moving up to the back of her neck. His thumbs pressed the taut cords on either side of her neck and her knees went weak. One strong arm came around, catching her just under her breasts and . . . she let him. Let him support her. Let him pull her against his body.

His very hard body. Hard in all the wrong places. She jerked forward, putting distance between them, suddenly tense again. Without a word he released his hold, moving his hands to her shoulders, starting all over again. *Gentling me,* she thought.

"Um-hm," he murmured and again she knew she'd spoken aloud. "And me," he added.

"You?"

"You're not the only one who's nervous here, Kristen."

She looked up at him over her shoulder. His face was stark, almost grim. "Why?" It came out a whisper and his hands stilled, and for a moment he said nothing.

Then he whispered back, "Because you say you have no family when your father is still alive, and you say you studied art in Florence, but I don't see anything in this house that you've painted. Because you said that victims never, ever forget. Because someone hurt you, and I'm terrified I'll do something to make you think I'd hurt you, too. Because I won't."

But he would. Her heart cracked as she acknowledged the fact inside. Outside, she nodded. "I know." Because he wouldn't mean to. And perhaps because some tiny part of her still wished with all her might that his words would be true.

His eyes bored into hers. "Do you?" His hands smoothed over her hair and she felt him feel for, then tug a pin from her hair. It clattered to the counter and he pulled out another.

"What are you doing?" her voice was low-pitched, raspy.

"Taking down your hair. These pins have driven me crazy all day." It was a low murmur and sent a new hard shiver racing through her body. His eyes flashed and he pulled out more pins. Her hair sprang free and his hands delved deep, his fingers scraping gently across her scalp. On a low moan her eyes slid shut and every bit of oxygen left her lungs. His hands felt so good, so absolutely necessary.

She'd been driving him crazy. The thought was nearly enough to make her giddy.

One hand slipped from her hair to bracket her jaw and his thumb swept across her cheek, much as it had her palm earlier. She opened her eyes with difficulty, feeling almost drowsy with pleasure. His face was closer now, much closer.

His lips brushed her temple and she stopped, simply stopped breathing.

"There's one more reason I'm scared," he murmured, his breath hot against her skin.

"What?" She mouthed the word, but her voice never emerged.

"I wanted you the first time I saw you. I want you now." His whispered admission shook her, shocked her. She should be afraid, terrified.

But I'm not. Instead she was tempted. Then his lips were on her cheek, scant inches from her mouth. So tempted. All she had to do was turn her head a little bit and his mouth would be on hers. And she wanted to. Wanted to feel the heat of his mouth, to know how it felt to be kissed by a man like him. "Abe."

He abruptly stilled. "Say it again," he demanded. "Say my name again."

She swallowed hard and somehow found her voice. "Abe."

He shuddered and the vibration of his body found its way into hers. Sharp little tingles singed her skin, sinking deep, making her yearn for more. Then all thought fled when he moved his head, closing those scant few inches to her lips. His mouth covered hers, hard and soft at the same time, impossibly hot. And she wanted more. She turned her body toward his and in one hard beat of her heart his arms were around her, hands splayed against her back, burning her skin. He slanted his head, deepening the kiss and her arms lifted, her forearms resting on the solid rock of his chest. His hands gently grasped her wrists, urging her arms up and around his neck. Then his hands were on her back again, his fingers pressing hard into her flesh, urgent. Desperate.

And the kiss went on and on and on.

Abruptly he broke it off. Disappointment crashed over her in a wave until he took one of her hands and placed it over his heart. Feeling the wild thunder under her palm, she looked up and knew as long as she lived, whatever happened in the next day, in the next minute that she'd never forget the way he was looking at her. *Like he can't get enough of me.*

"I can't." His eyes blazed, blue as the core of a flame and she knew she'd once again voiced her thoughts, but embarrassment was the farthest emotion from her mind. "Feel what you do to me, Kristen. Please, don't be afraid."

"I'm not." *I'm really not.* To prove it to him, and perhaps to herself, she pulled his head down for another kiss, this one shorter, but hers. Then pulled back to find him smiling and her heart took a great leap, then tumbled. There was such sweetness in his smile, such ease, such relief. She felt her own lips curve in response.

"I'm glad," he said.

"So am I."

"I have to go."

Startled, Kristen widened her eyes. "Why?"

His smile became rueful. "Because I want to do a hell of a lot more than kiss you."

Her breath caught in her throat at the image his words conveyed. It was more than she'd expected, more than she'd planned. "Abe, I—"

He pressed his fingertips to her lips. "It's okay, Kristen. I can wait."

She kissed his fingertips and his eyes heated. *I can make this man . . . burn.* And she had. She'd felt it in the brief brush of his body against hers as they'd kissed. He'd been aroused. But he hadn't pressed. Hadn't pushed. Hadn't thrust himself on her . . . Hurting her . . . And dammit, she was back *there,* twenty years old and scared out of her mind. *Be still. Don't fight me. You damn tease, you wanted this.* The ground was hard and the night was hot and the Ferris wheel went round and round, the lights bright and—

No, no, no. She closed her eyes, drew a breath, and made the memory stop. When she looked up, she could see that he knew. He understood. And he wasn't running away.

"One day at a time, Kristen," he murmured. "That's what we'll do."

We. Tears stung her eyes and she blinked them back. "Why do you care?"

He smiled so gently it made her heart want to break. "Because I like you. Now I'm going to kiss you good night because I have to go." He did, a hard stamp of possession. "Be ready tomorrow at four for dinner. Until then, don't leave the house without Truman, McIntyre, Mia, or me."

Sunday, February 22, 9:00 A.M.

It was too cold for many people to be out, but Abe could hear the rhythmic pounding of basketballs and knew someone in the neighborhood stirred. Hopefully they'd have more success finding the kid who'd dropped the Skinner box on Kristen's doorstep today than they had yesterday. If anybody knew this kid, nobody was telling. They might have to wait until tomorrow when school was open and ask the faculty if they knew the kid in their picture.

Mia was leaning up against her car, concentrating on tearing the tab off the plastic lid of her coffee cup. She gestured to a second steaming cup sitting on her hood. "Yours."

Abe took the coffee, grunting his thanks.

Mia shot him a deadpan look. "My, aren't we chipper this morning?"

"I didn't sleep well last night."

"Why not?"

Abe grimaced. *Because every time I closed my eyes I dreamed of kissing Kristen until she couldn't remember her own name, until whatever was done to hurt her was forced out of her mind, until she begged me for more.* The dreams had left him hard and aching and lonely. "Just this case catching up with me, I guess. Let's get started. I want to find this kid soon. I have dinner at my mother's tonight."

Mia brightened. "Will you save me some leftovers?"

Abe chuckled. "Let's go, Mia."

They followed the sound of the bouncing balls to the court across the street from King High School, the name that was clearly seen on the jacket the kid wore in the picture. Five young boys were on the blacktop. All five stopped when they saw them coming.

"Cops," Abe heard one of them hiss.

"Snoopin' around here yesterday," another muttered.

Abe held out his badge. "I'm Detective Reagan and this is Detective Mitchell. We're looking for a kid who goes to King High. Any of you kids go to King?"

The five looked at one another. They all looked to be

about sixteen. *Not too much younger than the punk that shot Debra.* "I asked you a question," Abe said, his voice going harder. "Do you go to King?"

They all nodded unwillingly.

Mia drew the picture from her pocket. "We're looking for this kid. If we don't find him today, we'll find him tomorrow when school's open. If you say today you don't know him and we find out later you did . . ." She let the thought trail off suggestively. "It'll be better for you guys if you help us out."

As a group they scowled at each other, and more mutters filled the air. But they looked at the picture, then again at each other.

"You know him," Mia said.

One of the boys nodded. "Yeah, we seen him around."

Abe looked down at the young boy who cradled a basketball under one arm. The young boy stared back, defiantly. "He didn't do nothing wrong."

"We didn't say he did," Mia said quietly. "Now, where can we find him?"

The boys looked down at their feet. "Don't know."

Abe sighed. "Okay, boys, everybody against the fence. We're going to call in a couple of cruisers to take you downtown."

The boy with the ball stomped. "We didn't do nothin'. Why we gotta go downtown?"

Mia shrugged, her cell phone in her hand. "You're material witnesses in a murder investigation. Don't you guys watch *Cops*?"

"Damn," one of the others whined. "My momma's gonna kill me if I go downtown again."

Abe kept his voice stern. "Then tell us where to find this guy and we'll go away."

The boy with the ball scowled. "His name's Aaron

Jenkins. Doesn't even go to King anymore. Lives three blocks up." He pointed a skinny finger. "That way."

"There's a lot of buildings three blocks up 'that way.' " Mia pointed in the same direction the boy had. "A little more information would be right friendly-like," she added, her expression sarcastic and dry.

The boy's scowl deepened. "It's the only building on that block with a green stoop. Old lady sits there all damn day, spyin' on us."

"Wears a poky-dotted cap, can't miss her," another added, rolling his eyes. "She's got the evil eye, y'know?"

Mia's mouth quirked up. "Thanks," she said, then held out her hand to the boy with the ball. "Can I?"

Clearly he didn't believe she could make it. He pushed her the ball and she caught it with one hand. Then from well into three-point range, she closed one eye and sent the ball sailing right through the hoop. The boys stood open-mouthed and Mia just grinned. "Stay outta trouble, boys, okay? I'd hate to take you downtown for real."

Abe could hear their exclamations as they walked away. "Where did you learn to play?"

"My dad." Mia shrugged. "He wanted sons and all he got was daughters."

Abe thought that was pretty sad, but let it go. They walked in the direction the boys had indicated, Abe remembering the cold look in Kristen's eyes the night before when she'd revealed her father was still alive and thought the trouble between Kristen and her father was a lot more complicated than a father who really wanted a son.

"Green stoop, old lady with the evil eye . . ." Mia muttered as they came up to the building, where sure enough an old lady with a polka-dotted cap sat eyeing them suspiciously. Even Mia's best smile did nothing to sweeten the old lady's grimace.

"This looks like the place," Abe agreed. "Let's cross our fingers Aaron Jenkins is home."

They found the Jenkins apartment and knocked. A woman holding a toddler on one hip opened the door and her eyes widened at the sight of them. "What is it?"

"We're looking for a young man named Aaron Jenkins, ma'am," Mia said politely.

The woman shifted the baby on her hip. "He's my son. Why? Is Aaron in trouble?"

Mia shook her head. "We just want to talk to him."

She looked over her shoulder uncertainly. "My husband is at work."

"This will only take a few minutes," Abe reassured her. "Then we'll be on our way."

"Aaron!" she called and the young man in the photo appeared from one of the bedrooms. He took one look at them and started to move backward.

"We only want to talk to you," Mia said and he paused.

"I didn't do nothin'."

"Aaron," his mother snapped. "Get over here." Feet dragging, he complied.

"You delivered a package Friday afternoon," Abe said.

Aaron frowned. "So what? I didn't do nothin' illegal."

"We didn't say you did. Where'd you get the package, Aaron?" Mia asked.

"From some white guy. He gave me a hundred bucks to deliver the box."

"What did he look like?" Abe asked.

Aaron shrugged. "I don' know. He had a jacket with a hood, so I couldn't see his face."

"Was he old? Young?" Mia pressed.

Aaron huffed impatiently. "I said he was wearin' a hood. I couldn't see his face."

"Was he in a car?" Abe asked.

"Nope, a van. A white one. Had a sign on the side. Had a little plug on it."

Abe frowned. "A plug?"

"Yeah, like you plug in the wall. Had a cute little happy face on it. The sign said . . . Banner Electronics." Aaron nodded, pleased with himself. "That's all I know."

Abe frowned harder. It wasn't the same van. Mia looked up at Abe, troubled. Then she turned her attention back to Aaron. "How did you know where to deliver the box?"

Aaron shrugged. "He gave me the address, then told me to tear it up, so I did. Listen, that's all I know." He looked at his mother. "Can I go now?"

Mrs. Jenkins jiggled the baby on her hip. "Can he?"

Mia nodded. "Yeah, sure." She was quiet until they'd reached the street. "That equipment that sandblasts stone? It can also make rubber signs."

"Magnetized to stick on a van." Abe blew a breath up his forehead. "Dammit."

Mia rolled her eyes. "I spent hours looking at florists. He's no florist. That's why Jack didn't find any flowers or pollen in the van. He can be anything he wants to be. Shit."

Abe's cell phone trilled. A look at the caller ID had the hairs rising on the back of his neck. "What's wrong, Kristen?"

Kristen's voice was shaky. "I got another box, Abe. McIntyre's caught the boy who dropped it off. He's holding him until you get here."

"We'll be right there," Abe said grimly, then turned to Mia. "Call Jack and tell him to meet us at Kristen's. I'll give Spinnelli the heads up. Our humble servant's hit again."

Sunday, February 22, 10:00 A.M.

"Oh, my God." Kristen's face drained of color as Jack slid the contents of the envelope onto her kitchen table. "It's Angelo Conti."

Mia put a comforting arm around her shoulders. "Don't faint on us now."

"I never faint."

Abe remembered she'd said the same thing the night they met at the elevator, after he'd scared her nearly senseless. But she'd shown them she was made of sterner stuff and Abe felt pride at her strength. Keeping his distance was costing him, but he knew she wanted to maintain her professional persona. Her hair was neatly tucked and pinned, although the pins he'd removed the night before were still scattered on the countertop where he'd left them.

"There aren't any Polaroids," Jack commented. "Just Conti's student ID card from Northwestern University. Why?"

"I don't know." Abe reached for the letter. " 'My dearest Kristen. Angelo Conti is dead. His crime was initially one of depraved indifference, crashing into Paula Garcia's car while intoxicated. But his blatant disregard for human life led him to beat the poor woman to death. His father's blatant disregard for the United States legal system caused Jacob Conti to taint the jury. Angelo Conti walked away a free man, at least until you would have tried him again. But if his original crimes weren't enough, he compounded them by publicly assassinating your character, and that could not be allowed. I hope his death is a signal to all who would make a mockery of the judicial system and its servants. As always, I remain Your Humble Servant.' "

Abe looked up to find Kristen gingerly lowering herself into a chair. "What's the P.S.?"

"It's a license plate number." Abe passed her the letter and her brows knit in confusion.

"It's not mine," she said. "That doesn't make any sense."

"I think we need to talk to the delivery boy," Mia said and Abe nodded.

He and Mia went out to McIntyre's cruiser where the boy waited in the backseat.

"His name is Tyrone Yates," McIntyre offered. "His parents are on their way."

"I didn't do nothin'," Yates growled.

"We didn't say you did," Mia growled back. Yates provided a story almost identical to the one told by Aaron Jenkins. Except this time the white van bore the name of a carpet store. By the time the boy was done, his parents had arrived to take him home.

Kristen was making tea when Abe and Mia came back in, followed by McIntyre. Mia dropped into a chair while Abe paced to the one window that looked out over the frozen backyard. McIntyre just stood in the kitchen doorway, his young face troubled.

"What did you find?" Kristen asked.

Abe tossed a frustrated look over his shoulder. "Not a whole hell of a lot."

McIntyre shifted uneasily. "About the white van—"

"The florist van?" Kristen asked and Mia shook her head.

"We think he uses different magnetic signs," she said. "The kid from King High swears it was an electrical contractor's van. This last kid says it was a carpet installer."

"That's why I didn't find any evidence of flowers or pollen on the crates," Jack said angrily, smacking the table. "Dammit. He can change the van at will."

Abe turned from the window, his face sober. "What about the white van, McIntyre?"

"The night Miss Mayhew was run off the road, I was moving traffic along. People stop to gawk, you know. One of the vehicles was a white van with an electrical contractor's sign."

Kristen's stomach churned. She knew what the P.S. meant now. She grabbed the letter on the table and showed it to McIntyre. "Do you recognize this number, Officer?"

McIntyre nodded. "That's the car that hit you. It had been stolen earlier that day."

Kristen set the letter on the table, her hands surprisingly steady. "I thought so."

Jack hissed a curse. "He was there."

Abe chuckled mirthlessly. "I was probably close enough to touch him. Do you remember what he looked like, McIntyre?"

McIntyre shook his head. "He had on one of those hats with the earflaps. Covered up most of his face. It was so cold that night, I didn't think anything about it. He was very polite, I remember that."

"Age?" Mia asked sharply.

McIntyre shrugged helplessly. "I don't know. Maybe forty? He didn't say much of anything, just nodded when I asked him to move along. I just figured he was embarrassed to be caught staring."

Nobody said anything for a long moment, then Jack stood up. "I've got to call my team to the spot on this map. And I'll call Julia to meet us there. You guys coming?"

"Wouldn't miss it," Abe said grimly. "Let's go."

Kristen started to follow, but Abe stopped her. "Stay here. Please."

"I want to be there," she said in a low voice, conscious of the others watching.

Abe looked at Jack, Mia, and McIntyre. "Give us a minute, okay?"

McIntyre bowed out instantly. "Got to get back on watch."

Mia raised her brows, eyeing them with open curiosity. "Okay."

Kristen felt her cheeks burn. "Reagan, please."

Jack gave her a hard look. "He's right. You've already had one accident this weekend. I don't want to see you get hurt." Then he followed Mia from the kitchen, leaving them alone.

Abe looked down at her with conviction. "Stay here."

Kristen felt frustration simmer. "Don't shut me out. Please. I need to be there."

His hands rose to cover her shoulders, kneading convulsively. "Do you know what will happen when Jacob Conti finds out his son has been murdered?" His blue eyes flashed. "Do you, Kristen? If you're at the site and the press shows up, your face will be all over the news, especially if it comes out that Angelo was killed because he verbally attacked you. Conti will strike out at you, and he isn't someone you want after you. Please, stay here for me."

His eyes were compelling, but in the end it was the emotion in his voice that won her acquiescence. "All right. I'll stay here."

His relief tangible, his hands loosened their grip. "I'll be back to get you for dinner."

"At four."

He leaned down and covered her lips with his in a hard kiss that left her mind reeling. "Call me if you need me."

Kristen sighed at the sound of her front door slamming. She'd become accustomed to doing just that. Calling him when she needed him. And in a flash of clarity his sister-in-law's words made sense. Ruth said Abe needed to take care of her. It didn't take a psychiatrist to pull the pieces together. Abe Reagan had watched his wife shot and had been able to do nothing. He, a man paid to keep the public safe, had not been able to keep his own wife alive.

Now he's keeping me safe. And even as the thought brought comfort, she wondered what would happen when this whole nightmare was over and she no longer needed to be kept safe any more. She pressed her fingertips to her mouth, still tender from his hard kiss.

I'll take what I can get and be grateful while it lasts. But for right now, there was a pile of half-sewn curtains she needed to finish.

Sunday, February 22, 11:30 A.M.

The spot that "x" marked was a patch of ground fifty yards from the spot Angelo Conti's car had struck Paula Garcia's. Appropriate. They found a marble marker inscribed with the names of Paula Garcia and her unborn son. Abe's eyes stung as he looked at the names, feeling an empathy for Thomas Garcia that the others couldn't possibly understand. Heavy silence hung over the grave, broken only by the clang of shovels and an occasional word from one of Jack's men.

"Ugh." Mia's face twisted in disgust as Jack's team brushed the dirt away from Conti's face. What was left of it, anyway.

Julia grimaced. "Your boy lost it this time."

The body was brought out of the shallow hole with care. Abe turned it gently, displaying a pattern of bruises across the lower back. "Tire iron?"

Julia knelt beside him. "Probably. I'll have a better idea once I've cleaned him up."

"Conti used a tire iron on Garcia," Mia said. "That part wasn't made public."

"More insider information," Abe muttered. "Wonderful."

Julia was looking over the body, her brow furrowed in concern. "He went off on Conti, Abe. I haven't seen a beating like this in a long time. Is he still watching Kristen?"

Abe's lips thinned. "Yeah. And we still have nothing."

Julia shrugged, her sigh vaporizing in the cold air. "Look on the bright side. He lost control. Maybe he wasn't so careful about physical evidence he left behind." She gave a nod to her assistant who efficiently loaded the body into a bag and zipped it closed. "I finished the autopsy on Skinner last night. I found blood in his lungs."

Mia huffed in frustration. "So it was like we thought."

Julia nodded. "I got pictures of the depressions in Skinner's skull to Jack this morning. He's trying to match them up with the particular model of the vise. Skinner's knees were shattered just like King's, and the bullet hole to the head was postmortem." She pulled off her rubber gloves and pulled on warm leather ones. "Oh, and I was able to make a plaster cast of the ligature marks on Ramey's throat. Jack's got that, too."

"Good work, Julia," Abe praised.

"Thanks. Just find this guy before he can send me any more business. I've got a date tonight with a three-year-old who doesn't understand why Mommy has to cancel to cut up dead people." With a little wave she headed off.

Abe turned to Mia. "She's got a kid?"

"A real cutie. Her husband left and she's been a struggling single mom ever since."

"That's tough." Abe looked over at Jack, who was watching Julia giving instructions to her assistants as they loaded the body bag into the ME's van. "And how does Jack factor in?"

"He doesn't." Mia rolled her eyes. "It's totally one-sided." Her expression went sly. "Although I can't say the same for someone else."

To his own consternation, Abe felt his cheeks burn. "That's enough, Mia. Let's get some pictures of this scene. I—"

He was interrupted by a cry of alarm and spun around to see Julia being shoved against her car by a man with silver hair. "Shit," he hissed, taking off at a run. "It's Jacob Conti."

Jack was faster and was pulling Conti off Julia as Abe reached the car, Mia at his heels. "Get your hands off her," Jack snarled and Abe stepped between them.

"Cool it, Jack," Abe muttered and Jack stepped back, rage still making him shake. Abe turned to Conti, who stared at him with wild eyes. "This is a crime scene, Mr. Conti. I'm afraid I'll have to ask you to step back."

"It's his son, dammit." Another man stepped up, large and menacing.

Mia pulled out her notepad. "And you are, sir?"

"Drake Edwards. I'm Mr. Conti's head of security. We want to see Angelo."

Mia drew a breath. "We planned to inform you of your son's death under other circumstances, Mr. Conti. Right now, I think it's best that you don't see him."

Conti closed his eyes, his body sagging, and Drake Edwards put an arm around his shoulders for support. "Then it's true?" Edwards murmured. "It is Angelo?"

Mia nodded. "Yes, sir. We believe so."

Conti's eyes flew open. "You *believe* so? Why don't you *know* so? You—" His eyes widened further as the horror of reality struck him. "He did something to his face. You didn't even recognize him." He lunged for the door of the ME van, but Edwards held him back, murmuring something in his ear that made Conti stop and visibly fight for control. It was a fascinating transformation. A moment later, a composed Conti turned to a still-ashen Julia and asked coolly, "When can we have his body? His mother will want to bury him."

"When the ME is finished," Jack snapped, but Julia put a hand on his arm.

"I'll do my best to complete my investigation with all speed, Mr. Conti," she said, her voice slightly trembling. "I'm very sorry for your loss."

Conti nodded stiffly and turned away, still supported by his head of security.

"How did he know?" Julia asked shakily. "How did he know it was Angelo?"

As Conti's limo rolled away, Abe's gaze fell on Zoe Richardson and her cameraman standing in the background, catching it all on tape. Without a moment's hesitation she approached, her damn microphone in her hand.

"Our own little bird," Julia said quietly.

"Our bird's a vulture," Abe responded caustically.

"Bitch," Jack snarled.

"God, she's cold," Mia marveled.

Abe stepped forward, his gut churning with rage he knew he had to suppress. This woman had systematically moved events from bad to worse. "Miss Richardson, I'm afraid I'll have to ask you to move along. This is a crime scene and you're not allowed here."

She ignored him. "Dr. VanderBeck, were you hurt by Mr. Conti's attack?"

Julia gaped at Richardson as if she had three heads.

"No comment," Mia snapped and stepped in front of the camera. "You'll leave now, Miss Richardson, or I'll arrest you for interfering with our investigation."

"But—"

"*Now*." Mia reached for her cuffs and the cameraman lowered his camera.

"We're going," he said, glancing at Richardson from the corner of his eye.

Richardson looked furious. "We're staying. You're the ones interfering with my First Amendment rights. The people have a right to the news."

"I said we're going," said the cameraman and Zoe slowly turned, shock slackening her normally perfect features.

"I think you're going," Abe said dryly.

Richardson looked at him, venom in her eyes. "By the way, where is Mayhew?"

"Out of your reach. Unless you'd like to surrender another tape, you should follow your cameraman's direction." He watched her stomp away. "I really hate that woman."

Julia straightened her coat. "I can see why. I'm going to the morgue where it's quiet. I'll call you if I find anything." She looked up at Jack. "Thank you," she said softly and drove away, leaving Jack red-faced.

"Maybe not so one-sided after all," Mia muttered with a grin. "When it rains it pours."

Chapter Fourteen

Sunday, February 22, 5:30 P.M.

Sunday dinner at the Reagans' was like being in the middle of a Kansas twister. Two televisions competed for mastery, a set in the living room tuned to some sport that had all the men present groaning in disgust. The second set was located in Mrs. Reagan's kitchen and was tuned to QVC where their stock of pearl strands was almost gone. Mrs. Reagan herself bustled around the kitchen, mashing potatoes and checking her ham. Every peek into the oven sent a whiff of incredible aroma through the kitchen and Kristen's stomach growled.

"It smells so good," Kristen said, sitting next to Rachel at the kitchen table where Rachel had laid a set of books and a small tape recorder in a semicircle.

"Mom is the best cook. All my friends think so." She flipped her notebook to a blank sheet. "Thanks for doing this interview with me. My mom says I shouldn't be bothering you. What with all the goings-on and everything."

"It's okay. I was going crazy sitting all by myself in my house anyway." A loud roar erupted from the living room. "I thought football season was over."

Rachel leaned back in her chair far enough to see around the corner into the living room. "It is. Right now they have a hockey game and a college basketball game going. Sean bought Dad one of those picture-in-a-picture TVs last Christmas." Her lips quirked up in adolescent amusement. "Mom was so pissed. So, do you mind if I tape this?"

"You really think you'll be able to hear anything you record?"

"Sure. I grew up in this house. I've developed excellent listening and not-listening skills." Rachel flipped on the recorder. "This is an interview with Assistant State's Attorney Kristen Mayhew. Can you start by telling us why you chose the law as your profession?"

Kristen opened her mouth, prepared to spout the response she always used. The one that wasn't nearly the truth. But something in Rachel Reagan's blue eyes stopped her. "I didn't, not at first," she said honestly. "I'd planned to

study art. I even had an art scholarship. But in my sophomore year someone I was very close to was the victim of a
serious crime."

Rachel's eyes grew wide. "Who?"

"I'd rather not say. She has the expectation of privacy,
you know? Anyway, the person who perpetrated the crime
was never punished and I didn't think that was fair."

"So you became a lawyer to make a difference?"

Kristen focused on the girl's earnest expression. Rachel
Reagan reminded her of herself, so many years ago. "I'd
like to think so."

Rachel had a whole list of questions. Kristen answered
each one, following Becca's movements around the kitchen,
remembering her own mother doing the same, the memories
bittersweet. Becca was rolling dough when the back door
opened and a man wearing a Bears sweatshirt and faded
jeans walked in, as tall and dark as Abe. Fondly, he dropped
a kiss on Becca's cheek and Kristen knew without asking
that this was Abe's other brother. She'd met Sean when
they'd arrived, so this could be none other than—

"Aidan!" Rachel dropped her pen. "We thought you
weren't coming."

Aidan had a CPD uniform on a hanger slung over his
shoulder. "I had to switch some shifts, but I didn't want to
miss ham." He plopped his hat on Rachel's head and gave
the brim a tug so that it covered her eyes. "What's new,
squirt?"

Rachel adjusted the hat so she could see. "I'm doing my
homework."

Aidan's gaze shifted to Kristen and she could feel his
cold blue eyes critically assessing her. "So I see," he said.
"You're ASA Mayhew."

Kristen wasn't sure he considered that a good thing, but
stuck out her hand. "Kristen."

He shook it. "Aidan." His eyes, so like Abe's, narrowed. "Why are you here?"

"Aidan." Becca's mouth bent in a disapproving frown. "What's gotten into you?"

"I'm sorry," Aidan replied, but it was clear from the taut clench of his jaw and his expression of disdain that he was anything but.

"Aidan."

Kristen turned instinctively to the sound of Abe's voice behind her. He filled the doorway to the living room and just the sight of him made her breath catch, made her lips tingle anew from the kiss he'd given her on returning from Angelo Conti's grave. He still wore a suit, but his tie was loosened and his shirt unbuttoned, revealing a strong throat and just the hint of dense chest hair. He stepped forward, a cautious look in his eye. "What's wrong?"

Aidan looked at Abe, then back at Kristen, disbelief mixing in with the disdain and Kristen wondered if she wore the fragile relationship with Abe on her chest like a scarlet letter. "No way," Aidan spat.

Rachel perked up. "No way what?"

"Be quiet, Rachel," Aidan snapped. "Tell me it isn't true, Abe."

Abe considered him evenly. "You've never been impolite to a guest. What happened?"

"Oh, nothing. Just that my partner and three other cops in our precinct got called into IA yesterday. Seems the SA's office is investigating cops for the murders of those lowlifes that deserved to be fried the first time around." Aidan glared at Kristen. "They're good men and good cops who wouldn't murder any man, even ones you guys were too inept to keep in jail."

Kristen wanted to deny it, but a look from Abe had her closing her mouth tightly.

"And now you have the nerve to bring her *here?*" Aidan sneered. "I'm gone."

"Don't you move one inch." Becca inserted herself between the brothers. "You aren't going anywhere, Aidan. Not until you've first apologized to Rachel's guest."

Aidan's eyes widened and he looked at Abe. "I thought—"

Abe's lips twitched. "I guess she's technically Rachel's guest." He let Aidan stew a moment, then added, "But next time she'll be mine."

Delighted, Becca and Rachel stared at Kristen, whose cheeks heated. Deliberately she ignored them and looked up at Aidan. "I'm sorry your friends were hassled, but anybody who's had any contact with those cases has had to account for their whereabouts on the nights of the murders. Everybody in the SA's office is getting questioned, even me. If they have alibis, we'll take them off the list. If not, they'll have to stay there a little longer." She lifted her hands, let them fall. "I'm sorry. I really am."

Aidan hesitated, then inclined his head in a single nod. "All right then."

"If we make her eat out on the back porch, can she stay for dinner?" Rachel asked dryly.

Aidan rolled his eyes. "Give me my hat, you smart-ass."

"Aidan!" Becca snapped. "Don't curse in my kitchen."

"Go in the living room and curse with Dad," Rachel said with a grin and after a moment Aidan grinned back, quickly checking the grin when his eyes met Kristen's.

"I'm sorry," he said quietly. "My partner was very upset after being called into IA. We're all afraid this is going to turn into a witch-hunt."

"Not on my watch," Kristen vowed and Aidan pursed his lips, considering.

"All right then." He lifted one black brow. "I guess you can stay."

Sunday, February 22, 8:00 P.M.

She'd held her own, Abe thought proudly. Kristen had survived a Sunday dinner with the Reagans. The ham was culinary history and everyone who remained gathered in the living room to watch a movie, so like old times it made his throat thicken. Sean sat on the sofa, while Ruth sat on the floor with their new baby, her back up against Sean's knees. For a long time after Debra's death Abe hadn't been able to watch Sean and Ruth together. It wasn't just that Ruth looked so much like Debra, because she did. They'd been cousins after all, their mothers were sisters. It was more the happiness Sean and Ruth exuded every time they were in the same room that was the hardest to bear. But over the years, Abe had become accustomed to the sharp pang of loss. It was a given. Just one of those things. Seeing Sean and Ruth together made his heart hurt.

Until today. Today he hadn't been alone. Today he'd brought Kristen to his family and she'd melded right in, as if she'd known them all her life. Now she and Rachel sat on the love seat watching the Steve Martin comedy Sean had rented. From his seat on the couch Abe could watch her face as she truly relaxed for the first time in five days.

She was intent on the movie when Rachel leaned over and whispered something in her ear. It must have been classic Rachel, irreverent and funny, because Kristen threw back her head and laughed that wonderful husky laugh that made him feel like he'd taken a kick to the gut. Looking back, he should have known he wouldn't be the only one to feel that way. Ruth twisted to stare, her face slack with shock. His parents also turned, pained.

Abe wanted to put the whole scene on freeze-frame and whisk Kristen out of the room before she noticed the family's reaction. But of course it was too late for that. Her smile at Rachel's witticism disappeared like mist in sunlight.

Her green eyes shot to his, wary once more. "What?" she asked.

"My God," Ruth breathed, then shook her head hard. "I'm so sorry, Kristen, I didn't mean to be rude, but . . . you sounded like someone I once knew."

Kristen grew very still, her eyes still on Abe's. "Debra?"

He'd seen fear and courage in her eyes, vulnerability and sadness. Now he saw hurt as she jumped to her own conclusions and it sliced at him like a knife. "Kristen—"

She held up her hand, a smile on her lips. "It's okay." But he could see it wasn't. She turned back to the television. "Can we rewind a bit, Sean? We missed the last minute or two."

Sean complied. Ruth sent Abe a silent message of acute apology. The movie went on, but Steve Martin just didn't seem as funny after that.

Sunday, February 22, 10:00 P.M.

Abe pulled past the cruiser in the street and into her driveway. She'd sincerely thanked his parents for dinner, wished Sean and Ruth congratulations on their new baby, and crossed her fingers for Rachel's good grade on the interview. But once in his SUV, she'd grown quiet and with every mile to her house, his heart grew heavier. He could almost hear the wheels turning in her mind and desperately wished she'd say something. Anything. Finally, she did.

"It's okay, Reagan," she said. He winced at the formality. Her eyes wouldn't meet his, focusing instead on her darkened windows with their new curtains. "I understand."

He put his hand on hers. "What do you understand?"

"I understood before tonight that you needed to take care of me, to keep me safe. Because you didn't keep Debra safe. Even though that wasn't your fault. I guess I didn't think that I was a substitute in every other way, though." She swallowed and looked out the window. "That hurt the old ego a little," she added wryly.

"You're not a substitute for Debra. Dammit, Kristen, look at me."

She shook her head firmly and opened the door. "Thank you. Really. I had a lovely time and you have a wonderful family. Call me tomorrow if you want to meet on the case. I've got Officer Truman here tonight. I'll be fine."

And she would be, Kristen thought. She'd been through a hell of a lot worse than this, after all. She slammed the SUV door, half-expecting him to follow her. She told herself she wasn't disappointed when he didn't. He backed out of her driveway with an engine roar that would most certainly make her neighbors complain. She entered her kitchen, not thinking about the fact it was the first time she'd entered her own house alone in the past five days. Not thinking about the kiss they'd shared over by her teapot. Not thinking about him at all.

It wasn't a bad outcome all in all. She'd discovered that she could tolerate, even anticipate feeling strong arms around her. That she could kiss a man without throwing up, that she could even yearn for the feel of his lips on hers. So it wasn't a total loss.

She dropped her coat on the kitchen chair. Bypassed the teapot. She didn't think she could stomach tea tonight. At least *he* wouldn't be able to peep in her windows anymore. Heavy curtains covered the glass.

She closed the door to her bedroom, not thinking about Abe Reagan at all.

But it was his name she screamed when the hand came out of the darkness to clamp over her mouth, muffling her scream, yanking her back against a large, hard body. She struggled violently, her nails raking against skin. A strangled cry met her ears and the hand left her mouth, an iron arm locking hard across her breasts, immobilizing her. She screamed again, kicking, her heel catching something hard. Then her body went still when cold, hard metal touched her temple. *I'm going to die.*

Lips grazed her ear and she swallowed back the bile. "That's better," a raspy voice declared. "Now, who is he?"

Sunday, February 22, 10:05 P.M.

She had a right to be hurt, Abe thought, pulling away from her house. A smart woman like Kristen had put two and two together. Unfortunately she got five. She was *not* a substitute for Debra. *Was she?* He thought about her walking into her house alone, all alone. *I should have followed her in, checked her closet.* But Charlie Truman was there, watching.

Abe went still, while every hair on his neck seemed to stand on end. *Wasn't he?* He'd seen the cruiser, but *had he seen Truman?*

Panic closed his throat and he turned a one-eighty in the middle of the road. A car blew its horn, but Abe was already halfway up the block. He brought the SUV to a screeching halt next to the cruiser. Jumped out to peer in the window.

The cruiser was dark and empty. He yanked at the cruiser's door, but it was locked. Truman was gone.

Kristen.

"Dammit." Abe ran up the driveway, his feet slipping on the ice. He fell and pulled himself back up to his feet, already running again. She'd locked her kitchen door. He pounded with his fists. "*Kristen!*"

He rounded the house to the back. The basement door was less secure. He could break it down. He threw himself at the door, again and again, until the frame cracked and he was inside. Mindlessly he took the stairs four at a time until he was stumbling into her bedroom, his weapon drawn and his heart hammering.

She knelt on the floor, her head down, gasping, the cordless phone from her nightstand in her hand. He went down on one knee, pulled her chin up. Her eyes were wide and glassy.

She looked at him, then looked at the phone in her hand and ironically his cell phone started to trill in his pocket. "I was calling you," she said, her voice oddly distant. "He's gone. Out the window."

Abe made it to the window in time to see a figure all in black against the snowy white of the backyard. The man took the back fence like a hurdle and sprinted away.

"Dammit," Abe snarled. He might have caught him had he stayed outside. But then again, his breaking in was probably what made the bastard flee. He turned to find Kristen struggling to her feet. In two long strides he was lifting her into his arms. He sank down onto her bed, holding her tight, feeling her body quake. She curled herself against him, her hands clutching the lapels of his coat. Her breath came fast, too fast, and he rocked her gently.

"It's okay. I'm here." He cradled her, pressing his cheek to the top of her head. *Oh, God, oh, God. I got here in time.* He drew a deep breath, realizing his own breathing was nearly as erratic as hers. He fumbled in his pocket for his cell phone and dialed Dispatch. "Officer Truman is missing."

The operator was calm. "Officer Truman called in a disturbance ten minutes ago. A young girl approached his vehicle to report her grandfather had fallen and was unconscious in her backyard. He went to help her. What's happened, Detective?"

"The woman he was supposed to be guarding was just attacked in her own bedroom," Abe bit out. "Radio him to return immediately." He hung up and dialed Mia. She picked up on the first ring.

"What is it?"

"Kristen's been attacked."

He could hear Mia moving around, drawers slamming. "Is she all right?"

"Don't know. Call Jack. I want a CSU team here ASAP. I'll call Spinnelli."

"Will do. Where's the uniform assigned to her?"

"Took another call. He'll be back soon. Get here as fast as you can."

He hung up and, his hand shaking, tossed the cell phone onto her bed. She hadn't said a single word since he'd picked her up. "Kristen, Kristen, honey, you need to concentrate. Listen to me, honey. Did he hurt you?"

She shook her head hard against his chest and he drew a breath of relief. Let it out. Started to feel his heart return to normal. "Okay, good. Did he say anything to you?"

She nodded.

"What, honey? What did he say?"

Her response was mumbled against his coat. He gently pulled her away from his chest and she valiantly attempted to control her breathing. "Who . . . is he?"

Shit. "He wanted to know who the killer was?"

She nodded, her eyes sliding closed. "He had . . . a gun. Cold. He . . . put it . . . to my head . . . said . . . he'd blow . . ." She shuddered and gathered fistfuls of his coat in her hands. "Said he'd . . . blow . . . brains out. Mine. He said . . . I was . . . getting letters. So . . . I . . . had to . . . had to . . . know him. Maybe . . . hired him."

Abe uttered a foul curse regarding Zoe Richardson and, unbelievably Kristen smiled. "Such . . . chivalry," she said, taking even breaths through her nose.

Abe brought her close again, holding her tight. "What else did he say?"

"Said if I didn't know . . . I'd better figure it out . . . Or people I cared about . . . would die."

A siren sounded in the distance, growing closer with each second. Abe gently settled her on the bed. "I've got to check the perimeter. Maybe he dropped something on his way in or out."

"But you don't think so."

"No. Stay here. I'll be back."

"Abe."

He turned at the doorway to find her staring down at her hands, her breath still hitching. "Send one of . . . Jack's guys in here to . . . scrape my nails." She looked up, her mouth set in a satisfied line. "I . . . got his face."

Abe smiled grimly. "That's my girl."

Monday, February 23, 12:30 A.M.

It was over now. All the police and CSU were gone. The only people left in her house were herself and Abe Reagan. They faced each other in her living room and he held out his hand. She walked into his arms.

"How did you know to come back?" she asked, her cheek pressed hard into his solid chest. A heartbeat later she was swung up into his arms and he settled on the sofa, holding her on his lap like she was a baby. To protest never entered her mind.

He pulled the pins from her hair with quick, efficient movements and she sighed as the pressure on her head disappeared and her curls sprang free. "I remembered I hadn't actually seen Truman in the cruiser." He shrugged. "I just knew."

"Thank you." One corner of her mouth lifted. "Either I'm getting good at playing the damsel in distress or you're getting good at playing the white knight."

He massaged her head with his big hand. "Do they have to be mutually exclusive?"

She closed her eyes and simply enjoyed the feel of his hand. "No. I called you again."

"Before you called 9-1-1," he said sternly and she just smiled.

"I guess I did. I knew you'd come." She sighed. "Thanks. For taking care of me."

He was quiet for a long moment. "You were lucky tonight."

She didn't want to think about it. "Will Officer Truman get into any trouble?"

Abe shook his head and Kristen felt relieved. Officer Truman looked as upset as she'd felt when he'd returned mere minutes after Abe had broken down the door to save her. "No. He did everything right. How was he to know he was being lured away from you by a false report? The girl who approached his vehicle seemed sincerely frantic."

"Who was she?"

"Truman will give a description to the sketch artists, but I'm not counting on anything. After he thought about it, he couldn't even say for certain she was a teenager. She told him her grandfather had gone out to walk the dog, that it was a while before she even realized he was gone. That she'd found her grandfather facedown in the snow, and he was unconscious. He chalked up her not calling 9-1-1 to the panic of a kid. Of course, there was no old man."

"Why didn't he take the cruiser to the girl's house?"

"She told him it would be faster to cross the backyards, that it was only a few houses away. She was crying and hysterical. Then she was gone. Disappeared into thin air when he'd turned his back to search for the old man. By the time he realized he'd been set up, I was here."

Kristen nuzzled her cheek against the crisp cotton of his shirt and once again his hand threaded through her curls, massaging the back of her head. She could feel the tension lessen by slow degrees. "Well, it's done and over and we're both all right. What a day."

His hand stilled, his palm cradling her head. "Kristen, I'm sorry."

She opened her eyes to find him staring down at her, his eyes desolate. "Why?"

"Because I made you feel bad in front of my family. Yes, you sound like Debra. But I swear to you, you are not a substitute for my dead wife."

She looked at his face, felt his strong arms around her. Remembered how it had felt when she heard him banging on the basement door. He'd come back. "It's okay."

His eyes widened. "It is?"

She nodded. "Abe, you've come every time I've called. You made me feel things I never thought I'd ever feel. I'm grateful for that. In the grand scheme of life, whether I sound like Debra or not really isn't that important." She narrowed her eyes. "Now if you want me to wear her clothes or wear my hair like her, I may start to get a little weirded out."

He chuckled. "You'd look like a kid playing dress-up if you tried to wear Debra's clothes. She was five-eleven without her shoes on."

Kristen returned her head to his shoulder, felt his arms tighten around her in response. "I liked your family, Abe. Even Aidan."

He snorted gently. "Aidan can be a real ass sometimes."

"Not like you."

He pulled back to glare down at her. "Excuse me?"

"It's not like you got mad at me for including cops on the list of suspects. Right?"

He yanked one of her curls. "Hush, or I won't give you a massage."

Her brows shot up. "A massage? Really?"

"I was considering it. You're still tighter than a drum."

She regarded him intently, thought about having his hands on her shoulders and her back and she wanted to melt. Conversely, she thought about his hands on her . . . elsewhere . . . and her stomach clenched. "I trust you, you know?"

His eyes heated with what she'd left unsaid. "I know. It kills me to know, but yeah, I know. Proper massage. No more. But I do want something in return."

She sucked in one cheek. "What?"

"Tell me about your family. I took you to mine, idiot brother and all. Tell me about yours."

Kristen sighed. It wasn't the same, not at all. But again, in the grand scheme of life, what did it really matter? "I grew up on a farm in Kansas a hundred miles from the nearest stoplight. There was just me and my sister, Kara."

"You said that your sister died in a drunk-driving accident."

She felt the familiar ache, as if it were yesterday instead of fifteen years ago. "I was sixteen, she was eighteen. Kara always was the wild one. We grew up in a very . . ." She searched for the right word. "Our house was rigid. My father liked rules. Kara didn't. When she was eighteen, she took a trip with some friends. They drove into Topeka, hotbed of sin."

Abe smiled and ruefully she smiled back. "After living on a little farm with wheat as far as the eye could see, even Topeka was like living on the edge." She sobered, remembering now. "Kara must have gone to some parties. Anyway, my parents got the call from the state police in the middle of the night. Kara was dead."

He'd sobered as well. "I'm sorry."

"So was I. On a number of levels. I loved my sister, and I missed her. I still do. But something happened to my parents after she was gone. My father grew more rigid and Mother just wound down. Before, she'd temper his rules. But after Kara died, she just went into this . . . I don't know. A dark place. She was never the same again."

"You must've been angry that she didn't care enough to be there for you."

Kristen considered it. "I suppose so. I was mad. Plus, my father cracked down even harder on me. You'd've thought it was me that was the wild child. He wouldn't let me leave the house except for school. I missed the football games, prom, everything. But I had a wonderful art teacher in high school who helped me get the work study program in Florence, set me up with a local family. Even asked my father for permission to let me go."

"He said no."

Kristen looked up at him. His eyes hadn't left her face. "He said no." She shrugged. "So I defied him and went anyway. I was eighteen by then and had saved my money from babysitting before Kara died. Plus, Kara had a nest egg set aside. I knew she'd want me to have it, so I took it and bought a ticket to Italy. One way. I knew I'd eventually have to come home, but I wasn't thinking that far ahead."

"I can't visualize you as an extemporaneous girl," Abe said softly.

Kristen thought of the girl she'd been. "Time changes people. Anyway, I came back from Italy and went to college. My father never changed, so I just . . . left." It was a partial truth, but all she was able or willing to tell at this point. Maybe ever.

He studied her face and she knew he knew she hadn't told the whole story, but he didn't press. "You said your father is still alive. When was the last time you saw him?"

"Last month."

Abe's brows shot up. "Last month?"

"Yes. My mom is in a nursing home." Her throat tightened. "She's in the advanced stages of Alzheimer's. She hasn't recognized me in three years, but I fly back to Kansas once a month to visit her. My dad was there the last time. He usually doesn't come on my Sundays, but my mom had a bad night and they'd called him in. He left the room when I arrived, so technically I saw him, but we didn't speak."

"I'm sorry."

"So am I. It's hard to see my mother like that. I enjoyed just watching your mother tonight. Before Kara died, my mom used to love being in her kitchen. After Kara died, she was too depressed. Now she just lies there, wasting away. She hasn't been my mom since I was sixteen."

He was quiet a moment. "I used to visit Debra and talk and talk and never know if she heard a word I said."

Kristen rested her forehead on his chest. "Sometimes," she said wearily, "I just wish she'd die and then I feel so guilty."

His chest rose and fell. "Yeah, I used to do the same. And I'd feel guilty, too."

"On Friday night you said she was in a coma for five years." Five years was one hell of a long time to watch someone you loved just exist.

"She wasn't in a coma. She was in a persistent vegetative state. It's different. Debra was clinically brain-dead from the moment they wheeled her into the ER."

Kristen hesitated, then blurted it out. "Did you ever consider pulling her life support?"

Another rise and fall of his massive chest. "Only every time I saw her or thought about her. But I couldn't. As long as she was alive, I just couldn't. But her parents wanted me to."

Kristen's eyes widened. "I thought parents were usually the ones to hold on."

"Not Debra's." His face shadowed. "Her father was suing me for custody when she died. They said she wouldn't want to go on like that and I knew it was true, but she was *alive*."

"And if she was alive there was hope."

"Yes. Then Debra's mother had a heart attack. Her father said seeing Debra like that year after year was killing her. He was desperate. I didn't know what to do, but I just couldn't do what he wanted. He filed for custody a month before Debra got an infection and died on her own. Her parents and I didn't part on what you'd call friendly terms."

"I guess not."

He sighed. "Debra and Ruth were cousins. That's how we met. Sean and Ruth set me up with Debra on a surprise blind date."

That was important for some reason, Kristen thought and searched her brain for a connection, nodding when she found it. "That's what Ruth was talking about the other night when she was here. Her mother invited Debra's parents to the christening."

Abe smiled ruefully. "Very good. Now if you can think of what I'm supposed to say when I see them, I'll be really impressed. But that's enough angst for one night." He stood up, letting her body slide against his until her feet hit the floor. He pressed his lips to her forehead, held them there for three hard beats of her heart. Then he pushed her gently toward her bedroom. "One massage. Then I'll get a lousy night's sleep on your sofa."

"It's uncomfortable?"

"No." He sounded regretfully amused, walking behind her. "I will be."

She stopped short, her whole body stiffening. He came closer and his heat burned her back. "I'm sorry." And she was. He would be, too, when the time finally came.

He pushed her curls off her neck and brushed his lips against her skin. She shuddered. "Don't be," he murmured. "I meant what I said. One day at a time. That's what we'll do."

She gathered up her courage. "You'll be . . . disappointed."

His breath was warm against her skin. "I don't think so. But don't worry about that now. Right now I'm going to get those knots out of your back and you're going to sleep like a baby." He gave her another little shove. "You have my personal guarantee."

She stopped next to her bed. Plucked at her blouse uncertainly. Felt like a fool. She was thirty-one years old, for God's sake.

"Whatever makes you most comfortable," he murmured. "You said you trust me."

She drew a deep breath and lay facedown on her bed, her clothes intact. "I do." *More than any man I've ever known.*

"Scoot over a little," he said and sat down at her hip. "I have to confess up front. I learned how to do massages for Debra. It kept her muscles from atrophying, and the hospice never had the staff to do it as often as needed to be done."

She tensed when he put his hands on her, but he said nothing, just started working her muscles with methodical skill until she began to relax. "Mmm. You're so good at this."

He still said nothing, just continued working the muscles on either side of her spine and she sighed. And wondered how it would feel to have his hands directly on her skin.

His hands paused. "It would feel much better, I think," he murmured, his voice warm and husky. "Take off your shirt."

Once again, she'd spoken her thoughts aloud. She should feel threatened that this man was able to draw her very thoughts into the open, but she wasn't. "Turn around." She stripped off her blouse, hesitated at her bra. That would stay. She resettled herself on her stomach. "Okay." Then waited expectantly for the first feel of his hands on her bare flesh. She sucked in a breath when he touched her, let it out on a long sigh. He was right. It was much better.

"You have a very pretty back," he said softly and she shivered. Hard.

"Cold?"

"No." Not even close. She was warm wherever he touched her and everywhere he didn't. Her breasts grew sensitized within the confines of her plain cotton bra and her pulse throbbed between her legs with an almost painful pressure. She arched her back, pressing her pelvis into the mattress.

He paused. "Did I hurt you?"

"No." Not like he meant anyway. It was more like an

ache. An ache only he could take away. *I want him to touch me.*

Abe stopped abruptly. She hadn't meant the words to be heard. He knew that. But he'd heard them nevertheless. She wanted him to touch her, and right here, right now, he could think of little else. But he'd promised her a proper massage. Nothing more. Even though he could just see the plump curve of her breast. Even though her spine dipped enticingly at the waist of her wool slacks. Even though right now he was harder and more ready than he thought he'd ever been before.

Drawing on every ounce of self-control, he pulled the quilt from the foot of her bed and covered her with it. She was almost asleep while he suspected he would do little sleeping tonight. He stood up. Watched her draw deep even breaths. Noted the way her dark lashes lay on her creamy skin like fans. He bent down and kissed her cheek.

"Sleep now," he whispered. He started to straighten, but her hand shot out and clamped over his wrist with surprising strength.

She half rolled to look up at him, her green eyes intense. "Don't go." His eyes, damn them, dipped lower, taking in her breasts, silently cursing the utilitarian white bra that hid them from his view. He needed to get out of here. Now.

He shook his head. "I'll sleep on the floor outside your door. You'll be safe."

"Don't go." Her grip tightened. "Please."

"Kristen, I . . ." He exhaled, and gently pried her fingers from his wrist. "You need to sleep. And I can't stay here. I promised you."

"I know." She grabbed a handful of his shirt, swung up, sitting on the edge of the bed. Her free hand captured his, and she brought his palm to her lips.

And he couldn't contain the groan. "Kristen, let me go. Now."

"No." She took his hand, placed it over her heart which pounded. "You can't possibly understand . . . I never thought I'd ever feel this way." She looked up and her eyes weren't afraid or wary or hurt. They were alive and bewitching. Compelling. Not taking her eyes from his, she moved his hand inch by inch until his palm covered white cotton. Covered his hand with her own, pressing his fingers until he held her breast cupped in his hand. "It's you," she breathed, so softly he almost didn't hear. Dropping her hand to her lap, her eyes slid closed.

And God help him, he couldn't say no. Gently he pushed her back against the bed and joined her there, his hand now freely exploring, his thumb seeking out the hard tip that the white cotton couldn't hide. "You are so beautiful," he whispered and bent to kiss her lips. Her hand came up and smoothed the hair at the nape of his neck so he deepened the kiss and felt her sigh. He moved his hand to her other breast and she arched to meet him. She was fluid grace and intoxicating innocence all at once and he knew whatever her past, whatever had turned her from the impulsive, spontaneous girl she'd once been to the wary woman he'd met just five days before, what she was feeling now was brand new. He bent his head to her breast and kissed her through her bra and her gasp made him feel proud, like he'd done something totally remarkable. And maybe he had.

She pulled his head closer and he opened his mouth, tonguing her stiff nipple, wishing there was nothing between his mouth and her skin. Then her hand left his head, tugged at the cotton and there wasn't. He drew her nipple into his mouth and sucked.

And she moaned his name. His pounding heart exploded. He wanted her. Wanted her naked, wanted to feel her sheathed around him. Wanted to feel her tighten, convulsing, his name on her lips. Before he realized his intentions, his hand was sliding lower, his fingers questing, finding. Claiming.

A startled little gasp surprised him and he raised his head. Confused panic warred with the passion in her eyes. "Sshh," he soothed. "It's just my hand. That's all. I'll stop."

Her eyes narrowed and her hand once again covered his, keeping him from making good on his offer. "No, you won't."

His lips quirked. She'd taken the reins. Good for her. "Whatever you say, lady."

"Don't call me lady." Then she closed her eyes, her lips pressed together. Her hand fell away from his, clutching the quilt. She frowned, focusing so hard he had to smile. He rubbed the heel of his hand across the hard bone of her pubis, watched her face change, soften, watched pleasure chase the frown away. She was beautiful like this, discovering her own capacity for passion. He fondled her through her slacks, saying nothing, showing her how good she could feel. Her eyes flew open and in them he saw amazement and urgency.

"Don't stop," she whispered.

He gritted his teeth against the sudden surge of his own body. Not now. *This time is Kristen's.* "I won't." He didn't, and she moved her hips, lifting against his hand, her breath coming in hard pants. She braced one foot on the mattress so she could push harder and then her body froze. Her hand dropped the quilt and clamped over his, pressing, pressing, and Abe knew he'd never seen anything sexier than Kristen caught up in climax. She slumped back, still panting. His body-hurt, his erection straining for release. But even the power of his own need was nothing compared to the look in her eyes when her lashes lifted.

"I did it." It was an awed whisper. "I really did it."

He had to smile despite the throbbing in his groin. "Yes, you did."

"Thank you." It was more than simple gratitude. This was a watershed moment in her life and he was humbled to have shared it with her. He could only hope she had another, more advanced watershed moment very soon. He wasn't sure his body could stand the strain of watching her again without participating a little more actively.

He tugged her bra up to cover her breast and pushed the tousled curls away from her face. "You're welcome."

She shuddered out a breath. "You didn't . . ."

He pressed a hard kiss to her mouth. "I didn't. But it's okay."

She bit her lip. "I'm sorry."

He laid a finger against her lips. "Be quiet. I'm fine."

"Abe . . ." Tears filled her eyes and her breath hitched. "I'm sorry, I—"

"Sshh." He gathered her in his arms, settling her on his lap for the second time that evening. He'd half expected this response, but still her tears tore at his heart. She pressed her cheek against his chest and her shoulders shook.

"I was so afraid."

He kissed the top of her head. "Of me?"

She shook her head. "Not you. That I'd never . . ." She lifted a shoulder. "You know."

He knew and he silently cursed whoever had made her lose confidence in her own body, who'd hurt her so badly that she'd all but buried whoever she'd once been.

Hurt her. What a pathetic euphemism that was. He was a cop, he'd seen everything and still he had trouble saying the word he knew she'd never forget. *Rape.* She'd been raped. He made himself think the word, forced himself to stay calm when what he really wanted to do was find out who'd done it and tear his guts out with his bare hands, and felt a flash of respect, gratitude to the killer who'd already removed one rapist from the planet. It was wrong to feel that way, but at the moment, if he knew who'd hurt the woman in his arms, he wasn't sure that he wasn't capable of cold-blooded retribution murder himself.

"Do you want to talk about it now?" he asked quietly and her body tensed.

She shook her head again, more vehemently this time. "No, not now. Not now."

Abe hugged her close. "Then sleep."

Monday, February 23, 1:30 A.M.

He'd lost control before, with Conti. That couldn't, wouldn't happen again. Not that the beast didn't deserve it, and a lot more. But it was dangerous. He'd left evidence behind on Conti's body, of that he was certain, but apart from dipping the man in a vat of lye, he didn't know how to rectify the situation. What was, was.

You could have just buried him and left his family to wonder, he thought. But that would have robbed him of precious closure. The world knew that Conti had been punished for his crimes against Paula Garcia, her unborn son, the American justice system, and last but far from least, Kristen Mayhew. Perhaps now the scum that paraded through her court would think twice before publicly defaming her name.

He shifted, trying to find a comfortable place on the concrete of the roof. He'd had to find a new rooftop. Who would have thought the police would use Skinner's car to guide them to the old rooftop? He had to give them credit. Mitchell and Reagan were no fools. Especially that Reagan. He frowned a little, thinking of how Reagan arrived to rescue Kristen from those thugs that ran her car off the road. Kristen had walked into his arms like she'd known him all her life instead of only a few days.

He sincerely hoped that Reagan wasn't the kind of man to push his advantage. If Reagan was foolish enough to try, he'd find Kristen had powerful allies in hidden places.

Aah, finally. He'd thought his target would never come. After his little detour with Conti, he'd gone back to the fishbowl and resumed his quest. Tonight's mark had been easy enough to lure. He'd found Arthur Monroe in a bar, quickly made friends by buying the man a beer. Then he'd made Monroe practically drool by bragging about a stash of pure cocaine and offering him some if Monroe met him here tonight. The lure had worked well in the past, bringing him every mark except for Skinner who'd required a slightly different candy. Skinner's lure had been the promise of discrediting information about a victim who was accusing one of Skinner's clients with sexual harassment. His lips curled in distaste. Killing Skinner had been one of his greater contributions to humanity.

But tonight was about Arthur Monroe, a man who'd justified his gross sexual imposition of the young daughter of his girlfriend by saying the five-year-old had "led him on," that he "hadn't been able to help himself," that it had been a "one time thing." Kristen pushed for a trial, but the mother refused to allow her child to testify. He gritted his teeth as he brought the mark into his sight. Most of the time parents refused to allow their children to testify to protect them from media exposure and further trauma. This little girl's mother didn't want her boyfriend to go to jail. To Kristen's shock, the judge in this case had sided with the boyfriend.

He'd known her by then and remembered that day well. She'd been devastated. She'd worked out a plea that she'd found repugnant enough, but the judge had unbelievably decided society in general had failed the pedophilic boyfriend and had rejected the plea, sentencing Monroe to probation and counseling.

Probation. For molesting a five-year-old. He smiled grimly as he tracked the man crossing the road. This time he'd get the boyfriend. Maybe next time he'd pull a judge's name out of the fishbowl. Because there were judges in there, waiting with all the others.

He inched the sight down, bringing the man's knees into view. He really wanted Monroe to pay, and with more than an easy death. But the vision of his own bloody hands after he'd killed Conti entered his mind, front and center. *His bloody, gloveless hands.* What a stupid mistake to make. He couldn't risk losing control again. The police already knew the florist sign on the van was a sham, and they'd recovered a bullet. That the bullet was too damaged to identify was a short-term boon. Sooner or later they'd figure it out and find him. He needed to hurry. There were many more names in the fishbowl.

He brought the sight up to Monroe's forehead and gently squeezed the trigger.

Nine down and still a million to go.

Chapter Fifteen

Monday, February 23, 5:00 A.M.

"Wake up."

Kristen heard the fly buzzing and swatted it away.

"Kristen, wake up."

No, not a buzzing fly. A rumbling voice. Abe. She rolled to her back, her eyes flying open. Abe sat on the edge of her bed, looking worried. And incredibly handsome. His shirt hung open partway, giving her a glimpse of his chest. It was hard, she knew. She'd felt his solid strength each time he'd held her against him. Now she wondered how it would feel to touch him there, to slide her fingers through the thick dark hair that covered his chest. Would it be coarse or soft? Would he like it? Would she feel his groan rumble beneath her hands?

As she contemplated, his hand lifted to smooth the hair away from her face so tenderly she wanted to sigh. He had such gentle hands. Such very nice hands. She shifted her body, feeling a warm throbbing between her legs that she now knew could become more than just a frustrating distraction. Much more. *So that's why everyone is so hooked on orgasms,* she thought. The feeling had been simply . . . indescribable. Exhilarating. Powerful. *I did it. I finally, really did it.* And she wanted to do it again.

How exactly did one go about making such a request? And if she did, when would he expect more? Eventually, he'd want . . . well, more. And despite his arguments to the contrary, he would be disappointed. Abruptly the warmth chilled. *So much for that.*

He bent his head a fraction closer. "Are you all right?"

"I'm fine."

He narrowed those blue eyes. "You don't look fine. You shouldn't go into work."

"I have to. I've got motion hour at nine." She struggled up onto her elbows and groaned at the resulting pain in her back. "It feels like I got hit with a truck."

"You did. A big truck with a gun."

Her stomach quivered and she glanced over at her bedroom window. She'd nearly forgotten about the attack. It should have been her first thought, waking up. But it hadn't been. Her first thought was of Reagan and his hands.

"You're safe now," Reagan said soothingly. "You don't have to be afraid." But she wasn't afraid. No man had ever made her feel truly safe. Not until this man.

She looked him straight in the eye. "I know. Thank you."

His eyes changed in a flash, going from worried to heated and the warm throbbing in her own body returned, intensifying almost to the point of pain. She watched his throat work. His jaw clenched. But he made no move to touch her. And she wanted him to.

She was in bed. With a man. And she wasn't afraid. Not taking her eyes from his, her lips curved. "Good morning."

His nostrils flared and she heard the quick intake of his breath. "Good morning."

He needed to shave, she thought. The beginning of a dark beard covered his cheeks, his chin. That space between his nose and his upper lip. Tentatively she reached up and trailed her fingertips along that space, then across his lips. And he swallowed hard.

"What?" she whispered, her fingertips resting on his lips. They were soft, but she knew they could be hard when they crushed against hers.

His eyes smoldered. "You're beautiful," he whispered back.

She had to remember to breathe. "No, I'm not."

He pressed a kiss to the inside of her wrist and she wondered if he could feel her pulse quicken. He leaned closer until their eyes were just inches apart. This close she could see the blue was rimmed in black. "Yes, you are." Then he tilted his head and his lips were on hers and it started all over again. The rushing, the pounding, the throbbing. The wanting. She heard herself hum in pleasure and he apparently heard it too because he took the kiss deeper, pressing her back, back into the pillows. Her hands reached, found his shoulders and held on. There was a tension in his shoulders. He was holding back, she realized dimly. He touched her only with his mouth, the rest of his body carefully held apart from hers. No pushing, no forcing. Strong, but gentle. The disparity was arousing.

He ended the kiss without really ending it at all, teasing the corners of her mouth with the tip of his tongue, brushing kisses across her cheeks, her chin, her forehead. "You're a beautiful woman, Kristen," he murmured into her ear and she shuddered hard, her hips arching upward, meeting nothing but blanket and air. Tensing, he pulled back until he was sitting in his original position. She opened her eyes to find him staring down at her, his powerful chest rising and falling as he worked to catch his breath.

So this *is what they mean by sexual tension,* she thought. *I like this.* "How do you do that?" she asked, her voice rough and husky.

His brows lifted. "Did you like it?"

She felt her cheeks heat and knew she'd bypassed peony pink and gone straight to ruby red. And by the look in his eyes, he didn't care that her face clashed with her hair. "Yes."

"Good," he said with such satisfaction that she had to smile.

She closed her eyes and screwed up her courage. "You make me want more."

A full beat passed. Then another. "Good," he finally said and this time it was his voice that was rough and husky. His fingertips skimmed her lips. The mattress shifted as he stood up. She opened her eyes and her mouth went dry at the sight of his body in profile. *His chest isn't the only thing that's hard,* she thought. And the thought didn't make her cringe. A mixture of pride and relief rushed through her as he chuckled wryly.

"Thank you," he said and she wished she could hide under the bed.

"I said that out loud?" she asked.

"Afraid so." He aimed an amused smile in her direction. "You have to get up now. I have to go by my apartment and change clothes, shower and shave before I take you to work."

She opened her mouth to say she could drive herself, then glanced at the window. There was pride and there was stupidity and Kristen was not a stupid woman. "Okay."

Monday, February 23, 8:00 A.M.

Spinnelli looked worried. He had a right to be, Abe thought. They didn't have shit.

Spinnelli leaned one hip against the conference room table, his bushy mustache bent in a painful frown. "So if I might summarize . . ." He lifted his hand and started counting with his fingers. "One, we have two more bodies. Two, one of the lead prosecutors in the city has been attacked twice, once in her own home. Three, it's open season on defense attorneys."

"That's not such a bad thing," Mia muttered and Spinnelli cut her off with a glare.

"Four, the captain's taken calls from Jacob Conti every other hour all weekend because the ME's office is, in Conti's words, carving up his son a second time, and five"—he held all five fingers extended—"we don't have a single goddamn suspect."

Mia shifted uneasily in her chair. "That's about the size of it."

"Kristen scratched her attacker last night," Abe said. "What about the scrapings from under her nails?"

From his seat beside Mia, Jack shrugged. "I can get DNA for you, but until you have a suspect, I don't have anything to compare it to."

Spinnelli stared at the whiteboard in frustration. "Julia found nothing on Skinner's body? No hairs, no fibers, no nothing?"

Jack shook his head. "Nothing. I did find some debris ground into Skinner's clothes, mud and some chemical residue from the factory in the dirt. I matched it to the site where we found the bullet, so we can confirm Skinner was there. The vise he used to keep Skinner's head immobilized was so tight it left an imprint of the model number. Julia was able to stain the skin so I could get a good photograph. It was a Craftsman."

"Solid as Sears," Mia muttered. "On every daddy's Christmas wish list."

"I have one," Spinnelli grumbled. "Wife gave it to me for my workshop three years ago."

"I bet half the workshops in Chicago have one," Jack said.

"What about the bullet?" Spinnelli asked.

"We've shown it to all the major gun stores in town," Mia said. "Nobody recognizes that maker's mark. It's too damaged. They also said nobody's been practicing at their range with homemade bullets. But I was thinking—"

"No," Spinnelli drawled and Mia shot him a look that was half annoyed and half hurt.

"Yes. I do that occasionally, Marc," she said quietly.

Spinnelli sighed. "I'm sorry, Mia. I know you guys worked most of the weekend on this one. I got a call from the captain's office this morning. He'd just hung up with the mayor, who'd been getting around the clock calls from

Conti demanding we put more men on this case. The mayor wasn't pleased, so the captain wasn't pleased. Plus it seems like every defense attorney in town's called to complain. They say we'd put more cops on the case if the prosecutors were targets." Spinnelli clenched his jaw. "That's just bull-shit."

"So you're in a shitty mood," Mia said. "Fine, just don't take it out on me."

"Fine." Spinnelli raised both brows. "So what were you thinking, Mia?"

Mia didn't look placated. "Just that if the guy has gone to all the trouble to make his own bullets, and he's a sharp-shooter who's not practicing at a public range, he's proba-bly rigged his own target range. He'd need some land to do that so that no neighbors would see him and call the cops. Ever since 9/11, people have been a little skittish about their next-door neighbors playing Rambo."

"That's good, Mia," Abe said. "If he does own land, his name will appear in deed records. We can cross-reference the list you got from the sandblasting company."

"But not the florist companies," Jack said.

"I'm still mad about that," Mia complained. "I looked at florists for hours. All wasted."

"Are we sure about that?" Spinnelli pressed. "We've got testimony from two kids saying they saw different signs on a white van. Are we sure they're telling the truth?"

"McIntyre saw it, too," Abe said and Spinnelli shrugged with regretful acceptance.

"And anyway, why would those kids lie?" Jack asked. "What's in it for them?"

"Especially since one of them walked right by a police cruiser to deliver the Conti package," Mia added. "McIntyre was sitting right outside Kristen's house when Tyrone Yates dropped off his box. If they were in cahoots with our guy, they wouldn't be so bold."

Abe had a sudden, terrible thought. "*They* might not be so bold. *He* might."

Mia turned around to look at him, her brows furrowed. "What?"

Abe sat down at the computer and brought up the department's criminal database. "How did our killer pick those two kids? They came from different neighborhoods, different schools. Did he pick them at random? By chance?"

Spinnelli's expression was grim. "He doesn't do anything by chance. He's too organized. Everything's connected, every loop closed. Abe, tell me those two boys were God-fearing angels that never gave the law a day's trouble. Please."

Abe typed in Tyrone Yates's name and waited for the computer to respond. And when it did, he sighed. "This boy's got a yellow sheet as long as my arm. Assault, plead down. Possession, plead down. Et cetera, et cetera."

Mia went very still. "And what about Aaron Jenkins?"

The only sound in the room was the clacking of the keyboard. "Same. Throw in a few misdemeanor petty thefts." He scrolled down. "He turned eighteen four months ago. He's got a sealed juvie record." Abe looked up, saw every eye looking at him. "He set these kids up."

Jack frowned. "I'm not following you."

Abe leaned back in the chair, crossing his arms over his chest. "He didn't just choose these kids at random. I'm sure of it. What if he has some personal beef with these kids? Maybe they did something to him, or to someone else who he wants to avenge. If he hires them, pays them, people will assume they know who he is. They're bad kids, they have reputations in the neighborhood. Word gets out, and suddenly they are the link to the killer. If somebody wants the killer, they go through the kids."

Jack shook his head. "But that doesn't make sense, Abe. Not only do you have one hell of a lot of 'ifs,' but if he has a beef with these kids, why not kill them himself?"

Abe shrugged. "I don't know. Maybe there's a vigilante code of ethics or something. Maybe whatever they did wasn't bad enough to warrant his kind of justice, but hey, if someone else does the honors, it's okay with him. I don't know. All I do know is right now, this is all we have."

Mia closed her eyes. "We showed everybody in that neighborhood Aaron Jenkins's picture. The whole freakin' neighborhood."

Jack massaged his temples. "And everybody who has a TV knows you guys are working this case, thanks to Zoe Richardson."

"She put Tyrone Yates's picture across the news last night," Spinnelli said grimly

Abe clenched his jaw. He'd missed tne news last nigh' He'd been too busy with Kristen's attacker. "How did Richardson get pictures of Tyrone Yates?"

Spinnelli ran his hand through his hair in frustration. "She must have been skulking around Kristen's neighborhood yesterday. She had really grainy video of Yates waiting in the back of McIntyre's cruiser. Then they ran the footage of Conti manhandling Julia. 'A father's grief,' Richardson called it," he said sardonically. "My wife videotaped it for me, since we were all a little busy at Kristen's house last night. I saw it when I got home."

Mia got up to pace "So between us and Richardson, the identities of those two delivery boys are common knowledge."

"The kids won't be able to ID the vigilante," Jack said. "Unless they lied to you about what they'd seen."

"Maybe they did lie," Abe said. "Maybe they didn't. If they did, I want them in here to get the truth. If not, if somebody wants to know who our humble servant is badly enough, they won't believe those kids and their lives are in serious danger. We know the Blades want to know, badly enough to risk attacking Kristen on a public street. Let's bring those two boys in for their own protection. In the meantime, I want to know what links these boys to our guy. Kristen wasn't involved in either of their cases."

Monday, February 23, 11:30 A.M.

Silence hung over the conference room in the State's Attorney's office. Kristen drew a deep breath. "That's about it." She scanned the twenty-odd faces in the room and found most registered shock or dismay. Greg and Lois were concerned.

At the head of the table, John looked tired. It had been John's request that she tell them about the Friday night attack in her car, the discovery of the Skinner box, the Conti box, the two delivery boys, and her attack last night. She omitted the more personal points, primarily the way Abe Reagan had come to her aid, in more ways than one.

"You're sure you don't know who this guy is?" Greg asked, apparent doubt in his voice and Kristen's mind abruptly left the topic of Abe Reagan.

"You think I'm keeping it to myself?" she said sharply, Greg's words a verbal slap.

Greg grimaced. "You know I didn't say that. What I'm saying is that this guy knows you. He has personal access to you. There are times he's probably close enough to touch you."

"Thank you for painting Kristen such a vivid picture," Lois said dryly and chuckles rippled through the room.

Kristen managed a small smile despite the chill that clenched her muscles. "Greg hasn't said anything I haven't already thought."

John cleared his throat. "The police have established some basic time frames on each of the murders. Because they believe that the killer has access to confidential court records, each of you will be asked to provide your whereabouts during those time frames. I've assured Lieutenant Spinnelli that you all will cooperate fully."

Angry murmurs reached Kristen's ears and she held up her hand to quiet them. "So many times we criticize the police for not crossing all the t's and dotting the i's. They are trying to do just that, trying to eliminate those of us who have access to the confidential court records John mentioned. Please cooperate with them when they come talk to you."

John wearily raised his hand. "For the record, I was interviewed by Spinnelli on Saturday for the same reason. When they ask you your whereabouts, just tell them. Remember, everything you've heard is confidential. You are not to discuss it outside this room. You are dismissed." He pointed a finger at Kristen. "I need you to stay."

He waited until everyone had filed out, leaving just the two of them at the table. He dragged his hands down his face and sighed. "How was motion hour this morning?"

Kristen raised her brows, surprised at the question. John never concerned himself with motion hour unless she had a major case, and this morning's cases were fairly routine. "Strained." That was an understatement. The defense crowded at the far end of their table as if her very air space was contaminated. "I managed."

"You always manage. You aren't going to like this."

The hairs rose on Kristen's neck. "Like what?"

"For what it's worth, I tried to fight this. I took it as high up on the ladder as I could." In his eyes Kristen saw weary resignation and her stomach clenched. "Milt got calls all weekend long, as soon as news of Skinner's murder broke." Milt was John's boss. His involvement either meant reprimand or raise. Kristen wasn't naive enough to expect a raise. "You're on administrative leave until this is all over."

Kristen froze, unable to believe what she'd heard. "Excuse me?"

John sighed again. "No defense attorney in town wants to appear in the same courtroom with you. They're all prepared to cite physical danger to themselves and their clients. Milt sees this as one big cause for appeal on any case that involves you. You're to turn over all your cases as of four P.M. today. We'll split your workload between the others."

Kristen sat there, stunned. Unable to utter a word.

John pushed himself to his feet. "I'm sorry, Kristen. I told Milt he was wrong, that this wasn't fair, but in the end it didn't matter. I feel responsible for this, but there's nothing I can do." He put a tentative hand on her shoulder and squeezed. She barely felt it. "Consider it a well-earned vacation," he said lamely. "No, I guess not."

A well-earned vacation. The very thought mocked. She rose, keeping her legs steady with the force of sheer will. She would be, as always, in control. "I'll gather my things."

"Kristen—" John reached out a hand and she stepped out of his way. His hand dropped and he sighed once more. "Let me know if you need any help."

"I won't."

Monday, February 23, 1:00 P.M.

Abe hated the smell of the ME's office. On a good day, it had the antiseptic smell of a hospital. He hated hospitals. On a bad day . . . Luckily Conti hadn't been dead long enough to call this a bad day.

"We came as soon as we could, Julia," Mia said, walking over to the table where Angelo Conti's body lay. "What's up?"

"I wanted you to see this." Julia joined them at the table. "Conti's body was in the worst shape of any of them so far. Your guy didn't just beat him, he pounded him into hamburger."

"Medium rare, hold the pickles," Mia quipped and Julia's lips twitched.

"Don't make me laugh. My ribs are still a little sore from yesterday."

Abe frowned. "Jacob Conti hurt you that badly?"

Julia gave a facial shrug. "A few bruises. It could have been worse."

"Yeah, Jack could have ripped off his face." Mia looked satisfied at the thought.

Julia's cheeks colored delicately. "Jack shouldn't have gone after Conti like that."

"Well, I'm glad he did," Mia said.

After a half beat of hesitation Julia admitted, "So am I."

"You could have pressed charges," Abe said.

"I could have, but the situation seemed inflamed enough as it was, what with that reporter filming every move. He'd just found out his son was dead, for God's sake."

"His murdering son," Mia muttered. "I wouldn't waste your tears on him, Julia. Angelo Conti died the same way Paula Garcia died, beaten to death with a tire iron."

Julia huffed out a sigh. "I suppose your guy does have a way with poetic justice. Well, anyway, take a look at this." She rolled the body slightly and pointed to a spot just above the back of Conti's knee. "It's faint and incomplete, but better than nothing."

Abe leaned closer to see, his pulse quickening. "A partial thumbprint."

Mia met his eyes, hers gleaming. "In Conti's blood. Nicely done, Julia."

"The body's lividity indicates the killer rolled Conti on his side shortly after his death. The blood still would have been wet."

"He didn't wear gloves," Mia murmured.

Abe felt a spark of excited hope. "He got so carried away he made a mistake."

"Yeah," Julia said with satisfaction. "For the severity of the beating, there was very little blood on the body. He must have known he'd screwed up and tried to clean him off afterward. But after laying Conti on his side, the body contracted up in rigor and this spot behind the knee would have been hidden. He missed it."

Abe whistled. "We're lucky the print wasn't blurred from the leg rubbing against it."

"That you are. I called Jack to help with the print. He should be here any minute."

"It's only a partial," Mia cautioned. "We shouldn't get our hopes up."

"We won't." Abe took another look at the partial print. "But he's made a mistake. He'll make others and that's how we'll find him."

Julia pulled off her gloves. "Good. I want this thing over, for all of our sakes, but especially for Kristen's. I heard about what happened last night. How is she?"

"Kristen," Mia said archly with a side look at Abe,

"seemed fine when I left her. But then *I* didn't stay all night."

Julia looked amused. "But you slept on the couch, right, Abe?"

Abe rolled his eyes. "Yes, I did, actually. It's a very uncomfortable foldout." He had, actually. She'd fallen asleep in his arms as he sat on the edge of her bed. He'd stayed there next to her for a long while, watching her take deep even breaths, wondering if his sudden and intense interest was due to the fact she was the first woman he'd met after a six-year dearth or if he secretly did compare her to Debra. He'd concluded neither was the case, that he was simply acting on the desire of a healthy red-blooded man for a beautiful, intelligent, sensitive woman. Then he'd retired to the relative discomfort of the foldout couch where he'd lain awake well into the night cursing the fact that he was a healthy red-blooded man with a beautiful, intelligent, sexy-as-hell woman in the next room. Stopping after a few morning kisses was one of the hardest things he'd ever done.

"Foldouts usually are," Julia commented dryly. Then she looked up when the door opened, her face changing from amusement to awareness. "Jack."

Jack closed the door behind him. "Your message said it was urgent."

"It is." Abe pulled on his jacket. "Take care with it, Jack. It's our best lead so far."

Monday, February 23, 2:30 P.M.

Taking care of business was less messy when he kept his head. There was a lot less cleanup required when the only mark on the body was a neat bullet hole in the forehead. The exit wound in the back of the head was a bit of a chore, but the best things in life were rarely the easiest. At least it was easier than it had been with Conti. He still shuddered at the thought of washing the body. Repugnant it had been. *Even for me.*

But enough about Angelo Conti. He'd moved on to Arthur Monroe now, the put-upon pedophile that society had failed. He'd chosen Arthur Monroe's final resting place with ironic care. The liberal bleeding-heart judge who had taken more pity on the offender than his five-year-old victim owned a small dry-cleaning business north of the city. It would serve as both a dumping ground for Monroe and a warning to the judge.

He pulled his van into the narrow access road behind the dry cleaners. The van sported a new sign that was a fine imitation of the one used by Chicago's Department of Water Management. It, like the electrical contractor sign, made a fine cover for digging a trench. Nobody would give a second thought to seeing a utility vehicle on the street.

And nobody did. It was almost anticlimactic, he thought as he got back in his van to drive away. Nobody challenged him, nobody said, "Hey, fella, what are you doing?"

But then again, it was better that way. His reward would come when the world found out that yet another repellent menace was off the streets.

Back to work now. Back to the fishbowl tonight. It was good to have a hobby.

Monday, February 23, 3:45 P.M.

"Kristen?"

She looked up at the sound of Greg's voice to find him standing in the doorway to her office, looking miserable.

She might have said he looked as miserable as she felt, but the human face was not capable of that kind of expression. She looked back down, concentrating on the files she was collecting, forcing her voice to be steady. "I'm almost finished, Greg. I'll be ready to get these cases to you in about an hour."

He sighed heavily. "You know that's not why I'm here." He came into her office, shutting the door. "I'm sorry this happened. I'm sorry it had to be you. I'm sorry it had to be me."

She looked up and met his kind eyes. "I know. I'm not upset at you, Greg. Really."

He flopped into the chair across from her desk. "This isn't fair. It isn't right. But then this whole past week hasn't been fair or right. Are you okay, Kristen? Physically?"

Her hands stilled on the file folders. "I'm fine, Greg."

"That's what you always say," he said bitterly. "We were afraid this would happen, Lois and I. That's why we wanted you to come stay with one of us."

"And have intruders with guns in your home, endangering your families? I don't think so."

He grimaced as her words hit home, then pounded his fist against his knee. "Dammit, somebody needs to be there for you. You shouldn't go through this all alone."

I'm not. The thought echoed in her mind, easing some of the tension from her shoulders. For however long it lasted, Abe Reagan was there. She still wasn't completely sure why, but at this point it was enough to know he would come when she called. "I'm fine, Greg," she said more firmly. "I have police protection, a home alarm—"

"Both of which served you well last night," he said sarcastically.

She conceded his point with a nod, not letting herself

think about how vulnerable she really was. "I'm considering a dog."

He looked unappeased. "A big one?"

"A nasty one with three heads. I'll name him Cerberus."

Greg frowned, then relaxed a little. "You'll get one soon?"

"Maybe tomorrow."

A knock interrupted them and Lois stuck her head in. "Kristen, you have a visitor."

Kristen's smile dimmed. "Refer them to John. I'm on vacation."

Lois shook her head. "Personal." She opened the door wider and Owen's face appeared, followed by the rest of him. He held a brown paper bag that smelled wonderful.

"You didn't come by for lunch," he said reproachfully and Greg stood up.

"Dog, tomorrow?" Greg urged.

"Promise." Greg left and Owen entered, frowning at the box on her desk.

"What is this?"

Kristen waved a careless hand. "Oh, I'm just cleaning up a few files."

"Why did that man say 'dog, tomorrow'?"

"I'm getting a dog," she said lightly. "What's inside the bag?"

"Soup and a Reuben. I didn't think you liked dogs. That blind guy came into the diner one day with a Seeing Eye dog and you sneezed your way into next week."

"Pie?" she asked, hoping she could redirect Owen with talk of food.

"Dutch apple, Vincent's family recipe. Why are you getting a dog?"

Kristen opened the bag and sniffed appreciatively. "I'm starving. I didn't have time for lunch." Truthfully, she'd been afraid to leave the office to get lunch, which added to the general annoyance hanging over the day.

He closed the bag just as she reached in. "Dog. Now. What happened?"

"Oh, I'm getting some annoying people at the house because of all this humble servant nonsense." She pasted a smile on her face to keep him from worrying. "I promised the guys I'd get a dog to scare them away."

His eyes narrowed. "That's all? Just annoying people?"

She nodded. "Totally annoying. So how's the new fry cook?"

Owen scowled and gave her the bag. "He quit. Hired a new one, but he's sorry, too. So why didn't you come by the diner all weekend? You're not on some fad diet, are you?"

Kristen chuckled. Between Reagan's gyros and Italian food and his mother's ham, she hadn't eaten so well in years. "No. Actually I'm . . ." She faltered. "I'm seeing someone." She shrugged when a delighted smile broke across Owen's face. "He feeds me."

"Excellent. Excellent news. And what's his name?"

"Abe Reagan."

Owen's eyes narrowed again. "The detective on this murder case?"

"Yes." She took the lid off the bowl of soup. "Why?"

"I don't know. Just seems dangerous."

No more dangerous than my own life, she thought.

Owen's face softened. "He's good to you?"

She thought of the night before, of this morning, of his patience and gentleness and felt her cheeks heat. "Yes. Yes, he is."

"That's good enough for me. Eat. I have to get back before Vincent kills the new cook."

Kristen smiled at that. "Somehow I can't see Vincent getting that mad ever."

"You'd be surprised. Man has quite a temper."

Kristen was genuinely astonished. "Vincent?" A temper? And her mind wandered, for just a moment, considering. A stupid moment. There was no way Vincent could hurt another soul. But still, stranger things had happened.

"Hmm." Owen backed up to the door. "He lost twenty bucks on the Bulls' game last night and actually said 'darn.' He was fit to be tied."

He was teasing her, Kristen realized and she laughed at herself for the split second she'd imagined Vincent in the role of the humble servant. "You're bad, Owen."

He grinned. "I know." He opened the door, nearly stumbling over Lois.

"Kristen, you have another visitor." She looked half-amused and half-harried, and a second later Kristen knew why.

"Kristen!" Rachel Reagan bounded into her office. "Ooh, food. Can I have some?"

Kristen laughed, the day suddenly sunnier. "Sure, but don't touch the apple pie. It's mine. Rachel, this is my friend Owen. Owen, this is Abe's younger sister, Rachel."

Rachel smiled up at him, a smile purely reserved to charm people she hadn't yet finagled into doing her bidding. "Nice to meet you, sir."

Owen tipped an imaginary hat. "And you. Kristen, I'll see you soon."

"Thanks, Owen." Kristen smiled at Lois who stood waiting. "The kid can stay."

Rachel unwrapped the Reuben. "I am so hungry. I was talking to my teacher and missed lunch." She took a huge bite, and said between chews, "We were talking about you."

"Me?"

Rachel nodded and swallowed. "Got anything to drink around here?"

Kristen handed her one of the bottles of water she kept in her desk drawer and Rachel gulped half a bottle before continuing. "Thanks. She loved my interview with you. She wanted to know if you would come in to talk to my class." She angled her head slyly. "Please?"

Kristen frowned at her because it seemed like the right thing to do. "Does your mother know you're here?"

"Kind of. I told her I was going to a friend's house after school. You said you practically live here, you work so many hours, so I wasn't exactly lying."

Kristen swallowed her smile and gave Rachel a stern look. "You weren't exactly telling the truth either. How did you get down here anyway?"

"I came on the El." She looked annoyed. "I'm not stupid, Kristen. I can get downtown."

But there were a lot of seedy places between Rachel's neighborhood and the El stop for the ASA's offices. Kristen shuddered at the thought of a thirteen-year-old roaming the streets by herself. "Rachel, your parents don't let you walk around town all by yourself, do they?"

Rachel's eyes dropped to the sandwich on her lap and Kristen realized she'd seen that same expression on Abe's face—the morning they'd found the first body and he'd been so angry that she'd put cops on the suspect list. She'd rebuked him and he'd been embarrassed. Now, Rachel wagged her dark head. "No. I'll probably get grounded again." She looked up, a gleam in her blue eyes. Abe's eyes. And in Abe's Kristen had seen that same gleam. "Unless you don't tell on me."

Kristen had to chuckle. "Actually, what's going to happen is that I'm going to see you home and your parents will wonder why I'm with you. Then you'll tell them yourself. You didn't think I'd let you waltz out of here alone, did you? It's going to be dark soon."

Rachel's pretty mouth pushed up in a frown. "I didn't think about that."

Kristen lifted a brow. "You'd better be thinking three steps ahead of everyone if you want to be a prosecutor. You have to determine all the possible outcomes and plan for each one."

Rachel perked back up. "So will you come to my school? Please?" She pressed her clasped hands to her heart. "I promise not to come see you alone on the El ever again."

"I notice you didn't promise not to take the El alone ever again," Kristen responded wryly and Rachel just grinned. Kristen looked at the files on her desk. They were Greg's problem now. She was on an "overdue vacation." "Why not? My calendar has suddenly been freed."

With a confident look that said she'd never really expected any other outcome, Rachel sat back and took another bite. "Extra credit, here I come."

Kristen looked at the young girl fondly. "Don't talk with your mouth full, Rachel."

Monday, February 23, 5:00 P.M.

Jacob Conti sat back in his chair, brooding. "So what do you know?"

Drake shot him a concerned look. "She's squeaky clean, Jacob. The woman hasn't had so much as a parking ticket. She seems to be the impossible. An honest lawyer."

Jacob turned his chair to face the wall, scowling. "You told me that before."

"It was true when Angelo was on trial, it's true now," Drake said with a patience that grated on his nerves. Drake thoroughly investigated Miss Mayhew when she was assigned Angelo's murder trial. They'd looked for something, anything to use against her then, to embarrass her, to blackmail her if necessary. There'd been nothing.

She was a sanctimonious little bitch.

He stared at Angelo's picture hanging on the wall before his eyes and felt the sting of tears. Stupid, stupid kid. Opening his mouth that way.

The man who took his son's life would pay dearly.

Elaine hadn't left her bed since he'd broken the news to her yesterday. Hardest thing he'd done in his life. She'd had to be sedated and the doctor even now waited at her bedside in case she woke up in hysterics again.

"She scratched Paglieri," Drake said and Jacob turned his head, staring.

"What?"

"Paglieri," Drake said tightly. "The guy you sent over last night to bully Mayhew with a gun without my knowledge."

Jacob turned the chair, narrowed his eyes at Drake. "I don't need your permission, Drake. I'm still the boss here, remember?"

Drake didn't blink. "I remember. I'm also telling you it was a damn stupid thing to have done, Jacob. You were thinking with your heart, not with your head."

An ashtray went flying across the room, shattering against the wall and splattering ash all over the floor. "Of course I'm thinking with my heart. My son is dead, Drake." A wave of grief hit him so immense he bowed from its weight. "Angelo's dead, Drake."

"I know, Jacob," Drake said gently. "But you can't harass a woman like Mayhew in her own home without consequences. She scratched Paglieri. Skin samples, Jacob. DNA. If he's caught, they'll follow him back to you. Let me handle this."

"You said you couldn't find anything."

"Nothing illegal, Jacob. That doesn't mean she can't be convinced to cooperate."

Jacob sighed. Drake was right. He wasn't doing Angelo any good by acting impulsively. "I'm listening."

Monday, February 23, 6:00 P.M.

Zoe squinted at the tape. Dammit, they'd been too far away and it was too grainy. She'd tried to get film of Mayhew's house last night from a couple of streets down because the damn cops in front of her house wouldn't let her any closer. Something had happened last night, and for once it was inside the house, not outside. Looked like Mayhew's castle had been scaled. Unfortunately, Mayhew appeared unhurt. How unsatisfying. That would have made great copy. Nevertheless, this little story was starting to percolate in all kinds of different directions. Good thing, too, because her lover hadn't come back. She guessed he actually did have a conscience after all.

She stopped the grainy video. It was worthless. She needed something new. CNN had called this morning and wanted rights to her tape. This was her one shot and she wasn't going to let Mayhew and her guard dogs ruin it.

Chapter Sixteen

Monday, February 23, 9:00 P.M.

Abe let himself into his mother's kitchen and took an appreciative breath. Whatever his mother had fixed for dinner smelled wonderful. He only hoped they'd saved him some.

"Well?" Kristen asked from behind him and suddenly dinner was the last thing on his mind. He turned to find her standing in the doorway to his parents' living room looking totally beautiful and thoughts of the newest box they'd found on her front porch slipped to the fringes of his mind. A glance over her shoulder revealed a grinning Rachel.

"Hiya, Abe."

He reached around Kristen to cover Rachel's face with one of his hands. Gently he pushed her, feeling her giggle under his palm. "Scram, kid."

Kristen's smile was wry. "We've been doing algebra. Actually, Rachel's been doing algebra, and I've been feeling old and stupid." She silently mouthed, "Save me. Please."

Abe slid his arm around Kristen's shoulders to Rachel's obvious glee. "I'm serious, Rach. Kristen and I have to talk about work. You go back to your algebra."

"Okay." Rachel winked broadly. "You go *talk* about *work*." She made a less-than-graceful exit, obviously entertained by very little.

"Oh, to be thirteen again," Kristen said.

Abe looked down at her. "Would you? Be thirteen again?"

She made a terrible face and he chuckled. "No way in hell." She sobered quickly. "What did you find?"

He shook his head. "Not here. Rachel has ears like a bat." He led her through the kitchen and into the laundry room and closed the door, shutting out the sound of the television, leaving only the sound of the dryer banging like it held a pair of running shoes.

"Now tell me," she said, but he shook his head, wanting to keep the real world at bay just a little longer.

"This first." He dipped his head and nuzzled her neck, taking in her soft scent, letting it soothe. She sighed and relaxed into him as if she'd been waiting all night for him to do just that. He pulled her arms around his neck and felt like sighing himself when her small hands settled on his skin, lightly playing with his hair. Her face lifted and he closed in, finding her lips exactly as he'd remembered. Better than he'd remembered.

"How are you?" he asked against her mouth and her lips curved.

"You saved me from algebra. What do you think?"

He kissed her again, then pulled back to look into her eyes. She'd been shocked today, hit hard with the administrative leave. But she didn't seem devastated. Not on the surface anyway, but she hadn't had a moment to herself since he'd dropped her and Rachel off four hours before. Maybe it had been a good thing. Rachel was enough to take anyone's mind off anything. "What was for dinner?"

"Pot roast." She licked her lips and he felt his body surge to life. He shuffled back a half step to put distance between them, not wanting to frighten her. Sooner or later she'd grow used to him, to the way his body responded to her. Hopefully much sooner than later. "With those little red potatoes," she added. "Your mom made you a plate." Her eyes danced at him. "Your father told stories at dinner."

Abe groaned. "I'll bet he did." He'd left her here under the capable protection of his father, who hadn't asked a question but who, Abe knew, had a damn good idea of what was going on. Kyle Reagan might be a retired cop, but his connections were as strong as the day he'd left the force. "Which stories? Or am I afraid to ask?"

"Oh, all kinds of stories." Her fingers stroked the back of his neck and his body clenched. Her eyes narrowing slightly, she repeated the motion, watching him. He splayed his hands wide across the middle of her back, forcing himself not to touch her the way he wanted to. She was testing, exploring her power over him.

"That feels good," he murmured and could see her confidence grow before his eyes. She did it again, then brought her hands around to his chest and pushed his overcoat from his shoulders. He let his arms drop to his sides and shrugged his coat onto the floor. She moved as if she'd pick it up, but his arms went around her again, holding her firm. "Leave it."

Her eyes grew warm, aware, and he drew in a steadying breath as her fingers pulled at his tie. Pulling it free, she dropped it over his shoulder, letting it fall.

"Your father told me that you and Sean fought all the time." Her voice was husky as her fingers struggled with the button at his throat and Abe made himself breathe. Made his hands rest calmly on her back.

"All the time," he said. "Drove my mom nuts." She finally worked the first button free and he let his arms drop to his sides, curling his hands into fists. This was about power, her taking power, and he'd be damned before he stole one iota of her show.

"Umm." She scrunched her brows, concentrating on the next button. "My favorite was the one when Sean was teasing you in the backseat of your mother's old car and you had the bright idea to throw the shoulder belt at him."

The next button slipped free, and he had trouble remembering his own name, much less the incident she described. "I had to have four stitches in my lip when the seat belt retracted and hit me in the face."

"Poor baby." Whether the murmured pity was for him as a seven-year-old with stitches in his lip or him as a fully grown man enduring torture at her hands, he wasn't sure. She pulled another button free and her fingertips gently stroked the hair at his open collar. She looked up at him in surprise. "It's soft."

Sweat was beginning to bead on his forehead. "What?"

Her fingers continued to stroke that one little spot while she stared up at him. "I wondered if it was coarse or soft. The hair on your chest."

Not taking his eyes from hers, he yanked at the buttons, opening his shirt to his waist. He took her hands and put them on his chest, gently pulling at her fingers until her hands were flat against him. He could see her pulse beating at the hollow of her throat as he moved her hands side to side, nearly groaning at the pleasure. It had been such a long time since he'd felt a woman's hands on him. Six long years. It was a homecoming of a different sort. He closed his eyes and just let himself feel. He dropped his hands from hers, and she continued to make wide, sweeping caresses. When he opened his eyes he found her staring up at him, her green eyes luminous with discovery.

"You like this," she whispered. He couldn't hear her voice over the sound of the dryer, but her lips moved and he somehow understood.

"Too damn much." He was harder than an iron rod and knew he'd scare her to death if he pressed her against the dryer like he was dying to. Then her thumbs found his nipples hidden under the thick mat of hair on his chest and he groaned.

Her tongue crept out to moisten her lips and he could

feel her arousal, a silken, throbbing web, suspended between them. "Kiss me, Kristen. Please."

She lifted on her toes and put her lips on his, just a whisper of a kiss. He leaned forward from the waist, his hands grabbing the dryer behind her. She was trapped between his arms and the shaking appliance, but his hips somehow remained an unyielding six inches from her body. "I want you," he ground out. "I don't want to scare you, but I want you so much—"

She lifted abruptly on her toes, throwing her arms around his neck and her lips into his. The kiss was wild and she opened her mouth, letting his tongue stroke hers, stroking back. He moved his head, getting the most he could from just the kiss. Her hands moved back to his chest, under his shirt and around to his bare back and he gripped the edge of the dryer as if it were his only lifeline and he was a drowning man.

He was drowning. And he never wanted to come up for air.

Then the door from the outside opened, letting in a burst of frigid air and an astonished Aidan. Aidan's eyes bugged out and his mouth dropped open and for a moment the three of them stared at each other. Then Aidan stepped back out the door. "Sorry. I'll go around front." He glanced over his shoulder, then back, grinning. "Heads up. Sean and Ruth's van just pulled up and it looks like they've got all five kids."

The door closed and the spell was broken. Kristen looked up at him, her hands still on his bare back. Her fingertips now stroked softly and he shuddered, damning Aidan and thanking him at the same time. Another minute and he wasn't sure he could have given Kristen the space he knew she needed.

"You've got company," she said. "We should go."

Her fingers still stroked his back. "Another minute. It

just feels so good." He pressed a kiss to her temple, her forehead, the corner of her mouth. "You feel so good."

"You're so patient with me."

He swallowed hard. "You're worth the wait."

She smiled at that, a sad little smile that tore at his heart. "We'll see," she said cryptically. She pulled her hands free of his shirt and slumped back against the dryer. "Well, that was an interesting way to work off the pie."

They were done for now, Abe thought and with regret he straightened and began buttoning his shirt. "There was pie?"

"Cherry. Better than Owen's, but never tell him I told you."

He smiled down at her. "Your secret's safe with me."

Her brows furrowed slightly. "Which one?"

He toyed with one of the pins in her hair. "Any. All."

She was quiet for a moment, then finally said, "Debra was a lucky woman."

He didn't know what to say to that. So he said, "Thank you."

"You're welcome." She tilted her head, regarding him soberly. "What did you find?"

The call had come just as they were sitting down to dinner. Truman had grabbed another kid leaving a box on her front porch. Once again the kid was a multiple offender, another teen with a yellow sheet as long as his arm. As if on cue, the dryer stopped and the room was quiet. "Arthur Monroe." Her eyes flickered.

"Little Katie Abrams," she said.

"Katie Abrams was the name on the stone," he confirmed.

"One of the worst of my career. I pulled the most liberal judge on the face of the earth who somehow believed a man molested a five-year-old because society had failed him."

She closed her eyes and he could see her bracing herself. "What was the P.S.?"

He clenched his jaw, anger building anew. *Sonofabitch. Acting like he cares about her when he's put her in this danger.* "He was worried about your safety. With me."

Her eyes flew open, wide and startled. "What?"

"He said, 'Be cautious about who you trust to stand guard over you at night.'"

Her eyes flashed, twin emeralds against her creamy skin. "I hate him."

"I know. I don't want you to sleep at your house tonight. Come to my apartment."

Her lips trembled. "I don't want him to throw me out of my house," she whispered. "I know you think it's crazy, but it's important for me to be in my own house. Please."

There was more, he knew. A reason she was so determined to stay in her home, that she'd chosen the words 'throw me out'. She'd tell him in her own time, just like she'd tell him everything else. "All right," he said. "But I'll stay with you."

Her eyes filled with tears and she dashed them angrily away. "I hate this."

He pulled her against his chest and she came willingly. "I know." His cell phone trilled in his pocket and he fished it out as she cuddled against him. "Reagan."

Mia's voice came through, shaky. But it wasn't the connection. It was Mia that was shaky. "Abe, they found Tyrone Yates. He's dead."

"Damn. How?"

"It was Blades. They left their mark carved into his face."

"What about the other one? Aaron Jenkins."

"Still looking," Mia said. "His parents are frantic. At

least this'll get the parents of tonight's kid off our backs for putting their precious junior in protective custody."

"Maybe this will be enough to get Jenkins's juvie record unsealed. Judge Rheinhold was so damn pious about it today. Let's see if he changes his tune now."

Mia sighed on the other end. "I think we might have better luck with Mrs. Jenkins. Until then, the Blades are serious trouble. Tell Kristen to take a vacation, go to Jamaica."

"I'll tell her," Abe said dryly. He dropped the phone in his pocket. "Mia says hello."

Kristen lifted a brow. "And what else does Mia say?"

He told her about Tyrone Yates and her shoulders sagged. "I'm ready for algebra now."

He pressed another kiss to her forehead. "How are you, really?"

"You mean after what happened today or last night?"

"Either. Both."

She drew a breath and straightened her spine. "I'm pissed as hell, quite honestly. But, there may be an upside. Now I'll have more time to go through all those old case records so I can help you figure out what's common here besides me."

Abe frowned. "But—" She gave him a self-satisfied smile.

"I burned a CD with all the information. I can work from home."

"That was probably against the rules."

Her smile went just a shade naughty and his heart skipped a beat. "You gonna arrest me, Reagan?"

He chuckled ruefully. "I'm tempted. Let's go before I get out the cuffs." With his arm around her shoulders he led her out of the laundry room back into the kitchen, where the volume was louder than the dryer had been. Sean and Ruth's kids were running around the kitchen like it was the

Indy 500. Abe dropped a kiss on his mother's cheek, then another on the cheek of the baby she held. His newest niece. "I'm back."

Becca looked amused and Abe knew Aidan had blabbed about the laundry room. "I can see that. Hi, Kristen."

Abe looked over to find Kristen staring at Ruth, a horrified expression on her face. "They're all yours?"

Ruth grinned, then cringed at the sound of broken glass. "Plus one other who will be losing his allowance for the rest of his life to pay for what he just broke."

Becca handed the baby to Ruth. "I'll go see. Abe, I fixed you a plate. Microwave it."

Abe snorted. "Hell, I'm eating the leftover pie before Aidan knows it's here."

Ruth shooed him. "Then eat it in the living room. I want to talk to Kristen. Coffee?"

Kristen shook her head. "No thank you."

"Then sit, please." Ruth gestured to the table and Kristen sat. "Becca told me you were here tonight. We were afraid you might not come back."

Kristen frowned. "Why?"

"Well, you seemed so hurt when you left last night. You were trying not to be, but we could tell you were."

Last night. Last night she'd been with Reagan. Kissing Reagan. Before that she'd been attacked in her own bedroom by an assailant with a gun. But before that— "Oh. The thing about Debra. I'm sorry. I was hurt, a little. But after Abe took me home . . ." She hesitated. "Someone broke into my house and threatened me. Abe chased them away."

Ruth went still. "The same men that pulled you out of your car Friday night?"

"Probably not." They all suspected Jacob Conti, but there was no proof. Nothing but the skin Jack had scraped from her fingernails, but without a suspect to compare, the evidence meant very little. Kristen shrugged. "I'm okay, really. Just shaken up."

"Abe stayed with you last night, right? He didn't leave you alone."

Kristen fought hard to keep her cheeks from flushing, but by the light in Ruth's eyes knew she'd failed. "No," she said, striving for some dignity. "He didn't leave me alone."

Ruth reached across the table and covered her hand. "Good. I mean it, Kristen. Abe's been alone for so long. He's a good man. He deserves someone who will make him happy."

Kristen couldn't stand the warm look in Ruth's eyes. She made Abe happy now, she knew. But it wouldn't last. "I don't want you all to get your hopes up, Ruth. Abe is watching out for me because of this whole . . . thing." She gestured aimlessly with one hand. "Media, killers, men with guns. I don't expect him to stick around when it's all over."

Ruth sighed. "This is your business, Kristen. Yours and Abe's. Whatever happens between you is between the two of you. I just wanted you to know I was sorry for reacting like I did last night. It was so rude of me, but when I heard you laugh, it was like having Debra right here in the room." She rocked the baby, and the sight tugged at Kristen's heart. "It's going to be hard for Abe, seeing Debra's parents on Saturday."

The baby's christening. Kristen dreaded the thought of christenings and had always managed to slide out of attending such ceremonies in the past, but she'd go with Abe if he asked her. It would dredge up still more old wounds, but she'd be there to support him even if it killed her inside. "Abe told me that they hadn't agreed on Debra's care."

Ruth stared pensively, then brushed a kiss on her baby's downy head and again Kristen's heart tugged at the sight. "Don't hold it against them. My aunt and uncle believed they were acting in Debra's best interest. I can't imagine having to make such a choice."

Kristen watched Ruth hold the baby close and considered her words. Acting in your child's best interest. Doing what was right even when it was enough to cut your own heart from your chest. She understood, better than anyone would know.

Ruth cleared her throat. "Anyway, it might be easier if Abe had someone with him on Saturday. Would you come to the christening? I know it's short notice, but . . ."

He'd been there for her, so many times. "Of course. Thank you for asking me."

"Asking you to do what?" Abe appeared in the doorway, holding Kristen's purse. He bent to kiss the baby's head. "Your purse is ringing."

Kristen pushed to her feet. "My cell phone." She dug it from her purse. "Mayhew."

Abe watched as she listened, his apprehension growing as her face paled. She sank into the chair, real fear in her eyes.

"She's all right?" Kristen said. She clutched the little cell phone so tightly that her knuckles were white. "You're sure." She listened, drew a deep breath. "I *am* calm. Do I need to come?" Her mouth twisted at the reply. "I suppose not. Did you call the police?" She gritted her teeth. "No, it's not a damn prank, Dad . . . Just don't touch the note or the flower, okay? I'm going to call the police. They'll want the note and descriptions of anyone who came to the nursing home tonight." Her lips pursed hard and she closed the flip phone with a hard snap. "Yeah," she said bitterly to no one. "Whatever."

Abe sat on the edge of the table next to her. "Your mother?"

She nodded. "Somebody left a black rose and a note on

her pillow at the nursing home." She flicked a glance at Ruth. "My mother's in the final stages of Alzheimer's."

Abe cupped her face in his hand and felt her tremble. "What did the note say?"

" 'Who is he?' " She lurched to her feet, her face stark. "Where's my coat?"

"Are you going to Kansas?" Abe asked.

Kristen shook her head, backing for the door. "No, I'm getting away from here. The guy last night said people close to me would die if I didn't tell him who he was. There's no way I'm putting your family in danger, Abe. Take me home."

From the corner of his eye Abe watched Ruth instinctively hold her baby closer to her chest. "Just calm down, Kristen," he said, realizing too late that was the wrong thing to have said. Her father had apparently said the same thing.

"I *am* calm," she said coldly. "I'll be calmer when you take me home."

Resigned, Abe stood up. "I'll get your coat."

Monday, February 23, 11:00 P.M.

It was too soon. He wasn't giving himself time to rest between, but he was running out of time. So many names in the fishbowl. Crooks, lawyers. Judges.

It was so cold. He shivered hard, his bones aching. He could feel his throat growing rawer by the minute. The rooftop was hard and icy under his stomach and his fingers were frozen. He'd been waiting for two hours. It didn't appear William Carson was going to show up. He smiled grimly, his lips cracking. Perhaps the attorneys were wising up. Perhaps Skinner's untimely demise had warned them against showing up at unseemly times of the night in seedy parts of town for damaging evidence against victims. Evidence that would help acquit the vermin they represented. But the media hadn't picked up on how he lured his marks, so there was no real reason for Carson to be wary of anonymous tips.

He scowled, bracing himself against the cold wind. If the media knew, that viper Zoe Richardson would have told it. Day after day she made her reports, day after day she suggested Kristen and the police knew more than they did. That woman should be stopped. Unfortunately, she hadn't done anything illegal or even immoral. Just trashy.

A movement caught his eye. He pushed himself to his aching elbows and peered into the darkness. So the rat had found the cheese too irresistible to pass up.

Excellent. He leaned down and pressed his eye to the sight, wincing when the frigid metal bit at his face. He centered on Carson's forehead. One pump of the trigger . . . There was another movement on the fringe of his eyesight and he flinched just as his trigger finger moved. A piercing scream rent the air and Carson fell.

I missed. He's still alive.

The thought had barely registered when another man appeared from the shadows, running to bend over Carson. He watched in horror as the man whipped out a cell phone. Carson hadn't come alone. As if guided by an unseen hand, he once again bent, set his sight on the crouching man and fired. The man dropped without a sound, but Carson still writhed. He set the sight on Carson's chest, pumped the trigger once. Carson's body went still.

Then he grabbed his rifle and ran.

Monday, February 23, 11:35 P.M.

Kristen stood at her front window, watching Abe's SUV disappear down the street. Another one. But this one was different. Their man had missed, and left a target alive.

Abe had struggled with leaving her, but in the end she'd insisted and knowing his duty, he'd gone. Now it was quiet again and she stood alone, unsettled and afraid in her own home. She went into the kitchen to make some tea, the routine movements providing some sparse comfort. Then she looked down to see her hairpins on the countertop where Reagan had left them. She thought back. Saturday night. Two nights ago. It seemed like twenty. He'd held her standing right here, kissed her for the first time and made her feel . . . alive. She wished he was here now.

The doorbell rang and she jumped. "Ridiculous," she murmured. "There's a cop sitting outside." *A lot of good that did last night,* she thought. The bell rang again, longer this time. Wishing the three-day waiting period was over and she had her new gun, she walked out of her own kitchen, her knees trembling. She pulled her cell phone from her pocket and punched in 9-1-1 and poised her thumb over the send button. Just in case. Although she doubted anyone with nefarious intent would be so bold as to ring the bell. But stranger things had happened. This week. *To me.*

She looked through the peephole in her door and exhaled in relief. "Kyle," she said, opening the door and clearing the 9-1-1 from her cell phone.

Kyle Reagan stepped inside, as large as his son. He was a quiet man, having said fewer than two dozen words to her the two times she'd visited the Reagan house. But he had an easy smile and a twinkle in his blue eyes that made her feel welcome each time. His blue eyes were sober now as he examined her face, likely for signs of strain. It was no secret that she'd left his house tonight in something less than a serene mood. He held out a bag. "Becca sent food."

Kristen's lips quirked. Food was Becca's panacea. "And Abe sent you?"

He shrugged. "Something like that. You got any coffee? It's cold out there."

"I was about to make myself some tea."

Kyle followed her into the kitchen and said nothing while she spooned tea into the teapot. "I suppose I should tell you that you shouldn't have come," she said. "But I'm glad you did." Her hands clenched on the countertop. "I hate being afraid in my own house."

"I know," he said quietly. "I'm not going to tell you not to be afraid, Kristen. It's a human response and in your case, a good one. It's keeping you aware."

"I bought a gun."

"I know. Abe told me. He said you're a pretty good shot."

She leaned back against the counter. "He did?"

"Sure. In fact, just about everyone in my family is singing your praises."

Kristen looked away. "I like your family, Kyle. I like them too much to drag them into all this."

"I know you do." He studied her across the room, not belittling her fear for his family and her respect for him went up. "How is your mother?" he asked.

"She's all right. Thanks." The kettle began to whistle and she lifted it from the stove. "I called the nursing home when we got back here." Sitting on her sofa with Abe next to her, his arm around her shoulders for support. "I needed to hear from the staff myself. My father tends . . . to keep things from me."

"Parents do that. For some reason we don't want our kids to worry."

Kristen shrugged. She knew better. "Perhaps." She joined him at the table with the teapot and two cups and changed the subject. "Then Abe called the police in Kansas."

"Did he get anywhere with them?"

"No. Nobody saw anything, and there aren't any cameras in the nursing home."

"What about the note and the flower?"

"Abe tried to get them to agree to ship it here, but they politely declined. They said they'd send it to their own crime lab in Topeka."

"If it was Conti, they won't find anything," Kyle said quietly.

"I know."

He slipped his hand in his pocket and brought out a deck of cards. "I'll stay here if you want to sleep. But if you can't . . ." He waved the deck.

Kristen knew she wouldn't sleep a wink until Abe came back with news on the latest shooting. "I don't know many card games," she said. "My dad didn't allow cards. But I need to get some work done anyway."

"Anything I can do to help?"

"Do you know anything about databases?

He grimaced. "About as much as you know about cards."

Kristen smiled. "Then just keep me company?"

He dealt himself a hand of solitaire. "That I can do."

Tuesday, February 24, 12:05 A.M.

Red lights flashed, creating a strobe effect as they reflected against no fewer than five police cars, six unmarked cars, a CSU van, and two ambulances.

Mia was crouching by one of the two men. When she saw Abe, she stood up and beckoned him closer.

"Sorry I'm late," he apologized. "I had to find somebody to stay with Kristen."

"No problem. This is Rafe Muñoz," she said, pointing to the big man lying on a stretcher, encased in an unzipped bodybag. "He's a bodyguard. Was, anyway. That"—she pointed at the stretcher being loaded into an ambulance— "is William Carson."

Abe grimaced. He knew the name. He'd been unfortunate enough to be cross-examined by Carson when he was still in uniform, years before "Another defense attorney. What's Carson's status?"

"Iffy. May make it, may not. He was conscious for a few minutes after the first cruiser arrived. He ID'd Muñoz before he passed out. They're taking him to Rush. Muñoz has a bullet hole in his head. Looks like he was kneeling next to Carson when he was hit. But Carson . . ." Even in the darkness Abe could see Mia's eyes gleam. "The first shot hit him here, barely grazed him." She tapped the top of her skull. "Second shot hit him square in the chest. We got an entry wound, but no exit."

Abe's pulse spiked. "The bullet's still in him."

"With any luck, before dawn we'll have a maker's mark to show Diana Givens."

"Where did the bullet come from?"

Mia turned and pointed to the four-story building across

the street. "He was waiting for Carson up there. Let's go take a look."

Armed with a bright searchlight, they climbed the fire escape to the roof and gingerly crossed to where their sniper would have lain in wait.

Mia whistled softly. "Do my eyes deceive me? Could I possibly be looking at what I think I'm looking at?"

Abe looked at the cup with the plastic lid, his own heart doing a little victory dance. Still he felt compelled to keep them from getting their hopes up. "It might not be his."

Mia bent down, sniffed at it, pressed her latex gloved fingers to the side of the cup. "It's coffee and it's still lukewarm." She grinned up at him. "Jack will be pleased."

Tuesday, February 24, 12:30 A.M.

He sat at his kitchen table, his hands still shaking uncontrollably. He'd missed.

He'd missed. And then he'd panicked and killed an innocent man.

Well, he reasoned, the man was probably not that innocent. He was hanging around Carson, after all. Carson was a dirty lawyer who represented murderers and drug dealers and rapists. Anyone accompanying such a pariah couldn't be entirely innocent.

But it was a regrettable loss, he had to admit. Worse yet, he'd run without making sure both men were dead. He'd turned tail and run down the fire escape like a common criminal, like a thug with the police at his heels.

The police still didn't know who he was. Not yet. But perhaps it was time to be considering the end. He picked up the three cards he hadn't added to the fishbowl. They were special names. He'd put off their executions, because as soon as all three were dead, the police would put two and two together and know exactly where to find him. He'd wanted to empty the fishbowl first, but time was growing shorter.

He stood, feeling the ache deep in his bones. It hurt to swallow and his head throbbed. Hours of waiting in the cold, digging graves and hauling bodies were taking its toll. He'd barely been able to hold on at his day job. Things had to come to an end, and soon. He began making coffee, hoping to return some warmth to his body. He peeled back the lid from the can, then froze when the aroma of ground coffee met his nostrils.

Coffee. He'd had a cup of coffee. *And he'd left it behind.*

Jerking himself back into motion, he continued his task, scooping the coffee into the filter basket. The police were not fools. Reagan and Mitchell would find the coffee cup and they'd be able to get his DNA. It was bound to have happened sooner or later. He was bound to leave some physical evidence behind at some point, no matter how careful he was. Now he had, and he would pay. He had to take care of the three key players before the police figured out who he was. He owed it to Leah.

Chapter Seventeen

Tuesday, February 24, 8:30 A.M.

Jack was pleased. "We got more than a DNA sample from the lid of that coffee cup," he announced. "Our guy's got a sore throat. We found traces of mentholyptis in the coffee, like he'd been sucking a cough drop at the same time he was drinking."

"Oh joy," Mia said sarcastically. "It's flu season. Let's round up everybody with a sniffle."

"It might be why he missed," Abe mused. "He's not feeling well."

"Poor baby," Kristen said unfeelingly. "My heart bleeds for him."

"Regardless, he might screw up again." Mia held up a plastic bag. "And now we've got a maker's mark. Hot off the press."

Spinnelli took the bag and held it up to the light. "It's in good shape this time."

"They recovered it from Carson's right lung," Abe offered. "The surgeon was able to get it out just a few hours ago."

"I'm glad we were there," Mia growled. "He almost threw it away."

"But he felt so bad about it he asked Mia out to dinner to apologize," Abe added with a grin and after another second of growling, Mia grinned, too.

"A doctor this time. I'm movin' up in the world."

Spinnelli shook his head with an unwilling smile. "So what's next, people?"

"Julia will autopsy Arthur Monroe today," Mia offered. "It's strange, you know? Conti's death was so brutal and Monroe . . ." She lifted a shoulder. "Just a pop to the head and he's done. Not what I would have expected him to do to a guy who molested a little girl."

"Conti was an aberration," Jack said. "He got so riled when Conti—what was it—'publicly assassinated' Kristen. That was . . . personal. Now he's back to business."

"Maybe he's rattled," Kristen said thoughtfully. "He lost control with Conti."

"Which could be another reason he missed Carson last night," Abe said. "I want to know how he lured Carson to the ambush. We know Skinner got a delivery the day he was murdered. Let's find out if Carson did, too."

Spinnelli frowned. "Ask him."

Mia shook her head. "We waited around after the surgery, just to see if he'd come to, but he didn't. The hospital's supposed to call us when he regains consciousness."

"What about Muñoz?" Spinnelli pressed. "How does he connect to Carson?"

Mia shrugged. "Carson told the guys at the scene he'd hired him as his bodyguard."

"Apparently a lot of the defense attorneys are doing that," Kristen said dryly. "One of them faxed me his bill just before I left the office yesterday afternoon."

"Hell of a bodyguard," Jack muttered. "Guy didn't even have a gun."

Mia frowned. "You didn't find a gun? He had a holster. I remember seeing it when they zipped up the body bag."

"We didn't take it," Jack said. "The only thing we got from Muñoz's body was his phone."

"Then somebody else took it," Abe said. "Somebody saw the shooting go down and took the gun before the cops got there."

"Maybe the killer took it," Jack said.

Mia shook her head. "Then why didn't he take Muñoz's cell phone, too? That's how we knew where to find them—the cell phone."

"GPS again," Jack said. "You're right, Mia. If he'd had the presence of mind to take the gun, he should have seen the cell phone, too. It was clutched in Muñoz's hand."

"That means we have a witness," Abe said.

"Who saw a van with a fictitious magnetic sign," Kristen sighed. "So what?"

"One of these days we're going to have a witness who actually sees something worthwhile," Abe insisted. "Marc, can you get somebody to sweep the pawnshops? My bet is that Muñoz's gun wasn't cheap, and whoever stole it will hock it."

Spinnelli wrote himself a note. "I'll ask Murphy to do it. He just closed a big case."

"Whoever took it probably has a couple guns of his own already," Mia muttered.

"Everybody does but me," Kristen grumbled.

Abe's lips curved. "You can pick yours up tomorrow, but if you want to visit it first, you can come see Diana Givens with us. Since you're on an 'overdue vacation.'"

"What?" Jack asked openmouthed. "What happened?"

"I got put on administrative leave. The defense attorneys say I'm a menace." She said it deadpan and Mia snickered.

Abe's lips twitched. "We're punchy, Marc. None of us got any sleep last night."

Spinnelli looked over at Kristen. "You didn't go to the scene, did you?"

Kristen shook her head. "No, I but I couldn't sleep either. I did some research last night while you were at the hospital with Carson." She tapped the stack of papers on the table in front of her. "With the exception of the Blade members and Angelo Conti, every one of the attacks has been related to a sexual assault. There doesn't seem to be a pattern, though. There's no chronology. He jumps a year forward, back, then forward. There's no commonality in sentence except that not one did any physical time. Some got off entirely, a few were plead down. He's got lawyers and defendants. I'd say he's choosing his victims at random, but that the deck's stacked with sex crimes."

"Okay." Spinnelli gestured to the papers in front of her. "So what's in those?"

"All the sexual assaults I prosecuted over the last five years where the perp did no physical time. I don't think there is a connection *between* the cases. But the killer has a connection to one of these cases, I'm sure of it. It may not be one of the victims he's already avenged. Maybe it's still to come. Maybe the others are . . ." She shrugged. "Public service."

"Our humble servant." Jack blew out a breath.

"Exactly. Anyway, chances are good that the next time he strikes, it will be someone on this list, either a perp or his lawyer."

Spinnelli recoiled. "Please tell me you're not suggesting we guard all those people."

"No, Marc. But remember how Westphalen thought there had been a trauma recently? Well, you've investigated all the original victims so far and found no real trauma around the time of the first killing—Anthony Ramey. I thought I'd start calling the victims of these cases and finding out how they are. Find out if any of them have experienced significant trauma."

"If it's the killer, they won't admit to any recent trauma," Jack said.

Kristen lifted a brow. "I thought of that. This isn't going to necessarily be a smoking gun. It may eliminate some of the names on this list. Do you have a better suggestion? You have DNA, one unconscious man, a partial fingerprint, and a bullet."

"The man may regain consciousness and the bullet we can trace," Abe said.

Kristen shrugged. "So trace it. My looking up old cases shouldn't affect that."

"It could help, Abe," Mia said slowly. "Besides, Kristen's on 'vacation.' If it were me, I'd be nuts without something to do."

"There is that," Kristen admitted. "Other than finishing my basement mantel, I'd just be twiddling my thumbs and that would drive me crazy. I'm not suspended from John's office, I'm just not working any active cases. Nobody said anything about archived cases."

Abe understood the need to keep busy. He'd thrown himself into the job when Debra was shot. Most days, it was the only thing that kept him going. "Do it from here," he told her. "I don't want anyone tracing calls to your house."

"There are a lot of names here," Spinnelli said. "This will take you hours. Days."

Kristen looked at each one of them sharply. "Look, we've got nine bodies. Nine. I don't plan to go to any of their funerals and cry, but they're dead nonetheless. Skinner left behind a wife and kids. They deserve justice if nobody else. My life is on hold and my mother was threatened last night. Until we catch this guy, I have all the time in the world."

Tuesday, February 24, 9:15 A.M.

Mia leaned against the glass countertop, staring at Diana Givens who stared at the bullet through a magnifying glass.

"Well?" she demanded. "Have you seen it or not?"

Diana glanced up, annoyed. "Keep your pants on." She bent her head down, squinting. "Intertwined M's or W's. I haven't seen anything like this, but one of my customers might."

"So where can we find your customers?" Mia pressed.

"Well, I told you I was going to invite them over, but I didn't think you'd be back with a good bullet so soon." She passed the bullet back to Mia and grabbed a sheet of paper from under the counter. "Here. I'll give you their names. You can talk to them if you want."

Mia gave Diana a smile. "Thanks. We'll owe you one."

Tuesday, February 24, 11:30 A.M.

"I hate hospitals almost as much as morgues," Abe grumbled.

Mia kept her eyes on the rising elevator display. "I know. You told me last night while we were waiting for Carson. Several times." The bell dinged and the doors opened. "Don't be such a baby. Come on, I want to talk to him before he goes unconscious again."

A nurse frowned as they came into Carson's room. "He's in no shape to talk."

"He's alive," Mia snapped. "That puts him in better shape than the nine bodies in the morgue."

Carson lay against the pillows, his face ashen. "Muñoz?"

"He's dead," Abe said quietly.

"Hell of a bodyguard," Carson mumbled. "I'll have to remember not to pay his bill."

Mia rolled her eyes, but her voice was professional when she stepped up to Carson's bedside. "We just have a few questions, Mr. Carson, then we'll leave you to rest. We need to know what brought you to that particular spot last night."

Carson closed his eyes and took a shallow breath. "Information," he said. "I got a call on my cell phone before dinner. Told me they had information about Melanie Rivers."

"Who is Melanie Rivers?" Abe asked and Carson grimaced.

"Little white trash." He breathed and they waited. "She filed a rape charge against my client, said he'd molested her at a party. She knows he's got money." He breathed some more. "She just wants a settlement. Her pound of flesh."

Abe bit back his distaste. "Maybe she's telling the truth."

"So what if she is?" Carson opened his eyes, sharp and canny despite his physical state. "I know what you think about me and frankly I don't care. I don't expect you to do much of anything anyway."

"And why is that?" Mia asked coldly.

Carson's gray lips twisted. "He's doing your dirty work for you, this killer. If the tables were turned, I'd look the other way, too."

Mia opened her mouth to say something then pursed her lips firmly. Abe stepped in to continue. "Who had your cell phone number, Mr. Carson?"

"Not many people. That's why I went to meet him. He said he'd gotten my number from a mutual friend and he wanted to help me out. For a fee." He breathed heavily, then batted away the nurse's hand when she tried to adjust the oxygen line in his nose. "Said he wanted two G's. If we'd won the case, it would have been cheap."

Abe was wondering what kind of friends a parasite like Carson would harbor when he had a sudden thought. "Would Trevor Skinner have known your cell phone number?" he asked. "Maybe had it in a phone book?"

"Probably." Carson drew a labored breath. "Trev kept his life in his BlackBerry."

"You mean his electronic organizer?" Mia asked.

Carson nodded. "Clever little thing. Trev could send e-mails from anywhere." He lifted a brow. "His BlackBerry wasn't on him when you found him, was it?"

"No." Abe shook his head. "No, it wasn't."

"Then I'd say you have your work cut out for you, Detectives. Trev knew the private lives of every one of his clients and half the lawyers in town. Judges, too."

Tuesday, February 24, 1:30 P.M.

Spinnelli frowned. "Judges, too? What did he mean by that?"

Mia squirted ketchup over her burger. "He just smiled and told us to figure it out. S.O.B."

"He's right, though." Abe considered the implications yet again. "If the killer has Skinner's organizer, he has enough ammunition to hold him for weeks."

"Speaking of ammunition," Spinnelli said, "what happened at the gun shop?"

"She gave us names of customers who make their own bullets," Mia said. "We'd visited the first two on the list when we got the call from the hospital saying Carson was awake. Neither had seen the mark before, but we still have four more names."

"Well, we got a reply on opening Aaron Jenkins's juvenile record." Spinnelli clenched his jaw. "No, no, and no."

Abe sighed. "Then let's visit the mother after we see the other old men."

Mia peeked in the bag. "One more burger. We brought it for Kristen. Where is she?"

Abe's eyes took yet another sweep of the office area. She'd been his first thought as he entered, occupying a corner of his mind even as they'd updated Spinnelli over lunch. But Mia had smirked at him smugly, so he'd held back his demand to know Kristen's whereabouts.

Spinnelli shrugged. "She took a break about an hour ago. She went to lunch."

Abe felt the hair on the back of his neck stand on end. "You let her go? Alone?"

"She's a grown woman, Abe," Spinnelli said mildly. "And not a stupid one. She told me where she was going and asked Murphy to take her there. Some place called Owen's. It's a diner, I take it."

Abe relaxed a bit. "It is."

"But you'll still call her to make sure she's all right," Mia added slyly.

Abe concentrated on his burger, well aware of the knowing glance passing between Marc and Mia and not giving a damn. "I will."

Tuesday, February 24, 1:30 P.M.

"You cleaned your plate," Vincent said approvingly.

Kristen looked down at the crumbs. "I was hungry." Which surprised her. After hours of accepting the pent-up anger of the victims she'd once represented, she'd thought her appetite gone. She'd come here to get away for a little while, agreeing to lunch only after Owen shook his finger in her face before disappearing to train his newest hire. Kristen winced at the crash of dishes and Owen's shout. "I'm not sure who I feel sorrier for. Owen or the new guy."

Vincent shook his shaggy head. "I think you should feel sorrier for me. I've got a mind to stop by Timothy's to ask his mom when he's coming home. How sick can one grandmother be? He needs to get back to work before I lose my temper."

"How long did Timothy work here?" Kristen asked and Vincent scratched his head.

"Well, I've been here for fifteen years. Owen bought the place about three years ago and hired Timothy about a year later. Anyway, you want some pie? I made it this morning."

"You twisted my arm, Vincent."

Vincent grinned his slow grin. "With ice cream?"

"Of course."

Vincent was heaping scoops of vanilla on her pie when the little bell on the glass door jangled. Kristen shivered at the blast of cold air at her back, then glanced over her shoulder when Vincent slowly lowered the ice-cream dipper and stared. Kristen stared, too, needing a minute to process the face above the calf-length fur coat that seemed out of place in a diner whose seats were cracked vinyl. Then realization clicked.

"Sara?" John's wife. *Oh, God,* she thought, looking at Sara Alden's stricken face and thinking the worst. "What's wrong? What's happened to John?"

Sara unbuttoned her coat with cool grace. "Can we talk privately, Kristen?"

"Of course." She led her boss's wife to a booth in the corner.

Sitting, Sara abruptly asked, "Why did you think something was wrong with John?"

"You went to a lot of trouble to find me here. I just assumed . . . How did you find me?"

"Lois said you might be here. She said you were out of the office indefinitely."

Kristen felt the sting, deep inside. "Yes, that's true."

"John is responsible." Sara's eyes flashed with anger.

Bewildered, Kristen shook her head. "No, John's boss made the call. John said he tried to keep him from putting me on leave, but Milt was determined."

Sara's lips curled. "Yeah, I'll just bet John tried real hard."

Kristen wasn't sure how to respond to that. "Sara, what's going on here?"

"Lieutenant Spinnelli's office called this morning. A Detective Murphy said they were confirming alibis for everyone in John's department for the nights those men were murdered. He asked about John."

"That's true, but it's standard procedure. Lieutenant Spinnelli's just making sure that they've looked at everyone who was involved in all those old cases. Is that what you're worried about, Sara? I can tell you, nobody suspects John. He's not involved in murder."

"He lied," Sara said flatly. "John told Spinnelli's man that he was home in bed with me. But he lied. He was with another woman. He thinks I sleep, but I know when he's gone."

Kristen sat back and drew a deep breath. John was on Spinnelli's list of sharpshooters. She knew that. She'd also dismissed it as soon as she'd seen his name on the list. Not once had she entertained the notion that John Alden could be involved in murder. John went to great lengths to follow procedure. To ensure all the statutes were followed, that every convicted man was convicted legally. He was a good prosecutor.

But apparently a bad husband.

"Oh, Sara." To her dismay Sara's eyes filled with tears. "I wish I knew what to say."

Sara dug into her purse for a handkerchief. "He actually expected me to lie for him."

"Did you?"

"No." Sara glared through her tears. "Well, not exactly. I told Detective Murphy that John never came to bed that night, that I couldn't say for sure where he was."

"But you know where he was?" Kristen asked gently.

Sara pulled her fur collar high on her neck, gathering her composure. "He's talked in his sleep for years, Kristen. He says all kinds of things. Sometimes things I shouldn't hear, but I've been a good wife all these years and haven't shared any of his confidences."

Kristen's eyes widened at the implications. "He talks about cases in his sleep?"

"Among other things."

"He said the other woman's name in his sleep?"

"He did. Have you wondered how Zoe Richardson found out about the letters addressed to you, Kristen? About how he signs the letters 'Your Humble Servant'?" Kristen's mouth fell open. "He muttered about it," Sara said softly, "in his sleep, a few nights after all this started, so I've known. So did Zoe Richardson."

Kristen swallowed, connecting the dots but still unable to believe the picture. "He's having an affair with Zoe Richardson? John? John Alden? My boss?"

"Your boss. My husband. Richardson's not his first, Kristen. But this is different. You're in danger and it's because that woman plastered your face all over the news as some kind of link to this killer. I know about Friday night and Sunday night. You've been attacked twice."

Kristen pressed her fingers to her lips, her brain reeling. "I . . ." She met Sara's eyes across the table. "Why didn't you call him on the cheating before?"

Sara lifted a shoulder, misery in her eyes. "I was humiliated, so I let it go."

"Until now." Kristen closed her eyes under the enormity of it all.

"I won't lie for him, Kristen. And he should pay for what he's done to you. The night you found the first letters, in your trunk? You tried to call him. Three times."

"He didn't have his phone on."

"Because he was with *her.* He came home in the middle of the night, sneaking in like the dog he is. Took a shower, thinking I was sound asleep. I turned his phone back on, listened to his messages. Then I deleted them so he wouldn't know what I'd done."

"He was mad at the phone service for losing his messages," Kristen remembered, her mind still reeling. "He was mad at me for not calling him."

Sara slid out of the booth. "Perhaps he'll be taking a 'vacation' soon, too."

Kristen watched her go, sighed, then took out her cell phone and dialed Spinnelli.

Tuesday, February 24, 5:30 P.M.

"Come in, sit down."

Abe looked around the little apartment owned by Grayson James. There was a small fireplace with a mantel upon which rested several trophies, all for marksmanship. "Thank you for taking time to talk to us, Mr. James."

"Diana said you'd be coming. She said you're interested in maker's marks." He put a small lamp on the kitchen table and flipped it on. "Let's have the bullet."

For the sixth and final time that day Mia drew out the plastic bag holding the bullet. No one else on Diana's list had been able to help them.

"Can I touch it?" James asked.

"By all means," Abe said and watched the old man handle the bullet with deft fingers. James held the bullet under the light.

Then sat down slowly. "Where did you get this?" he asked.

Mia looked at Abe, a new energy in her eyes. "You've seen it?"

"I have. More years ago than I'd like to remember." For a long moment, James stared at the bullet, his face taking on a faraway expression. Then he blinked and gave the bullet back to Mia. "I had a friend when I was a boy, back before the War. He and I would shoot together at his father's cabin.

His father made his own bullets, taught us to do it, too. That was his mark. I'd never seen it before and never seen it since. Where did you find it?"

"Your friend, Mr. James," Abe said as calmly as he could. "Can we talk to him?"

James's lips thinned. "Not unless you're into séances. Hank Worth died at Iwo Jima in 1944."

Mia exhaled, her disappointment as palpable as his own. "Any surviving children?"

"Nope. He was only eighteen when we joined up. Look, I've helped you. The least you can do is tell me where you found this bullet. You're detectives, so whatever it is, it can't be good. I hate to see someone tarnishing Hank's memory. He was my friend."

Abe hesitated. "I can't give you details, Mr. James, but we're homicide detectives. This bullet was used in an attempted homicide."

James's eyes widened as he put two and two together. "You're investigating that vigilante, the one killing criminals and lawyers."

Mia's back straightened at the implied accusation in James's voice. "We are."

"Seems like a quandary," James said. "He's poppin' off guys that deserve it, but still . . ."

"Still?" Mia asked.

"Still, it's killin' all the same. I did it, in the war, because I had to. But it changes you. When you take the life outta somebody else's body, it changes you."

Mia looked lost for a moment and Abe knew she was remembering the firefight the night her old partner was killed. She'd shot a man that night, killing him. The punk's pal shot both Mia and her partner. Mia was lucky to be alive. "Yes, Mr. James," she said, "it does. We need to find this guy. Please tell us anything else you remember."

James was regarding her soberly. "My friend had a sweetheart before he shipped out to the Pacific. They'd planned to get married when he came back, but she up and married somebody else not two months after he left. Killed him, it did. Wait here."

They waited in silence and a few minutes later James returned. "Here's the letter he sent me. It's dated December, 1943. Here's her name, his sweetheart, that is. Genny O'Reilly. Said he'd just gotten her letter, but the mail took forever in those days. It could have been months before that she actually married the guy." He handed them the yellowed page. "I'd like it back when you're done with it. Sometimes my memories are all I have left."

Tuesday, February 24, 6:00 P.M.

Zoe's boss, Alan Wainwright glared. "What were you thinking?"

Zoe glared back. "That if I got him drunk enough he'd let something slip."

Wainwright sneered. "Like his zipper? My God, he's the damn DA. Do you know how it feels to get reamed a new asshole by the mayor *and* the network execs?"

"Do you know how much our share has jumped since I broke the story?" Zoe shot back. Today hadn't been a picnic for her either, having to endure the catcalls and lewd 'requests' as she crossed the newsroom. It might as well have been a locker room. John Alden wasn't the first man she'd used her body to get close to, but she picked men who would be discreet specifically because she didn't want her story denigrated by sexual come-ons.

Wainwright paused, then smiled wolfishly. "Seven points."

"So get off my fucking case," Zoe snarled. "I did what I needed to do. And I'd do it again." She grabbed her briefcase and headed for the door. All she wanted at this point was a hot bath and a glass of wine.

"Spinnelli told the mayor. Two guesses as to who told Spinnelli."

Zoe froze. "Who?" she asked, even though she knew only one person would warrant the smugness she heard in Wainwright's tone.

"Kristen Mayhew."

Zoe's breath came out in a hiss and Wainwright chuckled.

"Just thought you'd want to know."

Tuesday, February 24, 6:30 P.M.

Jacob Conti sat at his desk in the darkened room. He heard the murmured voices in the hall and knew Drake had come with a report, his second of the day. He knew the killer had struck twice since killing his Angelo, this last time leaving alive a witness.

He knew that his wife hadn't left her bed since their son's murder. He knew that in her few hours of lucidity she'd wept for her son in great heaving sobs that tore his heart out. He knew that she slept now, the doctor having given her yet another sedative.

He knew that his son's body still lay nude and cold and butchered in the morgue.

More than anything else, he knew Angelo's killer would pay.

Drake slipped in and closed the door behind him. A moment of silence passed, then Drake's voice came through the darkness. "Can we turn on a light, Jacob?"

"Whatever. It doesn't matter."

Light flooded the room. Jacob blinked his eyes against the sudden glare.

Drake approached with a frown. "You aren't doing any good by sitting here in the dark."

Jacob returned the frown. "Save the advice and tell me what you have."

Drake drew a small notepad from his breast pocket. "She has very little family. A mother in a Kansas nursing home with Alzheimer's who she visits religiously once a month and a father who says they haven't spoken in years."

"Why not?"

"He wouldn't say, but I know there's bad blood between them."

"Then I take it he's not dead. Yet."

Drake shook his head. "I get the feeling his death wouldn't be the club you're looking for. I had a black rose and a note left on her mother's pillow last night."

Jacob's lips twisted in a sneer. "Melodramatic, Drake."

Drake shrugged. "It was meant to be. My man's posing as an investigator following up on the flower and the note. If my man can't dig anything up, there isn't anything there."

"Everybody's got something. Even squeaky clean ASA Mayhew."

Drake didn't look convinced. "We'll see. Your thug who attacked her Sunday night told her that if she didn't talk, people around her would die."

"Yeah. I told him to tell her that." He'd meant it, too. "So what?"

Drake grunted, still displeased with the maneuver. "So I built on that. She's had no significant others in the last five years that I've been able to trace, but lately she's been spending a lot of time with Detective Abe Reagan."

Jacob scowled. "If Reagan's guarding her, that'll make her harder to corner again. Mayhew's no dummy."

"Which is why I didn't want her attacked in her own home," Drake said angrily.

Knowing Drake was right just added to his frustration. "So what are you going to do about it?" Jacob demanded. "I want that vigilante." He clenched his fists. "I want the man who beat my son to death and Mayhew knows who he is. She has to."

"I really don't think she does, Jacob. I think if she did, he'd be in jail."

"I don't want him in jail. I want him here." Jacob thumped his desk.

Drake's brows lifted. "She's spent time with Detective Reagan *and* his family."

Jacob relaxed. Family always made for good leverage in any negotiation. "Good. I want an answer. I don't care where it comes from."

Drake's grin was wolfish, stirring his own blood. "That ball's in motion."

Tuesday, February 24, 7:00 P.M.

Abe pulled into his parents' driveway and shut off the motor, his hands shaking with a barely suppressed mixture of fear and fury. He looked over at Kristen who still peacefully slept in the passenger seat, her face slightly flushed, her chest rising and falling rhythmically. She'd been out like a light almost as soon as they'd pulled away from the station. She'd missed the trill of his cell phone, his muttered oaths in response to Aidan's urgent summons. Then she'd missed the melodic chiming of her own phone. And again more epithets as he answered, listened to the mocking voice of the caller who refused to give his name.

His eyes flicked over the collection of cars in front of his parents' house. Everyone was here. Sean and Ruth and Aidan and Annie. He and Kristen would simply add to the number that gathered in support.

She would blame herself. She would be wrong, but she'd blame herself nevertheless. He couldn't put it off any longer. He shook her shoulder briskly. "Kristen, wake up."

She turned in the seat, leaning into his arm, murmuring something unintelligible. She turned her face into his palm, so trustingly he felt his heart clench. When this was all over he was going to take her far away, to someplace where it would be just the two of them. Someplace where she could finally relax, take out those damn hairpins. Someplace where he could take her in his arms tenderly and teach her to unlock the mysteries of her own sensuality. Show her that she wouldn't, couldn't disappoint him. Ever.

"Kristen, honey, wake up."

He watched her lashes quiver, then lift. Slowly she came awake, then lifted her chin with a jerk when she realized where they were. "You said you were taking me home."

He closed his hand over the back of her neck and gently squeezed. "I will. First I have to see my folks." He hesitated and she sat up straighter in the seat.

"What's happened?" She studied his face in the darkness of the SUV's cab, then sagged back against the seat, her expression defeated and for that alone he wanted to catch both Conti and their humble servant and make them pay. "Who?"

"My dad," he said unevenly and she closed her eyes. "He says he's okay, but I didn't want to take his word for it. Aidan says he's pretty banged up, but . . ."

"Let me guess," she said bitterly. "Whoever did it wanted to know who 'he' is."

He wouldn't lie to her. "Yes."

Wearily she rubbed her forehead. "I told you I shouldn't
come around your family. I shouldn't be here right now. Go
in and see your father. I'll call a cab to take me home.
Truman's on tonight, I think. I'll be fine."

I'll be fine. The words echoed in his head and something
just snapped. He twisted, bringing his angry face within
inches of her startled one. For a second they stared, then he
took her mouth with a ferocity he immediately regretted. He
was angry, but not with her. She was fragile and vulnerable
enough without his making it worse. He pulled away, but
her hands pulled him back, holding on almost desperately.
She kissed him hard and long and when she finally let him
go they were both breathing like spent athletes.

"You are not fine," he whispered against her lips.
"You're scared and so am I."

"I'm sorry, Abe. I'm so sor—"

He cut off the apology with another hard kiss, gentling it
after the initial searing contact. He adjusted the angle, seeking a closer fit, finding it, backing off only long enough to
let them both catch their breath, then returning for more. He
ended it without ending it, pressing kisses to the corner of
her mouth, her temple. The hollow behind her ear and down
her neck, forcing himself to remain gentle when her body
shuddered.

"When this is over, I'm taking you far away," he murmured, the deep rumble of his voice shaking her down to
her core. "We'll lie on the beach and forget all about this."

Don't make promises, she wanted to say. They were here
because someone had beaten his father. *Because of me.* That
wasn't something even the Reagans could easily ignore and
she just didn't think she could bear their reproach, no mat-

ter how much they deserved to feel it. Kristen turned her face into his hand and kissed his palm. "Go see your father," she said. "I'll wait."

"You're not staying here by yourself. Come with me."

It wasn't a request, she knew. Just as she knew it would be foolish to tempt fate and stay in the car alone. Unprotected. So when he opened her car door, she slid down without a protest and walked, his strong arm around her shoulders.

From the laundry room she could smell Becca's dinner cooking, but there was a forbidding quiet that was foreign to the Reagan household. Abe pushed open the door to the kitchen. Five pairs of eyes turned to look at them, all filled with rioting emotions, Becca's with fear, Aidan's with fury. Sean and Annie's held disbelief. Ruth stood beside Kyle, holding a roll of gauze and she shook her head slightly. Kyle kept his face stubbornly averted and Kristen saw Abe swallow hard before approaching his father. His eyes slid closed and his throat worked as he struggled to keep his composure.

"How bad is it?" she heard him murmur to Ruth.

"I've had worse," Kyle snapped, but his speech was slurred. "I'm a bloody pulp, but I can still hear and talk."

"How?" Abe asked simply.

Becca drew in a breath. "He was leaving the grocery store and a man—"

"I can tell it, Becca." Kyle struggled to sit up in the chair and Aidan was there to help him, but Kyle pulled away. "I can do it. I was leaving the store and a man stuck a gun in my kidney. Told me to walk quietly and took me behind the store."

"How many were there?" Abe asked.

"Four," Kyle answered and Kristen shuddered from her spot in the laundry room. "Told me to tell you to figure out who the vigilante was or they'd move on to the rest of the family."

Abe looked around abruptly. "Where's Rachel?"

Ruth put a steadying hand on his shoulder. "She's in the bedroom with the kids."

"Where is Kristen?" Kyle asked. "You shouldn't have left her alone."

"I'm here," Kristen said quietly. "I'm fine."

Kyle raised a bandaged hand. "Come here."

On trembling legs Kristen complied. Whatever he had to say wouldn't be nearly bad enough. One look at Kyle's face made her trembles start all over again. Purple and black bruises covered his face and a patch of thick white hair had been shaved, a bandage in its place. Both hands were bandaged, his right more so than his left. She sank to her knees at his feet and stared up at him, blinking back tears. He'd sat with her all night, playing solitaire, keeping her company. Making her feel safe. And for his kindness he'd been beaten within an inch of his life. She opened her mouth and he made an impatient noise.

"If you say you're sorry, I'll be forced to kick your ass," Kyle said through swollen lips and a hysterical giggle bubbled up in her chest. Kristen forced it back and responded the only way she knew would preserve his dignity.

"I was going to ask how the other guys look," she lied dryly.

His blue eyes gleamed with appreciative humor. "Not as pretty as me," he said.

Standing behind him, Becca smiled tremulously. "You didn't cause this, Kristen. You're as much a victim as anyone else." Kyle nodded, then winced in discomfort.

"Is anything broken?" Kristen asked him.

"A few ribs. My pride." Kyle grew very serious. "You

will not tell them anything, Kristen. You have to promise me that."

Kristen huffed in frustration. "I don't *know* anything. If I did, the killer would be in prison. If I thought it would do any good, I'd call Conti and tell him I don't know anything."

"It won't do any good," Abe said and she looked up at him. "They called your cell phone while you were asleep. Said they'd be getting in touch with you every day until you had an answer. They don't care how you get it, they just want to know who the killer is."

Every day. She controlled the feeling of helpless panic and made her voice steady. "Can you trace the call?"

Abe shrugged. "I already made the request, but I can almost guarantee we're talking about a stolen or disposable cell phone."

"Can't you pick Conti up?" Aidan asked. "Use any excuse. You know it's him."

Abe's lips thinned. "It wouldn't do any good, and he'd sue us for false arrest. He's behind this, but he's not doing this himself. Spinnelli's already been warned by the brass not to pick him up until they have something that will stick."

Kristen stood up. "Well then, let's find out who's doing it for him. My first guess would be the man who was with him the day he pushed Julia up against her car. His name is Drake Edwards. He's Conti's right-hand man. Rumored to be one sick bastard." She looked down at Kyle. "Did you see any distinguishing marks on any of the men who did this?"

Kyle's swollen lips twisted in a grimace. "Only the ones I put on 'em myself. I didn't see any of their faces, but one of the guys should have a really bad bruise on his left cheekbone."

"I'll call it in," Abe said.

Becca waved her hands. "Enough of this sitting around. Sean, you get plates down to set the table. Aidan, you can carve the roast. Annie, I need you to help me peel some more potatoes. I've got to stretch dinner for four more plus the children."

Kristen took a step back. "Becca, I—"

Becca silenced her with another hand wave. "Hush, Kristen. You and Abe I planned for. It's the rest of my brood that I wasn't anticipating."

Becca's insistence was reflected in the faces of the other Reagans. They weren't throwing her out. She felt the knots in her stomach slide free. She was still part of this amazing family. "Then let me peel some potatoes." She glanced at Annie. "If you don't mind."

With an encouraging smile, Annie handed her a knife and they got to work.

Tuesday, February 24, 7:00 P.M.

The sun had gone down and still he sat, thinking, wondering, remembering in the darkness of his kitchen. The picture of Leah was to his left, the stack of bullets to his right, and in the center of the table, the fishbowl, still filled with names. So much evil in the world. He was only one man whose time was drawing to a close. Three cards sat in front of the fishbowl. He didn't need to turn on the light to be able to see their names. Their names were permanently etched in his memory. A judge, a defense lawyer and a serial rapist. He closed his eyes, remembering the look on Leah's face the last time he'd seen her alive. So very, very alone. Because of the judge, the lawyer, and the rapist. They all deserved to die.

And they would. But he'd have to be careful. Once he killed the judge, they'd start to narrow it down. Once he killed the defense attorney, they'd figure it out. The rapist himself would suspect and run away. And he'd be left without his vengeance.

That could not happen. So how to kill them all so that the others didn't suspect they were next? But he wanted them to suspect, just a little. He wanted the lawyer to hear the judge was dead and be afraid. He wanted the rapist to feel hunted, to feel terror as had his Leah.

He wanted each man to know why he was being killed.

And he wanted each one to feel a great deal of pain.

He sat there in the dark, running through various scenarios, finally returning to his original plan. He would hunt down each one like the dogs they were, disable them, then bring them here. He would hunt them quickly, efficiently. But once captive, he would kill each one slowly, until they begged for mercy.

The mercy they received would be equal to the mercy they showed Leah.

In other words, there would be none.

Tuesday, February 24, 10:00 P.M.

Kristen's eyes widened when they pulled into her driveway. The cruiser was conspicuously absent. "What happened to Truman?"

"They needed to pull him back onto patrol. Half a dozen guys called in with the flu and Central was scrambling to fill their shifts. I told them it was okay."

There was silence for a moment from the passenger seat. Then quietly she said, "Because you said you'd stay with me." They hadn't discussed it until now. In his mind it had been a given, but he could practically see the wheels of indecision turning in her head and he understood. The other two nights he'd stayed had been special cases. Both times she'd been attacked. Last night, his own father had stayed, a respectable guard. But tonight was different. Just a man and a woman alone in her house. To say he hadn't fantasized the possible outcomes would be a lie. One part of his brain was fantasizing at this very moment and he was grateful for the darkness that surrounded them. "I'll sleep on your couch."

She leaned back, turning only her head to look at him. "You would, wouldn't you?"

"Yes," he replied without hesitation. "Until you decide otherwise, yes."

One side of her mouth lifted. "So it's up to me?"

He didn't smile. "Totally."

"Will you at least kiss me good night?"

He did smile at that. "Just don't ask me to tuck you in. My principles are only so strong." Without giving her time to comment, he helped her down, then reached for the laptop bag she had in one hand and the Marshall Field's shopping bag in the other. "What's in the bag?"

"Magazines," she said over her shoulder. "Annie and I were talking about redoing my kitchen while we were peeling potatoes. She loaned me the magazines so I could get some ideas. I'm thinking about tearing out a wall and doubling the size. Maybe doing a French Provincial style. You can take a look at the pictures and tell me—"

She broke it off with a startled exclamation and a second later he saw why. The side of her house by her kitchen door was covered in black spray paint. Blade graffiti, six feet tall. A long horizontal line trailed toward the back of her house, a stylized arrowhead at its end.

"I'll get a light. Stay here." He deposited the bags at her

feet, got a heavy flashlight from the SUV, then carefully walked along the edge of her house, his weapon drawn, shining the light on the snow until he found what the gang had left behind. "Shit."

"What?" she said from behind him and he jumped.

"Dammit, Kristen, I told you to stay by the door." But it was too late. His admonition was interrupted by her sharp intake of breath.

"Oh, Abe, no."

"Hold this and don't move." He handed her the light and pulled out his cell phone and hit Mia's speed dial. "Come to Kristen's," he said. "We just found Aaron Jenkins."

Chapter Eighteen

Wednesday, February 25, 8:00 A.M.

"Let's get started," Spinnelli called from his position by the whiteboard. The side conversations ceased. There was a subdued energy in the room, Kristen thought. They finally, finally had a lead to follow, but they also had a new body in the morgue. Aaron Jenkins's throat had been slit, his body left to freeze in the shadows of her backyard. The gang members must have driven by her house and seeing no cruiser in front, seized their opportunity. The threat was clear. Anyone helping the vigilante was fair game for gang retribution. And Kristen was still at the top of their list.

The conference room table was filled. The core team was there plus Julia, Todd Murphy from Spinnelli's department, and Miles Westphalen, their staff psychologist. "What do we have, people? Abe?"

"A name to go with our bullet," Abe said. "Hank Worth. Problem is, he's been dead for sixty years."

Spinnelli's marker squeaked as he wrote the name. "And?"

"Genny O'Reilly, his intended," Mia said. "She up and married someone else two months after he shipped out. I may have seen too many old movies, but that sounds like she fell for the old I-may-not-come-back-from-the-war line and found herself eating for two. If that's the case, their child would be about sixty."

Spinnelli considered it. "Sixty seems a bit old for our humble servant."

"Many sixty-year-olds are quite fit," Westphalen said mildly.

Spinnelli smiled. "Point taken, Miles."

"Well, whoever we're dealing with," Jack said, "has to have above-average strength. How much did the heaviest victim weigh, Julia?"

Julia pulled out her notes. "Ramey weighed 220. Ross King, 251. The others were all lower. But I think he used a cart or gurney or something with wheels."

"Why?" Abe asked sharply.

"There were no signs of dragging the bodies. No scratches on their backs, no bruising at the ankles, wrists, or under the arms that would be consistent with grabbing and pulling with any force. There were marks from the rope he used to bind their wrists and ankles, but that looks very different from a grabbing bruise. If he used a gurney, he wouldn't need that much strength. He'd just need to roll them."

"But could a sixty-year-old even roll a man that big?" Jack asked.

Mia held up her hand. "First, let us check the records to

see if Genny O'Reilly had a child at all before we get carried away on his possible age. Then we'll check marriage and birth records on her children's children. Hank and Genny's grandchildren would be anywhere from twenty to forty years old and that's just the right age."

"If this lead proves true," said Miles thoughtfully, "your killer would have had to know his biological father's identity to get the bullet mold or at a minimum the Worth family's maker's mark. I'm wondering about the man Genny O'Reilly married. How would he react to having a child that wasn't his? How would the child be treated? If there were other children born later, would the first child, the bastard child, be singled out? It could lead to feelings of resentment and anger." Westphalen shrugged. "Or it could mean nothing."

"Get Genny O'Reilly's records and find out," Spinnelli said. "What else do we have?"

Abe leaned forward. "The old man, Grayson James, said he and Hank Worth would go up to Worth's father's property and practice their shooting. Mia, do you remember the other day when you thought he might have a private target range?"

Mia's eyes gleamed. "We can check property records for land owned by the Worths."

Spinnelli's marker squeaked as he wrote. "What else?"

"I've been working on identifying the chain he used to strangle Ramey," Jack said. "We made a cast of the ligature marks and I found a few men's chains that are similar in size." He laid three chains on the table. "The one closest to the plaster cast is the middle one."

"Dog tags," Spinnelli said. "I've seen men wear their dog tags on a chain like this."

Mia brought a chain from under her blouse. "Like this?" A set of military ID tags hung from the end of the chain.

"My dad gave me his tags when I joined the force. Said his tags kept him alive in 'Nam and hoped they'd keep me alive in uniform."

"We already thought he could have been military, being a sharpshooter," Abe said, excitement in his voice. "It makes sense."

Spinnelli paced from the whiteboard to the table and back again. "Good, good. Track him down and if you run into any problems with military records, let me know. I'll get the governor involved." He grimaced. "It'll give him something to do so he'll stop calling the mayor who'll stop calling me. Anything else?" No one said anything and Spinnelli pointed to Detective Murphy, who'd been sitting quietly. "Murphy, update us on Muñoz's gun."

"We canvassed the pawnshops," Murphy said. He was a serious man with a rumpled suit. Kristen knew him to be a good cop. Methodical. "We found the gun late last night."

"Any useful prints?" Abe asked.

Murphy nodded. "Yeah, they were in the system. Street punk, goes by Boom-Boom. We've got out an APB. Hopefully we'll find him and hopefully he saw something useful Monday night."

Spinnelli capped his markers. "And I'll get Aaron Jenkins's juvie record unsealed. Now that he's dead, there shouldn't be a problem."

Mia stood up. "Records opens at nine and I want to be first in line. You ready, Abe?"

Abe pulled on his coat and Kristen had to look away before her mouth started watering. They'd done nothing sexual the night before and somehow that made her wish they had. First they'd dealt with CSU, then the Medical Examiner's Office as they'd picked up Jenkins's body. Then when everyone had gone, Abe kissed her good night, a long, liquid, yearning kiss after which he patted her behind and sent her off to bed. He'd bedded down on the sofa, just as he'd promised, leaving her heart thundering and her mind wondering what would have happened had she asked him to tuck her into bed. He'd checked on her several times during the night and each time she'd been so tempted to ask him to stay. But she didn't, and when sleep finally came, her dreams were full of hot images that still had her nerves humming.

"I'm driving, Mitchell, so I can pick lunch." He stopped by Kristen's chair and bent down to murmur in her ear, "Don't go anywhere by yourself. Not even to Owen's. Please."

Her heart clenched at the tender worry in his eyes. "I promise. I'll stay here all day."

Abe straightened. "Maybe not all day," he said cryptically.

"Abe," Spinnelli said soberly, "I heard about what happened to your dad last night. Until we can get something concrete on Conti, be careful, all of you."

Wednesday, February 25, 10:00 A.M.

"All those?" Abe asked, eyeing the stack of huge volumes. "We'll be here for days."

The clerk, whose name was Tina, shot him a sympathetic look. "The marriage licenses from the forties aren't computerized yet," she said. "But it isn't as bad as it looks. What's the name and the date?"

"Genny O'Reilly," Mia answered, looking over the woman's shoulder. "She got married sometime in the fall of 1943."

Tina slid index cards in the volume to mark the pages. "It

will be between these cards. If you look yourselves I can find those property listings you were looking for."

"We'll look for Genny," said Mia. "You can help us find land owned by a man named Worth. We don't know exactly where it was, just that it was north of the city."

Tina bit her lip. "You have a first name, maybe?"

Abe shook his head. "Our source just called him Mr. Worth. His son's name was Hank, if that helps. Maybe Hank was a junior."

Tina shrugged. "I'll do my best. Happy hunting, Detectives."

When she'd gone, Mia slumped into a chair. "We have to stop all these late parties."

Abe opened the big book. "What'd the surgeon say when you left your date early?"

"He was a bore. I was ready for any excuse for him to take me home." She cocked a brow. "And you? Once the infantry marched away last night, how was your evening?"

Long. He thought of Kristen now, of the way she'd looked last night. She'd been at her kitchen door, locking it as the last person left, prudently setting the alarm. She'd turned and just that fast the very air was charged, practically sizzling as they'd stood at opposite ends of her kitchen, staring. Then she'd simply walked into his arms as if she'd been doing so all her life. He'd kissed her. And kissed her. And God help him, he'd kissed her some more, until she was trembling and so was he, his hands clamped on her hips, wrestling with his best intentions. In the end he hadn't dragged her against him as he'd so longed to do. He'd gently pushed her away, then turned her toward her bedroom with just a "good night." If she'd even hinted she wanted him to join her, he would have. He would have scooped her up in his arms and carried her to the bed and helped her have another . . . watershed moment.

But she hadn't hinted. She'd walked away, stopping once to look back and the look in her eyes was worth more than ten watershed moments. It was trust mingled with heated want, and the combination triggered something inside him so profound . . . So he'd let her walk away and listened to her get ready for bed, his body still clenched and aching. She hadn't slept until after three A.M. He knew because he'd checked on her, quietly, every half hour. He wanted to think he was checking because he'd been worried. She'd been shaken at finding Jenkins's body in her backyard, at the implicit threat. He wanted to think that, but he knew he was hoping that she'd change her mind and ask him to stay. She'd wanted to. He could see it in her eyes. But she hadn't and in the end she'd curled up and slept like an angel.

While he felt like anything but. He wanted her with a fierceness that left him breathless. He'd thought about it a great deal as he'd lain awake, staring at the blue-striped wallpaper from her uncomfortable sofa. She was a beautiful woman, no question of that, but he'd met other beautiful women in his life. Kristen had something more, something deeper—integrity, courage, kindness, a tender heart that she hid so well. A heart she was just now allowing to be seen. A heart that he wanted for his own.

In only a week she'd stolen his.

He looked over to find Mia studying him intently, understanding in her round blue eyes. She was an attractive woman as well, but he didn't want her. He wanted Kristen.

"I could tell you to be careful with her, but I think you know that," Mia said soberly.

Abe frowned. "Why? What do you know?"

Mia lifted a shoulder. "I've suspected for a long time that there was more to Kristen's dedication than simple zeal for justice. I went as far as to check once, to see if she'd filed a complaint. I have a very close friend who counsels women for these things. I thought maybe Dana could help Kristen. But there was no complaint here in Chicago."

"I wanted to check," Abe admitted.

"But you want her to tell you herself. Be patient, Abe. She's been alone for a long time. It takes some time to get used to having someone to lean on."

Abe heard something in Mia's voice, a yearning of her own. "Who do you lean on?"

One side of her mouth curved, a sad little half smile. "Me." She blew out an exaggerated sigh. "Even tomboys can dream of Prince Charming. Unfortunately, all I ever get is frogs." The half smile became a rueful grimace and she pulled the big book closer. "Well, let's get to it. How many Genny O'Reillys could have been married in 1943?"

Wednesday, February 25, 10:00 A.M.

Hunting the judge was proving easier than he'd anticipated. Funny how having a little insider information made all the difference in the world. Before, he'd planned to catch the judge getting into or out of his chauffeur-driven Lincoln with its bullet-resistant glass. It would have been difficult to say the least. He might have been caught.

But now . . . He smiled, thinking of the miracle of the little electronic gadget he'd found in Trevor Skinner's pocket. It was a cell phone, a date book, a phone book, and so much more. Apparently Skinner left little to chance and even less to the jury. There was enough dirt on every defense attorney and judge in the city to keep him busy for weeks and weeks. He was almost sorry he'd gone public. But he wasn't sorry. The criminals and the scum who defended them were shaking in their boots, afraid to leave their homes alone, looking over their shoulders like their victims did every day. Thanks to Zoe Richardson's tabloid-style reporting he knew the man with William Carson had been his bodyguard and that the prominent defense attorneys in town were fighting over the best hired guns to keep them safe.

But safety was an illusion, born in the mind. If a man was made paranoid enough, he'd be afraid even in the most secure place. And that was his goal. To make every man in the fishbowl afraid.

He fingered the card in his pocket. Judge Edmund Hillman. He'd tried Leah's case. Thanks to Skinner's BlackBerry, he knew that the Honorable Edmund Hillman had a mistress. He and Rosemary Quincy had been together for going on three years and met every Wednesday evening at a little hotel in Rosemont where the *Honorable* Judge Hillman was anything but. According to Skinner's notes, this was the only time Hillman drove alone.

He'd get to the hotel early, before Hillman was due. He'd wait and watch and then he'd make his move. Then it would be *his* turn to bang the gavel.

Wednesday, February 25, 11:30 A.M.

Kristen hung up the phone carefully, resisting the urge to slam it down as Ronette Smith had just done. Ronette was *fine,* thank you very much, and her family was *fine*, and her life was *fine*, no *thanks* to the U.S. justice system. *And me,* Kristen thought, rubbing her forehead. Ronette had been very clear on that fact.

As had most of the names on her list. Kristen looked at the list objectively. She'd managed to get in touch with over half. Three had lost jobs recently, which could be a traumatic event, but they didn't sound like she expected a killer to sound.

And how does a vigilante killer of nine sound? Cold? Dispassionate? Insane?

She was considering the question when a shadow fell over her papers. She looked up, expecting to see Spinnelli or Abe but her eyes widened when she saw Milt Hendricks standing before her. John's boss. Automatically she stood. "Mr. Hendricks."

He glanced down at her papers on Abe's desk, then back up to meet her gaze. "I won't beat around the bush. I wanted to be sure you knew why I pulled you out of the courtroom."

"Because the defense attorneys are afraid and you're worried about grounds for appeal on every case I was trying," Kristen said, parroting John's words.

Hendricks nodded. "That's true. But I also wanted you out of the spotlight. Somehow this vigilante has picked you. I told John to be sure you knew this was for your safety, not a punishment. But under the circumstances, I wasn't sure if he'd given you the entire message. This is temporary, Kristen. You've got the best conviction rate in the city. When this is over, I want you back at work. Although, from the looks of those papers, you're still working."

Kristen felt her face heat, but stood her ground. "I'm helping the police go through my old cases," she said. "We're certain there's a connection."

Hendricks lifted a brow. "Did John tell you that you could?"

"He didn't tell me that I couldn't. Sir," she added belatedly and his lips twitched.

"I see. Well, I don't see any issue with that. Just be careful." He sobered. "Stay safe. I've just lost one of my best prosecutors. I don't want to lose another."

Kristen paled. "John? Has something happened?"

"No, no. He's physically well," Hendricks assured her. "He offered his resignation this morning. I accepted it."

Kristen sat down and looked up at him. "I'm not sure what to say."

"He compromised his position," Hendricks said simply, "and the integrity of the office. Hopefully, this will all be over soon and we can get back to work. Oh, I understand you needed information on the Jenkins boy's juvenile record. Consider it done." With a tip of his head, Hendricks was gone, leaving Kristen staring after him.

"My mom would say if you let your mouth hang open long enough, birds will fly in."

Kristen looked to her left where Aidan Reagan leaned against a nearby desk. She closed her mouth with a snap and he grinned. "You free for lunch?" he asked.

"You're asking me?"

"Yeah. Abe said you had a purchase to pick up today and I'm between Rachels."

"Purchase? Oh," she remembered. "My gun. My three days are up." Then she frowned. "What do you mean 'between Rachels'? Is she all right?"

"She's fine. I'm just her shadow today because I'm on nights this week. I'll drop her off and pick her up from school until this is all over. And don't say you're sorry," he warned. "It would make Dad really mad and he'd have to kick your ass."

This tugged a rueful grin to her lips. "How is he?"

Aidan shrugged. "Sore. In a real pissy mood. I think he's more upset that he didn't hurt them worse. Blow to his pride and all. But he'll heal."

Kristen studied him carefully. "You change your mind about me or something?"

Aidan's cheeks darkened, just like Abe's did when he

was embarrassed. "I'm sorry I was rude when we first met. Look, I heard about the Blade graffiti on your house. Abe said you were thinking about a dog. I know a guy who trains dogs for the K-9 unit. You interested?"

Touched, Kristen grabbed her coat. "Let's go."

Wednesday, February 25, 12:00 P.M.

"Any success?" Tina the clerk asked.

Mia rolled her eyes. "Yes, but of course she was at the very end of the listings."

"That's the way it always is," Tina agreed.

"Genevieve O'Reilly," Abe read from his note pad. "Married Colin Barnett on September 15, 1943, in the parish of Sacred Heart by Father Thomas Reed."

Tina gave a satisfied nod. "Good. You could check the census to see if they had any children, but if they were members of their parish, the church would have a record of births."

"What about you?" Mia asked. "Any progress on our land search?"

Tina handed them a piece of paper. "I remembered Hank was short for Henry, and that's where I found it. Henry Worth. On his death it passed to a Paul Worth. It's all I could find. I hope it's enough."

Mia scanned the page, then looked up, a gleam in her eyes. "It's plenty. Let's call Spinnelli. We'll need full tactical gear, just in case he's there."

Abe grabbed his coat. "I hope he is," he said grimly. "I want a piece of him first."

Wednesday, February 25, 1:30 P.M.

"You should have told me you were allergic to dogs," Aidan said, his voice full of laughter as he helped her out to his car.

"Oh, that hurts." Gone was the satisfaction she'd felt as she test-fired her new gun back at Givens's target range. It disappeared once they'd reached their next destination—a kennel full of impeccably trained guard dogs. The first step inside had her sniffling. Five minutes later she was sneezing so hard she would have fallen over if Aidan hadn't held her up, chuckling all the time. "This really isn't funny, you know," she grumbled.

"Why the hell did you go into a kennel if you knew you had such severe allergies?"

Kristen leaned against his car to catch her breath. "I didn't know. I haven't been around that many dogs. Once a Seeing Eye dog came into the diner and I sneezed, but I'd hoped it was just that one dog." She wiped her watering eyes and got into the car. Unlike his brother, Aidan went for the smooth sleekness of a Camaro rather than the massive strength of Abe's SUV. She sniffled and shivered as he started the engine and the heater belched out ice-cold air. "I guess I won't be getting a guard dog after all."

Aidan's lips curved. "I guess you won't. But I don't imagine Abe will mind filling the role."

Her cheeks heated despite the cold air from the alleged heater. "Abe is very kind."

Aidan glanced over his shoulder before pulling out of the parking space. "I'm going to have to give him some pointers then, if all he can conjure is 'kind.'" Her face must have reflected her horror because he laughed. "I'm teasing,

Kristen. Number one, whatever is between you and Abe is your own business. Number two, he'd kick my ass."

"That seems to be a common theme in your family," Kristen commented.

"Hell, we're a family of boys."

"You have two sisters," Kristen pointed out.

"They have three brothers," Aidan corrected. "It's different."

"I stand corrected," she said dryly and he chuckled.

"Now you think I'm some Neanderthal whose knuckles scrape the ground."

Kristen pretended to study his unscraped knuckles. "No, I'd say you've advanced to the moderately stooped-over phase of evolution." She caught her breath as he made an erratic turn. "What the—" She looked over her shoulder, then back at Aidan who was checking his rearview mirror with a satisfied expression. "Reporters?"

"One bleached-blonde bitch and her camera-toting toady. No longer tailing."

"I really hate that woman," Kristen said wearily.

"I'd say the feeling is mutual."

Kristen frowned. "But I've never done anything to her. Why me?"

"She has to feed off someone else's misery and it might as well be yours."

"Well, still," Kristen grumbled.

Aidan leaned over to adjust the heater. "Better?"

"It's okay. I used to walk to school in weather colder than this."

"In Kansas, right?"

Kristen blew out a breath. "What didn't Abe tell you?"

Aidan just grinned wickedly and Kristen rolled her eyes. "For God's sake," she muttered, knowing her face was well past ruby red. Perhaps volcano violet. And for what? A little petting, that's all they'd done. And the promise of more, whenever she chose. She got to set the rules this time. It was enchanting. Enticing. Liberating.

"You'll have to get used to the teasing," he said. "It comes with the family."

Kristen felt a longing so strong, it was like a fist grabbing her heart. What a family to have. She felt a spear of jealousy for Debra, who'd obviously melded so effortlessly with the Reagans. "Tell me about Debra," she blurted and Aidan blinked, obviously taken aback.

"Debra?"

"Yeah, you know. The one I sound like. Your former sister-in-law?"

He suddenly began paying a great deal of attention to the road. "No need to get testy, Counselor. You want lunch or what? I'm starving."

Well, that was a smooth change of subject, she thought. It would appear Aidan wasn't comfortable discussing Debra. *Or maybe he just isn't comfortable discussing Debra around me.* "Sure. We're not too far from the diner where I normally eat." She gave him directions to Owen's, then sat back to try to think of something else to talk about.

"She was Abe's life," Aidan said abruptly. Kristen turned in her seat, studying his profile. His jaw was clenched hard and his knuckles were white where he clutched the steering wheel. "I thought he'd die when she was shot. I know he wanted to."

There was a curious lack of emotion in Aidan's voice that was more meaningful than if he'd broken down. "I'm sorry," she said. "I shouldn't have asked."

"It's all right. I suppose you have a right to know." He shrugged a powerful shoulder. "I'd been on the force a few years when it happened. I thought I'd seen it all." He shook his head and his throat worked as he tried to swallow. "But seeing her so lifeless, for so long . . ." He cleared his throat. "But I think burying the baby was the hardest part of all."

Poleaxed, Kristen's throat closed. "Baby?" she managed.

Aidan shot her a quick look. "Debra was eight months pregnant when she was shot. The baby didn't live. I thought you knew."

She shook her head and stared out the window, barely seeing the sign for Owen's diner when Aidan stopped the car. "No, Abe never mentioned a child."

"Don't let it bother you. He hasn't mentioned the baby since the funeral, to any of us. Even to Mom and Dad. I guess it was his way of coping. But he loves kids. You only have to look at how he is around Sean's kids. I know he wants a family of his own."

Kristen pursed her lips to keep them from trembling. Aidan thought she was upset because Abe might not want kids. How ironic. His child was taken from him while she . . . *How very ironic.* "Was it a boy or a girl?" she asked, unable to keep the question inside.

Aidan hesitated. "A little boy. Abe named him Kyle after Dad."

"Poor Abe," Kristen murmured. "To lose it all in one day." *And how will he feel when he learns the real truth about me?* she wondered. She didn't really want to know.

Aidan shut off the ignition and the car was quiet. "For what it's worth," he said, "I haven't seen him so happy in years than he's been in the last week. You put a light back in his eyes." Again he cleared his throat. "We're all grateful for that."

"Thank you." She forced a smile and gestured at Owen's diner. "Let's have lunch." On leaden feet she moved, then frowned when she tugged on the door and it didn't open. She peered inside where the lights were on, but every cracked vinyl seat was empty.

"The sign says they're closed," Aidan said.

"They're never closed in the middle of the day." Her heart started to beat harder as the possibilities struck home. "Oh, no. I should have warned him." She ran next door to the barber shop and stuck her head inside. "Mr. Poore, what's happened to Owen?"

Mr. Poore looked up from the hair he was trimming, his craggy old face pained. "He's at the hospital with Vincent, Kristen."

"Why? What happened?" she demanded and Mr. Poore slowly approached, wiping his hands on his white coat.

"Some thugs, they beat up Vincent in the alley behind the diner when he went to take out the trash. This used to be such a nice neighborhood. Now . . ." He held his hands up in defeat. "It's bad, Kristen. Real bad."

"No." She sagged and felt Aidan's arm go around her shoulders.

"Yes," Mr. Poore said soberly. "Owen, he went out to see what was the matter and they hit him, too, but not so bad. Me, I heard the yelling and called the cops and the men ran away." He shook his bald head. "Vincent, he didn't look good. Not good at all. The paramedics came and took him to the hospital."

"Do you know where they took him?" Aidan asked. Steadily. The voice of a cop asking questions. It gave Kristen the strength to stand on her own feet.

"The cops said they were going to County."

Aidan gave her a hard hug, pulling her upright. "Come on, Kristen. Let's go."

Wednesday, February 25, 2:15 P.M.

Aidan walked her into the hospital, standing silently behind her as she asked the closest nurse where she could find Vincent. He followed her to the elevator, punched the button for the surgical floor, still saying nothing. And when she walked out of the elevator and saw Owen sitting alone in the waiting room, Aidan stood to one side, watching.

She crossed the room to Owen's side, taking the chair next to his. He looked old. Old and tired and suddenly frail. Guilt mixed with fury and fear and she wasn't sure she could speak. "Are you hurt?" she whispered and he shook his head.

"Vincent . . ." Owen let the thought trail away, his throat working frantically. He looked away. "He never hurt anyone, never. He was the gentlest man I ever knew."

Kristen grabbed his arm. "Was? Owen, talk to me." He didn't budge and Kristen pulled his arm harder. "Dammit, Owen, tell me if he's still alive."

Owen turned and there were tears in his eyes. "His priest is in with him now."

It was like a fist hit her square in the chest. "Oh, God."

Silence hung between them, then Kristen heard the muted strain of Pachelbel's Canon inside her purse. She pulled out her cell phone to find no number on the caller ID.

"Hey, lady." A woman reading *Cosmo* glared at her. "You're not supposed to be using that here. Can't you read the sign?"

Cold with dread, Kristen put the phone to her ear. "Mayhew."

"You have any answers yet?" It was a male, that was all she could tell.

Kristen trembled, but held herself steady. "Who is this?"

"Answer yes or no, Miss Mayhew," the voice said mockingly. "Do you have an answer?"

Owen was motioning to the *Cosmo* lady to be quiet. "No," Kristen said. "I don't."

"Well," the voice said, "hurry up. Next time we won't go for old men and women. We'll go for youth." And he hung up.

Youth. "Rachel." Terrified, Kristin looked at her watch. Rachel's school was letting out in fifteen minutes. She'd be alone. *Because Aidan came here with me.* Her gaze shot to the wall where he'd last been standing, but he was gone. Frantically she searched, until she saw him at a phone by the nurses' station. She ran to him. "Where is Rachel?"

Aidan calmly hung up the phone. "Sean has her. She's all right, Kristen."

Kristen felt her knees give out and Aidan grabbed her shoulders. "You're sure?" Her voice shook and she didn't care. "He said next time they'd go for youth. I thought about Rachel and I—" Her throat closed and her eyes filled and Aidan pulled her against him, patting her back while she shuddered and tried to hold back what felt like a flood of tears.

"You can cry if you want to," he murmured. "I have two sisters, you know."

Kristen grabbed his sweatshirt and held on. "I thought they had three brothers," she said between her teeth and felt his chest move in a huff of silent laughter.

"It's all in your perspective, honey. Now, from where I'm standing, you've had a bad week. If you want to cry, you're entitled."

She gritted her teeth. "I won't cry."

"Then you won't be needing this." He pushed a tissue in her hand and she dabbed at her eyes as surreptitiously as possible.

She pulled back and drew a deep breath. "Thanks. When did you call Sean? You've been at my side all this time."

"I called downstairs when you were talking to the nurse."

"But I didn't hear you say anything."

Aidan held out his phone. "Instant messaged him. I IM'd Abe also, but he's out of the service area. I was just on the nurses' phone to Spinnelli, to let him know what had happened. He's got a team working these threats, Kristen. They'll catch whoever hurt Dad and your friend."

"It's Conti," she said grimly. "I know it."

"So do I. But Abe's right. Until we get hard evidence, knowing it means nothing."

Kristen looked over her shoulder at Owen, sitting alone. "I need to go back to him."

"I'll wait for you over here. We can stay as long as you need to."

She found a smile and tentatively touched his arm. "Thanks. I mean it."

Aidan's cheeks darkened. "It's okay. Go to your friend."

"Is the girl all right?" Owen asked when she'd rejoined him.

"Yes." He slumped back in his chair, relieved.

"Good. She seemed like a nice little girl."

"Owen, I'm sorry. I should have warned you and Vincent. I feel responsible for this."

His lips tightened. "You've been threatened, too?"

"Sunday night a man broke into my house." Owen paled and grabbed her hand. "It's okay," she said. "I'm fine. Abe scared him away. But the man said that if I didn't turn over the vigilante, then everyone I cared about would die. I should have warned you. I'm sorry."

"You could have been killed," he said thinly. "Dear God. Who else have they hurt?"

"They threatened my mother."

Owen's face registered surprise. "I assumed your parents were dead."

"My mother's got Alzheimer's. She . . . she doesn't know me anymore. I visit as often as I can, but my dad won't let me move her here. They didn't hurt her. Just a threat."

"Who else, Kristen? Who else have they hurt?"

"Abe's dad. They beat him, too, just like Vincent." Her lips trembled and she pursed them severely. "He was okay, though. Poor Vincent."

Owen took her chin in his hand. "You didn't cause this, Kristen." Kristen said nothing and he rolled his eyes. "You don't need to be hanging around the hospital. I'll call you when Vincent comes out of surgery. Go back to your young man. He's waiting for you."

Kristen looked at Aidan who stood leaning against the wall, quietly watching. "That's not Abe. That's his brother, Aidan. Abe asked him to keep an eye out for me today."

Owen took a long, measuring look at Aidan before nodding his approval. "The family has accepted you then. Good. Vincent and I have often worried about you, having no family, always hanging around two old men like us."

Kristen squeezed Owen's hands. "Don't be worrying about me. I'm not a minute out of anyone's sight." She grimaced, just a little. "It's starting to do a number on my nerves, never being alone. But it shouldn't be much longer. Look, I know Aidan has to get to work, so I'm going to have him take me home now. I'll ask him to get someone to see you home."

Owen smiled paternally. "That's not necessary. I'll see myself home."

Kristen sighed. "Please think about it, Owen. You could be in as much danger as Vincent." As one they looked at the doors to surgery, but they remained closed. "You'll call me as soon as he's out of surgery?"

"You have my word."

Wednesday, February 25, 3:55 P.M.

Abe crouched behind the cruiser. "It doesn't look like anyone's home." They'd found the old Worth property and on it a small shack. A stovepipe came through the roof, but there was no smoke. They'd been watching for twenty minutes and had seen not a hint of movement.

"Let's go in," Mia said evenly and Abe realized it was their first 'going in' together.

"I'll go first," he said. "You take my back."

"There's less of me to be a target," Mia protested. "With Ray I always went first."

Abe glanced down at her, mildly perturbed. "I'm not Ray."

"Flip a damn coin, people," Jack said irritably from his position behind a second cruiser. "I'd love to have some daylight to search the place since I'm sure this humble abode doesn't have any electricity."

"He's right," Abe said. "Watch my back. Please." Abe moved out from behind the cruiser, weapon drawn, conscious that a sniper might be hiding anywhere on the property. He was wearing full tactical gear, but there was vulnerability on any initial approach, this one more than others with its thick tree growth to provide cover to a shooter. He edged toward the front porch, gingerly testing the floorboards before putting his weight on the first step.

"Watch my back," Mia muttered behind him, but she did as he asked. Nimbly she followed him up the stairs and they each took position on either side of the wooden door.

"Police!" Abe said loudly. "Open up."

Dead silence. He tried the doorknob and it easily twisted.

"Unlocked," Mia murmured, following him in. "Nobody's been here in a long time."

"You're right." He moved to the doorway and motioned Jack and the others to come. "We're clear!" he shouted, then turned back to survey the shack's single-room interior. "He doesn't live here, that's for damn certain."

"And there's no cement floor like in the Polaroids, so he did his killing somewhere else." Mia opened a cabinet over a dry sink. "No running water, but here's a few cans of beans and a bar of soap." She took out a bar of soap and held it up to the light. "My grandmother had soap like this. It's an antique."

"What's an antique?" Jack asked from the doorway.

"Everything." Mia blew out a frustrated sigh. "I was so sure we had something."

"Patience isn't one of her virtues, is it?" Abe asked Jack.

Jack grinned. "Took you this long to figure that out? Hell of a detective you are."

Grinning back, Abe walked around the interior perimeter of the shack. "Somebody was here recently," he said and held up a newspaper. "It's dated December 28 of this past year."

"And lookee here." Mia bent over, then straightened, holding a bullet in her gloved hand. "It's clean as a whistle. Two intertwined W's, just like the others. W for Worth."

"Then it couldn't have been here long." Jack nudged a chair with his toe. "The cobwebs have cobwebs."

"He didn't use this place as a resort." Abe opened the back door and looked at the grounds beyond. "You were right, Mia. He's got himself a regular target range." He set out in the snow, still looking side to side, watching for any movement. He reached the makeshift moving target, a wire strung between two trees on which was suspended a piece of plywood the size of a door, covered with the familiar paper cutout of a man. Holes were clustered in the forehead and over the heart. Not a stray shot could be seen. "There's a battery-operated clip to move the target, watertight. Four speeds."

Mia walked around the target. "No bullets or footprints visible. Last time we had snow was a week ago, so he hasn't been here since then."

"Mia! Abe!" Jack stood in the back doorway waving. "Come and see." He held two picture frames in his hand. "We found these in that box beside the cot."

One was a family portrait—a father, a mother, and two sons. "Looks like early 1930's by the clothing," Mia said. "Could be the Worths."

"We'll take the photos out of the frames back at the lab," Jack said. "Maybe there's something written on the back. Look at this snapshot. It's the oldest son, ten years or so later, in uniform, with a girl on his arm."

"He's Navy," Abe said. "Genny O'Reilly and Hank Worth just before he went to war?"

"Could be. I'm also wondering about the younger son. Mr. James didn't mention him." Mia looked around. "You guys find anything else?"

The CSU man with the spotlight shook his head and switched off the light. "No. I've got the soap and the cans. We'll print them back at the lab. We can set up some spotlights and try for some more prints on the walls and furniture, but I wouldn't hold my breath."

Mia puckered her lips thoughtfully. "It's not a total waste. If that's Genny, that is."

Jack bagged the picture frames. "Let's cross our fingers because we got nothin' else."

"Detective Reagan?" A uniform appeared at the front door. "There's a call on the radio for you. It's Spinnelli. He says you need to call him when you're done here. It's important."

Kristen. Abe's heart dropped in his chest and he forced himself to take a calming breath. "Did he say important or urgent?"

"He said 'important.'"

Kristen was all right, he thought. If she'd been in trouble, Spinnelli would have said "urgent." Abe looked at Mia. "Are we done here?"

She nodded. "Yeah. Let's call Spinnelli."

Wednesday, February 25, 6:15 P.M.

He'd been late and missed the judge going into the hotel. He glanced up at the wall of windows. But it wouldn't matter. According to Skinner's notes, Hillman never stayed the night.

He'd used the waiting time productively, rerunning through his mind the transcripts of the trial that should have guaranteed Leah her justice. But there had been no justice. The jury had done their job, returning a guilty verdict. But in a rarely seen move, Hillman rejected the verdict, citing a technicality. The monster that raped Leah walked out of the court a free man.

He hadn't known Leah then. He'd met her after the trial, when she was just a shadow of the woman she'd been. He'd read the transcripts, felt the clawing anger of helplessness as he turned each page.

He wasn't helpless now. Now, it would be Hillman who would be helpless.

He waited patiently until Hillman came strolling out, a

distinctive spring to his step. Hillman stopped next to an old Dodge. A pathetic attempt at subterfuge that fooled no one. *Especially me.* He started the van and pulled up next to where Hillman had parked. His head ached, but he pushed the pain away and focused on his quarry.

He saw the alarm in Hillman's eyes in the instant he stepped from the van, his revolver in plain view, its silencer gleaming in the parking lot lights. "Keep your hands where I can see them," he said evenly. Hillman reached for his pockets and he poked the gun in the judge's gut, with much more force than necessary, but then again, he was angry both at the judge and the events of the day. "I said where I can see them. If I pull the trigger right now, you die. Right here in this parking lot next to a car you wouldn't be caught dead driving if it weren't so important to keep your wife from suspecting your affair."

Hillman's eyes widened. "If it's money you want—"

"I'm no mugger, Judge Hillman." He slid the side door open and watched Hillman pale as his eyes registered recognition of what was to come. "Take off your coat." He nudged the gun deeper into Hillman's gut when the judge just stood there. "Now, please."

Hillman tugged at the buttons on his expensive wool coat with shaking hands. "You won't get away with this," he said unevenly.

This made him smile. "I got away with Skinner. Of course it was a shame that Carson's bodyguard had to die instead of Carson, but one must break a few eggs to make an omelet. So I will most likely get away with this. And even if I don't, you'll still die."

Hillman went even more pale. "Oh, my God."

"I sincerely hope you're prepared to meet your Maker, Judge Hillman, because meet Him you shall. Climb in and have a seat."

Hillman looked around frantically, but of course there was no one around. It was as Hillman designed, week after week. A deserted parking lot where no one would see him meeting his mistress. "I'll scream," Hillman promised, his voice cracking.

"No one will hear you and you'll die just the same. Too bad you were so concerned with anonymity when meeting your Miss Quincy." He smiled cruelly. "Rather ironic, don't you think?" He shoved the gun harder. "If I squeeze the trigger, you're dead."

"If I go with you, I'm dead."

He raised his brows. "But you're a coward and you'll hope up until the end that someone will come and save you. On the count of three, Judge Hillman. One, two—"

The judge pulled himself into the van as he'd known he would. With practiced efficiency, he reached to fasten the handcuffs that would trap Hillman on the floor of his van. He fastened a second wrist cuff, then moved to Hillman's feet. Hillman kicked, sending an unexpected shudder of pain through his body.

"You'll pay for that, Hillman," he vowed. "Just like you'll pay for everything else."

Hillman's brow glistened. "But what have I done?"

He cut a piece of duct tape to cover Hillman's mouth. "Leah Broderick."

Hillman's eyes registered no recognition and that made him even more coldly furious. "You don't remember her, but you will. Before this is all over, you all will." He pressed the tape to Hillman's mouth, making sure to cover his pencil-thin mustache. It would hurt when he yanked the tape later. Such a small thing, some might call it petty.

But it had just been that kind of day.

Wednesday, February 25, 6:30 P.M.

Abe heard the pounding as soon as he got out of his SUV. He parked on the street as Aidan's Camaro filled Kristen's driveway. Abe stopped at the cruiser, back in position at the curb, and McIntyre rolled down the window.

"Anything new?" Abe asked and McIntyre shrugged.

"Nobody came close with any boxes. She had a visit from the man who lives two doors down, but she didn't let him inside. Your brother brought her home from the hospital a few hours ago. I did check on her when the pounding started, but your brother said she's all right, just working out some stress. I guess she's got a right."

Abe agreed. Spinnelli had told him about her friends, the men who ran the diner. He could only imagine what she was going through. "Thanks." Abe jogged up the driveway, slowing when he came to the carport. Behind the rental car was a pile of smashed cabinets and her ancient oven, turned on its side. Cautiously, he opened the kitchen door and saw Aidan pulling on her equally ancient refrigerator. Aidan caught his eye, breathing heavily.

"Damn thing doesn't have casters," Aidan grumbled. "Weighs a fucking ton. Close the door. You're going to give us pneumonia."

Abe obeyed, then blinked as the pounding stilled. A layer of white dust covered the kitchen and everything in it, including Aidan and Kristen, who stood at the far wall with a hammer in her hand. He could see part of the old parlor through the major hole in the wall.

Kristen turned around, her pinned-up hair no longer red, but white. Streams of sweat streaked her face, red from exertion, and her breasts rose and fell under a thin tank top. Under a very thin tank top. And a sports bra. And very tight biker shorts. In the space of two heartbeats the very thin tank top revealed how glad she was to see him. With an effort he jerked his eyes from her clearly visible nipples back up to her face. Her eyes were clear, green, and hot. Slowly she lowered the hammer, holding it limply at her side.

Aidan cleared his throat. "I'll be going to work now. Bye."

Abe just looked at Aidan as he backed out the kitchen door, noticing Aidan carefully averting his eyes from Kristen's very thin tank top. "See you. Call me if you need . . . anything." The last was uttered on a cough that Abe was quite certain muffled a laugh. The door closed behind Aidan and he and Kristen were alone in the wreck of her kitchen.

Abe wasn't sure what to say. He opened his mouth, closed it, then gave up and let his eyes drop back to her breasts.

"What did you find?" she asked, huskily.

Again he jerked his eyes back up to her face. "We found his target range, but he wasn't there." She absorbed this in silence, not moving a muscle. Awkwardly he gestured to the mess. "What is this?"

He watched her lips tremble, then she firmly controlled them, pursing them hard. Without answering she turned back to the wall, raised her hammer and the pounding began again. For a minute he watched her, then shrugged out of his overcoat, his suit jacket. He let them fall to the floor since they were destined to be covered in white plaster dust wherever he put them. He took off his tie, then his shirt. A crowbar lay on the table and he picked it up and began pulling the drywall from the hole she'd already started.

For ten minutes they worked together without speaking.

She pounded and he cleared away the debris. Then she stopped and once again there was silence.

"Vincent's in ICU," she whispered, and the hammer slid out of her hand to the floor. "Conti's men beat him up."

Abe blindly put the crowbar on the table behind him and reached for her. She came willingly, clenching her fists against his chest. He closed his arms around her and laid his cheek against the top of her head. "I know, honey. I'm so sorry."

She pounded her fist against him, once. A restrained blow. "He had a stroke on the operating table. Aidan had just brought me home and Owen called me. The doctors say he probably won't make it. Dammit to hell, Abe. Conti hurt him because of me." Her shoulders heaved, but she didn't cry. "Vincent's a good man. Gentle. He never hurt anyone."

He rocked her gently and her fists opened and closed against his chest. "This isn't your fault, Kristen. You know this."

Again she pounded, harder this time. "And then I came inside and Aidan closed the door . . ." Her tears were flowing now and he had no idea what to do, so he just held her. "And somebody knocked on the front door and I was afraid. Afraid to open my own damn door." She swallowed a sob, a horrible choking sound. "But it was just the man who does the neighborhood association. They signed a petition. All of them. They say I'm bad for the neighborhood. They want me to move. They want to throw me out of my own house."

Her shoulders heaved again and Abe wanted to find the neighbors and throttle them all. "They can't make you move, honey," he soothed. "We'll take care of that later."

"So I ripped up the petition and threw it in his face," she said, as if he hadn't even spoken. "Then I told him to go to hell and take his association with him."

He smiled against her plaster-covered hair. "Good for you," he murmured.

She pulled back, her face wet but her eyes clear. "Then I changed my clothes. I'll wear whatever the hell I want to wear in my own damn house. And I got a hammer and put that hole in the wall." She looked around with a frown. "And then the cats ran and hid."

He wiped her face with his thumb. "They'll come out when they get hungry."

"I know. Your brother asked me what I wanted him to do and I told him to get rid of the cabinets. And the appliances. They're old and ugly."

"They are." He felt for the pins in her hair and pulled them out one by one, freeing her curls. "But you're beautiful."

Her agitation seemed to dissipate before his eyes. "You really think so, don't you?"

"I know so."

She swallowed hard and his heart stuttered. "You make me feel beautiful." It was a husky whisper, as if she was afraid for anyone to hear. "And . . ."

He brushed her lips with his. "And desirable?"

Her eyes heated. "No one ever has before."

"Their loss, my gain," he muttered, pulling her back against him and taking possession of her mouth the way he'd been thinking about since sending her to bed last night alone. Her hands flattened against his chest, her fingers raking through his hair, then moving back and forth, pleasuring him as he'd taught her to do. His hands moved down her back, itching to catch her from behind and pull her into him. To thrust against her. To feel her writhe against him. But his mind regained control at the last moment and his hands detoured to anchor at her hips. He groaned against her lips and pulled away. "I don't want to push you."

She was breathing as hard as he was. "You're not." She stood on her toes to wrap her arms around his neck, pressing her breasts against him. "You came to my room last night," she breathed into his mouth, then kissed him softly. "Why?"

His mouth went dry as dust. "I was checking on you."

She shook her head, every movement grazing his lips with hers. "Try again."

He closed his eyes and his fingers stretched, half-touching her round rear end. The tight biker shorts showed off every curve. "I was hoping you'd ask me to stay."

"For what purpose?" It was practically a purr and a shudder racked him from head to toe. Once again she'd taken the reins, and once again he'd be damned before he stole one inch of her advantage. If this was a tease, he'd bear it. It might kill him, but he'd bear it. He could tell she wanted him. Her nipples were pebbled hard against his chest, but until she was ready, until she asked him, he would control himself.

Even if it killed him. And it just might.

She nipped at his lips. "What would you have done if I'd asked you to stay?"

He swallowed again. "Kristen, I don't think . . ."

"I dreamed about you all night," she murmured.

He opened his eyes and found himself drowning once again. "What did you dream?"

"I dreamed you put your hands on me and made me cry out."

His hands covered her buttocks and kneaded gently. "Like this?"

"Exactly like that. Then you made love to me." Then she hesitated, looking away.

He caught her chin with one hand, leaving the other firmly grasping her butt. "Look at me. Please." He waited until she lifted her lashes, shy uncertainty in her eyes. "You dreamed I made love to you. And then?"

She took several rapid breaths. "And I pleased you."

He felt as if he'd taken a physical blow. "Kristen . . . It's not about whether you please me. Haven't you figured that out by now? It's how we please each other." He kissed her, a rich melding of mouths and hearts. "Did you like that?"

She nodded, so slightly. "Yes."

He let go of her chin and covered her breast, heard her inhale sharply, felt her nipple grow rigid against his palm. "And you like this?"

She licked her lips, catching her lower lip between her teeth. "Yes."

He brushed his knuckles against the juncture of her thighs and felt her shiver. "And the other night, you liked that?"

"You know I did."

He took one of her hands from his neck and kissed her palm. "Then I promise you I'll like the same things." He brought her hand lower until her fingertips trailed the length of his erection and he tensed. "See? I like it, too."

Indecision clouded her eyes and once again he cursed whoever had hurt her in the past. Whoever had damaged her magnificent spirit. "But you don't have to do anything you don't want to do," he murmured and her mouth set in a determined line. It was as if he'd thrown down the gauntlet. "Kristen, I'm not daring you. We can stop right n—"

She pulled his head down for a kiss so hard he saw stars. "Don't," she whispered fiercely. "Don't treat me like spun glass. When you came into my room last night, what did you want from me? Be honest with me."

As if he could lie. "I wanted to be inside you. I wanted to feel you come around me. I wanted to hear you cry out and beg me for more. I wanted all that more than I wanted to breathe. Is that honest enough for you?"

Her eyes filled with tears and she defiantly blinked them away. "Yes. Now tell me this. If things were normal . . . If *I* were normal—"

This time he cut off her words with a hard kiss. "*Stop.* There is nothing wrong with you."

Her eyes flashed, impossibly, intensely green. "Then show me. Show me how it's supposed to be. Because I've always wanted to know."

For a moment they stood staring at each other and Abe realized a new gauntlet had been thrown down, by Kristen. She wanted to be romanced. Wooed. And he realized something else. He was scared to death. He drew in a lungful of air and slowly let it out. "Okay. How it's supposed to be. Well, first I'd be dressed better. Suit and a tie, maybe."

Her lips curved and her hands splayed wide against his bare chest. "I like you just like this. Then what?"

Her hands felt so incredibly good. "Then I'd ply you with a terrific meal."

She raised a brow. "You can cook?"

He smiled down at her. "Of course. Can't you?"

She scowled. "You're supposed to be making me swoon, not insulting me."

"Sorry. Then after dinner, I'd put on some soft music and pull you into my arms." He pulled her close and her hands slid up to his shoulders. "And I'd dance with you."

"I don't know how to dance," she admitted.

"Doesn't matter." He brushed a kiss across her lips. "The dancing's not important."

"What is important?" she asked breathlessly.

"Holding you. Touching you. Feeling your body against mine. Making you wish for just a little bit more." He moved with her, showing her how to follow his lead, letting his aroused body brush up against her lightly. She shuddered in his arms and he gritted his teeth against the sudden wave of lust.

"It's working," she said thickly. "What happens next?"

"Patience, patience." He kissed her dusty forehead. "We haven't finished our dance." But he slowed the motion until they were no more than swaying in place. He pressed kisses to her temple, her chin, the hollow of her throat. Heard her sigh. "Right about now I'd be wanting to feel you hard against me," he murmured. "I'd dance you backward until your back was against a wall and press against you." His brows lifted. "But you've knocked the wall down, so I can't do that."

She smiled at him, a siren's smile that set his hot blood to boiling. "Improvise."

He couldn't wait any longer. He took her mouth in a kiss that was everything he'd wanted and she returned it with equal fervor. Her arms slid around his neck and she pressed against him with her whole body and he filled his hands with her round ass and hauled her up into him, thrusting the way he'd dreamed. And she arched, sweetening the contact until he groaned and sank to his knees, bringing her with him. In a fluid movement he pressed her to the floor, cradling her head in his hands.

He lifted his head, every nerve in his body screaming for release. "This is what I wanted." He settled himself between her thighs and thrust his hips and watched her eyes flash. "It's what I wanted the first time I saw you."

"It's what I want now," she said. "Show me the rest, Abe. Please."

Rearing up on his knees, he pulled off her tank top, taking her bra with it. She lifted her arms in accommodation and then she was bared to the waist, open to his gaze. "You're beautiful, Kristen. But I knew you would be." He eased down to his elbows and looked his fill while she lay there, watching his every move. "When I got you like this, all hot and bothered, I'd tease you a little. Make you want a little more." He bent his head and gently licked her nipple and felt her jolt beneath him. He repeated the motion and she arched, offering him more. But he kept the caresses light, whispers only on her skin. Until she whimpered.

"Please."

He was truly going to die. "Please, what?"

She arched again. "Dammit, Abe, you know."

He ran his tongue under the fullness of her breast. Tasted the salt from her exertions. Purposed that she'd exert herself a hell of lot more before they were done. "Maybe I don't," he murmured. "I was showing you what I'd do, and there you go, rewriting the rules."

Her laugh was strangled, exasperated. "Abe."

He decided to have mercy and gave her what she was too shy to ask for, taking her breast into his mouth and sucking, tonguing her nipple and sucking some more. She moaned and threaded her fingers through his hair, pulling him closer and he lost it. He devoured, first one breast then the other, until she writhed beneath him.

"Oh, God," she gasped.

He lifted his head, panicked. "Please don't say you want me to stop."

She lifted her head from the floor, meeting his eyes. "If you stop, I'll hurt you."

His breath shuddered out in relief. He wasn't sure what he would have done had she asked him to stop. He would have stopped of course, but . . . He kissed each wet breast then continued down her stomach, slowing the pace, planting kisses down to her navel.

She lifted her hips against him. "Abe, I may be new at

this, but I think this is where we take off the rest of our clothes."

He'd been sliding down her body and now paused, his shoulders between her thighs. "Then you should be glad you have a master like me around," he said lightly. "You are so impatient." He pressed his mouth between her legs and she cried out. "God, you're already so wet," he muttered and looked up at her. She'd lifted herself on her elbows and now stared at him, her eyes heavy with need. "This is what I wanted last night," he said hoarsely. "Do you understand?" Wordlessly she nodded and his heart threatened to push out of his chest. "Can I?" And she nodded again. Unable to wait any longer he pulled her shorts, yanking in his haste, then dropped back down again, burying his mouth in her hot, wet heat. She fell back to the floor with another strangled moan, her arm covering her eyes, and he feasted. It had been so long and she tasted so good.

Raspy little staccato cries were coming from her mouth and he slowed down, drawing out her pleasure. "Do you like this?" he asked.

"Yes." Her hips arched. "Please." Then a few glorious minutes later, she began to tense and her hands reached for him. He reached to grab one of her hands, his other still under her, lifting her to him. "Abe." It was a high, keening cry and he intensified the pressure until she unraveled, coming with a long, low moan. He kept kissing her inner thighs, soft, plucking kisses until her breathing evened out.

His own body straining for release, he lifted his head and knew he'd never, ever forget the way she looked. Glowing, radiant. Awed. Covered in plaster dust.

She met his eyes. "And then what would you do?" she whispered.

He swallowed hard. "Then I'd ask you to help me with my belt, my zipper."

She sat up, tugging him to his knees. "Then I would." And she did, pulling at his belt, each movement making her breasts jiggle before his hungry eyes. The tip of her tongue appeared as she concentrated, finally loosening the belt when he covered her hands with his, halting their quest.

"Wait." He pulled his wallet out of his pants and found a condom. Her eyes widened and it was like he could hear the wheels turning in her mind. Did he always carry one? Did he do this with all the women? On this point he could allay all her misgivings. "Kristen, the last time I made love was six years ago, before . . ." He could see she understood. "I put the condom in my wallet last Wednesday night when I got back to my apartment."

"When you met me," she said softly.

"Again," he corrected, his voice husky. "Now, I would respectfully request you finish with my pants because I really, really want to be inside you." Her cheeks turned pink and she dipped her head, to focus on his waist. She accomplished the button of his pants with some difficulty, but he let her do it all. Gingerly, the zipper came down and she drew a deep breath. She pushed and tugged and his pants and boxers slid to his knees and when she drew another deep breath he realized he was holding his. Tentatively she stroked him and the breath he'd been holding came out as a guttural groan. "Oh, God. That feels so good."

It must have encouraged her, because she closed her hand around him and squeezed and he knew he was truly going to die. "Stop." He grabbed her wrist. "I want to be inside you when I come." He kicked off his pants and managed the condom, his hands shaking in his haste. Then he crawled between her legs and kissed her mouth until he felt her melt again. "Don't be afraid," he whispered, pushing her down to the floor.

She looked up at him, her eyes wide. "I'm not."

But she was. He knew she was. He could only make her fear disappear by showing her how it would be. He pressed deep, shuddering as her muscles contracted around him, accepting him. She was hot and tight. And beautiful. *And mine.* "Kristen?"

Her face had tensed, but the fear was gone. "Don't stop."

"I won't. I can't." He pulled out, then thrust deep and she caught her breath. "When we got to this point, I might suggest you—" He broke it off when she lifted her knees to hug his hips and he went deeper still. "Oh, God. Yes. Now move with me, Kristen." He set their bodies in rhythm. "Talk to me. Tell me what you feel."

"It's incredible." She cried out when he thrust and her hands reached to grab his shoulders. "I never knew . . ."

And somewhere he lost the thread of the conversation, his body taking control and he took, and took. In the distance he heard her muffled cry, felt her body contract around him, her pleasure catapulting him into his own. He gritted his teeth and thrust a final time.

Then there was peace. Panting, he rolled onto his side, still holding her, praying that now that it was over she wouldn't feel guilty or retreat back into herself. That he wouldn't accept. She was a most remarkable woman, although she would never admit it. He stopped just short of thinking she was *the* most remarkable woman, because in the stillness that followed completion, he knew he'd been a lucky man. He'd found two such women in his life. Debra was gone and he could never bring her back. But she of all people would want him to go on. And for the first time since holding his precious wife as she bled into a gutter, Abe allowed himself to imagine what the future would be like. To have a normal life again, with a wife to hold in the night and children with bouncy red curls. And it made him smile.

Kristen lay there, steeping in the kaleidoscope of sensations with which he'd gifted her, of all places on her kitchen floor. She pressed a lazy kiss to his hairy chest and settled her head back on his arm. Relief was a major emotion at the moment. He'd been pleased. More than pleased if she was any judge. Not that she was, but neither was she an idiot. He'd practically had heart failure toward the end, so hard was his pulse. The way he'd lunged, his teeth bared. The way his body had bucked and shaken. The groan as he climaxed. He'd been pleased. And so had she. She'd come not once, but twice and it had been like nothing she ever could have anticipated.

I'm not frigid after all. The thought was so exhilarating that she laughed out loud.

Abe drew a rasping breath. "Now, if we ever got to the place where we actually made love, I would suggest you not laugh afterward." His tone was teasing and her heart rolled over in her chest. "It's very bad for my ego."

She kissed the underside of his chin. "Your ego is safe. I'm happy. That's all."

He pulled her close in a hard hug. "That's not all, Kristen. That's everything."

"You're right." She lifted her head and looked down at their naked bodies. It was a sight she thought she would never see. Her naked with a man. That the man was Abe was . . . everything. She kissed his shoulder, then dropped her head back to rest on his arm. "Do you realize we're naked on my kitchen floor with a squad car parked out on my curb?"

He scratched his nose. "Do you realize I'm about to sneeze from all this dust and I'm lying on a piece of drywall?" he asked and she giggled. Giggled. She, Kristen Mayhew, formerly of frigid fame, was lying naked in a pile of plaster dust with a man who looked like Abe Reagan and giggling. He smiled and touched the tip of her nose. "You should laugh more often," he said. "And you've got plaster dust all over your nose."

She stretched lazily, feeling better than wonderful. "A shower will fix that."

"Hmm. The shower." There was laughter in his voice. "Do you want to know what I want to do in the shower?"

Chapter Nineteen

Wednesday, February 25, 8:30 P.M.

"Thanks." Zoe closed her cell phone with a snap. "Let's go."

Scott wearily put the minivan in gear. "Where?"

"County. She just went in with Detective Reagan."

Scott sighed and pulled away from the curb where they'd been parked. "Let me guess. Another one of your sources?"

"Hospital lobby," Zoe said with satisfaction, opening her compact. "She got away earlier today, but we'll catch her this time."

"Oh joy," Scott muttered.

Zoe glared at him. "Just drive, Scott."

Wednesday, February 25, 8:45 P.M.

Kristen stood outside the window to ICU watching Vincent's body lying motionless in the hospital bed. She and Abe had set out from her house to grab dinner, but with-

ut her asking he'd driven straight to the hospital, which
was so sweet of him.

"Thank you," she murmured.

"For what?"

She could feel the vibrations of his rumbling voice
through her back as he held her tightly against him, partly
possessive, mostly supportive. She leaned back into him,
feeling her hair catch on the stubble of his beard. For the
first time in years she'd actually left the house with her hair
down, because he'd asked her to and she didn't know if she
could ever tell him no. "For coming up with me. I know you
don't like hospitals."

"How could you tell?"

"I figured it out when you muttered in the elevator how
much you hate hospitals."

"Sorry. It's . . . ingrained."

"Still, thank you for bringing me to see him. It was
thoughtful."

She could feel him shrug. "I knew you were worried
about Vincent."

"And thanks for getting me in." At first they'd refused
her entry because she wasn't family, but Abe had gotten
them in by flashing his badge. She sighed heavily, looking
at Vincent just lying there. "I never thought of either of
them as being old, but I guess they are."

A nurse walked up. "Visiting hours are long since over,
Detective. You're going to need to go now." She raised a
brow. "Unless you have any more questions."

"No, you've told us there's no change. No more questions," Kristen said quietly.

"Wait. I have a question. Has anyone been in to see
him?" Abe asked in his cop voice, and Kristen twisted to
look at him over her shoulder in surprise.

"Two men, but neither of them were family," the nurse answered.

"*Two* men?" Kristen frowned at the nurse in confusion. "One would have been Owen Madden, but who was the other?"

"He didn't leave his name, and he was extremely distraught."

"Can you describe him?" Abe asked and the nurse's eyes softened.

"Twenty-five-year-old Caucasian male with mild Down's syndrome. Very functional. Said he'd heard about his friend on the news. I really wanted to let him in, but . . ."

Kristen sagged. "Timothy."

Abe lifted her chin to look in her eyes. "You know him?"

"He worked for Owen up until a month ago, but quit when his grandmother got sick."

Abe's eyes narrowed. "When did he quit? Exactly, Kristen?"

"I don't know. Mid-January maybe." His meaning struck her and she shook her head forcefully. "No way. There is no way Timothy could be involved in anything like what we're dealing with. No way, Abe."

"Mid-January, Kristen. Doesn't that strike you as strange?"

The nurse considered them. "If you're talking about your vigilante, I'm inclined to agree with Miss Mayhew. From everything I've read in the paper, the killer is highly intelligent, calculating. While this Timothy was highly functioning, we're talking two different planes."

Abe frowned. "I know. But I hate coincidences. If he comes back, will you call me?"

The nurse took his card. "Of course."

Wednesday, February 25, 9:05 P.M.

The elevator dinged and there they were. Zoe narrowed her eyes when Reagan put his arm around Mayhew's shoulders. She'd known there was more going on than Reagan just guarding Mayhew's house. Now her mind scrambled as to how to make the most of it.

"Here they come," Zoe hissed. "Scott, are you ready?"

"Rolling," he said tersely and she stepped in front of the couple, gauging their reactions. Mayhew's eyes flared and Reagan's teeth clenched. Very, very good.

"Miss Mayhew, can you comment on the condition of Vincent Potremski?"

"No." She and Reagan started walking and Zoe side-stepped them.

"How do you respond to recent allegations of impropriety in John Alden's office?"

Mayhew stopped dead and shot her a look of complete incredulity. She shook her head, sending her curls bounding. "No comment, Miss Richardson. Now if you'll excuse us." They started walking again, but Zoe spied the telltale tremble in Mayhew's hands that she'd come to look for in times of stress. Mayhew might look poised, but she wasn't.

"Isn't it true that your friend was nearly beaten to death because of you? That this is your fault? That he'll probably be a vegetable for the rest of his life?" she asked to Mayhew's back and once again Mayhew stopped dead. But when she turned, there was no incredulity on her face, only rage. Zoe waited, senses tingling. She'd broken Mayhew's control. Finally.

Mayhew advanced a step and Reagan tugged at her shoulder. "Kristen," he said quietly, but clearly enough to be heard. "She's not worth it."

For a moment it looked as though Reagan had won and Zoe felt the pang of disappointment. But then Mayhew took another trembling step forward. "First of all, Miss Richardson, the correct term is 'persistent vegetative state,' and I'm sure the families of those so afflicted would appreciate your consideration in this regard. Secondly, you wield a great deal of power with that microphone, Miss Richardson, and you, sir, with your camera. I'd hope that you'd use it to help bring justice to innocent victims rather than further fanning the flames." She walked away, Reagan's arm around her again, his hold proprietary and Zoe saw Mayhew lean against him.

And for just a brief moment, Zoe wished for someone to lean on, too. Then the brief moment was annihilated by the fire of fury. Little pompous bitch. "Stop film," she snapped. Scott lowered his camera, his gaze still on Mayhew's retreating back, his expression one of respect, making her even angrier. "Don't say a damn word," she hissed and pushed past him.

She had a piece to prepare.

Wednesday, February 25, 10:30 P.M.

"Who is Leah Broderick? Please."

He looked down at Hillman with contempt. The man was arrogant and powerful when he sat high above the courtroom. But now, when threatened, Hillman became a quivering mass of nothing. He wished Leah could be here to see him now.

He'd transferred Hillman from his van to his basement with relative ease. Hillman had resisted lying down on the table, though, and a little persuasion in the form of a blow to his head had been necessary. Hillman regained consciousness and spent the next hour fruitlessly pulling at his bonds. Then the begging had begun. It was rewarding to see such arrogance reduced.

He took out his gun and ignoring Hillman's pleas for mercy, methodically put a bullet in the judge's left knee. Hillman's scream was high and shrill, his body writhing. Hillman began to sob and again he wished Leah could be here.

"Just a precaution, Judge Hillman. I can't have you running away." The right knee exploded with the same force as the left and Hillman screamed again. He bent to inspect his work. Blood flowed, so he packed both knees with gauze. "I don't want you to bleed to death, Judge. Not just yet anyway. I'll check on you later. For now, I have a special treat." He walked over to the stereo and hit the play button. "I've taken the liberty of recording the transcript of a certain trial. Listen closely. Then you'll know what you've done."

Then he went upstairs to lie down on his bed, more exhausted than he should be. He had time for a few hours of sleep, then he had to get back to the hunt.

Wednesday, February 25, 11:40 P.M.

"How's Kristen?" Mia asked by way of greeting.

"She's fine." *Way better than fine,* Abe thought. "She's waiting at our desks."

Mia's eyes went sly. "Hope I didn't disturb anything. You know, calling so late."

Abe shook his head, willing his face not to break into a self-satisfied grin and not entirely succeeding. "Not really. I was dozing." Next to Kristen, in her bed. His hand cupping her bare breast, her butt tucked snugly against his groin. Life was good.

Mia tucked her tongue in her cheek. "On Kristen's sofa."

"Absolutely," he lied and saw her swallow her grin. He pointed to the window that looked into the interview room. "Who we got?"

"Craig Dunning. Driver and bodyguard to the Honorable Edmund Hillman."

"Who is missing."

Mia nodded. "Yep." She pushed the door open and sat down next to the thirty-something man who nervously twisted his chauffeur cap in his hands like a Frisbee. "This is my partner, Mr. Dunning."

Abe extended his hand. "Detective Reagan."

Dunning's hand was damp, but his grip was punishing. "I've seen you on TV."

"The life of celebrity," Abe said dryly. "So you last saw Judge Hillman when?"

"About five o'clock."

"And you were where?" Abe asked.

Dunning shifted uncomfortably. "In the parking lot of the limo company."

Mia rolled her eyes. "Come on, Dunning, it's late. Let's have the story."

Dunning glared, but complied. "Every Wednesday I pick up Judge Hillman at court and drive him to the limo yard. We . . . We switch cars. He takes my car and I sit with the limo until he returns. Tonight he never came back."

Mia gestured impatiently. "And he goes where?"

Dunning hesitated. "To meet his girlfriend."

Abe shook his head. "First Alden and now Hillman. Don't any of those guys sleep with their own wives? Okay, Mr. Dunning, let's have the details. What time does Judge Hillman normally return? And where does he meet this woman, and what is her name?"

"Her name is Rosemary Quincy, and they meet at a hotel

in Rosemont. He's normally back by six-thirty, seven at the latest."

Mia ran her tongue over her teeth, clearly biting back what probably would have been a fitting assessment of Hillman's staying power. "So how long did you wait?"

Again Dunning shifted. "Until nine-thirty. Then I went home. But at ten-thirty Rosemary called. She was leaving the hotel and saw his car—my car, that is—still in the lot. She said he'd left hours before, and she was scared, what with all the killings."

"Why didn't she call us herself?" Mia asked.

Dunning shrugged. "She was hoping to keep her name out of it."

"That's not likely," Abe said. "What about Mrs. Hillman? Does she know?"

Dunning licked his lips nervously. "About which? The affair or his being missing?"

"Both," Mia said.

"I don't think she knows about Rosemary. Hillman would be broke if she did. And about his being missing, yeah, she knew. She called me herself, about eight. I . . ."

"You told her that he was somewhere else," Mia finished, annoyed.

"Yeah. Look, I came here of my own free will. Can I leave now?"

Abe handed him a notepad and a pencil. "First write down Rosemary's name and number, your car description, license plate number. Then you can go." He gestured to Mia and together they left the room. Shutting the door behind them, Abe looked at Dunning through the window. "Hillman could be fine."

"Mrs. Hillman could have done him in for having an affair," Mia said.

"But you don't think so."

"No more than you do." Mia scrubbed her cheeks with her palms. "Damn, I'm tired of this. I guess it's back to Kristen's list."

Thursday, February 26, 8:00 A.M.

Their faces were grim, Kristen thought, looking around the table. They had a right to be. They were missing a judge. The press was in an uproar, the legal community even louder.

Spinnelli pressed his thumbs to his temples. "Please tell me you found something around the car."

"Nothing." Even Jack was discouraged. "Not one thing."

"And nobody saw anything," Abe added.

Kristen cleared her throat. "I know you all are tired of my lists, but here's another one. All the sexual assault cases I prosecuted in front of Hillman. I've already talked to a number of the former complainants. Most are still bitter. None reported trauma in the last three months."

"Any names we've seen before?" Mia asked.

"One. Katie Abrams."

"The five-year-old who 'came on' to her mother's boyfriend," Spinnelli said bitterly.

Familiar anger simmered at the memory of Katie Abrams and the gross miscarriage of justice. "Yes, that's the case." Kristen looked over at Todd Murphy who'd joined them again. "But Murphy checked out Katie's family after Arthur Monroe was killed. The mother's in prison for possession and Katie's been in foster care. I talked with her social worker who said she saw Katie two weeks ago. It's a good foster family and Katie's relatively happy."

"The foster parents?" Spinnelli asked. "Anything there?"

"Solid alibis, Marc," Murphy said quietly.

"Dammit," Spinnelli gritted. "What next? Miles?"

"It depends." Westphalen held up his hand when Spinnelli looked angry. "It depends on whether he picked Hillman at random or if Hillman's been his target all along. He hasn't hit anyone since he missed Carson on Monday night. Maybe he was shaken up. Maybe he's ready to tell us what his revenge is really all about."

"If Hillman's the next random target, we got nothing more than we had yesterday," Abe said. "If Hillman's his revenge, is he done?"

"I have to believe there is a pattern," Kristen insisted. "He's so regimented. Everything's always done the same way. And the focus is always on the victim."

"And you," Mia commented.

"And me. Somehow I factor into this. But it's more about the victims. Think about the headstones and the letters. I'm only the P.S. The victims are the focus. Maybe I'm just sensitive because I've been talking to these people for the last few days, but I hear the same things over and over again. The victims who've been denied justice blame the system. They blame the criminal, the defense attorney, me, the judge. It's a package."

"Just like the box he leaves for you," Miles said. "Interesting parallel."

"So where are you going with this, Kristen?" Jack asked. "What's the connection? Katie Abrams?"

Kristen shook her head. "I don't think so. For one, there's been no recent trigger with Katie Abrams. Second, there was no one who cared enough about Katie to avenge her. That was one of the things that made that case so hard. I think it's someone else."

"Maybe we're all wrong, and we just have a wild card," Mia said quietly. "Maybe he reads about you in the paper, Kristen, and decided to give you these gifts because he's crazy. Like John Hinckley, Jr., and Jodie Foster. Maybe there isn't a connection other than you."

"Then we have nothing," Kristen said flatly. "Because he's been too smart to leave us anything more than a bullet and a partial print and a cup of coffee."

Spinnelli sighed. "What about the shack yesterday? Any prints, Jack?"

"A few partials from the picture frames, but they were under layers of dust. We took a few from the newspaper. The prints on the newspaper could have been from anywhere, but we're running them. None match the partial we found on Conti's body. There was writing on the back of both pictures. One said, 'Worth: Henry, Callie, Hank and Paul.' The other said, 'Hank and Genny, 1943.'"

Abe noted it. "So Paul was the other son, which makes sense because the records clerk told us the Worth property had passed to Paul Worth when Henry the father died. And we know from the marriage certificate that Genny married some guy named Colin Barnett. We have the parish church where Genny and Barnett married and the year and a picture of Genny. I say we pursue it, because it's the only lead we have."

"We have Paul Worth," Mia inserted. "He would have had his father's old bullet molds. We should check him out, too."

Abe acknowledged the point with a rueful smile. "That would be more obvious than a child that may or may not have been born sixty years ago, wouldn't it?"

"I'll follow up on Paul Worth," Kristen said. "If he owns that property you found yesterday, there should be records in the tax assessor's office."

"Good." Spinnelli wrote it all on the whiteboard. "What else?"

"One more." From the end of the table Murphy spoke

up. "Marc asked me to get the details of the Aaron Jenkins's sealed record. Jenkins plead down to sexual imposition. He tried to rape a girl under the stairwell in middle school seven years ago. But she's not on any of your victim lists, Kristen. I checked. Her name is June Erickson."

Kristen searched her mind. "I've never heard the name. Can we talk to her?"

Murphy grimaced. "If we can find her. Her family moved soon after the complaint was filed. I found some neighbors who said the girl had a hard time in school after that. Kids pushed her around because she reported Jenkins. Apparently he was a pretty popular kid back then. I've got listings for people with the same names as her parents and I'll work through them today until I find them. I'll let you know when I have something."

"Then we have our direction," Spinnelli said. "Abe and Mia, find Genny O'Reilly. Murphy, find the Erickson girl. Kristen, you find Paul Worth, but don't leave the building without one of us. If anybody makes any deliveries to your house regarding Judge Hillman, the officer sitting in front of your house will let us know."

"And you?" Abe asked.

"I'll hold off the politicians and reporters that want to tell us how to do our jobs."

Kristen gave him her latest list. "The Hillman cases with defense attorneys and accused. Assuming there is a connection and this is his revenge, one of these guys will be next."

Thursday, February 26, 9:30 A.M.

Father Ted Delaney of the Sacred Heart Church fancied himself a bit of a detective, having watched *Columbo* religiously, as it were. So when Abe told him what they were looking for, the old priest plunged into the task with an enthusiasm that made them smile.

"I wasn't parish priest then, you understand," he said, adjusting his glasses on the edge of his nose. "I didn't arrive until 1965. Father Reed was two generations before me. He was old in 1943. I think he died before the war was over."

"We figured we wouldn't find the priest that married them alive," Abe said. "Do you remember any Barnetts in this parish? His name was Colin and hers was Genny."

"I can't say that I do, but the parish was much bigger then." He looked over his half-glasses with mild reproach. "People don't go to church like they used to."

Abe fought the urge to stare at his shoes. "Yes, sir," he said. "So how about the birth records? The baby would have been born around March 1944."

Delaney chose a bound volume and slowly flipped the pages, his fingers thick and twisted with age. Finally, he looked up. "A son. Christened Robert Henry Barnett on March 2, 1944."

One step closer. "Did they have any other children, Father?" Abe asked

"If you can wait, I'll look."

After what seemed like hours, Delaney's old fingers came to a stop again. "A daughter, christened Iris Anne, May 12, 1946." Again, his fingers crawled from page to page. "Another son christened Colin Patrick, September 30, 1949."

"Is it possible Genny is still alive?" Mia asked.

"She'd be close to eighty now," Delaney said. "The death records are in another room. If you wait here, I'll go check."

When he was gone, Abe turned to Mia. "They didn't name their firstborn Colin, Junior," Abe said, his voice barely a whisper.

Mia lifted a brow. "Seven-month baby. Jig was up. I wonder if Colin Senior knew ahead of time, or if he was surprised by a full-term son two months early."

"She named her firstborn Robert Henry."

"Hank is short for Henry."

Abe nodded. "Either Colin Senior was a most forgiving man, or Genny slid that one in on him. She gave her son his biological father's name."

"Let's hope at least one of the Barnett kids still lives in Chicago."

"When the good Father comes back, we'll check it out."

Thursday, February 26, 10:30 A.M.

Kristen hung up the phone, frustrated with her attempts to reach the final few people on her victim list. Some had moved, some had just disappeared.

Spinnelli approached her, his face grim. "I was waiting until you were off the phone."

"What's happened?"

He handed her the list she'd given him that morning. One of the names had been circled in red. "Gerald Simpson didn't show up for court this morning."

Kristen pursed her lips. Simpson was a dedicated defense attorney. In his mind, all offenders could be rehabilitated, and prosecutors were vindictive and power-mad, just looking to convict to hasten their promotions. He defended with great zeal, but with little compassion for the victim. "So maintaining our assumption that this is connected to Hillman, we just narrowed the field considerably. I only faced Simpson in Hillman's courtroom six times. Are we going to put any surveillance on those six defendants?"

"Already ordered. We've got a bulletin posted for

Simpson's car. I'm going to go interview his wife since Abe and Mia are still in the field. Maybe Mrs. Simpson will know something." But his expression clearly said he expected she would not.

"I'll call the six victims."

Spinnelli ran a frustrated hand through his hair. "Anything on Paul Worth, the son?"

"Records is checking. They said they'd call me back when they found anything."

Thursday, February 26, 2:30 P.M.

No Barnetts still lived in the parish, but Father Delaney had given them a list of his oldest parishioners. Viola Keene had been a member of Sacred Heart parish all her life. Church membership had done nothing to sweeten her disposition. "Sure, I remember the Barnetts. Why do you want to know?" Viola Keene frowned at their feet. "I just mopped in here. Can you shake the snow off your feet?"

"We're sorry, ma'am." Abe made an honest effort to clean his shoes and Mia did the same. "It's slushy out there."

"Maybe we're gonna have a thaw," the old woman said irritably. She really wasn't that old, Abe thought. She wasn't even sixty, but she seemed older. It was the way her mouth bent in a perpetual frown. The severe hairstyle and black wardrobe didn't help.

"One can only hope," Mia murmured and Abe bit back his smile.

"Well, what do you want to know?" Keene snapped. "I got a business to run."

She owned a small hat shop, but it appeared their privacy was assured. The layer of dust on the hats indicated Keene hadn't had customers in quite a while. Go figure.

"The Barnett family," Abe said. "How did you know them?"

"I went to school with Iris Anne. Foolish girl she was."

They approached the long counter where Miss Keene was bent over what looked like a big bow. "How so, ma'am?" Mia asked.

"Always worrying about boys and such. Never one much for her studies. Now her brother, he was a different tale."

Mia leaned closer to see the woman's face. "Which brother, Miss Keene?"

Keene looked affronted. "The older one, of course. Robert worked hard at his studies. He helped his father in their store, like a good son should." Impossibly, her face softened and she looked ten years younger. "He took good care of Iris and the other one." She frowned again. "The youngest . . ." She paused, trying to remember. "Colin. He was a spoiled one. Always gettin' into trouble, pickin' on kids in the neighborhood." She sniffed. "He got his."

Mia glanced up at him from the corner of her eye, then back to Keene. "How so?"

"Colin picked on the wrong kid." Keene picked up the bow and began fussing with the ribbon. "Kid beat him up, put him in the hospital. It was quite the neighborhood event."

"So what happened?"

"Colin died."

Mia blinked. "Wow. That was some neighborhood event."

Keene fluffed the bow. "The kid had a knife in his boot. Colin never saw it comin'."

Abe hid his surprise at the old woman's casual rendition of the tale. "What happened to Robert?"

Again her face softened, became almost wistful. "It got even worse for him at home after that. Finally, he ran away. Broke Iris Anne's heart."

Miss Keene's, too, he suspected. "What do you mean, it got worse? Was it bad before?"

Keene looked up, angry. "Mr. Barnett was hard on Robert. Iris and Colin could do whatever they liked, but Robert had to work hard. If he didn't breathe right, his father would take a cane to him. Like I said, he finally ran away. I never saw him again."

"Miss Keene," Mia said softly, "what happened to the kid who killed Colin?"

Keene dropped her eyes back to the bow. "He went to jail. One of those reform schools. But when he got out, he got in a bar fight and ended up stabbed, just like Colin." She held the bow up to the light. "Poetic justice, the papers called it. Never caught the guy who did it. Most people figured he'd made some enemies along the way, but me and Iris, we used to wonder if Robert came back." She sighed. "Of course it was just girlish wishing. I thought I saw him once, a few years later, but I was wrong."

"Where was that?"

"At the funeral. His parents and Iris Anne were killed in a car accident."

"I'm sorry," Mia murmured and Keene shrugged.

"It was almost twenty-five years ago." Then she surprised them both by smiling at Mia. "But thank you. She was my dearest friend."

"Why did you think you were wrong about seeing him, Miss Keene?" Abe asked.

"I called to him, but he didn't answer. My Robert never would have been so rude."

"One more question, Miss Keene," Mia said, "then we'll be on our way. Do you have any pictures, maybe a picture of Robert?"

"Oh, mercy. I may have an old annual or two from high school, but I'd have no clue where they'd be."

Mia gave her a business card. "It's really important we find a picture. My name and number's on here. If you find something, can you call us?"

Thursday, February 26, 3:00 P.M.

"Mr. Conti will see you now."

Zoe fidgeted nervously. Now that she was here, she was wondering how wise an idea this request for an interview had really been, especially since they'd refused to allow Scott to accompany her. He hadn't even been allowed to drive her here in the station van. She followed the butler, clad in a black pin-striped suit with a crisp white shirt and a black tie. *Shades of Al Capone,* she thought, glad she'd left word with the station on where she'd gone.

"Miss Richardson," the butler announced, gesturing her into Jacob Conti's private office. Conti himself sat behind his desk, staring at her through narrowed eyes. Drake Edwards stood to one side. She supposed Edwards intended to look casual, but the man exuded such coiled power that anything remotely resembling casual was an impossibility. For a moment she stared at him in fascination, then turned to Jacob Conti.

"Thank you for seeing me. Please accept my condolences on the death of your son."

Conti said nothing, but Edwards gestured toward the only other chair in the room. "Have a seat, Miss Richardson," Edwards said smoothly. "Stay a while."

His words had a distinctly ominous ring, but Zoe refused to be cowed. She sat, making sure she showed just enough leg. "I wanted to request a formal interview."

Edwards lifted a brow. "Why would Mr. Conti be interested in an interview?"

"There have been several attempts on the lives of Kristen Mayhew and her inner circle this week," Zoe said.

Conti's face remained impassive, while Edwards's grew amused. "And this concerns us how?" Edwards asked and Zoe knew she was being mocked.

"There are allegations that you are involved, Mr. Conti. The police were here to visit you just this morning."

"The police discussed no such allegations with us, Miss Richardson," Edwards said, again mocking her. "Perhaps your newest source is . . . incorrect." His eyes brazenly traveled the length of her body.

Zoe turned back to the silent Conti. "I wanted to give you the opportunity to address the allegations in a public forum," she said, as earnestly as she could muster while ignoring Edwards's blatant leer. Conti said not a single word. His expression had not changed once in the entire time she'd been in the room. If she hadn't seen his chest rise and fall, she might have believed he was dead. But he was very much alive.

And very much a threat. She stood up. "If you decide you're interested, please contact me." She placed one of her cards on the corner of his desk. "Again, my condolences."

She'd reached the door when Conti finally spoke. "Miss Richardson, I hold you as accountable for the death of my son as I do Miss Mayhew and his killer."

Unable to control the sudden tremble of her body, she turned to look at him. "Is that a threat, Mr. Conti?"

"Why would you think a thing like that?" Conti asked, his mouth curving in a truly horrible smile and she knew the true taste of fear. "Now leave before I have you forcibly removed."

On shaking legs she obeyed. Edwards followed her to the mansion's front entrance and opened the door. In his hand he held her card and a second later he'd deftly slid it down the neckline of her dress, between her breasts. "We know many things, Miss Richardson. Including how to reach you should we need to."

How she managed to start her car she didn't know. All she knew is she didn't draw a breath until she'd cleared the front gate. A mile away the nausea passed and fury swept in to take its place. She'd lost the upper hand. She'd just have to get it back.

Jacob didn't look up from his work when Drake reentered the room. "Kill her."

Thursday, February 26, 5:00 P.M.

Kristen laughed when a singularly atrocious hat landed on the desk in front of her. She looked up to find Mia wearing a grin. "What is this?"

"It's a gift for you."

Abe came up behind Mia, smirking. "She made friends with a hatmaker."

Mia sat behind her own desk and sighed. "I felt bad for her, all alone in that hat shop."

"She's alone because she's mean." Abe pulled up a chair and straddled it. He was almost close enough to touch and the sight of him straddling a chair brought back the memories in a flood. Kristen's fingers reached, then clenched and resolutely she focused on the ugly hat, but from the corner of her eye she saw him grin, enjoying knowing how much he affected her. "Except to you, Mia. You just charm everyone."

Mia made a face. "Shut up. You want to tell her or should I?"

Abe gestured broadly. "Be my guest."

Kristen listened as Mia recounted the conversation with Keene. "So Robert started early," she said, "assuming he really did come back to off the guy who'd killed his brother."

"The junior vigilante squad. Kind of like Boy Scouts, but not," Mia said.

Kristen shook her head with a rueful smile. "Mia. So what do you two think? Could Robert Barnett be our guy? That name's not on any of my lists but . . ."

Abe nodded. "I say he could be, but we hit a brick wall. Couldn't track Robert Barnett any farther than Keene. How did you do today?"

"I called everyone who was involved in a case Simpson defended and Hillman presided over. No obvious traumas, two invitations to celebration dinners, one nomination of the vigilante for the Nobel peace prize, and three I couldn't reach. I'll try them again tomorrow. Oh, and I found Paul Worth. I guess he'd be Robert Barnett's uncle through Hank."

Abe raised a brow. "And?"

"He's alive, but we can't talk to him. He's in a nursing home up by Lincoln Park. Not lucid. I did talk to his accountant, who's the executor of the estate. Paul Worth has no children and on his death that piece of land you found yesterday goes back to the state."

"I wonder how our guy found out about the property," Abe mused.

"I don't know. Maybe he knew the Worths." She handed him the sheet of paper on which she'd taken notes. "I asked the nursing home if you could see him. They said you were welcome to try. I wasn't going up there by myself and Spinnelli's gone."

Abe looked over at Spinnelli's empty office. "Where is he?"

Kristen sighed. "Mayor's office."

Mia winced. "Ooh."

"Yeah. He's got a press conference scheduled for seven. It's not going to be pretty."

They were quiet for a moment, then Abe's cell phone trilled. Kristen's heart skipped a beat. She'd been on edge all day, worrying about the Reagans, about Owen, about her mother, but everyone was accounted for. She'd warned Lois and Greg and knew she'd done her best to protect the people she cared about.

"Reagan." His face hardened and Kristen grabbed his arm.

"Rachel?"

He shook his head, covered her hand with his and gave a brief squeeze. "No, they're all fine. This is something else." He stood up and walked a few feet away. "This isn't a good time," he muttered, then, "No, I'm not free for dinner . . . Or drinks. Dammit, Jim, just say what's on your mind and be done with it."

Jim. Debra's father. *Poor Abe.*

"I'll try." Abe snapped his phone shut and stood there for a moment, all alone, and her heart cracked. Not caring who saw, she got up and smoothed her hand over his broad back. His muscles tensed under her palm and he turned to look at her, saw she understood. "They're in town for the christening. They want to meet me for dinner."

"Why?"

He moved his powerful shoulders restlessly. "I don't know. To talk, they said."

"Do you want me to go with you?"

One corner of his mouth turned up. "Thanks, but I don't think so. Don't be mad."

"I'm not." She leaned her forehead against his upper arm. "Just worried about you."

From behind them Mia cleared her throat meaningfully. "Hi, Marc."

As one, Kristen and Abe turned to meet Spinnelli's beleaguered stare. For a long awkward moment nobody said anything, then Spinnelli sighed. "At least there'll be one happy ending out of all this."

Kristen dropped her hand from Abe's back. "Mayor's not happy, huh?"

Spinnelli sank into a chair. "Well, let's see. We're incompetent, laughingstocks, the butt of jokes, an embarrassment. There was more, but those were the high points. Mia, call Murphy. Find out if he's gotten any closer to finding that girl." He snapped his fingers, his brow puckered. "Whatever her name was."

"June Erickson," Mia supplied. "Sure."

His gaze landed on the hat. "And what the hell is that?"

"Community outreach," Abe said. "I'll fill you in."

Thursday, February 26, 8:45 P.M.

"This is making me sick," Kristen said, feeling the room spin.

"This rocks," Rachel corrected. She was sitting in front of the Reagans's TV, careening down a mountain on a video snowboarding game that was entirely too real.

"Welcome to my world," Kyle said wryly. Becca chuckled.

Kristen covered her eyes. "I can't watch anymore. I'm going to throw up."

"Oh, man! Sixth place." Rachel shut off the video game. "My game is off tonight."

"It's a wonder you can still move your hands and your eyes aren't burned-out sockets," Kyle retorted. "You've been playing that fool game all day."

Because she'd stayed home from school. Just a precaution, Kyle said, and not her fault, Becca said, but Kristen felt responsible all the same. Rachel, on the other hand, was thrilled to have missed a test and to have the whispered admiration of her friends.

"Don't apologize," Kyle warned.

"Or you'll kick my ass," Kristen said with a weary smile. "I know. Has Abe called?"

"Not in the last five minutes since you asked before." Becca patted her hand. "He's fine, Kristen. He can take care of himself." It was said mechanically, in the voice of the wife and mother of cops. Kristen wondered if Becca had ever once believed it.

"Besides, it's just dinner," Kyle said. "The worst that can happen is he accidentally uses the wrong fork and Sharon cuts him up with that sharp tongue of hers."

Kristen looked up at him, curious. "Why do you say that?"

Kyle looked uneasy, but Becca huffed. "Debra was the sweetest, most generous woman in the world, but her parents were fond of money and the power that came with it." A look of pain crossed her face. "Abe wasn't good enough for Debra and her father never let an opportunity go by without telling him so."

"Becca," Kyle chided gently. "That's all past now. They can't hurt him anymore."

Kristen looked from one to the other, but neither

appeared to be prepared to impart additional detail. "Abe told me about the lawsuit. How they tried to get custody of Debra."

Kyle's eyes widened speculatively. "Did he now?"

Becca's jaw clenched. "Did he tell you that they never stopped blaming him for Debra getting shot? For five years Debra lay there and they never stopped blaming him."

Poor Abe. Poor Kyle and Becca, having to watch their son endure such torment. "He didn't want to meet them tonight."

Becca huffed again. "Of course he didn't."

"Then why did he?" Rachel asked from the floor and Kristen blinked. She'd almost forgotten the teenager was down there, listening to every word.

Kyle sighed. "I imagine he went to let them have their say and get it over with."

"So they wouldn't say it on Saturday and ruin the christening for Sean and Ruth," Kristen said. It added yet another layer of respect to the character of Abe Reagan.

Becca's eyes misted. "You really do understand him."

Kristen felt what was becoming a familiar wave of longing. For Abe, for his family. For the warmth of this house. "He's a good man," she said simply.

Kyle cleared his throat roughly and reached for the wallet he'd set on the lamp table.

"Kyle," Becca murmured. "Don't."

Kristen's mouth tipped. "Is he going to pay me?"

"No, he's going to show you Debra's picture," Rachel said and Kristen stiffened, but it was too late. Kyle held the worn snapshot and if she didn't look, she'd be rude.

So she made herself look down at the picture, at the woman who'd been Abe's everything. What she saw was a tall woman of average beauty and the protruding stomach of advanced pregnancy holding on to to a man who smiled as if he could never be happier. "She was lovely." It was true. Because beyond her average beauty was a glow, an expression that said Debra could never be happier either.

"This was taken two weeks before she was shot," Kyle said, a catch in his voice that made Kristen swallow hard. "I didn't think I'd ever see that look on my son's face again." His thumb swept over the plastic cover in a practiced caress. "But I have. Since he met you." His thumb grew blurry and Kristen bit the inside of her cheek, not daring to look up.

Rachel pushed a tissue in her hand, much as Aidan had done the day before. "Blow your nose before we all start bawling," she said and Kristen laughed unsteadily.

"Are you sure you're only thirteen?"

"Almost fourteen," Rachel returned archly.

Kyle groaned, the tender moment broken. "Going on twenty," he said.

"So can I go steady with Trent?"

Kyle scowled down at her. "No. Not till you're sixteen."

Rachel shrugged. "It was worth a try."

Grateful for the temporary respite from her worry, Kristen checked her watch and Kyle groaned again. "If you're so worried about Abe, call him on his cell phone."

"I don't want him to think I'm checking up on him."

Kyle huffed in disgust. "Women."

"We're all alike," Rachel sang and once again Kristen smiled.

"And you, having been a woman for so long, are an expert," Kristen said wryly.

"Hey, lady, I see what I see and I know what I know." Rachel grabbed the phone and handed it to her. "Call him. You know you want to."

Embarrassed, Kristen took the phone and dialed. And frowned. "He's turned it off."

Kyle's brows shot together. "He what?"

"He's turned off his cell phone. Or he's underground, because it's not picking up."

Kyle put out his hand, worry in his eyes. "Give me the phone."

Chapter Twenty

Thursday, February 26, 10:20 P.M.

Debra's parents had begged forgiveness. It was the one thing he hadn't expected. Abe rested his arms across the top of his steering wheel and stared at the bright lights of the Navy Pier's Ferris wheel. It was the one place where he could still see Debra smiling. They'd come here on that first blind date, set up by Sean and Ruth. He'd brought her here the night he proposed, bribing the Ferris wheel attendant to stop the wheel when their car was on the very top so that he could ask her to marry him with all Chicago at their feet. She'd brought him here the night she told him he'd be a father, bribing the attendant in the exact same way. So he came here tonight to think, to remember his wife as the happy woman she'd been. To try and find in his heart the forgiveness her parents had asked for.

He'd lost all track of time when a knock on his window nearly scared him to death.

Sean stood there scowling. "What the hell are you doing here? You had us worried sick."

Abe glanced at his watch in amazement. "I didn't realize I'd been here so long."

"Where's your damn phone? We've been calling you for an hour and a half."

Abe fished it out of his pocket and frowned. "No battery bars." It was the first time he'd been so careless. He plugged it into his cigarette lighter.

"Kristen's in the car."

His gaze snapped to Sean's car where Kristen sat staring at her hands. "Why?"

"She's been climbing the walls, afraid you'd been hurt by Conti's men."

Suddenly so weary, Abe dropped his head back against the seat. "I didn't think."

"Well, tell it to her yourself. I got to get back to my own woman."

A minute later Sean roared away and Kristen climbed up into the cab. She immediately dropped her eyes and he felt the pang of guilt. He'd been thoughtless.

"I'm sorry, Kristen. I didn't think you'd be worried."

"Well, I was, but it's all right." Her chin was practically digging into her chest.

"Can you look at me?"

She complied, twisting her neck at an odd angle and looking up from the corner of her eye, but still not meeting his gaze. She looked . . . strange.

"What's wrong?"

She closed her eyes, drew a strangled breath. "Can you please take me home?"

"Not until you tell me what this is all about. Open your eyes."

She shrank back in the seat, her eyes clenched shut. "Abe, please."

Suddenly alarmed, he pulled the SUV out of the parking place. "What's happened? Dammit, Kristen, if you're trying to get back at me for scaring you, it's working."

"I'm not. Just drive."

He started driving. "Is it Vincent?"

"No, he's unchanged. Owen called to tell me when I was in the car with Sean."

"Has that Timothy come back to see Vincent?"

"I didn't ask. I was too worried about you." He saw her open one eye, look in the passenger-side mirror, then shut her eyes again.

He looked in the rearview mirror and saw nothing but the blazing lights of the Navy Pier's Ferris wheel. "When we get to your house, you'll tell me?"

She nodded once. "Yes."

Thursday, February 26, 10:45 P.M.

He was relieved when Reagan's SUV pulled into her driveway. He could see between the houses from his position on the next block and watched as Reagan got out and crossed around to her side of the vehicle. Reagan was a gentleman. He approved.

He was glad they were home safely. He couldn't have forgiven himself if anything had happened to anyone else she cared about. He hadn't meant it to spiral out of control this way. He'd meant her to be comforted, knowing he was eliminating evil from the world, but instead her life had been turned upside down. She'd been threatened in her own home. He would have to find a way to make sure everyone knew she was uninvolved, that she knew nothing. He would write her no more letters.

He frowned. She should have been out of the car a long time ago. It was cold tonight. She'd get sick. Reagan needed to get her into the house, but he just stood there. Something was wrong. Finally, she climbed down and

Reagan put his arm around her and walked her into the house through the kitchen door. She appeared unhurt. But he needed to be certain.

Thursday, February 26, 10:45 P.M.

Kristen stopped short at the sight of her kitchen, visions of Ferris wheels temporarily dismissed. "It's clean. All the plaster dust is gone." So was the far wall. She and Abe hadn't finished ripping it down the night before, but now it was totally gone. As was the refrigerator, the sink, and the linoleum. The only thing remaining was her table, which was covered with magazines opened to layouts of beautiful kitchens. "Annie's magazines," she said, then understood. "Aidan and Annie were here. Did you know they were going to do this?"

Abe was grinning. "Where do you think they got the key?"

"Where did *you* get the key?"

"Mia stole it from your purse and I had a copy made. Are you surprised?"

She sank down into a chair and covered her mouth with her hand. Tears sprang to her eyes as Abe knelt beside her on one knee and pulled her into his arms.

"They wanted to do something for you. It was Aidan's idea."

"It's the nicest thing anyone's ever done for me. Oh, Abe."

His hands rubbed her back, great soothing circles. "Are you ready to talk now?"

She wiped her eyes on his coat. "I think so."

He pulled away, lifted her chin, kissed her mouth. Then

took the chair next to her and unbuttoned his coat. "I'm ready whenever you are."

It was time, she knew. Time to tell the story she'd told only once before. This time she'd be believed. Still . . . She'd harbored the secret for so long. Too long. It was time to let it go.

"I was twenty," she began with a sigh. "A sophomore at the University of Kansas. I'd spent a year in Italy and I was behind, so I was taking some summer classes so I could catch up. He was a guy in my statistics class. I was an art major, so he helped me with my homework. I didn't have a head for statistics." She smiled sadly. "And then I became one."

Abe's face was calm, but his blue eyes were turbulent. "You knew him, then."

"I thought I did. We'd gone out a few times, burger joints, pizza places. He'd have a few beers, I'd abstain. He'd tease me about being a prude, I'd just smile. Then one night we went to the county fair. It was a summer night. He wanted to walk, so we left the group we'd come with and walked out past the livestock barns. He kissed me, not for the first time. But then he wanted to . . ." She faltered, her throat closing.

"He wanted sex," Abe said flatly.

She nodded, relieved he'd said it for her. "Which was the first time."

"The first time he'd wanted to or the first time for you?"

"Both."

His eyes closed, his throat working behind the knotted tie. "You were a virgin."

"Probably the only one in my class. My father forbade drinking, dancing, rock and roll, card-playing, but sex was the epitome of sin. So I was waiting, but not for this guy."

"But he didn't take no for an answer."

"No. I fought and scratched, but he was too big. He over-powered me like I was nothing. Told me I wanted it, that I'd been asking for it. I told him I'd never . . . but he laughed. Said I'd been to Italy, I was a woman of the world. He pushed me to the ground and covered my mouth . . ." She lifted her eyes to the ceiling, unable to look at him as she said the words. "He raped me. I just kept thinking it would be over soon, it had to be over soon. I looked up and saw the Ferris wheel in the sky and watched it spin, count-ed the cars. And finally it was over." She dropped her eyes back to him and saw his hands fisted on the table. She cov-ered one of his fists with her hand, realizing for all his insis-tence on hearing the truth, it might be harder for him to hear than for her to tell. "He left me there, in the dirt behind the barns."

"Did you tell anyone?"

"Eventually."

"The police?" he asked tightly.

"No." She sighed. "We tell these girls to come forward, to tell the authorities, but they're scared. I was scared. I was afraid nobody would believe me. He told me he'd say it was consensual. We'd been dating for two months. Nobody would have doubted him. He wasn't a jock. He was a nor-mal regular guy who always went to class and turned his homework in on time. He was no womanizer. That was the reason I trusted him in the first place."

"So who did you tell?"

"My parents."

"And?"

She could see her father's face as if it were yesterday, scarlet and quivering in rage. She could still hear the sound of his palm whizzing through the air, just seconds before he slapped her to the ground. Where she lay, trembling and nauseous. *And pregnant.*

"He didn't believe me."

"What?" Abe lurched to his feet on the outraged cry. "He didn't believe you?"

"No. He accused me of being like my sister. Sinful and wild."

She watched as Abe paced the floor. "Is that why you left home?" he asked.

"I didn't leave home. He threw me out." *Terrified, penniless, and pregnant.*

Abe froze, then turned, his face a mask of disbelief. "He threw you out?"

"Yes."

"And your mother?" he demanded. "What did she do?"

"Nothing. She just looked at me. Maybe if Kara had still been alive, she might have had the strength to stand up to him, but by then, she just went through the motions. Anyway, it didn't matter. By that time the boy had told all his friends what had happened. They all thought I was easy." *And I knew by fall term I'd be showing.* "So at the end of the summer term, I left KU. One of my sister's old friends had moved to Chicago, so I came here to live with her. I transferred to University of Chicago and finished my degree."

Abe's hands were shaking and he shoved them in his pockets. "In art?"

She shook her head. "No, I couldn't paint after that. I majored in business and decided to go to law school." *And I had a baby. And I gave her away.* But when she opened her mouth to finish the story, all she could see was the photo of Abe and Debra, pregnant with the child that was stolen from them. *And I gave mine away.*

Abe sat down heavily and buried his face in his hands. "God."

"When I saw that Ferris wheel tonight . . ." She shuddered. "I can't look at Ferris wheels."

He said nothing, just kept his head bowed. She reached out and stroked his hair. "It's done, Abe. I went on with my life."

He lifted his head, his eyes piercing. "Alone."

She met his gaze, held it. "For a time."

"What happened to him?"

Kristen shook her head. "No, I won't tell you that."

He glared at her. "Tell me."

"Or what?" she asked calmly.

His shoulders sagged and his face suddenly looked haggard. "Please."

She should have known he'd need to know. She knew, after all. She'd kept tabs on him, even after all these years. "As irony would have it, he went to law school, too. He went into politics and is now the mayor of a small Kansas town." Her lips twisted. "He's running for a seat in the state legislature. Polls show he's ahead by ten points."

Abe's stomach churned. That the monster would prosper, never pay for his crime, never feel a fraction of her pain was more than he could take. "You could ruin him."

She sat very still. "But I won't. I didn't say anything then and I won't say anything now." She looked away, but not before he saw the glint of tears in her eyes. "Because the truth of it is, I'm a coward."

Abe stared, not believing the words coming out of her mouth. "You are not a coward."

She blinked, sending the tears down her face. "Yes, I am. These women that come forward, they're the brave ones. I make them live through it again and again, publicly humiliate themselves again, and most of the time it's for nothing."

He gripped her arms and urged her to her feet. "I don't ever want to hear you say that." She'd told him her story

with a clinical detachment, but she was weeping now and
while her rape filled him with helpless rage, her tears broke
his heart. He pulled her into his arms and held her tight.
"There are all kinds of courage, Kristen. You go into work
every day and relive your own experience. You make it possible for these women to get justice. You're the bravest
woman I've ever known." He kissed the top of her head,
rocking her gently, feeling her wave of emotion subside.
"After Debra was shot, I lived a day at a time. I volunteered
for all the most dangerous jobs because living didn't matter
anymore. I was afraid of the future, Kristen. I was afraid to
think about being happy again."

She'd gone very still in his arms. "Are you happy now,
Abe?"

He tugged on her chin until she lifted her face. "Yes." He
lowered his head and brushed a kiss against her lips. "Are
you?"

"Happier than ever in my life." She said it so gravely, it
squeezed his heart.

He needed to see her smile again. "I bet I could make
you happier," he teased lightly.

Her lips curved. "I bet you could."

Thursday, February 26, 11:15 P.M.

He waited until they'd left the kitchen before making his
way through her backyard to his van. At first he'd been
shocked, shaken, and unsure, but now he was filled with
cold rage and certainty. He'd hunted and bagged his quarry.
Three men now lay moaning in his basement, waiting for
him to mete out justice. He was ahead of schedule.

He had time to right one more wrong.

Friday, February 27, 8:45 A.M.

It was Friday, but nobody was thanking anybody, Abe thought. Spinnelli looked haggard after last night's press conference, like he'd rather be anywhere but leading their morning meeting, but he was there, marker in hand. There truly were all kinds of courage.

"What do we know, people?"

"I checked with the men you assigned to tail the six defendants common to Judge Hillman and Simpson," Abe said. "Four are accounted for, two can't be found. The two we can't find might be alive and kicking, but we don't know, so they'll keep looking."

"They found Simpson's car last night," Jack said. "The driver's window was smashed in from the outside, like maybe he locked himself in and our guy broke the glass to get him. Nine-one-one got a call from his cell phone about six yesterday morning, but the caller never said anything and ten seconds into the call they were disconnected. They tried to call back, but no luck. We found the phone smashed into pieces on the floorboard of Simpson's car. Apparently our boy is wising up to the danger of GPS."

"Where did you find the car, Jack?" Abe asked.

"Parked outside his health club. One of those twenty-four-hour places."

"His wife said he liked to work out before the morning rush," Spinnelli said. "Did you find anything on the health club's security tape?"

Jack's eyes gleamed. "White van. Plates registered to an Oldsmobile owned by Paul Worth."

A collective breath was drawn. "Finally," Mia said. "Something we can use."

"But we didn't get him on film," Jack said, disgusted. "The van blocked the camera."

Spinnelli rubbed his hands together. "Let's get a warrant for Paul Worth's house. Kristen, do you have the name of the accountant who's got his power of attorney?"

"No, I do," Abe said. From his notebook he pulled the piece of paper she'd given him the day before. "I'll call for a warrant."

The door to the conference room opened and Murphy came in, bags under his eyes and Mia winced. "You don't look so good, Todd."

"Thank you for noticing," Murphy returned dryly. "I found June Erickson, the girl who filed the attempted rape charge against Aaron Jenkins. She's a college student in Colorado."

Spinnelli stood a little straighter. "When did you find her?"

"This morning at about four A.M."

Mia whistled. "You called people at four A.M.? I bet you made some lifelong friends."

Murphy grimaced. "You could say that."

"Thanks, Todd," Spinnelli said. "I appreciate you sticking with it."

"Couldn't stomach being called incompetent," Murphy frowned. "Anyway, June's parents didn't want to talk to us, but when they found out Jenkins was dead, and woke up a little more, they changed their minds. I've got numbers for June's dorm and her parents' house. They're all expecting us to call at seven-thirty Mountain time so that June won't miss her first class. I thought a three-way call would be most efficient. It's almost time."

Spinnelli placed the speakerphone in the middle of the table. "Let's go."

Kristen reached under the table for Abe's hand and

squeezed as Murphy dialed one number, then the other, then made the introductions.

"Thank you for taking the time to talk with us," Abe said. "I'm Detective Reagan. Detective Mitchell and I have been working a serial homicide case for the last week."

There was silence on the other end. Then, a bewildered, "What does that have to do with us?" from Mr. Erickson.

"Aaron Jenkins was killed as a consequence of the other murders. After his death, we were able to look in his old record and your name came up. We're hoping you can give us some information that will let us figure out what connection Jenkins had to the killer."

"Is this the vigilante case we saw on CNN?" Mrs. Erickson asked.

"Yes, ma'am, it is," Abe said. "The record we opened showed your daughter filed a complaint against Jenkins for sexual misconduct."

Again silence, then a younger voice. "He cornered me under the stairs when I was in middle school." Her voice faltered. "I'm sorry. I don't like to remember it."

Kristen leaned toward the speaker. "I understand, June," she said. "I'm the prosecuting attorney working with the police. My name is Kristen. I meet lots of young women like you and it *is* hard to remember, but we really need your help. Can you tell us what happened?"

"He pushed me under the stairwell," June said and there was clear hesitation in her voice. "He tried to get . . . fresh."

"I understand. What did you do then, June? How did you get away?"

This time the silence was prolonged. Kristen frowned at the speaker. "June, it's Kristen. Are you still there?"

"Yes, I'm here." She sighed. "There was another girl who came along just then. I was screaming, but everybody was afraid of Aaron. This other girl was the only one who tried to help. She first tried to pull him off me, but she was small and he was big."

"They usually are, June," Kristen said. Abe nearly winced when her grip on his hand tightened. But her voice was steady and he was proud as hell. "What happened then?"

"She ran to get a teacher. They were . . . just in time. Nothing happened."

Abe knew from the report that something had indeed happened. Jenkins had ripped the girl's clothes off and was about ten seconds from rape when help arrived. But he said nothing to dispute the girl's words. Kristen was doing beautifully on her own.

"Well, I don't really agree with that," Kristen said pragmatically. "You were frightened and assaulted. That was something."

"Yeah, well, the teacher reported it. She said she had to. There were cops everywhere. It was terrible. Aaron was so popular. Anyone that crossed him . . . well, let's just say my life wasn't the same after that."

Mia passed her a note. *Ask her the name of the girl and why she wasn't in the report?*

Kristen nodded. "Believe me, June, I understand. One of the detectives here has a question. Who was the other girl, and why wasn't her name in the report?"

"Her name was Leah," June answered and Kristen closed her eyes briefly, clearly recognizing the name. "After the teacher came and Aaron ran, she begged us not to tell she'd been involved. She got made fun of so much anyway, she didn't want to be singled out."

"You never told us this, honey," Mrs. Erickson said.

"She asked me not to, Mom. She begged me not to. It was the least I could do. She put herself at risk to help me."

Kristen made a big circle on one of her lists and shoved

the paper into the middle of the table. Leah Broderick. One of the victims. They looked at one another with excitement. *Finally.*

"I've met Leah," Kristen said. "She grew up to be a remarkable young woman."

"I figured she would." June's voice faltered. "If you see her, tell her I said thank you."

A shadow passed over Kristen's face. "I will. Tell me one more thing, June, and then we'll let you go. What happened to you and to Leah after this incident?"

June sighed. "I never said a word to the police and neither did the teacher, but it didn't matter. Aaron made Leah's life a living hell. Her mother pulled her out of our school and put her somewhere else. My parents pulled me out and we came here."

"That's kind of what I thought. You've been an amazing help, June. Thank you."

"That's what you needed?" Mr. Erickson asked.

Abe looked around the table. There was an energy level higher than they'd had since this whole nightmare began. "Yes, it's exactly what we needed. Thank you."

"Kristen?" June's voice quavered a little.

"Yes, June?"

"I was really scared to talk about this again. But you made it easier."

Kristen bit her lips hard, but her eyes filled anyway. "I'm glad, June. Sometimes it helps to talk to somebody who's been there, too. Take care of yourself."

In stunned silence Murphy blindly disconnected the line. For several long beats, all eyes were on Kristen, then she stood up. "Excuse me. I need a few minutes."

Shaken, Mia started to follow, but Abe gently stopped her. "Let her go. She'll be all right."

Friday, February 27, 8:55 A.M.

They were waiting quietly when she came back. There was nothing makeup could do to fix her puffy face and red eyes, but she tried anyway. Abe met her eyes, his filled with pride. She took the seat next to him and looked around the table. Mia's face was quietly supportive, Jack's and Murphy's still shocked. Spinnelli looked torn between grief and rage. Miles Westphalen had joined them. She wasn't sure if this was because of the new information about Leah or because they were worried she was going to crack. She didn't plan to ask.

"I had Lois send over Leah's case file by courier." She placed the folder on the table and took a moment to collect her thoughts. "Leah Broderick was raped almost five years ago. She was one of my first sexual assault cases, but that's not why I remember her so clearly. Leah was cognitively challenged. She functioned at the level of about a twelve- or thirteen-year-old. She knew she was slow and hated it. She was a very proud young woman."

"You say 'was,' Kristen," Miles observed.

Kristen placed her palms flat on the table to control their trembling. "You were the one who suspected a trauma triggered this whole thing, Miles. I tried to call Leah yesterday, but her phone was disconnected. I called the supermarket where she worked and they hadn't seen her in over a year." She glanced up at Abe. "I don't like coincidences, either."

"It doesn't sound good," he murmured.

"So, about Leah. She had a job, she took the bus. She was active in her church. She helped teach Sunday school. Everybody who knew her loved her. Anyway, she'd been walking home from the bus stop when she was accosted by Clarence Terrill."

"One of the two men the plainclothes tails couldn't find," Abe said.

"Your package," Miles said. "Judge, defense, and accused, just like you thought."

Kristen wiped her damp palms on her slacks. "Clarence Terrill was a two-time offender already. Just one of those guys who slipped through the system. He raped her. Leah was able to give a good description and there was a witness who saw him pull her into his car. He'd bragged to his friends about the 'retard' he'd done. We had a good case. We had DNA. Simpson's strategy in rape cases was usually to have his client admit to the sex, but claim it was consensual. It clearly wasn't. Despite her handicap, Leah made a very credible witness. Until Simpson began his cross. He was ruthless. He broke every rule in the book and Judge Hillman let him get away with it. I objected so much that Hillman called me into chambers and told me if I didn't stop being so disruptive, he would hold me in contempt." She narrowed her eyes balefully. "I was green then. I'd like to see him try that now."

"If he's still alive," Abe said.

"One can only hope," Mia muttered.

"Simpson brought in witnesses who said they knew Leah from high school and everybody there knew she was easy. That she'd probably come on to Clarence Terrill, strengthening his claim that the sex was consensual." She opened the folder. "Tyrone Yates was one of the thirty names on his witness list. So was the last delivery boy, the one you have in protective custody."

"I say let him loose," Jack said, and didn't look apologetic in the least.

"They weren't in my database, because Simpson never called them to testify. I objected after three of the little bastards and it was only one of a handful of objections Hillman sustained. Then Simpson started in on Leah's appearance. She wore revealing clothes, which she didn't. Did she like boys? She was under oath, so she said yes. Did she want to get married some day, was she curious about sex? Had she had sex? Did she like sex? I objected and objected, and Hillman fined me. Anyway, the jury found Terrill guilty. Hillman thanked the jury, told them they could leave and when they were gone, he said Leah's testimony clearly showed she consented and that he was setting aside the jury's verdict."

Mia's jaw dropped. "Sonofabitch."

Kristen paused, remembering the day. "I was stunned. I remember Terrill high-fiving Simpson and giving Leah a wink as he left the courtroom. He *winked* at her. I couldn't believe it. Leah was devastated." She sighed and leafed though the documents in the folder. "Leah's only relative was her mother, but she had lots of friends. If one of them is our vigilante, we're going to have a very difficult search."

Friday, February 27, 11:30 A.M.

Drake closed the door to his office. "They're getting closer."

Jacob leaned back in his chair. "How do you know?"

"Spinnelli left the mayor's office without getting chewed out."

"Ah, yes. Your niece in the mayor's office. How is she?"

"As lovely and as loyal as ever."

Jacob fidgeted with his cuff link. Elaine had roused herself enough to lay out his clothes for him this morning before she'd gone back to bed. His wife was in a constant drug-induced stupor these days. Sometimes he envied her. But someone had to run the household.

"The Medical Examiner released Angelo's body this morning," he said.

Drake's shoulders sagged. "Jacob."

Jacob looked away, unable to bear the pain on his friend's face, knowing it was a reflection of his own. "There can be no viewing." There wasn't enough of Angelo's face left. The thought of it made him nauseous all over again. *My son.* "We'll have a closed casket ceremony tomorrow." But on the heels of his sorrow came blessed rage, cold and exacting. "I want Angelo's killer before then, Drake."

Drake stood up. "I'll call you when I know something."

"How is Miss Mayhew?"

"Scared. She's never without a bodyguard. Her circle's closed ranks, too. We almost got the little girl from the school, but one of the Reagans got there before we did."

"Disappointing."

"There's a family christening tomorrow."

"Better. Keep up your watch of Mayhew and Reagan. I want you to get to this parasite before they do. I don't want him to stand trial. Juries are terribly unreliable. Oh, and Drake?"

Drake stopped at the door. "Yes, Jacob?"

"What have we done with the Richardson woman?"

A slight pause. "She's no longer a problem."

Jacob regarded the defensive set of his friend's back, knew his . . . appetites. He'd always overlooked this side of Drake, because it was a man's own business how he found gratification. But perhaps now it could be put to good use. "You have her, then?"

"I do."

"Will she be missed?"

"She told her boss she needed time to let the Alden scandal die down because it was affecting her ability to get good interviews."

"Was she convincing?"

Drake half turned, a wolfish gleam in his eye. "Very."

"It's a closed casket, Drake." Jacob let the statement hover between them, then watched as Drake caught his meaning.

"She wanted an interview with a Conti," Drake murmured. "I'll see she gets one."

Jacob watched the door close behind Drake, knowing his oldest friend would see that business was done, then turned his mind to the matter of the investigation at hand. As soon as they knew the identity of Angelo's killer, Miss Mayhew would no longer be required. He hoped Drake's appetites extended to redheads.

Friday, February 27, 4:30 P.M.

"Detective Reagan."

On their way back into the station, Abe looked over his shoulder to see Richardson's cameraman hurrying behind him. "Haven't they done enough?" he gritted.

The cameraman jogged up to meet them, no camera in his hands. "I'm Scott Lowell."

Abe narrowed his eyes. "I know who you are. What do you want?"

"I know you hate me and I don't blame you. I just wanted you to know that Zoe's gone."

Abe and Mia exchanged a quick glance. "What do you mean, gone?" Mia asked.

"She went to request an interview with Jacob Conti yesterday."

"God, the woman's got balls," Mia marveled.

"She went alone," Scott said.

"More like rocks in her head," Mia amended. "So she didn't come back?"

"No, she came back. Mad as hell and muttering about how she'd nail Conti to the wall. Then this morning she calls in to say she's taking a leave of absence until this thing with John Alden blows over."

"And you don't believe her," Abe said.

"She would never walk away from a story. She wanted Conti, but she wanted Mayhew even more."

"You mean she wanted the vigilante story," Mia said.

"Sure she wanted the story. It was her ticket. She was getting calls from CNN and NBC, for God's sake. But she really hated Mayhew. She never would have just walked away."

"Why does she hate Kristen so much?" Mia asked.

Scott shook his head. "Don't know. Don't want to know. It was bad enough having to capture it all on film. I could say I was only doing my job, but I know that's no excuse. Please tell Miss Mayhew that I'm sorry."

Abe clenched his teeth and Mia continued. "I'll give her the message, Mr. Lowell. Did you report Richardson's disappearance?"

Scott shrugged. "Didn't seem to be any point. She made the call herself. I just wanted you to know in case it becomes important. I have to go. I got reassigned to a different reporter today. Good luck."

He walked away and Mia sighed. "A killer who takes out scum. Wealthy scum like Conti beat up old men, then take out Richardson. I'm not sure who the good guys are anymore."

Friday, February 27, 4:45 P.M.

"Leah's mother is dead," Abe announced when they'd gathered in the conference room. "She died of cancer three years ago."

"Leah hasn't been seen for a year by anyone we talked to," Mia went on. "Her pastor said she'd become more and more depressed, then one day she didn't come to church. They found she'd moved and left no forwarding address. I'm sorry, Kristen."

Kristen tried to push aside the sadness, but it was hard. "Poor Leah."

"We searched Paul Worth's house," Jack said. "Found a bunch of different prints, but still none that match the partial Julia found on Conti's body, which she released to the family today, by the way. In Worth's garage we found the Oldsmobile without its plates and between a table saw and a rolling tool chest there was an empty space just the right size for that Craftsman vise that was used on Skinner. The house itself was deserted. They have a cleaning service come in every other week. Nobody saw anything."

"Well, I can tell you Paul Worth himself is not involved," Miles said. "He's not lucid and hasn't been since his stroke last year. I saw him at the nursing home myself."

"Any visitors?" Abe said.

"None." Miles looked sad. "Hell of a way to spend the end of your life."

"Oh," Mia said, "and Zoe Richardson is missing."

This caused a bit of a buzz until Spinnelli raised his hand for silence. "Nothing we can do until she's declared a missing person. Let's not get sidetracked from our goal here, people. We know that Robert Barnett is the illegitimate son of Hank Worth and Genny O'Reilly, and that Barnett is Paul

Worth's nephew, but what is the connection between the Worth family and Leah Broderick?"

"We haven't been able to find any yet," Abe said tightly.

"There were no pictures of her anywhere in Worth's house," Jack added. "Sorry."

Spinnelli sighed. "What's next?"

"Murphy and I started checking area death certificates for Leah," Kristen said quietly. "Murphy sent out her picture to the State Police before I sent him home to sleep and Julia helped by sending copies to ME and county coroner's offices in Illinois. She was thinking there might have been an unclaimed Jane Doe." Kristen's throat closed. *Such a waste.*

Friday, February 27, 6:00 P.M.

"Looks like the gang's all here. Mom's having a little family party tonight. There's a big party following the christening tomorrow," Abe said, squeezing the SUV between Sean's minivan and Aidan's Camaro. Then he sighed. "This should be interesting."

There was a high-end Lexus parked in front of the minivan, and instinctively Kristen knew to whom it belonged. "Debra's parents?"

"Yeah."

"You never did tell me what happened last night," she said gently.

Abe rested his chin on the steering wheel. "They asked me to forgive them."

"Really?"

"Yeah, really. I about fell out of my chair. Said they'd been wrong. In everything. That they'd realized the day Debra finally died that they couldn't have ended her life either, even if I'd allowed them to. But that they couldn't get in touch with me to let me know because my parents weren't telling anybody where I was."

"So what did you say?"

"I said I'd have to think it over."

"And have you?"

He looked over to find her green eyes filled with gentle understanding and unrelenting support and something shifted inside him. He'd known it was coming from the start, from the moment she'd tried to fell him with a pathetic can of pepper spray.

He loved her. He watched her face heat and he knew what he was feeling was written on his face for her to see. "Yeah."

She reached out, letting her fingers trail down his cheek. "And?"

"Of course I will. Life's too short, Kristen. I'm ready to move on. With you."

Her mouth curved. "Are you now?"

"I am." He caught her behind her neck and pulled her closer. "Will you come?"

Her eyes danced. "Not in front of your parents' house. But maybe later."

Laughing, he kissed her hard. "Tart. Let's go in and join the others."

The kitchen was controlled chaos, as usual. Sean's kids ran circles around the floor, while his mother was smacking Aidan away from the pie she'd just pulled out of the oven. Annie was standing at the sink peeling potatoes and the television blared ESPN from the living room. The pie was cherry. All was right with the world.

"Hi, Mom," Abe said. "Got enough for two more?"

"We can't cook in my kitchen," Kristen added wryly. "Somebody stole it."

Aidan and Annie looked at each other, coconspirators, and Kristen surprised them all by walking right up to Aidan and pulling his head down to kiss his cheek.

"Thank you," she said. She put her arm around Annie's shoulders and hugged. "That was the nicest thing anyone's ever done for me."

Annie beamed and quickly recovering, Aidan grinned wickedly. "If that's the nicest thing anyone's done for you, then I really do need to have that talk with Abe."

Her cheeks crimson, Kristen looked at his mother. "Hit him, please."

Becca arched her brows. "You're no longer a guest. Hit him yourself." Sobering, she turned to Abe. "You've got company in the living room."

"Yeah, I know. I'll be back later."

Kristen watched him walk away. He was ready to put aside the last ugly remnants of his past so that he could get on with his future. A future he wanted to share. With her. *Will you come?* he'd asked. She knew where this was leading. A man like Abe Reagan didn't have affairs. He wanted a wife. A family. How desperately she'd wanted to say *yes*. But there were things he had to know first. Things that might change his mind. So she'd made light of his beautiful offer. She needed to tell him. Soon. And then, if he still wanted her, she'd give him the answer her heart was screaming.

Shaking herself, she turned to Annie. "So what do you think about the kitchen? Country hearth or French Provincial?"

Friday, February 27, 6:30 P.M.

Finding him had been no trouble at all. Few mayors of
small Kansas towns were running for the state legislature
and only one of them had gone to the University of Kansas.
Figuring out that Geoffrey Kaplan was the man who had
hurt Kristen had taken all of one hour. Getting from
Chicago to Kansas, unfortunately, had taken fourteen. He'd
managed to catch a few hours of sleep while Kaplan was in
town tending his mayoral duties.

He now waited for the man to come home to his pretty
house which sat isolated on ten acres of land. An old barn
made a handy cover for his van. Kaplan's trusting wife left
the garage door wide-open all day, so it was no problem to
slip inside and wait. It was a basement garage, like his own,
so there were lots of places to hide. At least two televisions
blared upstairs, and his gun had a silencer. There would be
no noise of consequence.

He felt a tightening in his chest when the bastard drove
in. In a few seconds, he'd see the face of the man who had
raped a young woman and left her in the dirt at the county
fair. The headlights switched off, leaving them in darkness.
The car door opened, the dome light illuminating the interi-
or and Kaplan climbed out. And his first thought on seeing
Kaplan was that Kristen had been right. He was a totally
ordinary-looking man. Five-ten, average build, slight
paunch. He was balding. Badly.

He waited until Kaplan had leaned into the backseat to
retrieve his briefcase, then emerged from his hiding place,
his revolver drawn. In his other hand he held Kaplan's own
tire iron. Soundlessly he approached.

"Stand up, Mr. Kaplan. Put your hands in the air."

Kaplan froze, then slowly straightened, his hands coming up. "Who are you?"

"Turn around, Mr. Kaplan. Slowly."

Kaplan obeyed and even in the dim light of the dome light, he could see terror in the man's eyes. Terror was good.

"Who the hell are you?" Kaplan hissed. Kaplan's terrified eyes dropped to the gun in his hand and then took a quick trip up to the ceiling to where Mrs. Kaplan moved about above.

For an instant he wavered, then stiffened. The wife would be better off in the end. Being a widow would be far better than to be the wife of a monster.

"Kristen Mayhew," he said, and waited.

"What?" Kaplan shook his head in bewildered panic. "Who is Kristen Mayhew?"

He didn't even remember. He stole the innocence of a beautiful young woman who trusted him and he *didn't even remember her name.* "Think back, Mr. Kaplan. College. Summer. The county fair."

He watched Kaplan desperately processing the information. "Kristen May—" His head came up, ever so slightly. "Oh, yeah. I remember her. She was just a girl I dated in college. So what?"

Just a girl? So what? "You raped her."

Kaplan's eyes widened, then narrowed. "She said that? That little bitch."

The tire iron swung up out of the darkness, hitting Kaplan just above the right temple. Kaplan sank to his knees, moaning.

"Watch your language, Mr. Kaplan."

Kaplan held his head and in the dim light he could see blood oozing between his fingers. "I didn't rape anybody. I swear it. She's trying to ruin my career. That's all."

That's all. "And why would she do a thing like that?" he asked tightly.

Kaplan looked up, furious. "Because I'm leading in the polls, that's why. Every bimbo I've ever fucked is comin' out of the damn woodwork."

Bimbo. Kristen's face crystallized in front of his face, then everything faded to red and the tire iron swung again and again and again.

"Daddy?"

He paused, the weapon above his head. His vision slowly cleared. And he heard the little voice again. "Daddy? There's a van parked behind the barn."

Panicked, he lurched to his feet, the gun and the tire iron dangling from his hands.

And over the car he looked into the horrified eyes of a child.

He looked down at himself. He was covered in blood. Her father's blood. She'd seen him covered in her father's blood.

She'd seen him. She'd run. She'd tell. He'd be caught.

I can't be caught. I'm not finished yet. Leah.

Slowly, he raised the gun.

Chapter Twenty-One

Friday, February 27, 10:00 P.M.

From his half-lounging position on her bed, Abe watched Kristen get ready for bed. It was the first time he'd had the opportunity. Every other time they'd ended up in her bedroom, they'd stumbled in, shedding clothes along the way, falling into bed to make incredible love. Now, tonight, he could just watch her. He used to love watching Debra get ready for bed. He'd missed the closeness, the knowing that soon she'd lie beside him.

That he'd found that closeness again was almost too hard to believe.

Kristen paused, her fingers stilling on the middle button of her blouse. She could feel the steady pressure of his eyes from the bed. He'd piled some pillows behind his head and sat up against the headboard, his long legs stretched out. She looked over her shoulder and shivered at the heated look in his eyes. "Why are you looking at me?"

His smile was at once sensual and beatific and stole her breath. "Because you're beautiful. Don't mind me. Just keep going."

She looked back down at her blouse, focusing on the buttons, willing her hands not to shake. She needed to tell him. *Now, Kristen.* Instead she concentrated on her clothes, taking them off, hanging them up as was her habit until she stood in nothing but her bra and panties. There was a rustle from the bed and he was behind her, almost scorching her back with his heat. He covered her shoulders with his hands and kissed the side of her neck. She tilted her head to give him better access and shivered again when he ran his tongue down her neck to the curve of her shoulder.

"Cold?" he murmured.

"No," she whispered.

"Mmm. Good." His hands capably kneaded the tight muscles in her back, then guided her to the little chair at her vanity. "Sit."

She sat and from under heavy lids watched in the mirror as he pulled the pins from her hair, knowing that he was creating traditions. One by one the pins dropped to the vanity surface until her hair sprang free. He picked up the brush and ran it through her hair, gently scraping her scalp. Her eyes drifted closed. *It felt so good.*

"Good," he said softly. "I'd stop if it felt bad."

Her eyes flew open and she stared up at him. "How do you do that? How do you make me say what I'm thinking out loud?"

"I think you say it out loud because in your heart you want me to hear it." The brush paused and he sobered. "What's wrong, Kristen? You've been so quiet tonight."

Now, Kristen. Don't be a coward now. She stood up, slipping around him to shrug into her robe. "I need to talk to you. I need you to listen, because it's hard to say."

His brow creased in a frown, he set the brush on the vanity and went back to sit on the bed. "I'm listening."

She opened the vanity drawer and found the little album. Holding it to her chest, she turned and looked into his very worried blue eyes. "I know about your baby."

He visibly blanched. "How?"

"Aidan let it slip. He didn't know I didn't know. Then your father showed me a picture of Debra right before . . . You know."

His nod was jerky, his skin pale beneath the dark stubble on his cheeks. "I'm sorry. I didn't mean to deceive you, Kristen. I just don't talk about it."

"I know." She sat on the bed facing him. "I understand." She swallowed, then put the album on the bed next to his hip and shot to her feet. He picked it up, looked at the first photo, an infant with tiny red curls and big green eyes. Instant recognition dawned.

"She's yours," he said dully. She said nothing and he flipped to the next photo and the next until he came to the end. "Eleven pictures."

Kristen's body was trembling and she couldn't make it stop. "One at birth and one for every birthday thereafter."

"She's pretty."

"Thank you."

He looked up, his eyes unreadable. "What's her name?"

She hugged herself, hoping to control her shaking. "They named her Savannah."

He nodded, still looking at her. "Where is she?"

"California."

"So far away."

"Her parents moved from Chicago when she was four."

He looked back down at the album and traced ten-year-old Savannah's smile with the tip of his forefinger. "What did you think I'd say, Kristen?"

She bit her lip. "I don't know."

"Did you think I would blame you?"

Hunching her shoulders, she dropped her gaze. "I didn't know. I blame myself."

"That I can believe." The warmth in his voice made her look up. He opened his arms and she crawled across the bed and into them. "Kristen, honey."

The tears came then and he pulled her onto his lap. "Oh, Abe, I didn't know what you'd say. You lost your baby and I gave mine away."

"No, you didn't. You gave your baby a chance to have a normal life." His hand was on her hair, stroking. Holding her until her tears slowed and his shirt was soaked. "I take it you got pregnant after . . ." He kissed the top of her head. "After."

"I hadn't planned to tell anyone. Then I missed one period, then two, and I didn't know what to do. So I told my parents."

His hold on her tightened. "And they didn't believe you."

"An unmarried pregnant daughter was worse than a drunken dead one."

There was a long, long pause. "I hate your father, Kristen."

She rested her cheek against the rock hardness of his chest. "So do I."

Another long pause. "Do you see her? Savannah?"

Kristen's heart squeezed. "No. We agreed they'd send me a picture every year on her birthday, and if she ever asked about me, they'd tell her that I was young and alone and couldn't care for a baby."

"Which is all true."

"Yes. When she's eighteen they'll let her choose whether she wants to meet me."

"They're good people, then."

Her eyes burned. "Yes. And they love her so much."

"Then you did the right thing," he murmured. Carefully he put the album in her nightstand drawer. Then tilted up her chin and claimed her lips in the sweetest, gentlest kiss. Her heart swelled in her chest and when he lifted his head she could only look at him as the words raced through her head.

That's not all I need to tell you. There's something wrong with me.

Please don't mind. Please don't let it matter.

I love you.

His eyes flashed, brilliant blue. "Say it again. I want to know you mean me to hear it."

To deny him was never an option. "I love you," she whispered.

Roughly he pushed her to her back and followed her down, his mouth taking unquestionable possession of hers, his hands cupping her face, his body insistently thrusting. "Tell me you want me."

"I want you." She did. Throbbing a primal rhythm in response to his passion, her body lifted against him. Her hands clumsily pulled at his shirt until she'd parted it to his waist, touching his chest, shuddering when he groaned.

He stripped away her robe and knelt between her legs, yanking at his cuffs until the buttons popped off. She sat up and holding his gaze, unhooked her bra and dropped it off the side of the bed. He did the rest, getting rid of her panties and his pants, then he stopped. And he stared. And her mouth went dry.

This wasn't the slow, considerate lover she'd known. He was frantic, shaking, hanging on to his control by a thread. She severed that thread when she grabbed his shoulders and pulled him down on her. Their kisses were wild and open-mouthed, lips and cheeks and any piece of skin they could reach until she was vibrating under him.

"Abe, do it. Now."

And he did, entering her hard and deep, groaning into her mouth when she cried out. He plunged wildly, taking them higher with every thrust into her body. She felt the now familiar tightening of her inner muscles, a miracle after so many years alone, then she fell into the heaven she'd found only with this man, her climax stunning in its strength. But what was the true gift was the expression on his face, the stark beauty of his features as he reached his own peak, the shudder of his body as he spilled himself into her.

He collapsed on top of her, his chest heaving as he struggled for breath. She stroked his broad back and waited, knowing the instant he came back to himself. He stilled, drew a deep breath. And said the words she'd waited a lifetime to hear.

"I love you, too." Then he rolled them to their sides, cupping her buttocks and pulling her close so they remained as one.

A long time later, well after she'd thought him asleep, she felt the rumble of his voice against her cheek. "Kristen, I'm sorry. I forgot about protection."

"It's all right," she murmured.

He didn't say anything for a minute. "So the timing's not right?" he asked, tentatively. She heard disappointment in his tone, faint, but there.

She swallowed convulsively. "No, it's not right."

And it never would be.

I'll never have the child you want, Abe.

She waited for the words to spill from her mouth, wished they would tumble as effortlessly as all the other thoughts had. But Abe was obviously right. That only worked when she really wanted him to hear it. Because this, she didn't. Not now, not ever.

Saturday, February 28, 9:00 A.M.

She hurt.

It was the first coherent thought Zoe had as she surfaced from the fog that enveloped her.

She was moving. That was the second thought. There was an eerie sense of floating. Then reality began to descend and with it the vile, unbearable images.

Oh, God, I hurt. He hurt me. She shuddered, remembering the brutality she'd endured at the hands of Drake Edwards. She tried to whimper, but her voice was gone. She blinked, tried to determine her surroundings. There was white. Lots of white. *Maybe I'm dead. Please let me be dead.* Death was preferable to Drake Edwards. The movement slowed and she became aware of doors, of passing through doors, then the movement stopped.

"How long before she comes to?"

Nooo. Again she wanted to whimper, again no voice. It was Edwards. He was here. Dammit. She wasn't dead.

"Looks like she's awake now. The drug should fully wear off in an hour." The other voice was new. *Who? What drug?* "Until then she won't move or speak."

"Good." There was satisfaction in Edwards's voice. She'd heard it often since he'd stolen her from her apartment. "I want her to be able to claw and scream."

There was silence from the other man and then Edwards's cruel chuckle.

"You're not paid to like it. You're paid to just do it."

A sigh. "If we take out the padding, they both will fit."

Padding? Frantically, she tried to look around, but her head wouldn't move. She strained her peripheral vision to the left. And her breath hitched.

It was a coffin. She wanted to scream.

"I don't care how you accomplish it," Edwards said. "Just do it." His face appeared above her and a wave of nausea threatened to choke her. He smiled, the same predatory smile she'd seen in Conti's office. When had that been? What was today?

"You asked for an interview with Jacob, Miss Richardson," he said mockingly. "Unfortunately, Mr. Conti is occupied this afternoon. It's his son's funeral. He has, however, arranged for an alternate interview. Talk as long as you like." He moved her head, turning it so that she could see his body to her right. "It's Emmy material."

He moved away, laughing softly, allowing her full view of what lay to her right.

Zoe's heart froze in her chest. It was a body in a black suit. With no face.

It was Angelo Conti. They were going to bury her with Angelo Conti. She screamed and screamed, but the sound echoed only inside her head.

Saturday, February 28, 11:15 A.M.

It was the first time Kristen had been in a Catholic church and she had no idea what to do. Luckily there were a lot of Reagans present, so all she had to do was follow along. There were benches on which to kneel and congregational readings to recite. There was the sacrament of Communion and the thundering organ. There was a priest in full regalia, swinging incense and a gold baptismal font next to which stood a beaming Sean and Ruth.

There was family. So much family it made Kristen's heart ache. There were also more than a dozen cops in the pews, all carrying firearms. Friends of Kyle, Aidan, and Abe, all there to ensure there was no trouble from Conti or anyone else. Mia came, as did Spinnelli. Todd Murphy was even there, his suit freshly pressed.

Kristen watched as the priest took the baby, smiling into her little face. The deep breath she drew didn't go unnoticed by Abe at her side. "Beautiful, isn't she?" he murmured.

Kristen felt the sting of tears. "Yes."

"This is where the godparents are recognized," he whispered. "Annie is godmother and Ruth's cousin Franklin is godfather."

Abe watched as Annie and Franklin took their places. He'd been the first choice as godfather for Jeannette, who was now five, but he'd just gone undercover and couldn't take full responsibility for his vows. Reagans took their vows seriously, after all. Aidan got to be Jeannette's godfather and Abe missed out on the joy of watching her grow from infancy to the happy child she was today.

He and Debra had chosen Ruth and Sean as their son's godparents. Of course they'd never gone through the ceremony. Perhaps they could be called on when he and Kristen christened their first child. Warmed within, he took her hand, squeezed it lovingly.

She looked up at him with a smile that didn't come close to reaching her wet eyes. She'd been through so much this week. It was hard to know what lurked in the shadows behind her brittle smile. So much pain. He thought of the little girl, Savannah. Thought of the pain Kristen must feel every year when a new photograph arrived in the mail. He knew it. It was the same pain he felt every year when his son's birthday came and went without celebration. He thought of the night before, how she'd told him she loved him. How natural it had been to love her. He looked down at her profile, felt his body stir. He'd come inside her last night with no barriers between them. She'd been so sure they were safe, that it was the wrong time. He smiled. He was Catholic after all. Half the people he knew got their start during the "safe" time of the month. Maybe she'd be wrong, too.

He slid his arm around her shoulders, pulled her close. And imagined the day they would stand next to the priest and the baby he held would have tiny red curls and big green eyes. His life had finally begun again. He felt reborn and Kristen was the reason.

Saturday, February 28, 12:00 P.M.

Drake slid into the pew next to Jacob and Elaine. Elaine sat numb, stoned out of her mind. Jacob held her hand and shouldered the grief for them both as he stared at the coffin. Perhaps the fact that a portion of his vengeance was complete would be a balm.

"It's done, Jacob," he murmured.

Jacob didn't move a muscle, just sat staring at the coffin. "Good."

Saturday, February 28, 12:15 P.M.

"Nice party, Abe," Mia said, walking up to him with a cup of punch in her hand. "Would be nicer if the punch were fortified, but it's still nice."

"It's a christening, Mia," Abe said with a smile.

"Hey, everybody's got to learn to party sometime." She looked around the church hall, her eyes sharp. "I think you've got enough coverage. I just got a call from Miss Keene, the hat lady. She found her high school annuals, and they have pictures of Robert Barnett."

Abe's pulse leaped. "Maybe we can finally figure out what ties Paul Worth, Robert Barnett, and those bullets to Leah Broderick. Do you want me to come?"

"Nah, you've got family stuff. I can handle Miss Keene. She likes me, you know."

Abe gave her a steady look. "Lots of people do."

Mia looked away. "Ray would have liked you, Abe. I'll bring the yearbooks back here."

Abe stared after her as she walked away, knowing approval from her former partner was one of the highest forms of praise he could ever expect. Then his own cell phone trilled, and he let the moment go. "Reagan." He listened, every nerve ending suddenly buzzing. "We'll be there as soon as we can."

He looked around and found Kristen talking with Aidan.

He made a beeline and watched her expression change as she read the urgency in his face.

"What now?" she asked, her tone low.

"You got another envelope. Aidan, can you tell Sean and Ruth how sorry we are? Let's get our coats and go."

Saturday, February 28, 12:50 P.M.

Kristen stood on her front porch, frowning at the envelope. "It's not a box. He always leaves a box."

A car pulled up behind the cruiser and Jack got out. "It's not a box," he said.

"We know, Jack," Abe said. "Let's open it and find out why."

"I hope this is fast," Jack muttered, waving to his car where Julia sat waiting. In the back was a small boy in a car seat. Jack blushed. "We're going to the circus."

Kristen's smile was weak, but sincere. "I'm glad, Jack. Let's get this over with so you don't disappoint him."

Jack stopped abruptly at the sight of her gutted kitchen. "Did you do this?"

"Only part of it. I had some help."

Jack spread white paper on her table. "Let's see now." He shook the envelope and two pieces of paper slid out. He handed the letter to Kristen and unfolded the other sheet.

"Oh, God," Kristen gasped. She held her hand over her mouth and looked sick.

Abe looked down at the unfolded paper and it was as if he'd taken a sledgehammer to the head. It was a political poster. *Geoffrey Kaplan for Kansas* it blazed, and below was a picture of a bland, balding man.

He was looking at Kristen's rapist. *Dear God.*

"This is him?" he asked and she nodded, her hand still

clamped over her mouth. "How did he know?" Abe demanded. "Dammit, Kristen, how did he know this?"

She sank into her chair, horrified. "I don't know." She looked over her shoulder at the window. "Was he listening?"

Jack squatted down to look up into Kristen's face. "Who is he?"

Her eyes flew to Abe's, silently beseeching.

"Think, Jack," Abe said quietly. "Think about what Kristen said to the Erickson girl on the phone yesterday morning."

Jack paled. "No."

Kristen's hands were shaking. "I only told you, Abe. The only time I've ever talked about him was sitting here in this kitchen with you on Thursday night. Either he was listening at the window or he's bugged this room."

Jack looked around the room, every wall picked clean. "The only place to hide it is under the table. Help me, Abe." Together they flipped the table and Jack searched. "Nothing here that I can see. Wait." He was gone for just a moment. "Somebody was out there at some point. The thaw started Thursday morning, so I could believe he was out there Thursday night. You've also had something going on by that shed out there."

"I can answer that." McIntyre came in from outside. "There was a small disturbance in the backyard and I saw smoke. When I went to investigate, I found a smoke bomb. I ran back around to the front porch and found the envelope."

"Diversion," Abe muttered. "When was this?"

"Two minutes before I called you," McIntyre said. "I called a unit to sweep the neighborhood, looking for a white van, but they haven't found anything yet."

"Read the letter, Kristen," Abe said.

"I can't." She was shaking like a leaf.

Abe took the letter. It was handwritten on a plain sheet of white paper in a flowing hand. " 'My dearest Kristen. I can't tell you how sorry I am to have caused you and your friends and family so much pain. My intention was only to make you feel safe and vindicated. I will not send you any more letters, but I wanted you to have this last ultimate retribution. I have avenged you, my dear. The man who stole your innocence and youth will never harm anyone again. I remain as always, Your Humble Servant.' "

Kristen's face was stunned. "And the P.S.?"

" 'Good-bye.' "

Saturday, February 28, 1:00 P.M.

He sat on the basement step, staring at the three men he'd bound to tables. All three stared back, eyes glassy with shock and pain.

Judge Edmund Hillman, attorney Gerald Simpson, and rapist Clarence Terrill.

He looked down at the gun in his right hand, then at his left. Leah's medallion. He'd worn it around his neck, on his own chain, since they'd removed it from her body at the morgue. He turned it, let it hit the light. Looked at the engraved initials as he'd done so many times before. WWJD. What would Jesus do?

He closed his eyes. Not what he'd done. Never what he'd done.

In the background droned the sound of his own voice, reading the transcript from Leah's trial. He'd made the CD weeks ago, when he'd planned this final scene. He'd left it to play on an endless loop while he'd driven to Kansas.

These men must have heard it play ten, twenty times by now. Maybe more.

Then he'd driven to Kansas. That he'd killed Kaplan was a foregone conclusion. The man deserved to die. That he'd done it in such a blind, animal rage . . .

Then he'd looked into the eyes of that child. She'd seen him.

And he actually lifted his gun to kill her, too.

She'd said nothing, Kaplan's child. She'd just stood there as he rose from the garage floor like a monster in a horror film, bloody and insane with the rage that had taken over his mind. She'd just stood there looking at him over her father's car, her eyes wide and frozen.

He'd almost killed a defenseless child. A child who'd harmed no one. An innocent. And in that moment he knew what he'd become.

He'd become just like those he'd come to hate.

He'd lowered the gun to his side. Dropped the tire iron, then run to his van, and driven for miles before stopping to wash himself in the snow. There was red all around as he scrubbed and scrubbed. Finally, he got back in his van and drove the long hours back to Chicago, back to Kristen's house, where he'd parked a block away, created a diversion, dropped off his final envelope and come home.

He was cold. He ached. But he still had a job to do. He always finished what he started. Heavily, he pulled himself to his feet and moved to switch off the CD player, feeling three sets of eyes watching his every move. Silence filled the room.

"I hope you remember Leah Broderick," he said. "She was my daughter. She's dead."

"I didn't kill her." This defiant little moan from Clarence Terrill. He turned to look at the man who'd defiled his child. Unremorseful until the bitter end.

He lifted the gun and pulled the trigger and Clarence Terrill was defiant no more. He turned to Simpson who was sobbing, begging for mercy. "And you portrayed her as a whore, stripping away what little self-esteem she had left." Another shot, and Simpson went limp. "There's your mercy." He turned to Hillman who could only stare back in terror.

"And you, Judge Hillman. I perhaps hold you at greatest fault of all. You swore to uphold the law, but you abused it. In the weeks that I've thought about this day, I planned to hold a mock trial where I would be the judge. But there's no point to such theatrics. I'm finished." With no further ado, he ended the judge's life with far more mercy than the man deserved.

He was so tired. But he had one more letter to write. He looked at the gun he held in his hand, smelled the acrid odor of discharged powder. Then he'd join Leah.

Saturday, February 28, 2:00 P.M.

Through all the horror of the past week and a half, Abe had never seen Kristen looking so fragile. She sat on her sofa, so pale. A phone call to Kaplan's town sheriff confirmed that Kaplan was indeed dead. His wife had found him savagely beaten to death in his own garage. The local authorities had thought it a robbery gone wrong. But what had seemed the final blow to Kristen's composure was finding out Kaplan's wife had found her child standing at the garage entrance, in shock. What the child had seen, nobody knew because she'd withdrawn, saying nothing. But there were prints this time. Bloody prints everywhere. He'd cracked. Their killer had finally cracked.

Kristen was hanging on to her own control by a slim, fragile thread.

Gingerly he sat next to her, put his arm around her shoulders. But she didn't melt into him. She sat rigid, staring straight ahead. "Kristen, what can I do for you?"

"I don't know." Her eyes closed. "I am so tired, Abe."

"I know you are, honey. But he's made a bad mistake this time. We'll catch him soon and this whole thing will be over." He rubbed her back with the flat of his palm. "We'll go someplace warm and forget any of this happened."

She said nothing and he groped for a new topic, for anything that would reanimate her face. She was scaring him. "The service was beautiful, wasn't it?" he murmured. "Sean and Ruth were so happy." If anything she stiffened. "I thought about my son today." She turned at that, looking up at him, her eyes so full of pain, it nearly broke his heart. "I guess you were thinking about your daughter. Savannah."

"Abe . . ."

He cupped her face, gently sweeping his thumb along the curve of her cheek. Back and forth. "Then I thought about us, standing in front of the church, holding our child."

But what he'd thought would give her ease had the opposite effect. She lurched to her feet and backed away from him, her eyes panicked. "Stop."

Standing, he reached for her, but she took another few stumbling steps back. "Abe, stop." She closed her eyes. "I need to tell you something and I need you to listen because it's hard to say."

They were the same words she'd used last night, before revealing the truth about her child. His heart chilled and he slowly lowered his hands. "All right."

She visibly schooled her features, straightened her posture and clasped her hands behind her back and all at once she was the woman he'd met ten days before. Her protective shields reerected. Untouchable. "I won't have any more children."

Her dispassionate words were a kick to the gut, sucking the air from his lungs. He could say nothing at first, then made himself breathe. "Kristen, I know you feel guilty about placing your daughter up for adoption, but that doesn't mean you won't be a good mother."

Her eyes flickered wildly and for a moment he thought she'd laugh hysterically. But her control was secure and when she spoke it was calmly. "No, Abe, you don't understand. I'm unable. I'm . . ." She swallowed hard. "After the baby was born, they took her away and I thought my life was over. I'd given away something so precious . . . But I told myself that I was still young. I might have another someday. Then six weeks later I came back for the follow-up exam and they found I'd developed a growth." Her lips twisted, but her posture remained controlled. "Kaplan had done more than rape and impregnate me. He apparently gave me a nasty little STD that over the months of my pregnancy had become cancerous."

His face must have shown his shock because she threw him a brittle smile. "Don't worry. It's all gone, along with half of my cervix."

Abe blindly felt for the sofa behind him and sat on the arm. He drew a breath and searched for the words that she would believe. That he believed himself.

It doesn't matter. Of course it did.

We can adopt. The irony there was just too much.

For a moment he grieved the loss. He'd never see her round and full with his child. He'd never splay his hands over her round belly and feel his child kick. He'd never stand beside her as she battled through labor. He'd never stand in front of the church holding his own child while his family and friends looked on in joy. All the things he'd watched Sean and Ruth do over the years. All those things he'd never do. *They'd* never do.

Because in the end, it would still be the two of them. Whether they had a house full of children or not. Because in the end, he loved her, and she'd said she loved him.

Kristen watched him, watched the truth sink in. Watched his dream slowly die in his eyes. And as he sat there, saying nothing, she could watch him no longer. She turned and walked to the bedroom to stare out the window.

Abe watched her go, so terribly afraid he'd say the wrong thing that he was unable to say anything at all. His cell phone trilled, echoing in the dreadful quiet.

"Reagan."

"Detective Reagan, this is the nurse from the ICU at County."

His heart sank. Vincent must have died. He didn't know how Kristen could take yet another blow. "I remember you. What's happened to Vincent?"

"Mr. Potremski's condition is unchanged. The reason I'm calling is that young man has returned. Timothy. He wants to see Vincent."

Abe jumped to his feet. "Can you keep him there for a half hour?"

"I'll try."

Abe ran back to the bedroom, then halted abruptly. Kristen stood at the window, hunched over, her arms wrapped around herself. From where he stood he could see the violent trembles that wracked her body. She was at the end of her rope. She didn't need to be dragged all over the city in this state. He knew by now how important control was to Kristen. The appearance of control, anyway. She needed to stay here, where she could regroup. He'd talk to this Timothy himself, then he'd come back and they'd talk and he'd make her believe that everything would be all right.

"Kristen, I need to go out for a little while." He made his voice as gentle as he could. "I'll call Aidan to come stay with you until I come back." He crossed the room and stood behind her, wishing he knew what to say or do. In the end he just drew her into his arms and held her there while she trembled and quaked. "Lie down and rest. And then we'll talk."

She nodded and allowed him to lead her to the bed, where she sat. So quietly. He tipped her face up and brushed a kiss across her lips and left her staring after him.

Saturday, February 28, 2:15 P.M.

Of course it mattered. Kristen had only to look at the desolation on his face to know it mattered. Still she'd waited for him to say it was all right. That he loved her anyway, that they could still be happy. But he hadn't said any of those things.

He didn't say it was over, either. Logic started to break through, but logic was a poor substitute for the words she'd so desperately needed to hear. With a sigh she got up and walked through the house. It was so quiet. For the first time in a week, she was alone in her own house. It was unnerving.

"Here, kitty, kitty," she said, just to hear the sound of her own voice. It had always been this quiet before she'd met Abe Reagan, but she hadn't realized before just how much she despised it. She wished she was back at Kyle and Becca's, with its blaring TVs and constant activity. She jumped when Nostrodamus rubbed against her legs. She hadn't seen either cat since she'd torn down the wall. "Let's go get you some dinner."

But she had no kitchen. She looked around and for the first time wondered what had become of her dishes. She supposed Annie had stored them somewhere. So she cleaned out a potpourri dish and filled it with cat kibble. Then wondered what to do next.

The muted strains of her cell phone caught her ear and she grabbed it from her purse, her heart stuttering. The last call to her phone had been a threat, and even though the church hall was filled with cops, the Reagans would be at risk until this whole nightmare was over. "Kristen Mayhew."

"Miss Mayhew, you don't know me, but my name is Dr. Porter. I'm with the Lake County Coroner's Office. I was told you were searching for Leah Broderick."

Her pulse scrambling, Kristen sat down at her desk and pulled out a notepad. Lake County was where they'd found the Worth shack along with the sniper's practice paraphernalia. "Yes, we are. What can you tell me?"

"Well, I signed her death certificate on December 27 of last year. It was a suicide."

Kristen sighed. "That doesn't surprise me at this point. Can you tell me who made the identification and arranged for burial?"

"It was her father, I remember that." Kristen heard a file cabinet opening in the background. "I'll check his name." That was strange, she thought. She distinctly remembered Leah's mother as a single parent. Still, it was worth a try . . .

"Was it Robert Barnett by chance? Or maybe someone named Worth?"

"No, I know that wasn't it. Hold on . . . Here it is. Owen Madden."

Kristen's hand went limp, the pen rolling out of her

grasp. Instant denial sprang from her lips. "No, that can't be right."

"I can assure you it is." He sounded offended. "I remember him well. I did the ID by closed-circuit video because the body was so disfigured. He stood there as stoic as a Marine."

For a moment Kristen could only stare, her breath coming fast and shallow. Owen. It simply wasn't possible.

My God. "Um, thank you, Dr. Porter. I'm sorry, this is just a bit of a shock." A bit? She struggled not to hyperventilate. "Thank you."

"I made a copy of his photo ID," Porter said. "I can fax you a copy if you like."

"Yes, thank you." She gave Porter her fax number. "Thank you for calling me."

Her heart now pounding frantically, Kristen closed her phone. *I have to think. Think.*

Owen. How could it be true?

At this point, how could it not?

"I have to call Abe," she murmured and flipped her phone open with shaking hands.

"Maybe later," a gravelly voice said from behind her and before she could scream, one large hand had covered her mouth while another grabbed her cell phone and pulled her back against a rock-hard body. "For now, just shut up and do as I say."

Kristen struggled, but the man was big and strong. She thought of Vincent and Kyle and knew she would be next. *Where was McIntyre?*

"Stop struggling," he bit out, "or you'll be sorry."

She thought of her new gun, safely stored in her desk drawer. She might as well not have it at all. She wrenched, trying to kick backward and the hand lifted from her mouth and cuffed the side of her head.

Blinking, she saw stars. Still, she drew a breath and screamed as loud as she could. Miraculously, the front door opened and there stood Aidan, key in hand. His face registered shock, then he leaped, pulling the man to the floor and setting her free. Kristen backed away, stopping when the edge of her desk bit into her back. Horrified she watched the men fight.

Police. *Call the police.* The man had her cell phone so she grabbed the land line. It was dead, the cord cut, so she grabbed her gun instead. The two men rolled across the floor, grappling for control, then Aidan gave a mighty shove and pushed the intruder into a wall. Not thinking, she acted. She squeezed the trigger, again and again and again and the man slumped to the floor. Aidan raised up on all fours and stared, breathing hard. She seemed frozen in place, her arms still extended, the gun still pointing at the wall where a line of blood now streaked her blue-striped wallpaper.

"My God." Aidan pushed himself to his feet and came to her, gently taking the gun from her hands. He pulled her into his arms and together they took great shuddering breaths. Then his body jerked and Aidan crumpled to the floor. As if disconnected from her body, she watched him fall, then looked up, taking in shoes, trousers, an overcoat. A hand holding a small club. And the annoyed face of Drake Edwards.

"If you want something done right," he muttered. Bending, he scooped her gun from the floor, pulled Aidan's from its holster, then rolled the dead body and took the intruder's gun from the waistband at his back. "Miss Mayhew, you're coming with me."

"No."

He looked amused. "No? And how do you propose to stop me?"

Her heart hammering like a wild thing, she took a step

back, then cried out when he grabbed her arm. The phone rang, the double ring of her fax machine, and they both turned. The first man had disabled her phone, but not her fax. Fascinated, Edwards watched as the printer spit out the page.

Kristen's stomach turned over. It was Owen's driver's license. Edwards's brows shot up in surprise and his mouth curved in a wicked smile. "Working overtime, Miss Mayhew? Is this someone special?"

Her mouth dry, Kristen couldn't think of a reply.

"I knew you were close, but is this the cigar? The grand prize?" He folded the paper and slid it in his pocket. "Come. I make a practice never to kill cops. A dead cop makes me a lot of enemies and cops never forget. However, if you make so much as a peep, I'll make an exception for him." With a last desperate look at Aidan's unconscious form, she helplessly walked out of her house to the cruiser parked at the curb. Behind the wheel sat a stranger in uniform. The stranger saluted her with a mocking smile. *Where was McIntyre?*

Drake Edwards was kidnapping her in broad daylight in a police cruiser. Her eyes shot up to his face in disbelief, finding his mouth curved in genuine amusement. "So many comings and goings at your house lately, Miss Mayhew. So many bodyguards. Nobody will notice one more." He was right. Nobody noticed anything. Edwards opened the rear driver's side door, and she saw the slumped form of McIntyre in the front passenger seat, blood trickling from one ear. But his chest rose and fell, so at least he was still alive. Edwards bent down, his mouth next to her ear. "Don't try anything or those two little boys riding bicycles down the street will die." She watched the children ride by and knew Edwards would do as he promised. He was Conti's main henchman, rumored to be a sick bastard. But the authorities had never been able to find evidence to make a charge stick. She wondered if they would now, or if she herself would become just one of the rumors.

"Where are you taking me?" she asked when he climbed in.

"You have an appointment, Miss Mayhew. I'm sure you don't want to be late."

Saturday, February 28, 2:15 *P.M.*

Mia returned to the church hall, Miss Keene's high school annual under her arm, seeking Spinnelli. "Abe's not back from talking to that man at the hospital?"

Spinnelli shook his head. "Not yet. He said he called you and gave you the update on the latest." He shook his head. "Poor Kristen."

Yeah, after everything else, and now a shock like this. She looked around with a frown. "Where is Kristen?"

"Back at her house resting. Abe's brother went over there to sit with her."

"Well, at least she's not alone."

"What did you find out at the hat lady's? You were gone forever."

Mia sighed, opening the annual to the page she'd marked. "This is him. Robert Barnett. I stopped by the art department and got them to mock up a picture of what he might look like forty years older." She showed him the sketch. "I've never seen him."

"Neither have I," Spinnelli frowned. "I was hoping it would be the big ah-ha."

"Me, too. We know he's Genny O'Reilly's son and the nephew of Paul Worth, the old guy in the nursing home, but other than that, I'm still stymied on the connection."

"Hi." A young girl bounded up to them, a social smile on her face. "I'm supposed to mingle and make sure everyone has enough to eat. I'm Rachel." She scrutinized them. "And I bet you're Mia and you're Lieutenant Spinnelli."

Mia needed no introduction to recognize Abe's little sister. They had the same eyes. "It's nice to meet you, Rachel. This is a nice party your family's put on."

"It's okay. It would have been better with pizza." She looked curiously at the annual, then bent closer, her expression intent on the sketch. "Is that Kristen's?"

Startled, Mia glanced up at Spinnelli, then back at Rachel. "Why would you ask that?"

She shrugged. "That looks like her friend."

"You've seen this man?" Mia exploded and Rachel's eyes widened in alarm.

"I think so. Why?"

"Where did you meet him, honey?" Spinnelli asked soothingly.

"He brought her a sandwich last week. I'd gone to see her at work and he was just leaving. His name was Owen something." She looked anxious. "Why?"

Mia grabbed her phone. "I need to call Abe." She grimaced when it went right to his voice mail. "He's still in the ICU ward talking to Kristen's friend Vincent. His phone's off."

"Call Kristen." Spinnelli was gesturing for Todd Murphy.

Kyle Reagan approached, frowning. "What's wrong?" He was a retired cop. He knew when something was up.

Mia clenched her teeth. "It's just ringing. Dammit. Kristen's not answering."

Kyle grabbed the phone. "I'll call Aidan." A few moments later, he paled. "He's not answering either."

Spinnelli pulled out his own phone and punched numbers furiously. "Send a unit out to ASA Mayhew's house. Full sirens, as fast as possible."

Spinnelli looked at Murphy and Kyle Reagan. "Keep everyone calm and keep them *here*. Mia, let's go."

Saturday, February 28, 2:45 P.M.

The phone rang, surprising him. No one ever called him at home, except for telemarketers. In fact, the last legitimate call he'd received had been from the Lake County Sheriff's Office about Leah's suicide. Setting aside his pen, he answered. "Hello?"

"Mr. Madden, this is Zoe Richardson. I take it you've heard of me?"

His jaw clenched, his hand tightening over the telephone. "I have."

"Well, the jig's up, Mr. Madden. I know who you are."

Don't panic. "I don't know what you're talking about."

She chuckled throatily. "That's fine. I just wanted you to know I'm preparing tonight's report. I've uncovered evidence that ASA Mayhew has a personal relationship with the vigilante killer and she's directing his efforts. It should be a fascinating piece."

In spite of his fatigue, his blood started to pound. "You know that's ludicrous. Kristen has done nothing wrong."

"Perhaps, but her career was in jeopardy before. After this, no courtroom in the country will have her." Her voice grew clipped. "I'll have a report on the air tonight, Mr. Madden, one way or another, if you catch my meaning. I can hide your face and disguise your voice. You can go right on doing your deeds, I just want an exclusive when you do. Do you have a pen?"

"Yes," he gritted.

"Good. Write down this address. I'll be waiting."

He flipped the page he'd been writing on and took down the address. "You're filth."

"Well, birds of a feather, Mr. Madden. Birds of a feather."

He stared at the address, then made his decision. Kristen's life would not be ruined by his actions. He ripped the paper from the notepad and stuffed it in his pocket. Then opened the glass cover of his gun rack. He'd killed so many. At this point, what was one more?

She handed him the cell phone. "How'd I do?"

Drake smiled. "Perfect, just perfect." He slipped a hundred-dollar bill in her coat pocket. "Buy yourself something nice. And be sure to give your mother my love."

"Thanks, Uncle Drake." She rose up and kissed his cheek.

Jacob waited until Drake's niece was out of the limo. "She has promise, that one."

"She does." He smirked. "It's almost showtime, Jacob."

Saturday, February 28, 2:45 P.M.

Mia and Spinnelli burst into Kristen's house. Jack and his men were searching for any clue as to where she'd been taken. The room was a shambles and blood stained her blue-striped wallpaper. Controlling her panic, Mia knelt next to Abe's brother and pressed her fingers to his throat. His pulse was steady. *Thank God.*

"Which one of you called me?" Spinnelli demanded. An officer stepped forward.

"I did, sir. I found Officer Reagan unconscious and

called for an ambulance. This other guy has no ID and he's dead. Reagan's gun is gone."

Mia looked up. "And McIntyre?"

"No sign of him or his cruiser. We've searched the house and the shed in the back. He doesn't respond to radio communication. One of the neighbors saw Miss Mayhew leave in the cruiser. She said there was a big man with her. Hat hid his face. Nobody else saw anything."

Spinnelli swore. "Did you ask her why she didn't call the police?"

"She said there'd been so many police around the last week, she didn't give it a second thought," the officer said grimly.

"Did anybody hear a damn gun?" Mia demanded.

"She said there'd been so much pounding here the last few days, she didn't think a thing about that either."

Jack's face was tight. "I checked with Aidan's CO. He carries a Glock .38. This guy was killed with a .22."

"Kristen just bought a .22." Mia hit the redial on her phone, with no more success than the last ten times. "Shit, where's Abe?"

"Did you call the hospital?" Jack asked as Spinnelli knelt to check the dead body.

"They're looking for him," Spinnelli said. "Apparently this Timothy guy was terrified when he saw Abe and they had to remove him from the ICU. Abe's got him somewhere else, calming him down so he can talk to him."

Mia tilted her head, listening. "Quiet. That's Kristen's cell phone."

Spinnelli pulled the dead guy's coat, tipping him over. "It's in his pocket." He flipped open Kristen's phone. "Yes? . . . This is her phone . . . This is Lieutenant Marc Spinnelli of CPD. Who are you?" He listened, then jumped o his feet. "Was there anything on the fax machine when ʷou guys came in?"

The officers looked at one another. "No, sir."

"No," Spinnelli said, "she didn't get it. Can you send it ₐgain? Quickly? Thanks." He looked at Mia. "That was the ∟ake County coroner. He called Kristen with the name of ₕhe man who ID'd Leah Broderick's body, then faxed her a ᵦhoto ID. It was Owen Madden."

Mia closed her eyes. "Then she knows."

"Yeah," Jack said. "And whoever has her knows, too."

"And assuming that's Conti . . . ." Spinnelli didn't finish ₕhe thought.

He didn't have to. Conti wanted the killer. Now he had ₕim. And he had Kristen, too.

Chapter Twenty-Two

Saturday, February 28, 3:00 P.M.

'Are you okay now?"

Timothy nodded, but Abe was unconvinced. All he'd ᵦeen able to learn was that Timothy had seen something that ₕad terrified him. Every time they got close to the truth, Timothy would begin trembling so violently he couldn't speak. Abe was getting ready to call Miles. But of two ₕhings he was certain. This man had a strong affection for ₖristen and Vincent, and he was not capable of being their ᵥigilante killer. The nurse's assessment had been complete-∤y accurate. Timothy was a high-functioning man with ᴅown's.

High-functioning. That was the same phrase Kristen had used to describe Leah Broderick. There were no coincidences.

"Let's try this again. You used to work at the diner where Kristen eats?"

In agony the young man closed his eyes. "Yes," he whispered.

"Timothy, did you know a woman named Leah Broderick?"

Timothy nodded. "Yes. We went to church together. Sometimes we'd go to socials at the community center together."

"Was she your girlfriend?"

He frowned. "No. Just my friend."

"Okay. So when did you last see Leah?"

He looked down at his knees. "A long time ago. She's dead now."

"Can you tell me how she died?"

Timothy picked at a stray thread on his slacks. "She killed herself."

They'd been looking for trauma. The suicide of a loved-one was an event traumatic enough to trigger intense emotion. "I'm sorry." Timothy said nothing so Abe pressed on. "Did she have family?"

Timothy paled. "Yes."

"Timothy, look, I know you're scared, but this is important. It could keep Kristen safe. Did Leah have anyone in her family named Robert Barnett?"

"I don't know. Her mom died of cancer. It was just her dad, but that's not his name."

"Did you know her dad?"

Again Timothy began to tremble. "He was my boss."

Abe's heart stopped. "Your boss? At the diner? *Owen* is Leah's father?"

Miserably Timothy nodded.

"Timothy, what did you see? Please tell me."

"The freezer. I'd go to his house and he had ice cream in he freezer, so I went in the freezer." He began to rock himelf. "Two men. They were dead in the freezer."

Oh, God. Timothy had seen the two Blade members dead 1 Owen's freezer. "Did Owen know you saw the dead peo- le in the freezer?"

"No. I ran, so fast. Ran to the bus."

"It's okay, Timothy. It's okay. He won't hurt you. Can ou tell me where he lives?"

Abe dialed Mia as soon as he hit the hospital lobby.

"Where have you been?" Mia demanded.

"Talking to Timothy." Abe took off at a run for the park- ng lot. "Mia, Kristen's friend Owen is Leah Broderick's ather."

There was a beat of silence. "I know, Abe. Owen is Robert Barnett."

The connection, finally. But Mia was too quiet, too con- ained. His heart began to race even faster and it had noth- ng to do with his sprint. "Mia, what's happened?"

"Abe, Kristen's gone. Someone took her from her ouse."

He'd reached his SUV and stood frozen, his hand clutch- ng air. "Oh, God." *Conti.*

"She knew it was Owen, Abe. Whoever took her knew it, oo, along with Owen's address. Marc and I are on our way o Owen's house now."

Abe made himself take a breath, then another. Made his ands open the SUV door. Conti could have her anywhere, ut it would be poetic justice to take her to the place his son ad died for his revenge. "I'm closer. I'll meet you there."

Saturday, February 28, 3:30 P.M.

Kristen looked around. The warehouse was filled with huge stacks of crates, forty, fifty feet high. Some of the boxes were stacked on themselves, others on silver racks that stretched to the ceiling. The brand names on the boxes were familiar due to the hours of investigating Conti's business when she was prosecuting Angelo for the murder of Paula Garcia. This was Jacob Conti's turf. And she was a sitting duck.

They'd driven the cruiser only a few miles before pulling out of sight where Conti's limo waited. Edwards had left her with the mocking stranger, getting into the limo. A few minutes later, a young woman got out, wearing a satisfied expression. A minute after that Kristen was forced into the limo where Jacob Conti regarded her with a reptilian stare. She hadn't looked away, which seemed to amuse him.

But now she was here, amid the boxes. It was no use pulling at the ties that bound her wrists and ankles. Drake Edwards had done a thorough job. It was no use trying to scream. The gag kept her silent. Something was going to happen soon. It was clear from the way Edwards chuckled as he left her here.

"Richardson!" The shout came from a familiar voice.

Owen. *I was bait,* she thought. *They've lured him here.*

"Richardson, I'm tired of your games. Come out and let's get this over with."

She was torn. Owen Madden was a killer.

He was my friend. But he's killed thirteen *people.* Assuming the final three were dead—Hillman, Simpson, and Terrill. There was no reason to believe otherwise.

Still, she didn't want him to fall into Conti's hands.

He appeared between the stacks, a dark figure half a

warehouse away. It was clear when he saw her. His gasp echoed in the cavernous quiet, the pounding of his boots like booming cannon fire as he ran to her. He ripped the gag from her mouth.

"Owen, it's a trap. Run."

Saturday, February 28, 3:30 P.M.

Abe shot the lock off Owen Madden's front door. The house was quiet, not a sound. Still, he moved cautiously, his weapon drawn.

He cleared each deserted room, then walked past the kitchen table and stopped. A fishbowl sat in the middle of the table, filled with folded pieces of paper. Thirteen one-by-four-inch strips were lined up next to the fishbowl, each with a typed name, one for every body in the morgue, plus strips for Hillman, Simpson, and Terrill. There was a stack of bullets and a picture of Leah Broderick. Abe recognized her from the pictures Jack and Kristen and Julia had circulated yesterday. A cup of coffee sat next to the pile of bullets. It wasn't yet cold.

A notepad sat in front of the fishbowl, the page facing him empty. Abe flipped back a few pages and recognized the flowing handwriting from the Kaplan note. The first page in the notebook started out, *My dearest Kristen.* He felt the rage bubble and shoved it back down. Madden had put Kristen in danger and still had the nerve to use endearments.

He kept moving, finding the door to the basement. He took each step one at a time, his finger alongside his trigger. If Conti was waiting below, he'd be a prime target coming down the stairs like this. But there were no shots, no sounds of any kind as he reached the basement floor. Three male bodies lay lifeless, bound to tables. Each had a bullet hole in the forehead. His eyes took a quick trip around the room, noting the Craftsman vise, the bullet molds, the neatly stacked slabs of marble, the rolls of rubber standing like rolled-up carpets. There was a device of some kind in the corner and he approached, still careful. There was a fine layer of dust around the six-foot-tall box with a Plexiglas front and a pair of built-in gloves so that the user could work behind the Plexiglas. He peered in and saw a finished grave marker that read simply LEAH BRODERICK.

There was a freezer in one corner, a big chest model. He lifted the lid. It was empty. There was no one here.

Conti had taken Kristen elsewhere. Viciously Abe put aside the rising panic that threatened to choke off his very breath and made his way back up to the first floor. He walked around again, stopping to stare at the photo on top of the television. Genny O'Reilly Barnett, older, more mature. She was Owen's mother. Then back to the table where he again flipped the pages of the notepad. Three pages were filled, but the fourth stopped midway, midsentence, as if Owen had been interrupted. Frowning, Abe turned the fourth page, noting fringed remnants of a fifth page torn out. He ran his finger over the empty page, his pulse quickening. It was one of the oldest tricks in the book. *Please, God, let it work.*

Lightly, he fanned a pencil over the empty page and watched another handwritten note appear. He recognized the address. It was on the lake, at the port.

It was a warehouse. Conti's. His old boss in Narcotics was certain that Conti used the merchandise in the warehouse as a cover, to hide shipments of drugs. But not one police search had turned up a single gram of illicit substances and Conti continued to walk around, a free man, cloaked in respectability and wealth. Until now.

"Thank you," he murmured and pulled out his phone. "Mia, meet me at Conti's warehouse at the port." He rattled off the address and ran for the door. "Send for backup."

"Abe, wait for me. Don't go in alone." Her voice was urgent and Abe heard male mumbling in the background and Spinnelli took the phone.

"Abe, don't you go in that warehouse until backup arrives. That is an order."

Abe said nothing. Kristen was in there, he was certain of it. He'd do anything he had to do bring her out alive. And untouched. His hands trembled as he jumped behind the wheel of the SUV. *God, please let her be untouched.*

"Abe," Spinnelli spat. "Did you hear me?"

Tires squealed as he raced away from Madden's house like a bat out of hell. "Yeah. I heard you."

Saturday, February 28, 3:45 P.M.

Owen looked up from slicing the bonds at her feet. "You knew?"

"Since about an hour ago."

He straightened. "Who did this?"

"Jacob Conti." Kristen stood, rubbing her wrists. "He objected to the murder of his son."

Owen looked down at her and she wondered if she'd ever seen that cold, determined look in his eyes before. No, but she'd honestly never looked. He was Owen, her friend. He owned a diner. He made fried chicken and cherry pie.

He'd ruthlessly killed thirteen people.

"If it wouldn't have put you in danger, I'd do it again."

"And for that you'll pay."

Unsurprised, she and Owen turned to find both Jacob Conti and Drake Edwards standing at the end of the row of boxes. Edwards had spoken and now came closer, a semi-automatic in his hand and a predatory leer in his eye.

Kristen's blood ran cold. *Abe, please know I'm gone. Please come find me. Please.*

"Drake, search him for weapons. Then let's go somewhere where we'll all be more comfortable, shall we?" Conti said smoothly.

Edwards patted Owen down, retrieving two large semi-automatics, one from his shoulder holster, the other from his back waistband. He then forced them to walk until they reached the wide corridor where forklift trucks normally went about creating the huge stacks of boxes. At the end of the corridor were large loading bays, deserted. All was quiet now.

Owen stopped. "Kill me here," he announced. "I'm not going any farther."

"You'll do what we say," Edwards snapped.

"You've got me now," Owen said as if Edwards hadn't spoken. "Let her go."

Conti's lips curved. "And lose the best part of my revenge? I don't think so."

Again Kristen saw Edwards's predatory leer. And understood. Owen had killed for her. Now she'd be used to make him suffer.

Edwards chuckled. "You gotta love smart women, Jacob. She's figured it all out."

Owen paled, but said nothing and Conti laughed. "You see, just killing you wouldn't be enough. You're going to suffer as you made my son suffer. Drake will have her and you will watch. Then Drake will kill her and you will watch. Then . . . you'll wish you were dead."

"Come, Miss Mayhew." Edwards took her arm and horrified, Kristen yanked away. Edwards's expression grew dark and he grabbed her arm hard, his fingers digging into her flesh. "I said come." He pulled her to him and she struggled, pushing at his chest, twisting her head when he would have kissed her.

Conti laughed again. "So, Drake, will she be as entertaining as Richardson?"

Edwards grabbed her shoulders and shook her until she saw little white lights in front of her eyes. "I think so, Jacob. I like them with a little piss and vinegar."

Kristen blinked hard, trying to still her swaying senses, thinking it was a trick of her imagination when Owen went down on one knee and Edwards jerked. He hung there for a split second, a neat little hole in his forehead, then crashed to the floor. Before she could draw her next breath Conti's arm was locked around her neck, his gun at her temple.

Owen was still on one knee, a small gun in his hand. He must have hidden it in his boot. He was breathing hard, his eyes narrowed and deadly and Kristen realized she was indeed looking at the man who'd ruthlessly murdered thirteen people. She looked at Edwards's body from the corner of her eye and her stomach heaved.

Fourteen people.

"You sonofabitch," Conti snarled. "Throw down the gun or she dies."

"He's going to kill me anyway," Kristen said. "Get help. Please."

Conti shoved the gun harder into her temple. "Shut up. The gun, Madden. Now."

Owen dropped the gun on the floor.

"Now stand up and kick it this way."

Owen obeyed. Then there was another shot and Owen fell to the floor, writhing in pain, his knee bleeding. But he uttered not one cry. She remembered the words of the Lake County coroner. He was indeed as stoic as a Marine. A sharpshooting Marine.

"Now watch her die, Madden."

Kristen closed her eyes, preparing herself, wishing she had just one more day with Abe. *He'll find me here,* she thought. Shot just like Debra. *Oh, Abe, I'm so sorry.*

And then, Abe's voice boomed. "Let her go, Conti."

Kristen sagged. *Abe.* Conti jerked her so she stood on her own two feet, his gun still at her temple. Abe stepped out from behind a stack of boxes near the loading bay, his own gun drawn.

"Why would I do that?" Conti called back.

"Because I'll kill you where you stand if you harm one hair on her head." He approached slowly. "Let her go."

Conti retreated a step, dragging her with him, calling the names of several men in an authoritative voice.

Abe walked steadily closer. "If you're calling the men who were standing guard outside, you'll have to yell a hell of a lot louder. Let's just say they're out of the range of your voice."

Kristen felt the change in Conti, his body stiffening in rage. "I'll kill her. I swear I will." Fighting panic, Kristen looked at Owen lying on the floor, clutching at his knee, then saw him pointedly look to his right. She followed his line of sight and nearly fainted in relief.

Barely visible through the boxes was Spinnelli, his gun steadily trained on Conti.

And me, she thought. Frantically she tried to think of a way to get away from Conti so that Abe and Spinnelli would have a clear shot.

Then Owen looked up and again Kristen followed his line of sight. To where Mia knelt on one of the metal racks, her hands poised on a box. Mia held up three fingers, then two. Her breath trapped in her chest, Kristen waited . . . waited . . . until one of the boxes thudded to the floor behind them with a crash. Startled, Conti faltered and

Kristen lunged, kicking, squirming, scratching, biting, dropping, and rolling when he lost his grip. Three shots rang out in quick succession and Conti fell.

He wouldn't be getting up again.

Then she was in Abe's arms and he was rocking her. "Oh, God, oh, God," he kept saying, his face buried in her hair. "I thought I'd lost you."

He thought he'd have to watch another woman he loved killed before his eyes. A shudder ran through his body and he tightened his arms around her. Kristen ran her hands up and down his back. "I'm fine. I'm fine. Abe, I'm really fine."

Her words gradually sank through his fear and Abe loosened his grip. He held her at arm's length, his eyes narrowed, searching for any sign of abuse, closing his eyes in relief when there appeared to be none. "I wanted to kill Edwards for touching you."

"It's okay. He's dead. Owen killed him."

"I know. I was standing behind those boxes from the time you all came out of the stacks, watching the whole thing." Abe shuddered again, knowing he'd never forget the sight of those bastards' hands on her. "If you hadn't stopped where you did, we couldn't have gotten to you in time."

Kristen twisted around to look at Owen, who lay silently observing, his face contorted in pain. "You stopped us here. You said you wouldn't go any farther."

Mia swung down from the metal rack. "He saw us at the loading bay door." She looked at Owen, her expression unreadable. "You must have one hell of an eye."

Kristen let out a breath. "You saved me. Owen . . ." Her face twisted pathetically. Her eyes filled with tears. "How could you do it? How could you kill all those people?"

He said nothing, just lay looking at her. "I can't let you go," she said brokenly, as if there weren't three armed cops

surrounding her who would allow her to do so if she wanted to.

"I know." It was gritted from behind clenched teeth. "I
couldn't respect you if you did." He struggled to sit up, then
like lightning pulled a second Beretta from his other boot.
"I also won't go to prison. Good-bye, Kristen."

"Owen, no." In horror Kristen watched as he put the
small gun under his chin. Abe pulled her around, crushing
her face against his shoulder as a final shot rang out.

"Don't look, honey," Abe murmured against her hair.
"Just don't look."

She wouldn't. She'd seen more than enough.

Saturday, February 28, 6:15 P.M.

She shouldn't be here. The thought echoed in Abe's mind as
he watched Kristen reading the note Owen had been writing
just before being called to Conti's warehouse. She should
be at the hospital with Aidan and McIntyre, who were conscious but under observation. Kristen should be there, too,
being treated for shock. But she'd refused to remain at the
hospital, even with every Reagan begging or demanding
she stay. Instead she'd insisted on accompanying him and
Mia back here, to Owen's house. Where this whole nightmare began.

Now she sat at Owen's kitchen table, her face pale, her
gloved hands trembling even though they were flattened
against the tabletop. He trembled himself and felt no shame
in doing so. He'd nearly lost her today. He didn't think he'd
ever get over the sight of Conti's hands on her, his gun to
her head. But she was alive. Unhurt. Physically, anyway.
Who knew how long it would take for the emotional scars
to heal? Almost being killed by Conti. Finding out a man

she'd trusted was a cold-blooded murderer. Seeing him put a .38 under his chin and hearing him take his own life.

He felt Mia's hand on his back. "She's all right," she murmured from his side.

"I know. It's just . . ." Helplessly he let the thought trail away and Mia patted his back.

"I know. Come and see what Jack's found. She'll be fine by herself for a few minutes."

Reluctantly he let Mia guide him into a back bedroom where Jack sat at a computer.

"What did you find?" Abe asked and Jack looked over his shoulder, his expression grim.

"Kristen's database," Jack said. "How the hell did Madden get this on his computer?"

"He stole it," Kristen said from behind them, her voice flat. She gently pushed past Abe, Owen's notebook in her hand. "He put something in my tea one evening when I was there for dinner, made me fall asleep." Her lips twisted. "I remember waking up, thinking I must have been more tired than I thought. I hadn't slept well for a few nights. I remember my first thought when I woke up was my laptop, where was my laptop? Then I realized it was in the bag at my feet, right where I'd put it, that Owen was watching over me and wouldn't let anyone steal my computer while I was asleep." She handed Abe the notebook. "It's all in here. He copied my database while I was asleep. It would have been right after New Year's."

Yet another betrayal. "I'm sorry, Kristen," he said softly and she swallowed hard.

"He used me to murder all those people," she whispered harshly.

"You were as much a victim as anyone else in this whole nightmare," Mia insisted.

Kristen's chuckle was mirthless. "Tell that to the families

of all the people Owen murdered. I think they'd see it differently." She lifted her eyes to the wall behind the computer where several framed certificates hung. His Chicago certificates were all for volunteer work with the developmentally disabled. He'd taught woodworking and stone carving and metal shop at the local community center where Leah had socialized. His Pittsburgh certificates were for outstanding service during his thirty-year career as a police officer. A single medal hung in the middle of all the certificates. Owen's Purple Heart. He'd been wounded serving as a Marine in Vietnam in 1965.

"I still can't believe it," Kristen said, her voice nearly toneless. "I can't believe he was a cop. I still can't believe he killed all those people. But he did. And he said he'd do it again."

Mia took the notebook from Abe's hands, scanned the final letter. "Well, at least he told us almost everything before he was interrupted. All the pieces are starting to fit."

"What pieces?" Spinnelli asked from the doorway. He, too, looked grim. "What's in the notebook?"

"A letter to Kristen," Abe answered. Kristen was still numbly staring at the certificates on the wall. "He explained a number of things, like the fact he was born Robert Henry Barnett but he changed his name in the early sixties due to some 'unpleasantness' in his family."

"That was right about the time of the murder of the boy who stabbed Colin Barnett to death," Mia said. "The hatmaker, Miss Keene, said she'd always wondered if Robert came back to avenge his brother's death. It makes sense that he did."

"He was a Marine in 'Nam," Spinnelli said, then his eyes settled on the Purple Heart on the wall. "But I guess you figured that out already."

"How did you know?" Abe asked, still watching Kristen who still stared at the wall.

"We got a match on the prints from Kaplan's garage." Spinnelli stepped up to the wall to examine the certificates. "Owen Madden got an honorable discharge from the Marines after one tour in 'Nam, came back to the States where he got a job as a cop. Commendations out the ying-yang. He retired five years ago and bought a cop bar in downtown Pittsburgh. I called his old CO, who said about three years ago he up and left with no explanation. One day the bar was open, the next there was a FOR SALE sign in the window."

"He'd found out about Leah," Kristen said quietly. She turned away from the wall, her expression carefully reserved. It was her way of holding on to the last thread of her control, and Abe couldn't fault her for it. "Leah's mother was dying of cancer and was afraid of who would care for Leah when she was gone. She hired a private investigator to track Owen down. Apparently he'd come to Chicago twenty-three years before and met Leah's mother. He was only here for a week or so, but in that time he met Leah's mother. They had a short affair, but when the week was over, he had to go back to Pittsburgh."

"Twenty-three years ago," Mia mused. "He was back in Chicago for the funeral of his parents and sister, Iris Anne. Remember, Miss Keene thought she saw him, but he never acknowledged her when she called his name."

"That makes sense," Kristen agreed dully. "Apparently Leah's mother got pregnant, but she didn't know where to find Owen. He never planned to come back to Chicago. She finally found him right before she died. Leah had already been through the trial and was starting to sink into depression. Her mother was afraid of what would happen when she was gone."

"Well, he got involved in his daughter's life way too late," Spinnelli said tightly, looking at the certificates recognizing Owen's volunteer activities. "How did you meet him, Kristen?"

Kristen shrugged. "Pure chance. I was upset over a case I'd just had to plead down and I'd gone for a walk to clear my head. I walked into Owen's diner and we started to talk. I never had any clue he was Leah's father. I never had any clue he'd been a cop."

She said it like she thought she should have. "Why would you?" Abe asked reasonably. "He ran a diner, served food. Why would you think he was a retired cop?"

Kristen shook her head. "I know up here that I couldn't have known." She tapped her head. "But knowing it down deep is something entirely different. Anyway, apparently Leah got more and more depressed until Owen moved her to an apartment away from the city to give her a change of scenery. To keep her from having to walk the same streets that she'd been walking the day she was raped. He got her a place up in Lake County, not too far from the Worth property you found."

"But it was too late," Mia added. "Leah ended up committing suicide."

"The trauma we were looking for," Spinnelli said.

"How is the little girl?" Kristen asked. "Kaplan's daughter? She's been weighing on my mind all day."

Spinnelli clenched his jaw. "From what they can get out of her, she didn't see her father killed. They don't think she saw his body, just Madden. He was bloody and crazy. That's what she keeps saying. Bloody and crazy."

"She's traumatized for life," Kristen murmured, guilt blatantly obvious on her face.

"It is not your fault," Abe said firmly.

"How did he know about his uncle, Paul Worth?" Spinnelli asked.

Kristen shrugged. "He didn't get that far. He stopped while he was writing about how he drugged me and copied my database from my hard drive. He must have gotten a call from Zoe Richardson, because that's who he was looking for when he came into the warehouse."

Spinnelli's expression became even grimmer, his bushy mustache bunching as he frowned. "He may have gotten a call from someone saying she was Richardson, but it wasn't Richardson."

Kristen closed her eyes. "She's dead."

Spinnelli hesitated. "Yes."

"How?" Kristen asked.

Spinnelli exchanged a glance with Abe that spoke volumes. This was not something Kristen needed to know. At the prolonged silence Kristen opened her eyes. *Tell me.*"

"Conti killed her, Kristen. That's all you need to know."

Kristen's eyes flashed. "How did she die? Dammit, Marc, I have a right to know."

Spinnelli sighed. "She suffocated."

Mia frowned. "Suffocated? But—"

"Jack, are you done here?" Spinnelli interrupted. "Because I need to schedule a press conference and I'll need a summary of everything you've found. Kristen, there was a stack of books on Madden's nightstand. He stuck a sticky note with your name on the top of the stack. Poetry, I think. Keats and Browning. Mia, will you take Kristen to look through them?"

Kristen regarded him steadily. "It doesn't matter if you tell me or not, Marc. Sooner or later one of the reporters will find out and all I'll have to do is watch the ten o'clock news." She left the room, Mia at her heels. When they were gone, Spinnelli sighed again.

"When news broke that both Edwards and Conti were dead, we got an anonymous tip that if we stopped them from burying Angelo Conti, we'd find a missing person. Luckily the ground is so soggy from the thaw that they couldn't get the diggers out to the burial plot."

Abe grimaced as Spinnelli's meaning hit home. "No."

Spinnelli nodded. "Yes. Kristen's right. This will be all over the news sooner or later. I'll leave it up to you how you tell her. Now, get her out of here and get back to your family. How is your brother?"

Abe checked his watch. "They should be letting him go home any minute. I'm taking Kristen home."

"Not to her house," Spinnelli cautioned. "We'll need to get someone to clean up her living room. There's blood all over the wallpaper."

Blue stripes. Fighting a shudder Abe visualized the scene Mia and Spinnelli had found, the dead body in her living room, the blood streaking the blue-striped wallpaper. Visualized Kristen shooting the man who'd intruded into her home. Who'd put his hands on her. And even through the horror, was fiercely proud that she'd acted with such precise calm. She hadn't been able to fight her attacker ten years ago. Today, she'd more than made up for it.

"No," Abe said, his voice unsteady. "I won't take her to her house. I'll take her to my parents'. Everyone will be there." He turned to go when Spinnelli's hand closed over his shoulder.

"I was proud of you today, Abe. You waited for us at the warehouse instead of charging in to save the day yourself. You did the right thing."

And how hard it had been to sit there, hearing the seconds tick away in his mind, knowing Conti had Kristen, that he might be killing her at that very moment. But it *had* been the right thing to do. He never could have saved her alone. "Thank you," he whispered.

Spinnelli gave him one of those long hard looks that once again made Abe feel as if the man was looking straight into his soul. "You're welcome."

Saturday, February 28, 7:30 P.M.

The noise was such a welcome relief that Kristen felt tears sting her eyes. By unspoken mutual consent, she and Abe had not returned to her house, instead coming to the only place it made sense to come. Abe opened the door to Becca's kitchen from the laundry room and it was like she'd come home. Sean and Ruth's kids chased each other across the kitchen, Becca was watching QVC and Annie was peeling potatoes. Rachel sat at the kitchen table, working on what appeared to be algebra. The television in the living room was blaring some sports event, accompanied by the outraged shouts of Reagan men.

With a tearful cry, Rachel leaped from the table and rushed Kristen, nearly knocking her down with the ferocity of her embrace. Kristen hugged her close, rocking her gently. Rachel hadn't been at the hospital when she and Abe had gone to see Aidan. Kristen understood the girl needed the reassurance that she was indeed unharmed. Perhaps Kristen needed the reassurance as well. She swallowed hard and drew Rachel's head against her shoulder.

"It's all right now, honey. I promise. It's all over."

"I was so scared," Rachel whispered, trembling. "When they said you were missing, I . . ."

"I was scared, too." She could admit that now, now that everything was over. She'd seen four men die this afternoon, one at her own hand. Somehow the reality that she'd killed a man in her own living room hadn't yet sunk in. She supposed it would in time. For now, she held on tight to Rachel. "But you, honey, you helped save my life. Detective Mitchell told me how you recognized Owen from my office. Without you, they wouldn't have known who he was. You helped them find Aidan, so they could get him to the hospital."

Rachel pulled back, her lips curving in a faltering smile even as tears streaked her cheeks. "I did, didn't I? He owes me big time."

Kristen cupped Rachel's cheek, wiping the girl's tears away with her thumb. "Yes, he does. And so do I. Thank you, Rachel."

"You're all right?" she asked anxiously. "Really all right? You're not lying or anything?"

Kristen's lips twitched. "I'm not lying. I'm really okay. Better now that I'm here with you."

Rachel tilted her head to one side, studying her. "Aidan said you shot some guy and killed him."

Kristen drew a breath. "Yes, I did."

Rachel's eyes narrowed. "Good. He deserved it."

"Rachel, I don't think Kristen really wants to talk about that right now," Becca said. She put her own arms around Kristen and brought her close. "We were so worried," she whispered. "I'm so glad you're back here where you belong." She pressed a kiss to the top of Kristen's head, then pulled away, briskly moving about her kitchen. "Abe, make yourself useful. Take that pie into your brother. He's resting on the sofa in the living room."

Abe frowned. "Aidan gets pie? That's not fair."

"He has a concussion. Of course it's fair." She put the plate of pie in Abe's hands. "And don't be sneaking any on the way. Go on, now. Those boys," she clucked after him. "Kristen, we have a house full of people tonight. If you feel up to it, there's lettuce and salad makings in the fridge. I could use your help, too."

"Mother," Annie whispered and Becca shot her a frown. And Kristen knew Becca didn't need any help at all. It was just Becca's way of making her feel like family.

She was digging cucumbers out of the vegetable drawer in the refrigerator when Ruth appeared in the doorway, the baby on her shoulder. Her eyes assessed Kristen carefully, then she smiled. "I hear you had a bit of excitement today."

Kristen heard the words, but had eyes only for the infant in Ruth's arms. Not for one moment had she forgotten that she and Abe still had issues to discuss. She'd anticipated having a reaction to the sight of Ruth's baby, but she was unprepared for the wave of emotion that nearly cut her at the knees, a rushing combination of yearning and fear. Yearning that she, too, could hold a child in her arms, Abe's child. And fear that her inability to do so would come between them and she'd lose her place in this incredible family.

"Kristen?" Ruth approached, tilting Kristen's chin up with her free hand. "Say something."

Kristen made her eyes blink, her lungs breathe and her mouth move. "I'm fine. It's just the day catching up to me." She dropped the vegetables on the table. "But I think staying busy is the best thing. The christening was lovely, Ruth. I'm just sorry the party was ruined."

Ruth looked unconvinced. "If you need anything, you *will* let me know."

"I will. I promise." Kristen settled at the kitchen table and started ripping lettuce, a remarkably cathartic activity all in all. "So, Rachel, more algebra?"

Rachel grimaced. "Makeup work from all the days I missed. You'd think they'd cut me some slack, under the circumstances. But nooo. It's all due on Monday."

Kristen concentrated on the lettuce. "Welcome to the real world, honey." *Where life rarely cuts you any slack. But couldn't it, please? Just this once?*

Saturday, February 28, 10:45 P.M.

The house was quiet, relatively speaking. Sean and Ruth had gone home, taking all five children which eliminated 80 percent of the noise right there. Aidan had gone off to his old bedroom where Becca insisted he sleep for the night. Annie had also gone home, but not before quietly telling Kristen not to worry about her living room. She had some wallpaper that would be just perfect, and she'd fix it all up, better than new.

Now she and Abe sat with Becca and Kyle, the television showing pets doing amazing tricks. Abe's arm was around her, holding her tight when she remembered. *Pets.* Damn. "I need to go to my house," she said, dreading the thought. "I have to feed the cats."

Abe just tightened his hold. "Mia fed them. They're fine."

So Kristen indulged herself, putting off the nagging knowledge that there was still one major unresolved issue for just a little while longer. Then the program ended and Kyle stood with a groan.

"I'm sorry, but I have to go to bed. I'm getting too old for all this excitement. Becca?"

Becca rose, bent to kiss Abe's cheek, then Kristen's. "Where will you go tonight?"

"My apartment," Abe said firmly. Kristen was in no mood to disagree and a few minutes later they were sitting in the cab of his SUV, staring at his parents' house. Abe hadn't started the engine and the quiet was almost deafening. Kristen knew he'd been wrestling with the unresolved issues as well. It would appear the time of reckoning had arrived.

"We need to talk, Kristen," he said quietly, "but not here." In silence he drove to the apartment she'd seen only once, the morning after she'd been attacked in her room. Abe's place was empty and sterile and Kristen found she dreaded it almost as much as returning to her own house. But perhaps it was the conversation she dreaded more than the location.

He took her coat and turned on some lights. Flipped a switch and the gas fireplace ignited with a whoosh. He stood with his back to her for a long moment while she waited.

"Last night I told you I loved you," he said abruptly and she was acutely conscious that he hadn't said so since. "You said you loved me." He turned and focused those piercing blue eyes on her face. "Did you mean it?"

Kristen swallowed. "Yes."

His eyes flashed. "What did you think I would say, Kristen? That my love was conditional? I love you, but only if you bear my children? That if you can't, the deal is off?"

Kristen's eyes stung at his brusque tone. "I told you I'd disappoint you."

He looked up at the ceiling, blew out a sigh. "I'm disappointed," he admitted, then brought his gaze back down to hers. "But not with you." He crossed the distance between them and put his arms around her. "Never with you. How can I make you believe that?"

His arms were around her again and suddenly it was all too much. The dam broke and the tears rushed and she grabbed handfuls of his shirt and held on. And cried and cried. He scooped her up and settled her on his lap on the sofa and held her until the wave passed and the tears dwindled to a trickle. He lifted her chin and kissed her then, long and deep and . . . permanent. That's what it was. Permanence. Possession. His stake.

Her breath shuddered out in relief. "I'm sorry, Abe. I wish I could change it, but I can't."

He delved into her eyes, his gaze intense. "We are who we are because of what we've been through, Kristen, and we can't go back and change things, no matter how hard we wish. We are *where* we are because of what we've been through. Somehow, our lives came together. We're together. And right here, right now, I wouldn't change a thing."

His face became blurry and she blinked, sending tears down her cheeks. "And later? When you want a child of your own?"

"Any child we have will be a child of our own. We can adopt. I wanted to say that this morning, but I didn't think you wanted to hear it then."

"There are long waiting periods," she murmured, still unwilling to let herself entirely believe what seemed too perfect to be true. "It's not easy to adopt a baby."

"Who said anything about a baby?" he responded gently. "There are children everywhere that need homes, families to love them. We can be a family, Kristen. You and me. Even if we never biologically reproduce, I love you. Even if we never have any children, I love you." He kissed her mouth so tenderly she thought her heart would break. "Marry me."

Marriage. To a man with a heart like Abe's. It was more than she'd ever dared to hope for. "Are you sure, Abe?" *Please be sure. Please.*

"I'm very sure." He said it quietly, so that it rumbled from deep within his chest.

"I love you," she whispered, tracing his lips with her finger, watching his eyes heat. "I never believed I'd ever find anyone like you. I just want you to be happy."

His eyes burned, blue as flames, and she wondered how she ever could have thought them cold. "Answer the question, Counselor."

She smiled up into his face. "Yes."

His shoulders sagged and she realized he hadn't been entirely sure she'd say yes. Abruptly he rose, swinging her to her feet. Without saying a word he switched on the big-screen TV, changing stations while she watched, bewildered. Finally he came to the end of the stations, to the ones that only played music to solid background screens. He stopped changing channels and a smooth voice filled the room. Oldies. Turning, he held out his hand. "Dance with me."

She walked into his arms and they held one another, swaying to the music. She let herself drift in the sheer nearness of him until her back hit the wall. Abe's body pressed against her, hot and hard and very ready.

"Are you hungry?" he asked and she looked up and drew a quick breath. He was, but not for food. It was evident. In so many ways.

Her lips curved as she remembered the first time they'd made love and he'd told her how it would be. First dinner, then a dance, then . . . Even if she were hungry, she'd lie. "No."

"Good." He kissed her until the room spun. "I didn't want to have to cook for you first."

Her eyes danced up at him as he lifted his head. "But I do have a taste for dessert."

His smile sent her pulse skyrocketing. "So do I, Counselor. So do I."

Epilogue

Saturday, July 17, 1:30 P.M.

Abe tightened the final screw in the easel the box claimed would take only ten minutes to assemble, but in reality had required two hours. That the easel arrived with a video that described assembly and operation instructions should have been his first clue that this would be harder than it looked. But it didn't matter. It was a present for Kristen.

The whole room was a present for Kristen.

It was the spare bedroom in the house they'd closed on just the week before. He'd turned it into an art studio, complete with all the paints she could ever want. The clerk at the art store nearly kissed him, Abe thought wryly, with good cause. Paints were damn expensive. But again, it didn't matter. It was a present for Kristen and they could afford it now that they no longer had to worry about the mortgage on her old house.

Luckily Kristen's old house had sold quickly, Annie helping with more than a few required repairs. Like rewallpapering the living room and hastily building a new kitchen. Still, time and expense aside, both Kristen and her old neighbors were happy the house now held a new couple who found the house's recent history compelling. The husband was a reporter, the wife a writer. Abe shuddered. Let them have the house and good riddance.

Owen's house had been sold as well, again to people who were welcome to it. He'd left it to Kristen with the stipulation she keep a portion of the proceeds from its sale and donate the rest to the community center where Leah and Timothy had socialized. She'd donated the portion to the community center, then used the rest to set up a fund for Kaplan's child and Vincent's ongoing physical therapy. Vincent had proved tougher than they'd thought, and though he'd never work in a diner again, with therapy he could have a somewhat normal life.

Abe stood back, looking at his handiwork. Double-masted with a hand crank to raise and lower her canvases, the easel could hold a canvas up to eight feet tall. Abe looked around at the canvases he'd pulled from the storage shed in Kristen's old backyard. It had been what she'd hidden out there, locked with the enormous padlock. The canvases she'd completed in Italy and during her early years as an art major, portraits and landscapes so stunning they made his heart clench. Of course, he was the least little bit biased.

His wife was gifted. On so many levels. Her most recent work in progress sat on a makeshift easel in the corner of the room. She'd captured the beauty of Florence so effortlessly. It was the view from the hotel room where they'd honeymooned, making the piece that much more special.

The house itself wasn't much to look at. Yet. Abe had no doubt that between them, Kristen and Annie would change that quickly. But at least she'd get along with their neighbors this time around. Their new house was located just a half a block away from his parents. Sean and Ruth lived just a few blocks farther. Life was good.

"Abe?" The front door slammed downstairs.

"I'm up here, honey. Spare bedroom." Anxiously he

watched as she climbed the stairs, anticipating her reaction to the new studio. But his anticipation quickly became a frown as she reached the landing. She was pale and trembling, despite the heat of the July day. "What's wrong?"

She just looked at him, her expression distant and unreadable. He grabbed her arm and pulled her into the spare bedroom, gently forcing her into a soft chair. He crouched down to stare at her pale face. "I said, what's wrong?"

Her eyes traveled around the room and her breath caught. "Oh, Abe . . . Thank you."

But the thank-you was said in a voice so paper-thin, it didn't sound like hers. "Kristen, you're scaring me. What is wrong?"

Her russet brows knit as she seemed to concentrate. "I've just come from the doctor."

His heart stopped. *Oh, God.* His brain spun, his mind landing on the possibility he'd kept buried in the back of his mind. Her cancer had returned. "It's back?"

She frowned at him. "What's back?"

"Cervical cancer."

Her face blanched, her shoulders sagging. "No, oh, no, Abe. I'm so sorry. I didn't mean to worry you like that. No, I'm fine, really." As his pulse slowed to normal, she looked around the room again, her mouth curving into a little smile. "You've been busy this morning. Too bad you're going to have to move it all back down to the basement."

Abe shook his head. "No way. I've been working on this all—" He stopped himself, captured by the look in her eyes. It was a gleam he'd never seen before. Hope and . . . something else. His heart stuttered in his chest and he gently pushed the curls from her face, not wanting to hope himself. "Which doctor did you go see?"

Her eyes held his. "I went to the doctor to get tested for

anemia. My mother used to have it, and I've been so tired since I got back from my last trip to Kansas."

Abe didn't want to think about that trip, about the showdown with her father who still refused to give her the love she deserved. Abe had wanted to break the man's face, but in the end Kristen had just said good-bye. She'd continue going back to see her mother for as long as her mother lived, but she'd given up on her father as a lost cause. Her father's loss. He'd end up alone. Kristen, on the other hand, had more relatives than she could count, having been absorbed into the Reagan family.

"And he said?"

"*She* said my iron was fine." An expression of wonder crossed her face. "Then she said I was pregnant."

Pregnant. The word just exploded inside his head. His heart. Elated, Abe wanted to shout, laugh, turn cartwheels, but she seemed so still. So he waited.

"I told her it was impossible, that I'd had most of my cervix removed. But she said they'd done something called a cone biopsy, and though it removed a lot, it didn't interfere with conception." She said the words as if by rote, as if she still didn't believe them. "She said the doctor should have explained all this to me ten years ago."

"Did he?"

"Maybe. I was so devastated by the whole birth, adoption, and surgery experience that I probably didn't listen. I just assumed . . . Then later, I just didn't want to think about it."

Abe couldn't help it. A grin spread across his face and with a whoop he grabbed her into his arms and spun her around as if she was little Jeannette's age. She laughed breathlessly as she threw her arms around his neck and clung.

He tilted her head back so he could look into her eyes. Green and glinting with tears. "I love you, you know."

She blinked, sending the tears down her face. "I know. I love you, too. Oh, Abe, I just can't believe it's true."

"When?"

"January."

He quickly did the math. "Then you're three months already?"

Her face looked awed again. "I heard the heartbeat, Abe." She spread a tentative hand across her belly. "We're having a baby."

He covered her hand with his, desperately wishing he'd been there at her side. "Next time I'm going with you so I can hear it, too. And every time after that."

She grinned unexpectedly. "You'll have to pay Mia back for covering for you during all those doctors' appointments."

"I'll let her pick lunch." Abe leaned his forehead against hers, so happy he thought he would burst from it. "I love you."

"I love you, too."

"Can we tell everybody?"

Kristen pulled away and started for the door. "If Ruth hasn't already."

Abe grinned. "She was the doctor?"

Kristen grinned back. "What can I say? I get a family rate."

About the Author

KAREN ROSE is an award-winning author who fell in love with books from the time she learned to read. She started writing stories of her own when the characters in her head started talking and just wouldn't be silenced. A former chemical engineer and high school chemistry and physics teacher, Karen lives in Florida with her husband of twenty years, their two children, and the family cat, Bella. When she's not writing, Karen is practicing for her next karate belt test! Karen would be thrilled to receive your email at karen@karenrosebooks.com.

Enjoy a new tale of romantic
suspense by master storyteller

KAREN ROSE!

Please turn this page
for a preview of

DIE FOR ME

available in mass market.

Prologue

The first thing that hit Warren Keyes was the smell. Ammonia, disinfectant . . . and something else. What else? *Open your eyes, Keyes.* He could hear his own voice echo inside his head and he struggled to lift his eyelids. *Heavy.* They were so heavy, but he fought until they stayed open. It was dark. No. There was a little light. Warren blinked once, then again with more force until a flickering light came into focus.

It was a torch, mounted on the wall. His heart started thudding hard in his chest. The wall was rock. *I'm in a cave.* His heart began to race. *What the hell is this?* He lunged forward and white-hot pain speared down his arms to his back. Gasping, he fell back against something flat and hard.

He was tied. *Oh God.* His hands and feet were tied. And he was naked. *Trapped.* Fear rose from his belly, clawing his insides. He twisted like a wild animal, then fell back again, panting, tasting the disinfectant as k sucked in air. Disinfectant and . . .

His breath hitched as he recognized the odor und the disinfectant. Something dead. Rotting. *Somethir died here.* He closed his eyes, willing himself not panic. *This isn't happening. This is just a dream, nightmare. In a minute I'll wake up.*

But he wasn't dreaming. This, whatever it was, w real. He was stretched out on a board on a slight inclin his wrists tied together and his arms pulled up ar behind his head. *Why?* He tried to think, to remember There was something . . . a picture in his mind, ju beyond his reach. He strained for the memory and rea ized his head ached—he winced as the pain sent litt black spots dancing across his eyes. God, it was like really bad hangover. But he hadn't been drinking. Ha he?

Coffee. He remembered drinking coffee, his hand closing around the cup to get warm. He'd been col He'd been outside. *Running.* Why was he running? H rotated his wrists, feeling his raw skin burn, reachin until the tips of his fingers touched rope.

"So you're finally awake."

The voice came from behind him and he craned hi neck, trying to see. Then he remembered and the pres sure on his chest lessened a fraction. It was a movie. *I' an actor and we were making a movie.* A history docu mentary. He'd been running with . . . with what? H grimaced, focusing. *A sword, that's it.* He'd been i medieval costume, a knight with a helmet and shield . . even chain mail, for God's sake. The entire scene cam back now. He'd changed his clothes, even his under wear, for some scratchy, shapeless burlap that irritate

his crotch. He'd had a sword, and he'd carried it as he
ran through the woods outside Munch's studio, yelling
at the top of his lungs. He'd felt like a damn idiot, but
he'd done it all because it was in the damn script.

But this—he jerked at the ropes again with no success—*this was* not *in the script.*

"Munch." Warren's voice was thick, grating on his
dry throat. "What the hell is this?"

Ed Munch appeared to his left. "I didn't think you'd
ever wake up."

Warren blinked as the dim light from the torch flickered across the man's face. His heart skipped a beat.
Munch had changed. Before he'd been old, shoulders
stooped. White hair and a trim mustache. Warren swallowed, his breath shallow. Now Munch stood straight.
His mustache was gone. So was his hair, his head
shaved shiny bald.

Munch wasn't old. Dread coiled in his gut, seething
and roiling. The deal was five hundred for the docu-
mentary. Cash if he came that day. Warren had been
suspicious—it was a lot of money for a history docu-
mentary they'd show on PBS if he was lucky. But he'd
agreed. One odd old man was no threat.

But Munch wasn't old. Bile rose, choking him. *What
have I done?* Close on the heels of that question came
the next, more terrifying. *What will he do to me?*

"Who are you?" Warren croaked out and Munch held
a bottle of water to his lips. Warren pulled away, but
Munch grabbed his chin with surprising strength. His
dark eyes narrowed and fear made Warren freeze.

"It's just water this time," Munch ground out. "Drink
it."

Warren spat the mouthful of water back in the man's

face and held himself rigid when Munch raised his fist
But the fist lowered and Munch shrugged.

"You'll drink eventually. I need your throat moist."

Warren licked his lips. "Why?"

Munch disappeared behind him again and Warren
could hear something rolling. A video camera, Warren
saw when Munch rolled it past him, stopping about five
feet away. The camera was pointing straight at his face
"Why?" Warren repeated, louder.

Munch peered through the lens and stepped back
"Because I need you to scream." He lifted a brow, his
expression surreally bland. "They all screamed. So will
you."

Horror bubbled up and Warren fought it back. *Stay
calm. Treat him nice and maybe you can talk your way
out of this.* He made his lips curve. "Look, Munch, let
me go and we'll call it even. You can keep the sword
fight scenes I did already at no charge."

Munch just looked at him, his expression still bland
"I never planned to pay you anyway." He disappeared
again and reappeared, pushing another video camera.

Warren remembered the coffee, remembered Munch's
insistence that he drink it. *Just water this time.* Rage
geysered inside him, momentarily eclipsing the fear.
"You drugged me," he hissed, and he filled his lungs
with air. "*Somebody help me!*" he yelled as loud as he
could, but the hoarse sound from his throat was pathetically useless.

Munch said nothing, just set up a third camera on a
boom so that it pointed down. Every movement was
methodical, precise. Unhurried. Unconcerned. Unafraid.

And then Warren knew no one could hear him. The
hot rage drained away, leaving only fear, cold and

absolute. Warren's voice shook. There had to be something . . . some way out. Something he could say. Do. Offer. Beg. He'd beg. "Please, Munch, I'll do anything . . ." His words trailed away as Munch's words replayed in his mind.

They all screamed. Ed Munch. Warren's chest constricted, despair making it difficult to breathe. "Munch isn't your real name. Edvard Munch, the artist." The painting of a ghoulish figure clutching its face in agony flashed into his mind. *"The Scream."*

"Actually, it's pronounced 'Moonk,' not 'Munch,' but nobody ever gets it right. Nobody gets the details right," he added in a disgusted voice.

Details. The man had been all about details earlier, frowning when Warren argued against the scratchy underwear. The sword had been real, too. *I should have used it on the bastard when I had the chance.* "Authenticity," Warren murmured, repeating what he'd thought had been the ramblings of a crazy old man.

Munch nodded. "Now you understand."

"What will you do?" His own voice was eerily calm.

One corner of Munch's mouth lifted. "You'll see soon enough."

Warren dragged in each breath. "Please. *Please,* I'll do anything. Just let me go."

Munch said nothing. He pushed a cart with a television just beyond the camera at his feet, then checked the focus of each camera with calm precision.

"You won't get away with this," Warren said desperately, once again pulling at the ropes, struggling until his wrists burned and his arms strained in their sockets. The ropes were thick, the knots unyielding. He would not break free.

"That's what all the others said. But I have, and I wil
continue to do so."

Others. There had been others. The smell of death
was all around, mocking him. Others had died here. He
would die here, too. From somewhere deep inside him
courage rallied. He lifted his chin. "My friends wil
come looking for me. I told my fiancée I was meeting
you."

Finished with the cameras, Munch turned. His eyes
held a contempt that said he knew it was a last, desperate bluff. "No, you didn't. You told your fiancée you
were meeting a friend to help him read lines. You told
me so when we met this afternoon. You said this money
would pay for a surprise for her birthday. You wanted it
to stay a secret. That and your tattoo were the reasons I
chose you." He lifted one shoulder. "Plus, you fit the
suit. Not everyone can wear chain mail correctly. So no
one will be looking for you. And if they do, they'll never
find you. Accept it—you belong to me."

Everything inside him went deathly still. It was true.
He had told Munch the money was for a surprise for
Sherry. Nobody knew where he was. Nobody would
save him. He thought of Sherry, of his mom and dad, of
everyone he cared about. They'd wonder where he was.
A sob rose in his throat. "You bastard," he whispered. "I
hate you."

One side of Munch's mouth quirked, but his eyes lit
up with an amusement that was more terrifying than his
smile. "The others said that, too." He shoved the water
bottle at Warren's mouth again, pinching his nose until
he gasped for air. Wildly Warren fought, but Munch
forced the water down. "Now, Mr. Keyes, we begin.
Don't forget to scream."

Chapter One

Detective Vito Ciccotelli got out of his truck, his skin still vibrating. The beat-up old dirt road that led to the crime scene had only served to further rile his already churning stomach. He sucked in a breath and immediately regretted it. After fourteen years on the force, the odor of death still came as a putrid and unwelcome surprise.

"That shot my shocks to holy hell." Nick Lawrence grimaced, slamming the door of his sensible sedan. "Shit." His Carolina drawl drew the curse out to four full syllables.

Two uniforms stood staring down into a hole halfway across the snow-covered field. Handkerchiefs covered their faces. A woman was crouched down in the hole, the top of her head barely visible. "I guess CSU's already uncovered the body," Vito said dryly.

"Y'think?" Nick bent down and shoved the cuffs of

his pants into the cowboy boots he kept polished to a spit shine. "Well, Chick, let's get this show on the road."

"In a minute." Vito reached behind his seat for his snow boots, then flinched when a thorn jabbed deep into his thumb. "Dammit." For a few seconds he sucked on the tiny wound, then with care moved the bouquet of roses out of the way to get to his boots. From the corner of his eye he could see Nick sober. But his partner said nothing.

"It's been two years. Today," Vito added bitterly. "How time flies."

Nick's voice was quiet. "It's supposed to heal, too."

And Nick was right. Two years had dulled the edge of Vito's grief. But guilt . . . that was a different matter entirely. "I'm going out to the cemetery this afternoon."

"You want me to go with you?"

"Thanks, but no." Vito shoved his feet into his boots. "Let's go see what they found."

Six years as a homicide detective had taught Vito that there were no simple murders, just varying degrees of hard ones. As soon as he stopped at the edge of the grave the crime scene unit had just unearthed in the snow-covered field, he knew this would be one of the harder ones.

Neither Vito nor Nick said a word as they studied the victim who might have remained hidden forever were it not for an elderly man and his metal detector. The roses, the cemetery, and everything else was pushed aside as Vito focused on the body in the hole. He dragged his gaze from her hands to what was left of her face.

Their Jane Doe had been small, five-two or five-three, and appeared to have been young. Short, dark hair framed a face too decomposed to be easily identifiable and Vito wondered how long she'd been here. He wondered who she belonged to. If anyone had missed her. If anyone still waited for her to come home.

He felt the familiar surge of pity and sadness and pushed it to the edge of his mind along with all the other things he wanted to forget. For now he'd focus on the body, the evidence. Later, he and Nick would consider the woman—who she'd been and who she'd known. They'd do so as a means to catch the sick sonofabitch who'd left her nude body to rot in an unmarked grave in an open field, who'd violated her even after death. Pity shifted to outrage as Vito's gaze returned to the victim's hands.

"He posed her," Nick murmured beside him and in the soft words Vito heard the same outrage he felt. "He fucking posed her."

Indeed he had. Her hands were pressed together between her breasts, her fingertips pointing to her chin. "Permanently folded in prayer," Vito said grimly.

"Religious murderer?" Nick mused.

"God, I hope not." A buzz of apprehension tickled his spine. "Religious murderers tend not to stop with just one. There could be more."

"Maybe." Nick crouched down to peer into the grave which was about three feet deep. "How did he permanently pose her hands, Jen?"

CSU Sergeant Jen McFain looked up, her eyes covered with goggles, her nose and mouth by a mask. "Wire," she said. "Looks like steel, but very fine. It's wound around her fingers. You'll be able to see it better once the ME cleans her up."

Vito frowned. "Doesn't seem like wire that thin

would be enough to trip the sensor on a metal detector, especially under a couple feet of dirt."

"You're right, the wire wouldn't have set it off. For that we can thank the rods your perp ran under the victim's arms." Jen traced one gloved finger along the underside of her own arm, down to her wrist. "They're thin and bendable, but have enough mass to set off a metal detector. It's how he kept her arms fixed in position."

Vito shook his head. "Why?" he asked and Jen shrugged.

"Maybe we'll get more from the body. I haven't gotten much from the hole so far. Except . . ." She nimbly climbed from the grave. "The old man uncovered one of her arms using his garden spade. Now, he's in pretty good shape, but even I couldn't have dug that deep with a garden spade this time of year."

Nick looked into the grave. "The ground must not have been frozen."

Jen nodded. "Exactly. When he found the arm he stopped digging and called 911. When we got here, we started moving dirt to see what we had. The fill was easy to move until we got to the grave wall, then it was hard as a rock. Look at the corners. They look like they were cut using a T square. They're frozen solid."

Vito felt a sick tug at his gut. "He dug the grave before the ground froze. He planned this pretty far in advance."

Nick was frowning. "And nobody noticed a gaping hole?"

"Perp might've covered it with something," Jen said. "Also, I don't think the fill dirt came from this field. I'll run the tests to tell you for sure. That's all I got for now. I can't do anything more until the ME gets here."

"Thanks, Jen," Vito said. "Let's talk to the property owner," he said to Nick.

Harlan Winchester was about seventy, but his eyes were clear and sharp. He'd been waiting in the back seat of the police cruiser and got out when he saw them coming. "I suppose I'll have to tell you detectives the same thing I told the officers."

Vito put a little sympathy into his nod. "I'm afraid so. I'm Detective Ciccotelli and this is my partner, Detective Lawrence. Can you take us through what happened?"

"Hell, I didn't even want that damn metal detector. It was a present from my wife. She's worried I don't get enough exercise since I retired."

"So you got out this morning and walked?" Vito prompted and Winchester scowled.

"'Harlan P. Winchester,'" he mimicked in a high, nasal voice, "'you've been in that good-for-nothin' chair for the last ten years. Get your moldy butt up and walk.' So I did, 'cause I couldn't stand to listen to her nag me anymore. I thought I might find something interesting to make Ginny shut up. But . . . I never dreamed I'd find a *person*."

"Was the body the first object your detector picked up?" Nick asked.

"Yeah." His mouth set grimly. "I took out my garden spade. It was then I thought about how hard the ground would be. I didn't think I'd be able to break the surface, much less dig deep. I almost put my spade away before I started, but I'd only been gone fifteen minutes and Ginny would have nagged me some more. So I started digging." He closed his eyes, swallowed hard, his bravado gone like so much mist. "My spade . . . it hit her arm. So I stopped digging and called 911."

"Can you tell us a little more about this land?" Vito asked. "Who has access to it?"

"Anybody with an ATV or four-wheel drive, I guess. You can't see this field from the highway and the little drive that connects to the main road isn't even paved."

Vito nodded, grateful he'd driven his truck, leaving his Mustang parked safely in his garage alongside his bike. "It's definitely a rugged road. How do you get back here?"

"Today I walked." He pointed to the tree line where a single set of footprints emerged. "But this was the first time I've been back here. We only moved in a month ago. This land was my aunt's," he explained. "She died and left it to me."

"So, did your aunt come out to this field often?"

"I wouldn't think so. She was a recluse, never left the house. That's all I know."

"Sir, you've been a big help," Vito said. "Thank you."

Winchester's shoulders sagged. "Then I can go home?"

"Sure. The officers will drive you home."

Winchester got in the cruiser and it headed out, passing a gray Volvo on its way in. The Volvo parked behind Nick's sedan and a trim woman in her midfifties got out and started across the field. ME Katherine Bauer was here. It was time to face Jane Doe.

Vito started toward the grave, but Nick didn't move. He was looking at Winchester's metal detector sitting inside the CSU van. "We should check the rest of the field, Chick."

"You think there are more."

"I think we can't leave until we know there aren't."

Another shiver of apprehension raced down Vito's back. In his heart he already knew what they would find. "You're right. Let's see what else is out there."